C000262211

IAN HEY

NO LIFT
and NO
STAIRS

The Book Guild Ltd

First published in Great Britain in 2022 by
The Book Guild Ltd
Unit E2 Airfield Business Park,
Harrison Road, Market Harborough,
Leicestershire. LE16 7UL
Tel: 0116 2792299
www.bookguild.co.uk
Email: info@bookguild.co.uk
Twitter: @bookguild

Copyright © 2022 Ian Hey

The right of Ian Hey to be identified as the author of this
work has been asserted by him in accordance with the
Copyright, Design and Patents Act 1988.

All rights reserved. No part of this publication may be
reproduced, transmitted, or stored in a retrieval system, in any form or by any means,
without permission in writing from the publisher, nor be otherwise circulated in
any form of binding or cover other than that in which it is published and without
a similar condition being imposed on the subsequent purchaser.

This work is entirely fictitious and bears no resemblance to any persons living or dead.

Typeset in 11pt Minion Pro

Printed and bound by CPI Group (UK) Ltd, Croydon, CR0 4YY

ISBN 978 1914471 698

British Library Cataloguing in Publication Data.
A catalogue record for this book is available from the British Library.

MIX
Paper from
responsible sources
FSC® C013604

To Anna

One

AN EARLY START

I shot up in bed, sweating, heart pounding, the residue of a disturbing dream vanishing slowly from my consciousness.

John Lennon was singing about cavities in a northern town, and I reached over and hit the 'STOP' button on the radio alarm. 5.30am, the skeletal, blue figures grinned at me.

'I blew my lights out in a traffic car,' I mumbled, and swung my barely awake carcass into an upright position on the side of the bed. Sarah always said this was one of my many annoying habits, me trying to sing the lyrics of a song and always getting them wrong.

I sat on the loo trying to wipe out the sleep from my eyes. I did like The Beatles. OK, I'd only got the *Red* and *Blue* compilation albums of all their main hits, but they wrote good songs. I can't abide all these trendy, so-called music lovers who say they were crap. They were massively influential and it wasn't only the countless classics such as 'Ticket to Ride', 'Hey Jude' and 'Here Comes the Sun' but also the hidden gems that made them so great.

I remembered getting off the bus on the Broadway when I still lived with Sarah and a busker sat outside Blockbusters playing a hauntingly beautiful song which I recognised but couldn't quite

1

place. When I got home, I began to hum the melody in the kitchen and Sarah came in and said, 'I love that song' – the first words she'd spoken to me in two days. I said to her I thought it was Donovan or Dylan. She tutted at my ignorance and corrected me: '"You've Got to Hide Your Love Away" by The Beatles, stupid.'

I showered quickly and got changed, picked up a £20 note from the bedside table and walked outside into the November rain at twenty-five to six.

The bus was on time and, yes, I did go upstairs but didn't have a cigarette.

Maurice Bagley sat in the Stoneways' restroom in his usual seat at the table nearest the toilets: glasses on, perusing the *Daily Mirror* and sipping occasionally from a can of Tizer.

I checked the clock on the wall above the 1974 Health and Safety Act and worked out I had three minutes to make and drink a coffee before the one-man wrecking ball which was Maurice Bagley sprang into life at six on the dot. I hurriedly flicked on the kettle in the kitchenette and grabbed an upside-down mug off the draining board. It wasn't brilliantly clean, but it would have to do.

We didn't have coffee jars in our restroom, just a very large cash-and-carry tub which, give the boss his due, was always Nescafe. As soon as I'd pierced the lid off with a spoon from the drawer underneath the microwave, Maurice was by my side, bustling his short but solid frame about, flicking off the kettle and grabbing one side of the tub.

I held the tub fast. 'Maurice,' I told him, 'I'm having a cup of coffee before I do anything else, OK?'

Maurice had hands like a bear. I was not to be undone and tightened my grip, but he was too strong and a great scree of coffee granules leapt out of the tub and landed on the lino floor just as Daz Oatridge, the operations manager, walked in through the office door.

I'll give Maurice his due: for a man who'd never been near a gymnasium in his entire life, he could certainly move fast. A muffled,

'Morning,' to Daz and he vanished through the restroom fire door to the yard like a *Harry Potter* character who'd just been vaporised by the ugly baddie's wand.

Daz allowed me a few slurps of very strong, black coffee while I hoovered up the mess. The reason for the 6am start, he explained, was because we had to be at a self-storage depot the other side of London by half eight.

Maurice was putting his mobile phone back into his pocket as I climbed up into the passenger seat of STONE 42.

'Daz has just phoned to tell me Unsworth's running late,' he said.

I shrugged; I was still annoyed about the coffee incident.

'We've got to pick him up at the station.'

'Great,' I muttered, and stared straight ahead.

We drove out of the industrial estate in silence and turned left onto the London Road. There were no cars, just a lone figure in a bright, yellow hi-vis top and a flashing light strapped to his forehead, jogging along the pavement on the other side of the road towards us. For some reason, Maurice beeped him. It was an HGV truck's horn and the jogger stumbled and nearly fell over. Maurice beeped him again, gave him a wave and chuckled. He looked at me, but I maintained a moody countenance.

We parked in the bus stop opposite Fleet Town Station to wait for Jeff Unsworth and Maurice quickly became bored. Although he was nearing fifty-three, bundles of boundless, inquisitive energy infused his very being. Before long, he was fiddling with the sun visors and switching on the windscreen wipers, testing their three speeds and then switching them off again. He pressed a button on his armrest which opened and shut both his and my passenger window and then cranked his chair forwards and backwards before reclining himself almost horizontal.

I continued to feign ignorance but did experience a moment of panic when Maurice righted himself, pulled out a fire extinguisher from beneath his driver's seat and began to read the instructions.

A thin straggle of bodies emerged through the as-yet-unmanned barriers in the station's forecourt. 6.30am, second train heading for Waterloo and not a suit in sight. Half-asleep cleaners, shift workers and a removal man: could be the name of a song.

Early morning, mid-afternoon or late at night, Jeff Unsworth always looked the same: gaunt, bedraggled and unshaven. However, a combination of failed relationships, a nomadic lifestyle and too many years working in the removal trade had bestowed upon Jeff a steely cynicism which enabled him to still walk across the stage of life. He flopped his Stoneways Removals bomber jacket over his head to ward off the rain and hurried over the road to the truck.

I clambered onto the bunk behind and Jeff sat in the passenger seat. He closed the door and grunted a barely audible greeting, but that was Jeff's way. Yes, he was late and it was his fault, but nobody was going to tell him that, not now at any rate, at such a stupidly early hour on a Friday morning. He wound down the passenger window, lit a cigarette and Maurice let him have it full blast with the fire extinguisher.

I had to admit, I found it quite funny, but Jeff wasn't happy, especially because his cigarette was now completely un-smokable. Luckily for him, the extinguisher was of the foam variety and he could wipe off most of the bubbles, except for some tiddlers, which stuck to his hair and ears.

Maurice checked his mirrors and began to manoeuvre the truck out of the bus stop.

Jeff was irate. 'What the fuck did you do that for?'

Maurice switched off the indicator and placed both hands on the steering wheel. 'Mr Unsworth,' he said, 'are you familiar with the 1985 Fire and Safety Act?'

'No, and neither are fucking you.'

'Are you sure it was 1985?' I asked.

Maurice aimed a cursory glance back towards me and then pressed the button which opened the passenger window fully down. The top of the van hit the foliage of an overhanging tree and a solid sheet of water sprayed onto Jeff.

'Oh, sorry,' Maurice apologised. 'Just checking you were fully out.'

We reached the Purfleet roundabout and Maurice drove all the way round twice before I asked him what he was doing.

Maurice spoke out loud as he drove. 'Well, Mr Modern History expert, there's a job sheet in here somewhere with an address and a map telling us where we're going.'

Jeff looked at me. 'Well, I can't read it. I left my bins at home.'

I didn't want to read the map. I'd dived into the bunk so I could try and have a kip.

A car beeped us as Maurice began to drive around the roundabout for a third time.

I was pissed off with Jeff but realised I had no choice; I'd have to navigate from the bunk.

'Give it to me, then,' I said to Jeff.

'No, no,' Maurice butted in. 'One of you can hold the map up so I can see it and I'll navigate while also driving this rather large vehicle.'

The same car beeped us again as we completed our third circle. The driver pulled up level and downed his window.

Maurice downed his and shouted across to make himself heard. 'Don't mess with me, sonny; I'm a member of the X-Men.'

The driver gave us the finger and sped off back towards Fleet Town.

'M25,' I told Maurice.

'Clockwise or anti-clockwise?'

'Anti-clockwise,' I told him. 'We're heading for the East End.'

The address was: S&S's Super Storage, Unit 3, Bernstein's Industrial Park, The Old Kent Road . I worked out the easiest way was round the M25 and come off at Junction 2 where, at some point, the A2 itself, became Old Kent Road.

I made a makeshift pillow out of my bomber jacket and told Jeff to wake me up when we reached Junction 2.

It's not the most pleasant bed, the bunk of STONE 42, but at least it was long enough for me to lie down on fully. The truck's steady drone of governed, fifty-five miles an hour indicated to me we were on the M25 and I closed my eyes only to reopen them a minute later and stare at the top of the cab where several clumps of mould hung from the underlay of grey felt.

According to a psychiatrist I used to chat to in the pub, one way of determining the state of a person's mental health could be gauged by what golden bough they'd reached in life and how far they'd fallen off it. For example, when Ricky Hatton lost his one chance of boxing immortality after he got decked by Floyd Mayweather, he sank into a deep depression. OK, I hadn't fallen as steeply as Hatton had, but being kicked out of Sarah's flat and landing in the present humble hovel I was presently renting was definitely on a downward trajectory, so yes, I was feeling a little blue and those clumps of mould weren't helping.

I shifted onto my right side so my head was snuggled up behind Jeff's seat. *Just get on with it*, I thought, and tried to think of happier things, but sadly, the chances of a tip and a few beers at the end of the day's play seemed to be the only potential pleasures that came to mind. I rolled back over to my left and buried my head in my jacket.

There was something I'd forgotten about Maurice – he seemed to know exactly what moment you were going to drift off and I'd never worked out how he did this.

The early start finally caught up with me and I closed my eyes, my weary mind succumbing to the deliciousness of approaching sleep. Maurice beeped the horn and slammed on the brakes, forcing my head to bounce upwards and collide painfully with the mildewed roof of the cab.

It had stopped raining when we pulled up outside the closed gates to Bernstein's Industrial Park and the November dawn was full in the grey skies above the relentless concrete of the Old Kent Road. An Audi sports car sat on the other side of the gates directly opposite us and beeped its horn.

It was funny with Maurice. He possessed an enviable vocabulary, but when irked, he was always a touch more direct. He leant his head out of the window and shouted, 'Are you some kind of fucking idiot?'

The car door opened and a well-dressed, dapper man emerged. 'No,' he said, 'I'm Alan Curdley.'

'I don't give a fuck who you are. Just get your silly little wanker's car out of my fucking way.'

There was a moment of almost perfect silence before I tapped Maurice on his shoulder and pointed out the name of the customer printed at the top of the worksheet. 'ALAN CURDLEY'.

Fortunately, dear old Alan either hadn't actually heard what Maurice had said or just found it so ridiculous that its meaning had not yet fully computed in his head. He smiled. 'Oh, come on, Mike; you must remember me?'

'Mike?' I echoed.

'Shut up,' Maurice hissed.

'Is he someone who wants to kill you?' Jeff asked.

'I thought I'd wait for you here,' Alan said, 'so I could let you in and show you where to park the lorry.'

'Ah, Alan,' Maurice spoke out of the window again, 'didn't recognise you.' He paused. 'Have you lost some weight?'

We backed Maurice in and stopped him a tail lift length away from the main shutters of Unit 4, headquarters of S&S's Super Storage.

Maurice got out of the cab and Alan formally greeted us all with a fleeting handshake.

I'd have put him in his early fifties, of similar age to Maurice and Jeff, but he looked a hell of a lot better. He wore designer clothes and boasted a full crop of carefully manicured, grey-free, dark hair. One would call him handsome, although on closer inspection, his face appeared unusually tanned.

'Sunbed overload,' Jeff said.

I heard the sound of a forklift levitating a heavy pallet off a vehicle somewhere on the estate and the opening riff of 'Orgone

Accumulator' began to play in my head. Sarah says this is another of my most annoying traits: my love of Hawkwind.

I must have been six or seven when I sat cross-legged on my mum's lounge floor and watched grimy footage of Hawkwind playing 'Silver Machine' on a *Top of the Pops* repeat. The music meant nothing to me – it was their hair that fascinated me. It was the longest hair I'd ever seen and it wasn't carefully corkscrewed nor painstakingly curled. It was long, unruly and greasy.

The image stayed with me till I was thirteen when I found one of their LPs round Paranoid Ian's house in his older brother's bedroom. I nicked it and took it home. The music was incredibly repetitive and the songs went on forever, but they looked so damned cool on the inner sleeve I played the album again and again until I finally began to like it and knew all the lyrics.

The receptionist for S&S's was a heavily made-up girl who looked like she'd machine-gunned herself several times with a staple gun. 'JANE', her nametag read.

Alan introduced himself and she studied her computer. After a moment, eyes still glued to the screen, she asked Alan how he'd like to pay.

Alan flashed an American Express card and placed it in the machine between Jane's telephone and a brightly lit plastic contraption selling multicoloured gobstoppers.

Jane blew out her bubblegum, exploded it and said, 'You can take your card out now.'

She authorised Alan a key for Lock-Up 6 and we followed him through a door marked 'CUSTOMER STORAGE'.

It wasn't quite one of the tunnels on the spaceship in the first *Alien* film, where everything was dripping wet and scarily lit, but it certainly didn't remind me of any of the self-storage units I'd ever been in.

Alan stopped by a peeling wall where somebody had sprayed 'I DID JANE OVER THE PHOTOCOPIER' in fluorescent red and we all stopped. He turned to Maurice. 'Guess what, Mike?'

'Yes, Alan?'

'Your chap at Stoneways – Darren Oatridge?'

'Could well be.'

'Do you know what he quoted me for two years' storage?'

It was a rhetorical question, so Maurice didn't answer.

'Seven thousand pounds!' Alan announced dramatically. 'Seven thousand pounds,' he repeated in a lower tone, and whistled to himself at the ridiculousness of the figure. 'Bill Scar, who co-owns this place with his son, Lee, quoted me two and a half thousand – four and a half less than Stoneways. To be quite frank, Mike, it's a wonder your boss has any storage customers at all.'

Maurice nodded his head in agreement and we all turned left down another poorly lit corridor. The rotten-apple smell of damp strengthened until we reached a rusting, metal door. LO K-U 6 was displayed in fading blue letters at the top and underneath somebody had written 'THE BOSS IS A TWAT' in indelible black marker pen.

Alan pulled out a key from his Armani windbreaker.

Maurice said, 'I don't think you'll be needing that, Alan,' and leant down and picked up a padlock off the floor which lay beside the missing C and P.

Alan studied it for a moment before exclaiming, 'My God, it's been sawn in half!'

'Certainly has,' Jeff said, and pushed open the door.

I found a bank of light switches to my left, flicked them all on and, slowly, the interior of LO K-U 6 began to light up.

It was a large cube-shaped room with an impressively high ceiling. Intermittent splashes of water from the morning's rain dripped down through holes in the corrugated roof onto Alan's storage below.

Or, should I say, what was left of Alan's storage.

Open cartons lay on their sides, spewing torn tape, packing paper and broken ornaments. A chest of drawers lay face down in a puddle of water and a dining table with only one leg rested on top of a severely gouged, antique-looking sideboard.

Maurice nudged me and said, 'Looks like you stacked it.'

Jeff let out a ferocious cry and we all turned to look at him.

'I don't believe it,' he said. 'It's just terrible.'

'Thank you,' Alan said quietly.

Jeff strode over and picked up a flat Pack6 which leant against a ripped-apart Wardrobe Carton. He held it up to Alan.

'This!' he shouted.

Oh shit, it was Jeff's thing. He detested anybody packing a picture in a flat Pack6. He's told me it's one of the only things that can keep him awake at night.

Maurice suggested to Alan that the best way forward would be if we helped repack what remained of his storage as we loaded it. 'At no extra cost,' Maurice assured Alan, and his right knee began to tremble. This was one of Maurice's famous quirks: his right knee beginning to tremble at the prospect of a gratuity. It had also been known, on occasion, to indicate impending violence.

I think our Alan was too traumatised to grasp any ulterior motive behind Maurice's offer of help, but he agreed and, for the next two hours, we repacked and trundled Alan's storage on the creaking trolleys provided by S&S's along the dim, dank-smelling, corridors of Unit 4 and out to the back of the truck.

We were generally happy in our work – there were no stairs. While Maurice stacked the van, he composed a lengthy ditty, sang in his surprisingly tuneful baritone, concerning Alan's misfortune. 'Two and a half grand well spent,' he named it.

Jeff and I wheeled the two last trolley-loads to the back of the truck at ten-thirty, leaving Alan in the lock-up, sobbing quietly and clutching a broken knob off a Davenport which had previously been standing upside down on an obliterated Georgian mirror.

We leant against the tail lift as Maurice tied the tabletop with only one leg to the side of the van.

Jeff lit up a fag and said, 'Think that's it, Boss.'

'What about the Stone Lion?' Maurice asked matter-of-factly as he pushed a couple of Pack2s into place with his right foot.

'What are you on about?' I said.

Maurice faced us. 'You see, I remember this job now. We bought some stuff into store a couple of years ago for this feller. Not a bad job – he was a bit of a prat but no real problems.'

'Why does he keep calling you Mike?' Jeff interrupted.

'Just shut up and listen. As I said, it wasn't a bad job except for this Stone Lion.'

'Is this one of your jokes?' I asked.

Maurice put up his hands. 'OK, take the piss, but I know that monster came into store. So, if you two shit-for-brains think that's it, take the job sheet and go and ask my great mate Al to sign underneath the "we've got everything" bit.'

'But I thought Al said he didn't store his stuff with us?' Jeff said.

'He did!' Maurice raised his voice and then calmed himself. 'At first.'

He was like an actor, his stage the back of a removal truck. He turned to check his load, grabbed a couple of van blankets and stuffed them into a gap between two Pack3s.

He spoke again. 'We placed the thing by the diesel tank back at the yard where all the other oversized outside storage items lie and, every morning and every evening, I'd check it was still there. I'd become as obsessed as Captain Ahab.'

'Captain who?' I asked.

Maurice tutted at my apparent denseness and continued. 'And then, one miserable, rainy April afternoon, I discovered it had gone. Where, I didn't bloody well care. The rain suddenly stopped and the sun burst through the clouds, somehow reflecting the joyous relief in my heart.'

'Oh, please,' Jeff said.

Maurice ignored him. 'I made enquiries the following day. Daz informed me Alan hired a firm to deliver all his storage, including the

Stone Lion, to another warehouse somewhere in London.' He paused to let his words sink in. 'Obviously, here.'

'Well, I haven't seen a Stone Lion,' I said. 'Nor a burial mound for that matter.'

'OK, Mr Modern *and* Ancient History expert,' Maurice said, and grabbed the side of the van and pointed. 'What's that fucking thing over there, then?'

I followed his finger to an old, broken-down truck which sat rusting against a cast-iron fence to the side of S&S's reception. Placed in front were some heavy-looking pots and a Stone Lion.

Two

CURLY

We walked over and looked at it.

Its body was at least two feet high, head a good foot higher and was roughly five feet long. It would have been longer but half its tail was missing. It sat on a plinth at least six inches thick and the whole moss-greened structure was made entirely of stone.

'Fuck,' I said. 'Are you sure it's his?'

Maurice didn't bother replying and I began to mentally try and work out how we could shift the base out of the weeds growing through the gravel. Two years standing there, that bastard must have sunk in. We'd have to rock it slowly from side to side to try and loosen it, and then what?

'Would Al remember it's here?' Jeff asked out loud to no one in particular.

Alan had to drop the key for the lock-up back at reception. We followed him and there was still no mention of the Stone Lion. I didn't think any of us were brazen enough to get Al to sign the 'we've got everything' bit on the sheet – we were just going with the flow.

It was the pierced receptionist who spoilt it.

She detonated another sugary bubble and said to Alan, 'The boss told me to tell you not to forget your garden ornament.'

Alan gave her a puzzled look.

Jane pointed. 'That stone thing over there in front of the old van.'

'Oh, goodness me, yes,' said Alan. 'I'd completely forgotten about Curly.'

Police sirens sounded on The Old Kent Road as we once more stood in front of the Stone Lion.

'Oh, crikey, that's the final straw,' Alan said. 'His tail's broken.'

Maurice reversed the van over and we dropped the tail lift down a foot away from the beast.

I managed to persuade Alan to return to reception and enquire about possible financial recompense for his damaged and missing goods while we three stood and studied the Lion again.

It's funny, this old removal lark. You go through your head all the scenarios and alternatives – piano wheels, sack barrows, webs – and then gradually you convince yourself you'll never be able to move the fucker so you phone the office. Or, at least, Jeff and I insisted on Maurice phoning the office.

'But I've moved it before,' Maurice argued. 'Daz'll say, "It must be lighter cos half its tail's missing, so just get on with it."'

It was Jeff who asked the obvious question. 'So how did you move it before?'

Maurice pursed his lips and scratched at a spot below his left ear. 'Do you know,' he said, 'and I'm being completely honest with you, I got so drunk the night after we'd moved it, I can't remember.'

'Who helped you, then?' I asked. 'We could give them a call.'

'A load of blokes who were building Al's new conservatory and Andy Brett and Bod Smalldick.'

Jeff and I were quiet.

Andy Brett had been a qualified electrician who'd worked part-time with us for a couple of months before he and his family emigrated to New Zealand. Bod Smalldick (whose real name escaped me) had also been part-time, a law student who must have graduated to the Bar shortly after the initial removal of Curly. Even if we could have somehow obtained a contact number for him, he'd probably charge us £200 for the privilege of talking to him.

Jeff broke the silence. 'Phone the office then. That thing's unreal.'

Maurice shook his head but pulled out his mobile and went and sat in the truck.

I grabbed the Lion's neck between both arms and attempted to rock it. There was no movement.

Jeff stood to one side of the tail and grabbed the backside. After a count of three, we both attempted to tilt the thing to one side, but again, there was no movement.

Maurice got out of the cab.

'What did he say?'

'Funnily enough,' Maurice replied. '"If half its tail's missing, it must be a lot lighter. You've moved it before so just get on with it."'

We worked out the head was the key and all three of us surrounded it and pushed it one way. A trembling of tiny stones and earth fell off the plinth. We pushed again, this time the other way. The plinth visibly moved.

Maurice began to get excited. 'Right. What we need to do is keep rocking it until its head rests on the side of this fence, giving us some point of balance. We then shove some piano wheels under the base and push it back over.'

We tried, by Christ we tried, but we didn't have sufficient combined strength nor weight to push the Lion over. We needed help.

Maurice approached the forklift driver, who walked around Curly twice before telling us we were having a laugh. 'You need a diesel-powered forklift to shift that,' he explained. His was only electric but he did offer to give us a hand if required.

Jane, the receptionist, S&S's cleaner, Dave, Alan himself and an Italian called Alonso who owned the estate's mobile snack bar were also enlisted.

The first part of the plan worked and the Lion rested at an angle on the side of the fence. However, a new problem arose due to one of us, Jeff, having to break off and hold the piano wheels tight against the base as the remainder of us tried to tip the thing back over. We couldn't do it – another body was needed.

A Class 1 driver called Ralph, who had been taking his statuary forty-five-minute break whilst parked up outside the builder's merchants at Unit 5, waddled over and offered his assistance. Like many professional, articulated drivers, Ralph had substantial girth and talked complete bollocks, but his extra bulk was a godsend.

After several more minutes of sweaty exertion, Curly stood proudly on the piano wheels.

Jane and Alan returned to reception to sort out the bill, the forklift driver back to his forklift, Dave to his hoover and Alonso back to his burgers. Ralph stayed to help wheel Curly onto the tail lift and began to tell us a story about how he and his platoon once lifted a tank over a wall in Baghdad. Maurice thanked him for his help and then told him to, 'Fuck off,' or else he'd hit him.

Jeff and I stood with Curly while Maurice worked the control panel at the side of the truck. The hydraulics shrieked and, for one agonising moment, the tail lift refused to budge. Maurice made a comment about my weight and then, very slowly, Jeff, myself and the Lion began to judder upwards until we were level with the back of the truck.

With the aid of a small stepladder, Maurice climbed onto the tail lift (age was beginning to take its toll) and all three of us pushed Curly into position in front of the remaining pile of van blankets.

I was the biggest worrier – the 'what if' member of the crew – and queried the unequal weight distribution if we were to tie Curly where we'd just placed him.

Maurice said he'd tie an overweight pillock like me to the opposite side of the van to nullify the problem.

'I'm not fat,' I protested.

'Fatter than Jeff,' Maurice said. 'Now, stop making such stupid comments and give us a hand.'

We decided to leave Curly on the piano wheels – the reason being the logistics of getting him back on them at the delivery address were too much to think about – and secured him to the side of the van with five webs.

As I had to read the map, I insisted on sitting in the passenger seat. Jeff didn't seem to mind and jumped on the bunk. The unload was in Sunningford and I told Maurice to head back round the '25 clockwise and come off at Junction 12.

Although the storage facilities at S&S's had tickled the three of us, the mood was muted. Curly weighed on our minds like the dense blanket of grey cloud overhead.

Maurice quickly became bored with the doom and gloom and composed several ditties mostly concerning my recent split with Sarah. A twisted version of the operatic middle section of 'Bohemian Rhapsody' ended in:

'*Sarah Raines, Sarah Raines,*
Can you wash Peter's Y-fronts?'

We came off the motorway and parked up outside a café in Engleford. Maurice and I both ordered the special with extra fried pots while Jeff had a bacon sandwich which he didn't finish and went outside to smoke a fag.

When we got back to the truck, Jeff told me he knew the way to Sunningford so I let him sit in the passenger seat.

Maurice was curious. 'How do you know Sunningford?'

'I went out with a bird who lived there.'

'You?'

'Yes.' Jeff was indignant.

'But you're from North Bitton.'

On the way to Sunningford, expertly directed by Jeff, Maurice kept quizzing him about his posh bird from Sunningford.

'So where did you meet her?'

'In a pub in Camwell.' Jeff paused. 'Left at these lights.'

Maurice pulled up at the lights and indicated left. 'West Camwell?'

'No, the other bit.'

'There's no posh birds in the other bit.'

'I don't bloody know, but she lived in Sunningford.'

The lights changed and Maurice lifted the handbrake.

I sat up in the bunk to watch. This was a skill.

Maurice shifted gears and checked both his mirrors before swinging the seventeen-and-a-half-ton removal truck onto the Bragstone Road. The lorry couldn't quite make the turn and Maurice stopped and began to reverse the truck to try and line up the right swing.

The mirrors were his all-important eyes and I saw, with him, a Porsche beginning to overtake. The car sped past and Maurice slammed on the anchors and beeped his horn as long and as loudly as he possibly could. It managed to prevent anything behind attempting something similar and allowed Maurice the space and time to reverse the remaining few feet necessary and swing the lorry into the Bragstone Road.

The gear box smoked and a back wheel jumped a kerb, but it was good driving.

'What pub were you in?' Maurice asked Jeff.

'The White Hart.'

'Was she a prostitute?'

We arrived outside the delivery address at just gone two in the afternoon: 'The Keep, Fullers Avenue, Sunningford'.

The electric gates opened and Maurice steered the truck into an oversized gravel driveway. The gates closed behind us and we faced a very large house, recently built, five storeys high and topped by squiggly brick turrets.

There were slits in the turrets which Maurice said Al had specially designed so he could practise shooting a bow and arrow.

'At what?' Jeff asked.

'At the local peasants when they revolt from time to time.'

A four-door garage stood to the left of the house, fire-escape stairs spiralling up one side to the roof above.

Alan stood in front of us waving his arms exaggeratedly like a solitary man standing on a runway directing a plane in.

Maurice sent Jeff over to find out where Alan wanted us to park and I slid into the passenger seat. After a brief tête-à-tête with Alan, Jeff wandered back to the lorry and stuck his head through Maurice's window.

'All the stuff's going into the house,' he said.

I got out and helped Jeff back Maurice up to the enormous front door. I noticed a switch on the opposite side to the doorbell which I worked out you had to press to lock the top bolts because they were too high for a standing human to reach.

'What about the Lion?' I asked Jeff.

'He didn't say and I didn't ask.'

Alan led us through the front door and into a vast hallway. A marble staircase swept upwards, curving off either side to an imposing landing where a plaster-cast bust of Margaret Thatcher glared down at us from an enclave in the landing wall.

Alan pointed to a door in the hallway and said, 'Cloakroom's there, by the way.'

'Sorry, Al,' Maurice said. 'But I had a mug of tea about an hour ago and wouldn't mind hanging up my coat.'

Alan gave Maurice a puzzled look and then led us left along a passageway, wooden-floored this time, past several closed doors and bowls of scented, dried flowers sitting on ridges underneath electric candles, up two steps and into the kitchen.

I never watched much TV, but when I did, I was always amazed at the size of the kitchens in the adverts. Were these people who sat around enormous coffee tables, eating Special K, Alpen Deluxe, or even securing a loan from Wonga.com, really that wealthy?

Al's was such a kitchen.

What really got me was how sparkling the chrome was. Most likely polished daily by the Filipino maid I could see, ironing away in the utility room which didn't look much smaller than my flat.

'All the boxes,' Alan told us, 'are to be stacked here.' He pointed to an area in the breakfast room by the eight-door French windows. 'Is that enough room, Mike?'

I sensed a tiny flash in Maurice at the continued misuse of his name, but he controlled himself and muttered, 'Fine, Alan, fine.'

'The four items of furniture that…' Alan's voice wavered a touch, but he recovered and etched out an 'oh well' smile. 'That made it. Could they be stored in the games room on the top floor?'

My worst and most annoying trait, according to Sarah, is my unfailing inability to engage my brain fully before I opened my mouth. I'd also worked in removals long enough to know better, but I still had to blurt it out.

'Where do you want your…' I began, and then squeaked in pain as Maurice flicked out his left fist and tapped me on my right testicle, not too hard but not too softly either.

'Are you alright?' Alan asked me.

'Ulcer,' I replied quietly.

'Sorry, Alan,' Maurice said. 'He's been drinking quite a lot recently. Haven't you, Peter?'

We set the van up and carried the cartons through to the kitchen. Maurice reminded us he'd been driving all day and made Jeff and I carry the chest of drawers, sideboard, one-legged table and the knobless Davenport up to the top of the shop.

Jeff and I didn't mind. After we'd leant the Davenport against a wall underneath the sixty-inch flat-screen TV, Jeff racked the reds on the full-sized snooker table while I sorted out the upper-end colours – God Bless You is how I always remembered it.

We tossed a coin and Jeff broke, completely missing everything.

I picked up the white ball and had a go myself. The cue I had was rubbish, but I managed to clip the reds and return the white back up the table just in line with the blue. Jeff reached underneath the table and produced one of those extended crab things. He leant it on the baize, lined up his cue and walloped the white into the pack as hard as possible. He obviously committed a foul as at least two reds and the pink hit the crab thing and one of his arms before he could get them off the table.

'Foul and four to me,' I declared.

Thanks to Jeff's shot, there were several reds sprayed around the baulk cushion nearest me, but I noticed a red at the other end of the table balanced over the bottom-left pocket. I found some chalk and chalked my cue. It was a long way, but I wanted to hit the white slowly, tap in the red and leave myself for the black into the opposite pocket.

I positioned myself and Jeff's phone rang.

'How do you know we're playing snooker?' he asked.

The moment had arrived – there was no escaping it – and we stood on the back of the van with the Stone Lion.

'Peter,' Maurice said to me. 'Go and ask Alan where he wants Burnley.'

'Curly,' Jeff corrected him.

'Curly,' Maurice repeated.

I walked through to the French windows where Alan stood, tearing the tape off a Pack2.

'Excuse me, Alan, but it might be easier if you use this,' I said, and handed him a knife from out of a block on one of the kitchen worktops. 'It also preserves the boxes better.'

I could see that Alan was the type of customer who didn't give a flying fuck about our boxes, but recycling was a potent word to allude to these days and he murmured a, 'Thank you,' and accepted the knife.

He sliced off the rest of the tape and then noticed I still stood there.

'Did you want to ask me something?' he ventured.

'Well, yes. We've unloaded everything off the van except...' I paused.

'Except what?' Alan asked.

We hovered around the Lion while Alan leaned against the tail lift, hands clasped together in thought.

'I think,' he eventually said, and we all looked at him.

Perhaps the unconscious shift in our demeanour from generally amiable removal blokes to something far more potentially threatening affected Alan's decision, or perhaps he was essentially a decent person who could not possibly inflict so much pain on his fellow human beings. Whatever, after another agonising moment of hesitancy, he instructed us to position Curly at the foot of the spiral staircase by the garage.

Maurice untied the webs and, although two had begun to fray, they'd done their job; the Lion hadn't moved an inch. However, the hazards of lowering the tail lift with the beast on it were plain to see. Gravity, itself, had now become an issue.

Maurice decided that Jeff should be the only one to stand on the tail lift and steady the Lion. It was to do with our conjugal states, he reasoned. 'Myself,' he began, 'has been married for thirty years. Peter has only been single for a matter of months which means, Jeff, that you have been the most single.'

'What the fuck are you on about?' Jeff asked.

Maurice smiled. 'Basically, my old mucker, it means you're the lightest.'

It was funny watching Jeff, standing on top of the tail lift and really not looking very happy.

'Don't you dare tilt it,' he said to Maurice, and I saw the devil grin appear.

'I mean it!' Jeff hissed.

Maurice hit the 'DOWN' button and the tail lift shot to the gravel. Jeff was visibly shaking: truly a white-knuckle ride.

We carefully trundled the Lion over to where Alan stood by the side of the garage. The plan was to tilt Curly so his head rested on the wall. Point of balance achieved, we'd then whip out the piano wheels and push the beast back over onto its plinth. Basically, the same method we employed at S&S's but in reverse.

I taped two van blankets to Curly's head to try and nullify any potential damage to the wall, and we all stood back and looked at it again.

'Sorry about this, Alan,' Maurice eventually said, 'but I think we're going to need a hand.'

Including himself, Alan recruited Rosa, the Filipino maid, Bob the gardener and Hugo, a tall feller in a suit who we later found out was Alan's personal tax consultant.

Bob the gardener fetched a spade and Maurice instructed him to build a pile of gravel the same height as the piano wheels. This done, we all tilted Curly on the piano wheels into the pile and then over, ever so gently until its blanketed head rested against the garage wall. I whipped out the piano wheels while Bob hastily removed the pile of gravel and all seven of us positioned ourselves around Curly's head and body. We heaved but the bastard wouldn't move.

Maurice tapped the suit on his shoulder. 'Sorry, mate, but I've forgotten your name.'

'Hugo,' Hugo replied.

'Well, Hugo, would you mind putting a bit more effort in?'

'I do have a bad back, you know,' Hugo retorted.

'Hitting the golf ball too hard?'

'Now, look here...' Hugo hesitated for a fraction of a second. 'My man. I've offered my assistance, haven't I? I don't have to be doing this.'

Maurice wasn't finished. 'Did a pen roll off your desk and you cricked your back bending down to pick it up?'

Hugo's face took on a bright crimson hue. 'Right!' he declared, took off his jacket and handed it to Rosa. He realised we were all looking at him so he took it back off her and hung it over what was left of Curly's tail. He rolled up his sleeves and wagged his finger at Maurice. 'I'll show you,' he said, and grabbed Curly's underside.

Undoubtedly aided by Hugo's new-found strength, we finally managed to stand Curly upright on his plinth.

Hugo brushed down his jacket and glared at Maurice.

Maurice glared back.

Hugo stropped off to the house while Rosa asked the rest of us if we wanted tea.

'Wouldn't mind, love,' Bob said.

'That reminds me, Alan,' Maurice announced, 'I still haven't hung my coat up yet.'

Maurice went to visit the cloakroom and Alan announced he had to make a call and disappeared into the garden.

Rosa bought out the teas on a tray with a little bowl of sugar lumps and a pair of tiny tongs. Bob, Jeff and I thanked her, and she smiled at us and walked back to the house.

We sipped our tea and Bob said, 'Heavy bugger.'

Glimpses of the sun began to flash through scattering clouds and, for a moment, Curly was bathed in light. Its jaws were open in a growl and I, too, wanted to growl. We've won, I wanted to shout; we've fucking moved you.

The clouds thickened and Curly darkened.

What's the point? I thought. Maybe, one day, I'd meet another girl, a good person who I knew I could love and live with and, on our first date, she'd ask me what I did for a living and I'd tell her.

I'd heard Sarah's new feller was a builder. Probably drives her round well-to-do neighbourhoods, pointing at extensions and houses saying, 'I built that.' What could I do? Take the new girl of my dreams up here, ask Alan or the maid if they could open the gates, walk up, show her Curly and say, 'I moved that bastard.'

'Do you mow the lawn, Bob?' Jeff asked.

'Aye, I do.'

'A sit-on?'

'Two.'

'In case one breaks down?'

'No.' Bob smiled, a nice smile in a weather-beaten face. 'There's another lawn you can't see down by the brook. I keep the other mover down there in the other shed.'

Rosa appeared with the tray to collect our cups.

We thanked her again and she smiled her sweet smile and glanced at Curly.

'I help, yes?' she asked us.

'Of course!' we enthused.

'Better than sir?'

'Oh, definitely.'

Rosa beamed.

'Before you go,' Jeff said, 'do you do the hoovering in the house?'

'Oh yes,' she replied.

'She's only got one sit-on,' Bob commented with a wry grin.

Three

MRS CURDLEY

Maurice passed Rosa on his way out of the house and sat in the cab. He put on his glasses and began to study the job sheet.

'If you don't need me anymore, I'll be off home,' Bob said to me and Jeff.

We shook his hand and he walked over to a bicycle padlocked to the fence by the main gates.

Alan reappeared from the garden. 'Everything OK, chaps?'

'Fine.'

'Just one slight thing,' Alan began, a tone of nervousness evident in his voice.

He paused as Bob rode off past the house on his bike and Maurice got out of the cab and walked over towards us, pen and job sheet in hand.

'Any problems, Alan?' Maurice enquired.

'Well, Mike, as I was just about to tell the lads here, my wife has been on the phone. She'll be arriving in a couple of minutes and would like to see you before you go.'

'That's very nice of her,' Maurice said. 'But, while we're waiting, if you'd just like to sign our job sheet acknowledging everything has been delivered to your satisfaction.' He held up the pen.

Alan hesitated.

'Just here.' Maurice pointed to the bottom of the job sheet and his right knee began to tremble.

'I… I… my wife…' Alan stuttered.

'Take your time to unpack,' Maurice continued, 'and when you've finished, give the office a ring and somebody will pop out in a day or two to collect the empty cartons. Our yard's only round the proverbial corner.'

Alan reluctantly took the pen from Maurice's hand but hesitated again. The electric gates began to clank open behind us and we all turned to look.

A metallic-grey, 4x4 BMW began to nose its way into the driveway.

Maurice returned his attention to Alan. 'We would be grateful if you put all the packing paper into one or two of the larger cartons and flatten all the others, preferably with a sharp knife.'

The BMW pulled up to our left.

'Perhaps you could get your maid to do this,' Maurice added.

'Just a mo, please, Mike, my wife has just arrived,' Alan said, and walked over to the BMW, pen still in hand.

'Or even a passing pigeon or wayward hippopotami,' Maurice said under his breath. 'Both they and the maid would undoubtedly possess a lot more common sense than you do.'

I'm not a sexist, I swear, but I am a heterosexual man.

Alan opened the door of the passenger seat and a pair of shapely legs topped by a most exquisite, jean-clad bum appeared. A voluptuous, perfectly formed torso, wrapped in a clinging jumper, came next, followed by a mop of beautifully wild blonde hair.

Mrs Curdley stood upright, clutching her handbag, and turned towards us. The face too was stunning. Exquisitely chiselled features, a perfect nose and wonderful dimples all highlighted by a light touch of superbly applied make-up. Mrs Curdley might have been in her mid-forties, but she was definitely a bit of alright.

Until you got up close.

Her greeting smile to us was a quick stretch of the lips, crow marks fleetingly scarring her cheeks and forehead. She walked over to Curly and rested a slender, ringed hand on the stump of his tail. Her face and eyes quivered imperceptibly, and she shook her head in displeasure. She circled the Lion, one hand cupping her chin in thought and then, for some reason, she looked directly at me.

I held her gaze and caught a glimpse of her very ugly, shallow soul before she raised her eyebrows and shrugged. Even Maurice seemed cowed by her presence; it was as if we were prisoners on death row and she was our executioner.

She walked up the metal staircase by the garage, jiggling that lovely behind, but this time I could detect a small ripple of protruding flesh below either buttock.

'Pleasant lady,' Maurice said, and offered up the job sheet to Alan again. 'If you'd just like to sign here then, please, Alan.'

Mrs Curdley paced along the top of the garage, eyes down, chin still clenched in thought.

Alan was stuttering again. 'I'm not sure... my wife...'

'Darling,' Mrs Curdley called down, 'could you tell the men to bring the Lion up here, please?'

I've never believed in telepathy or anything psychic, but Maurice, Jeff and I changed our posture at exactly the same moment.

For me, this is where I have to admit, the Customer Service NVQ training sessions kicked in and my own personal reaction wasn't as bad as it could have been. Maurice and Jeff didn't care about things like that. I sat next to Maurice during the classes and he drew a big willy on the stick man in my NVQ logbook. Jeff, meanwhile, phoned in sick on both days of the course.

Maurice finally spoke from a more important source: experience. 'She's funny, isn't she?' he said to Alan. 'Now, if you'd just like to sign here, please.'

'I've got to walk away,' Jeff said, and put his hands in his pockets and walked over to the passenger door of the lorry.

'Did you hear me?' Mrs Curdley called out again.

Alan looked at me and Maurice, and once more, I felt some faraway empathy. He was like a man torn between two conflicting emotions. Good and Evil, the romantic in me would have liked to have thought, but perhaps the renewed trembling of Maurice's right knee might have helped tip the balance.

He took hold of the sheet and signed.

Once again, I was astonished by the speed Maurice could move. He shook Alan's hand and was off like a sprinter on something better than steroids, the driver's door to the truck opening and shutting as quickly as a gnat's jazzer.

I stood on my own with Alan and I wanted to say something profound, to communicate my feelings of gratitude and sympathy towards his plight, but in the end, all I could manage was, 'Thanks for the tea,' and shook his hand.

Jeff slid into the bunk while I climbed into the passenger seat.

Mrs Curdley waved at us in fury.

Maurice waved happily back.

'Alan, the men are leaving!' she cried.

Alan approached the driver's door, a tortured look on his handsome features.

Maurice wound down his window.

'Tell them to carry Curly up here immediately!' Mrs Curdley yelled.

'Mike,' Alan began.

'Yes, Alan?'

'Mike,' Alan repeated. 'My wife would like—'

'A snooker cue up her arse?' Jeff said from the bunk.

'Sorry, what was that?'

'Nothing,' Maurice said. 'Jeff here was having a bit of a wheeze.'

'A wheeze?'

'A bit of a laugh.'

'Oh.'

Maurice switched on the ignition.

'It's just my wife would like Curly situated on top of the garage.'

Maurice raised his voice above the engine. 'Would she indeed? Perhaps you and Hugo could carry it up there for her.' He reversed the truck back in front of the garage, changed gears and drove up to the gates.

'Stop them, Alan!' we heard Mrs Curdley scream.

The gates juddered open and we began to drive out. Alan chased after us and Jeff said, 'I'm going to smack the twat.'

'Patience, dear boy, patience,' Maurice told him, and indicated right.

Alan appeared at my window.

I wound it down and Maurice leant across. 'The office will send you the bill for the extra boxes we used to repack your wares, Alan,' he said.

'Tell them to come back here and do as they're bloody well told!' Mrs Curdley hollered from the rooftop.

'I see,' Alan said. 'It's just… my wife—'

'When was the last time you had sex, Alan?' Jeff asked.

Of course, Alan didn't hear him. He was transfixed, a helpless fly caught on a sticky web waiting to be eaten. He pulled out his wallet.

Mrs Curdley bellowed out something and Maurice beeped his horn.

Alan pulled out three notes, folded them in half and said, 'For the extra boxes, Mike.'

He held up the folding to me. I didn't know what to do.

'Thank you very much, Al,' Maurice said.

I remained frozen.

'Thank the man, Peter, please.'

I took the notes and said, 'Thank you very much, Alan.'

We drove down the road under a sinking sun, a few whispery white clouds tinging red in the darkening blue. We passed a school at chucking-out time and a couple of kids tried stepping out in front of us and making faces. Maurice beeped his horn and they sprang back, alarmed.

Alan had given me three £20 notes.

Maurice pulled up at the Bragstone lights. He put the handbrake on and rested his elbows on the steering wheel. He looked tired, older, I suppose.

I handed him a twenty.

'Give it me back at the yard,' he said.

I clipped the note to the top of the job sheet and put one of the other notes in my back pocket. I turned and handed the last one to Jeff.

The lights changed.

Was it because I used to smoke weed or was it because I had a GCSE in Religious Education? I'm not sure, but the twenty didn't feel right in my pocket, and I took it out.

'Do you think we should chuck two quid in each for charity?' I asked.

Maurice eased off the handbrake.

'You know, for Rosa and the gardener and all?'

Jeff sat up on the bunk.

Maurice shifted gears and turned to me. 'Booth, you can give as much as you like to charity, but I, personally, am spending all twenty sobs on myself.'

'Me too,' said Jeff.

'Sorry, Rosa and Bob,' I said, and returned the twenty to my back pocket.

'Amen,' said Maurice, and we drove back to the yard.

Four

THE FRIDAY NIGHT CLUB

We were the last crew back, the other vans lying silent under the dark sky. Although it was a clear evening, stars were rarely visible on the Fleet Town industrial estate.

Maurice parked up the lorry and sorted out his tachograph. Jeff and I got out and walked along the fag-strewn, pebbled passageway dividing the east side of our warehouse with the barbed-wire fence of Majestic Wine depot and turned left through the fire door and into the restroom.

Dressed in his perennial shorts and sunglasses, Leo Wainwright leant against the counter underneath the glass shutter, dividing the restroom from the office, with his back towards us. He purposefully tensed his gym-fuelled biceps as he pointed at something on his job sheet to another much shorter and slimmer person standing next to him, also with their back towards us.

Leo turned. 'Heard you had a spot of bother with a garden ornament today, Unsworth.'

'Not as much bother as you're going to have after I've booted you in the slats,' Jeff replied.

Leo chuckled annoyingly.

The figure beside him also turned to face us.

'This is Emily,' Leo announced.

Emily nodded shyly.

I'd have put her in her mid-thirties, but she was difficult to age. Her hair was tied back in a ponytail and I couldn't detect any make-up.

Leo introduced us in his 'I know more than anybody else' monotone. 'This is Jeff Unsworth and Peter Booth, both senior members of staff, although,' he paused and winked at Emily, 'unlike myself, neither of them are qualitied, confessional HGV drivers.'

Emily looked a little puzzled – she obviously hadn't yet registered Leo's insistence on trying to use long words and, more often than not, mispronouncing them.

Leo droned on. 'This has been Emily's first day with us: her induckment day.'

'Induction,' I corrected him under my breath, and then cursed myself.

Leo joined Stoneways two years ago and, after a couple of weeks, I worked out that it wasn't worth trying to tell him anything. This was mainly due to the fact that he didn't possess any listening capacity unless he was actually shouted at, and even then, very little information would register in the murky depths of that large, square, rugby-playing head.

The Stoneways uniform didn't do Emily any favours. The black trousers and red sweatshirt, obviously several sizes too big, made her appear baggy and shapeless, but her brown eyes and fresh face belied a pleasing attractiveness. As the saying goes, she looked like she could scrub up well.

'She spent the morning with Daz and the secretary, Ross Keating,' Leo rolled on, 'filling in the necessary forms and studying the various nodules on health and safety, fire awareness and other technocratic stuff. Luckily for the office, I, as usual, finished my job miles earlier than anyone else would have done and this afternoon I've been showing her around the warehouse and lorries to give her a feel of how things get done here. I've also given Emily an extensive tour of the new and second-hand carton area and have already demonstrocated taping up a Pack6, *and*,' Leo stressed, 'a Pack4.'

'Pardon my language, Emily,' Jeff interrupted, 'but Leo, could you please shut the fuck up?'

Emily blushed and I noticed a couple of quite sexy dimples appear. *Oh Christ*, I thought, *I'm beginning to fancy her.*

Daz Oatridge stepped through the office door. 'Lads,' he greeted us. 'Take it Leo's introduced you to Emily, our new member of staff.'

I nodded and formally shook hands with Emily. Her hand was soft, a tad clammy due to nerves, maybe, but I didn't mind. She smiled and her brown eyes seemed to me to become larger and glow a touch.

Jeff held up a hand in greeting.

Emily gave him a little wave back and said to Daz, 'Everybody's so friendly here.' Her voice was gentle with a slight London twang but not common-sounding.

'Fortunately, Emily,' Daz addressed her, 'we've managed to create a happy, working environment at Stoneways and possess an admittedly diverse but exceptionally cheerful and helpful collection of staff.' I gave Daz his due, he did actually pause before he added, 'Haven't we, boys?'

Maurice appeared through the restroom door. 'Ah, Mr Oatridge,' he said. 'On Monday morning, shall we all come in early, line up against the wall by the front entrance while you and the other office staff climb up on the roof and throw several buckets of freshly laid cow pat over our heads?'

During the eighteen years I'd worked for Stoneways, Friday night had always been pub night.

The boss, Kye Stoneway himself, would place his plastic over the jump of a local hostelry for an hour or so or instruct one of the other managers to do so in his absence. This enabled his staff to enjoy a couple of free pints and ease tensions which may have surfaced during the week.

An intelligent stab at team-bonding, I would call it, although, on occasion, the tab had been kept open too long and been readily abused by several members of staff, resulting in drunkenness, excessive tomfoolery, vandalism, violence twice and arrest three times. After such events, the Friday Night Club, as it became commonly known, would be suspended until a particularly busy period – usually punctuated with bouts of atrocious estimating – necessitated its reinstatement in order to ward off the threat of serious mutiny.

The venue had also changed over the years mainly due to such disturbances resulting in bans for certain members of staff. The current watering hole was the Queens Head in Purfleet, where Maurice had been barred from back in 2004 for throwing a chair at the television screen when Arsenal were beaten 2-0 in the cup by Macclesfield. However, the ownership had changed several times since so his bar had naturally been lifted.

There'd also been an increase in trouble in the local area mainly due to the construction of the Redbridge Estate in Fleet Town in 2006. Consequently, it was actually impossible to lift up a barstool in the pub because they'd all been nailed to the floor.

Maurice gave me and Jeff a lift down to the Queens in his wonderfully messy Citroen. Jeff got in the back and I swept two empty cans of Tizer, four chocolate bar wrappers and three copies of the *Daily Mirror* off the front passenger seat and sat down. Despite a fair amount of effort on my part, the seatbelt refused to click into its designated slot and I settled with holding it across my stomach. I'd recently been fined £30 for not wearing one in Sarah's VW by an over-zealous female PC in North Bitton and didn't want it to happen again.

It started to rain when we turned left down the London Road. Maurice switched on the windscreen wipers, opened his window and held out his free hand. The right wiper hadn't worked properly for over a month and his hand was the only obstacle deflecting the wiper back across the windscreen.

The Queens Head was a large pub set back off the Mossford Road heading out of Purfleet. Although the pub was built in the late 1800s and boasted several attractive features such as the criss-cross of overhead wooden beams and the original Victorian fireplace, it had never elevated its status beyond a reasonably agreeable establishment frequented by local people. In other words, it was probably the best pub in Purfleet, but that wasn't saying much.

The Stoneways crowd occupied two pushed together tables in the far corner of the dining area by the window. This wasn't a problem. The Queens was a traditional pub in the sense that Friday evenings were for drinking not eating.

Maurice ordered himself a Fosters while Jeff and I went for the Stella – make the most of the free alcohol, was Jeff and I's motto.

Sat at the head of the table was sixteen-year-old Freddie Keating, currently the youngest member of staff. Freddie, like most people of his age, was immersed in his mobile phone. Ross, his mother and company secretary sat to his left engaged in conversation with Stoneways' main estimator opposite: the aptly named Trevor Blind. Next to them, on either side, sat Daz Oatridge and the forklift driver, Barry Noble.

On the second table, one of the other HGV drivers, a red-eyed Steve Woodgit, was playing a game on his phone. Opposite him sat Emily, quiet and attentive to the lumbering charms of the colossal Leo, who sat next to her, invading her space with elbow and arm outstretched.

Maurice and Jeff sat down at the end of their table while I decided to hover by the window between Barry Noble and Steve Woodgit, stealing the odd glance towards Emily and hoping she wouldn't catch me.

Now in his mid-fifties, Barry Noble was the second longest-serving member of staff after Maurice and the only person amongst us who drank real ale. As he often liked to remind us, the first spoon ever placed in his mouth was definitely of the plastic variety.

His parents separated when he was young and he was thrown out onto the streets by his mother when he was fifteen. Angry throughout the rest of his teens and his twenties, he seemed to become even angrier in his thirties before fortune eventually decided to give him a break. He met the lovely Angela, a divorcée with a caring heart and an all-encompassing devotion towards her new beaux.

Shortly after we moved to the new warehouse in Fleet Town, Barry leapfrogged Maurice in the seniority stakes and was taken off the vans and promoted to forklift driver and warehouse manager. His advancement was understandable – a vision of Maurice rampaging through the warehouse on a potentially, highly lethal forklift truck would disturb any sane person's mind. The absence of the mental and physical stress of frontline removals, combined with his new-found love, mellowed Barry beyond recognition. At heart, he still remained a naturally cynical man but possessed a very subtle wit and a turn of phrase to be envied.

In front of Steve Woodgit was a bottled, pseudo-Mexican concoction with a slice of lemon in its neck. C-drinks, Jeff called them, but Steve didn't really care about alcohol; weed was his thing.

Barry was questioning Daz Oatridge where the boss was.

Daz was evasive. 'I think he went to have a look at a new truck in Farnborough.'

'Is that what they call Cindy Sutcliffe these days: a new truck in Farnborough?' Barry asked. The boss was not renowned for his fidelity.

'I don't think Emily really needs to hear that, Barry.'

Emily heard her name mentioned. 'I'm sorry?' she said.

'We were just talking about the boss's new truck,' Barry told her. 'Quite impressive, I'm led to believe.'

'Oh,' she said. 'I suppose he'd always be on the lookout for new vehicles.'

'Indeed, he always is,' Barry replied.

Leo excitedly reached into the man bag he always carried around with him and produced a copy of *Truckers Monthly*. He flicked it open to an earmarked page and held up a picture of the latest Scania for Emily to peruse.

'Now this is the sort of truck I keep telling the boss to buy.'

'Yes,' Barry said, 'but he pays about as much attention to you as a vegan does to a sausage roll.'

I could see Emily was embarrassed: an indication to me of her general niceness. She murmured an, 'Excuse me,' and began to fiddle with her hairband. She undid it, shook her head and a wonderfully thick sheen of dark, kinked hair tumbled down around her shoulders. She blew a few strands of stray wisps off her forehead and caught my eye, perhaps for the first time since I'd been in the pub.

A nervous, icy tingling hit me in the chest. I tried to smile but I think it came out as a sort of toothy grimace. Jesus, I was acting like a spotty teenager.

The initial shine of her face vanished and I saw a confused look cross her eyes. She gave me a tiny, almost infinitesimal shrug and turned back to look at the photograph of the Scania.

Maurice, meanwhile, was busy tearing up his bar mat into bits. When finished, he brushed the pile of torn pieces onto the carpet.

'Why have you done that?' Jeff asked.

'Because, Mr Unsworth, I'm ensuring continued employment for the pub's cleaner. This is the back end of 2010 and, despite Mr Cameron's recent pledge that we're all in it together, we are currently embroiled in a rather challenging recession, in case you hadn't noticed. Persons such as us, factory workers, those employed in the building trade *and* cleaners, are rightfully worried about their jobs. Thus, by purposefully littering the floor of this establishment, I am thereby ensuring that the cleaner will still be gainfully employed. My take on Keynsian economics,' Maurice finished, and tapped Steve Woodgit on his shoulder. 'Don't you agree, Mr Woodgit?'

'Whatever,' Steve said, and went back to his game.

'You don't half talk some old shite,' Jeff said.

'Intelligent and constructive shite,' Maurice replied, and wiped his hands. He took a large gulp of his Fosters and shook his head quickly from side to side in appreciation. He emitted a long, 'aaaaah'-type noise and looked over at Emily, who was now holding the copy of *Truckers Weekly* while Leo explained to her some finer points of the new Scania.

'Young lady,' Maurice addressed her.

'Yes?' Emily looked up.

'I don't think we've been properly introduced. I'm Maurice Bagley, pleased to meet you.'

'Emily Richards,' she politely replied.

'First of all, Emily Richards, do you take it—'

'Maurice!' I shouted.

He guffawed and had another swig of his pint.

Alarmed, I looked over at Emily, but she bore a mild, confused expression as though she hadn't heard Maurice properly or, perhaps, like many other people who didn't know him very well, could not truly believe what he'd just said.

Daz Oatridge stood up and asked everybody if they'd like another drink. It was obviously his plastic behind the jump.

I offered to give him a hand and began to take the order.

Ross said she had to get home and offered her son a lift, but Freddie said he'd like to stay and asked for a Coke. Barry drained his ale and put on his yellow hi-viz; he only ever had one pint if he was driving. Leo put his hand over his glass and said, 'In training, Pete,' but made no sign he was leaving. That man could make a solitary pint last hours.

I didn't bother asking Steve – conversation wasn't his bag. If he wanted another drink, he'd go to the bar on his own steam, most probably after he'd nipped out to his car for his hourly reefer. I also didn't bother asking Jeff. That man would be in Stella mode till half eight when he'd order a Queens Special Mixed Grill before they stopped serving. Not great on quality but high on quantity; Jeff was never sure when he'd eat next.

Maurice stood up and said he had to go.

'Are you alright?' Jeff, Daz, Trevor Blind and myself asked at the same time.

'Wife's birthday,' Maurice informed us.

Occasions such as birthdays had never stopped Maurice from having that extra pint. Something wasn't right and I recalled his tired look at the Bragstone lights on the way back this evening. I had mixed feelings. I did genuinely care for Maurice and worried about him, but I was also relieved. Sometimes, I'm afraid to say, I was happier to see Maurice Bagley leaving a pub rather than entering one.

Trevor Blind signalled for another Peroni and I looked over at Emily with enquiring eyes as coolly and as uninterestedly as I possibly could.

'I'd really better get going,' she said.

'Oh, come on,' Trevor said. 'Have another one.'

She glanced at her near-empty glass of red wine and said to me, 'Could I just have a tonic water, please?'

Daz noticed my dazed silence and said, 'Course you can,' and he and I walked up to the bar.

It was busy but Ruth, the landlady, spotted us and asked what we were having. I began to relay the order and she pulled three empty pint glasses from underneath the bar and began to pour out the two Stellas.

Daz said to me, 'Mrs Curdley rang up and registered a complaint about you, Jeff and Maurice.'

I felt the rage but didn't want to argue. Daz had been good to me when I'd told him about the split from Sarah and given me the necessary time off to sort things out. I owed him.

'She's a silly cow,' I said.

'I know, mate. Don't worry about it.'

Ruth placed two pints of Stella on the bar. 'Peroni?' she asked.

I nodded and heard a commotion behind me.

Maurice had collapsed on the floor by the door Barry Noble was currently holding open for him.

Nobody moved except Emily, who sprang over and frantically began to pump Maurice's chest. 'I'm a trained first aider!' she cried. She pummelled his chest some more and then leant down and pressed her lips on Maurice's.

I actually saw Maurice's tongue flick into her mouth.

Emily was fraught. She made a small gagging sound, got up, grabbed her coat and bolted out to the car park.

'Looks like Emily's completed her induction day,' Jeff said.

Barry wished us all 'Goodnight' while Maurice upended himself and said, 'Pint of Fosters, please, Booth.'

I couldn't be arsed to get the bus, so I asked Steve Woodgit to give me a lift home back to South Bitton at half seven. I noticed, with some consternation, that young Freddie had jumped in the back. He lived with his mum in West Purfleet and had obviously only come along for a toke of Steve's ganja.

It wasn't that I was anti-weed. I'd smoked it for several years until I noticed a paranoid type of near psychosis beginning to develop. I also became aware that if I didn't have any, I'd become irritable and dull to the point of thinking what the point of getting up in the morning was. The days of hysterical laughter and Tangerine Dream sounding brilliant began to seem far away, and I hadn't smoked any cannabis for a long while. But those were my issues, nobody else's.

Steve was a lovely feller: no temper, no aggression, no back-stabbing and always ready to help somebody out. Maybe my only criticism of him was that he was too laidback. Like now, as he sat hunched over the steering wheel, eyes glazed, staring straight ahead. It was as if nobody was at home which I found fairly alarming when he was driving.

I was concerned for Freddie because I treated him like a son. Ever since I'd first started working for Stoneways, his mum, Ross, and her husband, Bill, had always been nice to me, and when Bill tragically died when Freddie was eight, I'd kept my eye out for him. Perhaps this was the first time I was seeing Freddie shed the shackles of his naive and endearing youth and taking his first bite of an apple from the Tree of Life.

Oh well, beyond my control now, I thought.

I gave Steve a fiver and got him to drop me off on the Broadway. I watched as he sped off back to the A3, handing Freddie his joint, which the latter greedily sucked on.

My original plan had been to stop off in the Wetherspoons and imbibe a cheap pint. Finances weren't strong since my split from Sarah, but I decided against it. The pub had once been a cinema and I found the music-free atmosphere in the cavernous space depressing. Sitting on my own at a dimly lit table, listening to other people's chit-chat, the clinking of glasses, the paying-out of fruit machines and the constant low murmur of the pub's fridges didn't appeal to me right now.

Instead, I stopped in Sanjays and bought a cheap bottle of red wine and two microwave meals – macaroni cheese and spaghetti Bolognaise. 'Meal for Two', both sets of packaging declared so, combined, they should be just about enough.

The flat hadn't changed since I'd left it that morning. Perhaps that was the most depressing thing: no evidence of any other human life except for me.

I put the meals in the fridge; I'd eat them later. Right now, I just wanted to open the wine, pour a decent-sized draught into one of the pint glasses I'd purloined from various pubs since I'd lived there and lie down on the bed to rest my aching bones.

I stretched myself out, enjoying that tiny crumb of comfort even that single bed could provide.

After a couple of minutes, I raised myself up on the pillow. The silence was too much. I didn't want television but I needed sound.

Most of my CD collection still lay unpacked in a Pack6 underneath the bed apart from a few scattered around the CD player on the chair beside the bed. Tom Petty's *Damn the Torpedoes*. Yes, it was a good album, but I wanted something harder. Early AC/DC?

No. Motorhead? Maybe. The Jam? *Why the fuck did I buy that?* I thought. The hypocrite writes 'The Eton Rifles' and then sends his own kids to private school.

I drank more of the wine and studied the Van Gogh print on the wall above the telly. I wasn't really into art but I liked this picture: a ladder lying flat down in the snow outside an old farmhouse. It was simple, understated, rustic, but the lack of people bothered me.

A sound flashed through my mind and I sat up on the bed and pulled out the Pack6. After a couple of minutes, I finally found what I was looking for, and it wasn't a U2 album.

The Best of Black Sabbath.

I put it on.

I love Sabbath: the guitar, the drums, the bass, the voice and the vitriol.

I stood.

Darkness and beauty.

Sarah telling me she wanted me to leave.

I finished the wine in my glass and clicked the stop button on the CD player. Even the Sabs couldn't keep me in.

I still couldn't face the Spoons, so I headed for the Lazy Lion. It was a considerably more expensive pub, but right now, I wanted some life and some noise.

I tripped slightly as I walked up the three steps to the entrance and a suited skinhead bouncer gave me a disapproving look but let me in.

I bought a pint of some unpronounceable Belgian lager and sidled up to a couple I vaguely knew who were standing by a wall-length picture of a packet of cheese and onion crisps. I suppose I should have heeded the warning signs when I kept swaying into people and noticing, in general, that my mouth was getting way too far ahead of my brain, but I'd moved a Stone Lion today and the only place I was going back to was a dingy flat, two microwave meals and half a bottle of undrinkable red wine.

Five

THE FOOTBALL MATCH

My mobile phone woke me up.

I was lying on the bed, fully clothed with my steel-capped boots on. The alarm clock read 8.43am. My head hurt but I was more aware of being incredibly thirsty and dying for a pee. I checked the name on the screen: *Sarah*. I didn't answer and headed for the loo, the phone falling silent as I peed.

I washed my hands, drank two pints of cold water, one straight after the other, and opened the fridge door. The ready meals still lay there untouched, their only company a tub of margarine and the half bottle of wine.

I showered and got changed into my jeans, fleece and Stoneways bomber jacket, found thirty quid and some shrapnel in the pockets of my work trousers, threw the strides into the open Pack3 I was using as a laundry basket and silently thanked Alan Curdley for his tip.

I stopped in Sanjays to buy ten Benson and Hedges – for some reason, I always had to smoke when I had a hangover, and I realised with no sense of pride that hangovers were becoming more and more frequent since Sarah had kicked me out.

There were two cafés on the Broadway but the Sunshine Eat was my preferred one. The owners, Frank and Manny, were Turkish and the food always seemed a little less greasy than George's next to Iceland. I should have ordered a salad or even something with scrambled eggs, slightly healthier fare to combat the booze, but couldn't resist my usual: the Special with chips and extra black pudding. The other thing I liked about the Sunshine was the coffee: proper strong filtered stuff and not overly expensive.

My phone rang when I was eating: *Sarah*. I pressed the silent button and promised myself I'd phone her later. I picked at a gap between two of my teeth with one of my fingernails and it rang again.

I glanced down, registered the name and picked it up. 'Ross,' I said into the phone. 'How are you?'

'I'm fine, Pete. And you?'

'All good my end,' I answered cheerily.

'Really?'

'Well, yeah. Why?'

'You phoned me twice last night. At half ten and at quarter to midnight.'

'Ah,' was all I could come out with.

'I didn't answer.'

'Ah,' I repeated.

'Pissed?' she asked.

'More than likely,' I admitted.

There was a pause on the line.

'Ross? You still there?'

'Yes, of course.' There was another pause. 'Look, Pete. Why don't you come over this afternoon? Fred's playing a game at three. He likes you to come. We could watch the football and have a quick drink afterwards. I worry about you in that tiny flat.'

I looked out of the café window: no sign of rain. 'Sounds good,' I said.

'Do you want me to pick you up?'

I thought about this. Ross was undoubtedly one of my best friends and I enjoyed her company but just recently – unless I was working – Saturdays had become a slow dissolving into a mild alcoholic stupor. A full breakfast, a few pints at lunchtime, a leisurely kip back at the flat, another couple of pints, late afternoon/early evening in the company of an old acquaintance or even a complete stranger, and then back to the flat once more with a four-pack or bottle of wine, a DVD or a touch of Saturday-night telly and, perhaps, a trawl through my CD collection, a microwave meal or a takeaway if I could afford one, and a steady drift into oblivion.

Depressing, some might say, but strangely comforting. No emotional commitments nor shocks, the life of a single man existing solely on a removal wage.

I hedged my bets. 'Thanks, but I'll make my own way. Home game?'

'It is.'

'OK. See you there.'

'You will come, won't you, Peter?' Ross's voice was sceptical.

'Definitely,' I said, and hung up. I grimaced – Ross was like a mind reader.

I finished my breakfast and went to the till to pay.

Frank stood there as usual. A stocky, unshaven man with a bull-like neck, Frank was in charge of the money. It was rumoured he once owned a Turkish restaurant in Haywards Heath and cut two fingers off a drunk with a kebab knife who was trying to steal from the till.

I gave him a tenner and Frank sorted me out the change.

'Oh, shit,' I said. 'Sorry, Frank, could I have a black coffee to take away?' I offered him back two of the pound coins.

'On house,' Frank told me.

This was unexpected and I thanked him.

He turned to his daughter, Tula, who was putting dirty plates into the dishwasher. 'Black coffee for Peter, takeaway.'

Tula stopped what she was doing and filled up a styrofoam cup from the pot on the hob. She fastened on a lid and handed it to me. She was a pretty girl and she smiled, and I smiled back. Oh, shit, I was beginning to fancy any woman who showed even the slightest interest in me.

'Second thoughts,' Frank said, and looked at me with dark eyes. 'One pound twenty, please.'

It was cold but the sun was high in the sky. I walked down to the park and saw Kilo sitting on an otherwise empty bench by the old Scout Hut and sat down beside him.

Kilo was an off-and-on acquaintance I'd known over many years. We'd never become close enough to exchange phone numbers but he was a colourful character and I always enjoyed our irregular chats.

'Pete.'

'Kilo,' I acknowledged.

'How's Sarah?'

'She's kicked me out.' I undid the lid off my coffee, took a sip and placed it on the ground. I pulled out the packet of fags and offered them to Kilo.

He took one, produced a monstrous contraption from his jacket pocket and pressed a button. A huge blue flame erupted. I bent over, lit my fag and moved quickly away, my eyebrows singeing.

Kilo lit his and we sat in silence.

A woman and two children were throwing pieces of bread to the ducks and two swans floating in the pond. A man with a ponytail wearing a trench coat sat on another bench reading a book and a couple cycled past on the pathway.

My phone began to ring. I checked the screen. *Sarah* glared back at me. I let it ring.

'Not going to answer it?' Kilo asked.

'Not yet,' I said, and the phone stopped ringing. I picked up my coffee, took a sip and offered it to Kilo, who shook his head.

Coffee wasn't really Kilo's bag nor, for that matter, were alcohol or drugs, which was surprising since his reputation was built on his own phrase that he could get you a kilo of anything. He told me once he'd been a roadie for Judas Priest and I'd never had any reason to disbelieve him.

'Had to go to the doc the other day,' Kilo said. 'Reckons I've got cancer.'

'Kilo!' I was alarmed and turned to look at him. He possessed a healthy crop of hair greased back into a rocker's quiff.

'S'OK, chemo doesn't bother me. Buster Bloodvessel did alright and so did Phil Collins.' He looked at me and I saw the easy, friendly sparkle in his eyes countered by that tiny glimpse of darkness which hinted at a different person I always hoped I'd never meet.

It was 11.30am when I finally relented and decided to have a pint in the Spoons.

I really didn't like the dimness of the place and I could hear another noise above the fridges: a loud bleep which sounded every three seconds. Where the fuck had that come from?

I checked the beer pumps along the bar and spotted Aunty's Cornish Banger. *A rich, fruity ale from Pasty Country*, the blurb declared. I was more interested in the price, £1.25, and the alcohol content, 7.5%.

A tall kid in a black shirt approached me.

'Pint of one of them, please,' I said, and pointed at the pump.

I looked round as the barman poured and counted five people sitting at tables on their own, reading the paper or just staring into space. There was a sound of coins clattering onto a metal tray and I saw Paranoid Ian standing by one of the fruit machines, sunglasses on, woolly scarf pulled up to just below his nose.

Legend has it, Ian once ate four hundred magic mushrooms, which subsequently caused a few psychological problems. I'd known him since infant's school, but he was an acquired taste, so I paid for the beer and headed for the furthest corner of the pub away from him.

I settled on a table by a pillar which I could hide behind if Ian decided to wander. Half a burnt sausage, a pile of untouched beans and an unfinished fried egg sat amongst a slew of brown sauce on a chipped white plate. A fork was balanced on the sausage, but the knife was nowhere to be seen. I picked up the plate, placed it on an adjacent table and sat behind the pillar.

A copy of *The Sun* lay on the chair beside me, but I didn't touch it. It wasn't so much that the paper was a rag; it was more my unnatural fear of Maurice suddenly appearing in front of me and committing some extremely painful act of violence to one of the more sensitive regions of my anatomy because I dared peruse such right-wing, sensationalist bollocks.

I took a swig of my pint. Christ almighty, where the hell did they get the *rich, fruity ale* bit? The beer tasted like the water from a bucket after somebody had washed a scaffolder's two-week-old pair of underpants in it.

I pulled out my phone and scrolled down the contact list to *Sarah*. I should ring her, I knew, but I still wasn't in the mood. The split had been coming for a long time and, as far as I knew, there'd been no third party involved. There was no great shouting match; she showed me the door and I left, but certain words still stung.

I put the phone down on the table and took another drink. God, it was awful, but the alcohol content was beginning to dull me. Another couple of these and I'd quite happily stagger back to the flat and sleep.

I thought about Kilo and hoped he'd be alright. I drank again and the looseness began to envelop me. Even the three-second beep sounded comforting.

I picked up the copy of *The Sun*. 'WE'RE BETTER OFF WITH THE TORIES!' the headline shouted. I put it back on the chair and had another drink. It was still quite foul but getting better.

Paranoid Ian stood at the bar with his winnings.

I should go and say hello, I thought and then heard a new, more consistent bleep. A text message from Ross.

just letting you know. charlie playing today. his mum emily our new employee also coming X

I shot back to the flat, poured out a pint of water and lay on the bed.

My head was still swimming from the pint of Aunty's Cornish Banger and I realised I needed some form of kip before I went to the game. I switched on the telly to *Football Focus* on BBC1, which was fortunately showing extended highlights of Chelsea's midweek goalless draw away to Spartak Moscow in the Champion's League.

I woke up at half one, sober and reasonably refreshed. I worked out I could catch a bus from the bowling alley in an hour which would get me to Leysham Village for just after three, allowing me plenty of time to get ready.

I was quite happy with the jeans and fleece but became a bit of a tart over my choice of T-shirt. Every single shirt I owned had a band logo on it. What would Emily be into?

Outwardly, there'd been no clues. No orange, pink, blue, green or red dye in her hair, no piercings and no visible tattoos. She might not even like music, but I had to try and look sophisticated.

Napalm Death and Social Distortion definitely had cool factor but were too obscure, while AC/DC and Motorhead pigeonholed me too much. I tried on a Hawkwind *Levitation* 1979 tour T-shirt I bought in a head shop during a night out in Bristol a few years back – one of my favourites – but it cried out self-righteous, crusty hippy.

Funkadelic, the same.

A stroke of inspiration finally hit me when I was brushing my teeth at two-fifteen.

I found it lying at the bottom of the chest of drawers: a Kenny Rogers T-shirt. I wouldn't say everybody I'd ever met loved Kenny, but I couldn't think of anybody who passionately disliked him.

I put on a fleece and my leather jacket and checked myself one last time in the bathroom mirror, squinting slightly to blur some of the more unattractive features of my thirty-eight-year-old countenance.

The game had already started when I got to the ground.

Ross and Emily stood together on the halfway line with a gaggle of other parents and I moseyed my way over.

Ross pecked me on the cheek and squeezed my hands with hers.

Emily turned and gave me a half-smile; I didn't think she recognised me.

'What's the score?' I asked Ross.

'Nil-nil,' she replied. 'They've only been playing ten minutes.'

I tried to concentrate on the game but couldn't help glancing over at Emily. She was wearing a cagoul and even baggier trousers than her Stoneways pair, but her face looked decidedly pretty underneath her blue and red bobble hat.

'Don't scare her,' Ross whispered in my ear. 'Watch the game.'

The opposition, Broughton under-19s, had a free kick just outside Leysham's penalty area. Freddie stood on the goal line by one of the posts, jostling with one of their strikers. The ref blew the whistle and Freddie saw me and waved as the ball floated over his stationary head into the top of the net.

Emily's boy Charlie looked quite useful. He played in central midfield and, despite appearing to be too small and lightweight, he was fast and tricky. After an impressive run, beating two defenders, he lost the ball in Broughton's penalty area, but Leysham's captain reacted before anyone else and slotted the ball calmly past the keeper for the equaliser.

Emily jumped for joy, and Ross and I clapped.

Despite another scintillating run by Charlie and a terrific foul by Freddie on the oppo's right-winger, the rest of the half dissolved into a pretty uninspiring spectacle – lots of aerial stuff but not much ground control.

'Do either of you want a coffee?' I asked after the ref blew the half-time whistle.

Emily looked at me. 'Oh, sorry,' she said, 'I didn't recognise you. You're Jeff, aren't you?'

'Pete,' I told her, trying not to sound too deflated.

'Oh, I'm terribly sorry; I apologise again.'

'Don't worry about it.' I adopted a thoughtful stance. 'And you're...?'

'Peter,' Ross interrupted, 'stop being such a pillock.'

After Ross had firmly sledgehammered my nose into place, I went to the clubhouse and bought her and myself a coffee; Emily said she had her own thermos.

I could never get properly angry with Ross. She was like the sister I'd never had, but I do wish she'd sometimes stop being so brutally honest with me. Especially in front of other people who didn't yet know me very well.

The man who served me was a permanently grumpy feller I recognised as one of the Leysham Village Dad's – Pod, I think he called himself. He poured half a teaspoonful of insipid-looking, granule-free instant into two plastic cups.

I stopped him before he added boiling water. 'Could you put a bit more coffee into those, please?'

Pod sighed exaggeratedly and shook his head. 'It's not a fucking charity, you know,' he said but did add another quarter teaspoonful to each cup.

The wind had gotten up and it was beginning to feel a lot colder. I noticed Emily hopping up and down on one foot as she chatted to Ross.

I walked over and Emily started to speak to me straightaway.

'Ross tells me you're one of the nicest people she knows.'

'Well, that's very kind of her,' I said, and handed Ross her coffee.

Emily was jumping up and down fairly rapidly now, and wisps of her dark hair began to escape from her bobble hat and drift quite sexily around her face.

I thought of Leo and Maurice. 'Probably not much competition,' I joked.

'The guys at Stoneways?' she said. 'Oh, they all seemed alright; a bit childish, maybe, but nothing I can't handle.'

She hopped up and down again, and I noticed a globule of snot appear at the bottom of her left nostril.

'I've mainly always worked with other girls,' Emily continued, 'and, believe me, they can be a lot worse. I was just telling Ross here that I'm quite looking forward to Monday.'

I had to tell her. 'Sorry, Emily, but I think you've got a little…' I stopped and wiped at my nose.

She looked at me as though I was a nutter.

I flicked a finger at my nose again.

'Oh, I see,' she said, and dabbed at her face with a hanky.

'I'm really sorry, Emily,' I heard Ross say. 'I really am.'

There were a couple of chances for both sides in the opening twenty minutes of the second half and Freddie, up for a corner from the back, had a header cleared off the line. Ross told me this was quite a grudge match. For reasons unknown, both managers couldn't stand each other and both teams were second and third from the bottom of the league: the archetypal six-pointer.

The more the half went on, the nigglier the game got. I noticed Freddie and the winger he'd so gloriously fouled in the first half, constantly pushing and generally mouthing each other.

With ten minutes left to go, Emily's Charlie made another great run and forced a throw-in down the right, five feet shy of the Broughton corner flag. Freddie raced up from his left back position presumably with the intention of taking the throw-in quickly. The winger got there first and booted the ball as far as he could in the direction of the toilet block. Freddie lost his rag and pushed the lad in his chest. The latter went down dramatically, clutching his face, and the ref showed Freddie the red card.

Ross was furious: a red card meant a £50 fine.

'Make him pay it,' I told her.

'Trying to get money out of Fred is bloody impossible,' she retorted. 'He's as tight as his father was.'

Freddie ignored us as he left the field and stomped off to the changing rooms. I knew his strops well – leave him alone for half an hour and he'd be fine.

With the advantage of the extra man, Broughton lay siege to Leysham's goal. With no less than two minutes to go and still 1-1, Freddie's winger went down like a sack of shit in the box. The ref pointed to the penalty spot and pandemonium broke out on the touchline opposite us.

I'm afraid to say these were some of the bits I enjoyed the most about watching Freddie play football on a Saturday afternoon.

The opposing managers began pointing and yelling at each other from a foot away. An ineffectual punch was swung and an ample amount of coat pulling ensued before the linesman got involved. He grabbed the arms of the Leysham manager from behind – a short, bald-headed man called Dave Whitlock who owned the MOT garage on Garrison Lane. Unfortunately, nobody else made any attempt to restrain the Broughton manager, who took his time before grabbing Dave's coat lapels and kneeing him extremely hard in the nuts.

'I bet that hurt,' a man behind me said, and we both watched Dave collapse onto the grass clutching his nadgers. Two parents finally took action and jumped on the Broughton manager's back, forcing him face down onto the ground. The ref ran over, blowing his whistle and threatening to abandon the game unless both managers calmed themselves.

'They look pretty calm to me,' I said to Ross, and she smiled. I looked over at Emily, who was hiding her face in her hands.

Some semblance of order was achieved and a Broughton player

placed the ball on the penalty spot. Ross and I booed loudly as he stepped back, and I could see Emily peering through her fingers.

The pressure must have got to the penalty taker because he fluffed his shot and the keeper easily gathered up the ball in his arms. The Leysham players surrounded him with hugs and pats, but the keeper shooed them away. He bounced the ball a couple of times before booting it up field. There was a definite foul on little Charlie by the Broughton centre-back, but the ref had understandably had enough and blew the full-time whistle.

We sat at a table by the window in the clubhouse overlooking the football pitch. The ends of the goal nets blew in the wind, but it was a nice evening and the sky was a dark, starry blue above the sycamores to the west.

Emily insisted on buying the drinks. Ross and I had a can of Budweiser each and Emily, a small glass of rosé. I poured the contents of my Budweiser carefully into my plastic pint glass and took a sip. I wasn't particularly fond of the stuff but at least it was cold. Ross drank hers straight from the can.

Fortunately, Emily and Ross seemed to have already established a bond and chatted happily away. This meant I could sit back and observe Emily without saying anything stupid, cringe-worthy or just plain embarrassing.

Emily said she'd enjoyed the game but had been a bit put off by the aggro after the penalty decision. Her husband had been a violent man and, since their divorce, she'd found any form of aggression abhorrent. It reminded her of 'dark times', she said.

I had mixed feelings about this revelation. I was pleased she was divorced (although I knew that did not necessarily mean she was single) but perturbed at the suggestion her ex was a 'violent' man.

My own fighting career hadn't lasted much longer than my early teens. I'd won a few fights in my third year at secondary school and began to consider myself a bit tasty. One night at the local youth club, I decided to have a pop at Simon Ravenhead (in later years, known as Simon Ravingmad), the acknowledged 'hardest man' in our year. I walked up and walloped him in the ear when he was playing table tennis. He didn't appear to flinch and then proceeded to blacken one of my eyes, break my nose and knock two of my teeth out. For one of the very few times in my life, I did learn my lesson and have always tried to talk my way out of any potential trouble ever since.

The Leysham players began to drift in from the changing rooms, the opposition nowhere to be seen. Football, through all its levels and ages, never seemed to have the same social solidarity and mutual respect of cricket or even rugby.

Young Charlie appeared and gave his mum an affectionate kiss on her cheek. Emily ruffled his hair – they were obviously close.

She introduced us. Ross smiled while I clumsily shook Charlie's hand and said, 'Well played,' rather like some stuffy geography teacher with brown patches sewn onto the elbows of his faded green, stripy jacket.

Freddie walked moodily over, purposefully trying to be off with his mum so she wouldn't mention the red card and the £50 fine.

'You're paying the fine,' Ross told him straightaway.

'Dave Whitlock says he's going to challenge it.'

'How high's he going to go?' I asked, and glanced at Emily, but she, like Charlie and Ross, was looking at Freddie.

'I don't know,' Freddie said. 'To the top, I suppose.'

'Can the league rescind these things?' Emily asked.

'They should do.' Charlie spoke for the first time. 'Their winger was a wanker.'

'Charlie!'

'Sorry, Mum.'

I decided to give it another go. 'After this afternoon, I don't think Dave would have the balls to do it.'

'He said he would,' said Freddie.

I gave up and asked everybody if they'd like another drink.

Freddie and Charlie wandered off to talk to their teammates. Ross and Emily declined my offer of a drink but said they'd stay while I drank another Budweiser.

Emily told us she was a hairdresser but the shop she'd worked in closed a couple of weeks ago. Most probably due to the recession, she said. She'd still got some private clients, but she was very pleased Stoneways had offered her a job.

'Did Darren Oatridge interview you?' Ross asked.

'Kye Stoneway.'

'Oh, right,' Ross said, and glanced at me.

Randy old bastard, I thought.

The combination of the central heating and the increased mass of bodies in the clubhouse had begun to warm us up from the cold November wind, and Emily took off her cagoul. Even though she wore a polar-necked jumper underneath, her chest line was still impressive. *God knows how high the boss had turned the heating up in his office when he'd interviewed her*, I thought.

Emily's glass was nearly empty and I realised she'd be going soon. It was time to reveal Kenny Rogers.

'It is hot in here,' I said, and draped my leather jacket around the back of my chair.

'Mr Stoneway was extremely nice and explained what would be expected of me very clearly and succinctly,' Emily said to Ross.

I took off my fleece, folded it and placed it on the table.

Emily took a sip of her rosé and gave a small laugh. 'Only thing was,' she said, 'his mobile went off halfway through and his ring tone was a Tammy Wynette song. I'm sorry, but I can't take anyone even remotely seriously who likes country and western.'

I quickly grabbed my fleece and covered my chest with it.

She finished her wine. 'Look, I'd better get moving; taking Charlie to the cinema tonight.'

'I'll walk you to your car,' Ross said, and they both stood up.

Emily held out her hand to me. 'It's been lovely seeing you…'

'Pete,' Ross reminded her.

'Pete.'

I shook Emily's hand and tried to smile in my most unaffected way. Emily called Charlie over and the three of them walked out to the car park. I watched them go and dropped my fleece back onto the table and put my head in my hands.

Ross came back in a few minutes later. 'You're such an idiot,' she said, 'but I do love you.'

Ross lived in a flat in West Purfleet, a short walk from the ground, and she invited me back for something to eat.

I visualised my own flat, heard the bleep in the Wetherspoons and wondered if I'd been barred from The Lazy Lion. 'If that's OK?' I asked.

'Of course it is,' she said.

I bought a bottle of red wine in the local Londis and Ross made a chilli. We drank the wine, listened to some Motown and played several games of crib. She tried to quiz me about what I thought of Emily, but I played it cool. At one point she ejected a CD and put on *The Gambler* by Kenny Rogers. I told her to bugger off and we fought over the CD controls. We were laughing and I suddenly realised how physically close we were. Ross was a good-looking woman, slim and petite, her hair cropped spikily short, and, for one fleeting moment, our eyes met but I moved away. My friendship with her was too precious to try and complicate.

Freddie had one of his football mates round and, during lulls on Ross's stereo, we could hear Machine Gun Kelly and Kanye West blaring out through his bedroom door. At one point, him and his mate said they were popping out for a wander and, when they came back in, they were glassy-eyed and giggling and I could detect the high, sweet smell of cannabis.

I didn't say anything but wondered if Ross knew.

Freddie's mate went home and the three of us watched *Match of the Day*. Ross made up the sofa bed for me and kissed me goodnight. Before Freddie went to bed, I asked him if he got my two jokes about Dave Whitlock and he replied, 'What jokes?'

I lay there in the dark, thinking about Emily and how lucky I was to have Ross as a friend. The lights of cars passing by on the dual carriageway occasionally lit up the front room, but the sofa bed was comfortable, the duvet warm, the pillows soft, and I quickly fell asleep.

Six

CANNED BEETROOT

In the morning, Ross made me a cup of tea and a piece of toast and offered me a lift home.

I told her, thanks, but I'd be OK. It was sunny outside and the walk back over Oxam Common and through the woods to the back of the Broadway appealed to me.

I gave Ross a hug and told her how much she meant to me. She told me to sod off and said she'd see me tomorrow at work. Freddie was still in bed: a smoked-up sixteen-year-old who'd probably sleep through till the afternoon.

The wind had dropped overnight but it was still cold. I walked to the end of Ross's road and left through an alleyway and out on to the common. It was Sunday morning and I knew I should have been planning my day ahead: launderette, proper food shopping and phoning Sarah.

But I loved to dream.

I'd taken Emily to a gig at the Black Horse in North Bitton. A local band called Canned Beetroot were playing. A tight three-piece – guitar, bass and drums – they played mainly covers but gave them such a spiky twist, the tunes always sounded fresh and original. Feedback regularly featured but the band possessed an R&B sensibility which could make the listener dance.

Emily clapped enthusiastically after a punky cover of 'Keep the Customer Satisfied' by Simon and Garfunkel. Mat, the lead guitarist and singer, spotted me and waved. I waved back.

'Do you know them?' Emily asked me excitedly.

'Played with them,' I told her. I sipped my pint and could see her looking at me with a new respect.

'Played with them?' she repeated.

I nodded and Mat spoke into his microphone.

'Peter Booth,' he said. 'Fancy giving us a hand?'

'Can you hold on to this, please?' I said to Emily, and handed her my pint.

Mat lent me his Fender and strapped on an acoustic. Josh, the drummer, gave us the one-two on his sticks and Mat launched into the intro of 'Pinball Wizard'.

I was Pete Townsend, all swirling arms, power chords and explosive solos. Josh let me smash up his drum kit at the end of the song and the crowd went crazy.

My phone vibrated in my pocket when I reached the woods: a text message from Kate: *can I come over and c u today x*

course x, I texted back.

A small terrier came bounding through the trees towards me. I liked dogs and bent down to pat him. The dog stopped before I could reach him and dropped a much-chewed tennis ball at my feet. It looked up at me, barked and wagged its tail.

where? my phone replied.

I thought about this. There was a launderette near the Spoons and I could have a drink with Kate in between the washing and the drying. The atmosphere wouldn't be so depressing if I was with Kate and it was cheap. I could do the food shopping afterwards.

12.30 outside the wetherspoons on the broadway, I texted.

The dog barked again and growled in a playful, challenging manner, but I really didn't want to pick up the ball.

'Monty!' a male voice called, and an elderly man appeared. 'Sorry about that,' he said, and picked up the tennis ball with a blue scooper.

Monty lost interest in me and barked at his owner. The man launched the ball out onto the common and the terrier happily flew after it.

c u there xx

I put my phone back in my pocket and carried on into the woods.

We had a quick drink with the band and left the Black Horse at closing time.

'Fancy some chips?' I asked.

'That would be nice,' Emily said, and slipped her arm through mine.

Three teenage lads stood at the counter in the chip shop, boisterous and sweary and obviously a bit worse for wear from their evening. I stood next to them and ordered two portions of chips and a single helping of curry sauce.

Tony, the owner, saw me and gave me a high five.

The biggest lad in the group told Tony he was a smelly spic and I told him to leave it out.

The kid was immediately in my face. 'What you gonna do about it?'

I ignored him and Tony grabbed a couple of paper bags and began filling them with piping-hot chips.

'Salt and vinegar?' Tony asked me.

'Please,' I told him.

'I said, what you gonna do about it?' the kid repeated.

Tony was smiling as he ladled the curry sauce into a plastic container. He knew me well.

The kid threw a punch which I caught in my left hand. I chinned him with a right uppercut and he stumbled backwards into one of the chairs by the yucca plant. I crouched into a martial arts stance, but his two mates seemed to know better and backed off.

Tony handed me our takeout and said, 'On the house, Pete,' but I insisted on paying. I took a couple of wooden forks from the 'PLEASE HELP YOURSELF' box and turned to the three lads.

'Tony tells me of any more trouble from you lot and I'll be seeing you again.'

The boy I'd chinned grumbled under his breath but he, like the other two, avoided any eye contact with me.

Emily and I sat on a bench by the river and dipped our chips into the curry sauce container. She told me about her ex and his constant threats since she'd kicked him out. I told her not to worry and she snuggled up to me.

The river was calm and we watched the ripples glittering in the neon light of the street lamps on North Bitton bridge. The ripples became tiny waves as a party boat passed by. It sounded its horn and the party-goers waved at us from the deck.

We waved back and Emily put our chips and curry sauce to one side and reached up and kissed me.

My phone rang: *Sarah.*

I let it ring but decided I'd better text her: *sorry, really busy. 24-hour office move. will phone this evening.*

We'd never actually done a twenty-four-hour office move – although the odd one had felt like it – but it sounded plausible.

I put my phone away and stopped walking. I'd come to a clearing between the trees and in front of me stood a twenty-foot-tall electric pylon. Whenever I'd come across one of these things, I was always reminded of the picture of the Martian War Machine on the cover of Jeff Wayne's *War of the Worlds*, but I'd never seen one in these woods before.

I was lost.

Where had I gone wrong? I could hear a fairly constant stream of traffic coming from beyond the woods to my left which I assumed must be the A3. No viable alternative struck me, so I headed in that direction.

I must have walked for over an hour through thickening foliage and dense bracken. Small clouds began to form and play hide and seek with the sun's rays. The effect was eerie and sinister, and I felt the first pangs of anxiety and doubt. Even the sound of traffic seemed to be becoming less distinct, but I kept walking.

After another mile, I came to a single-track road. I soldiered on and houses began to appear, washing on lines blowing in the November wind, a park and a flower shop, and I suddenly realised where I was.

Cheston, two miles south of the Broadway.

I stopped at a deserted bus stop – a request stop with no timetable on display. After waiting for ten minutes, I realised, although Cheston might only be fifteen miles from the centre of London itself, the odds of getting a bus there on a Sunday morning were probably about the same as getting one in that place in Somerset where Susan George was gang-banged in *Straw Dogs*.

I eventually decided it would be quicker to carry on walking and finally got back to the flat at 12.20. I rang Kate but she didn't answer so I left a message telling her I was running late. If it was too cold outside, I added, she should go in the pub and find a table to sit at quietly while she waited for me.

I had a quick shower and threw the clothes I was wearing plus the stuff from the Pack3 into my stripy laundry bag. One particular pair of socks really did smell.

When I'd lived with Sarah in our pleasant, two-bedroomed flat on the Berryfields estate in South Bitton, I was a regular at the Fox and Flowerpot, the local pub and only hostelry within a two-mile radius.

The pub stood at the top of a small parade of shops which included a newsagents, two hairdressers and a launderette.

One Sunday lunchtime, a cheerful Irish lad called Jerry, who rented some digs across the road, bustled in with an empty laundry bag and an opened box of Persil. He bought a pint and said to Warren, the barman, 'Can't you cut out the middleman?'

'Explain, please,' Warren replied in his usual deadpan manner.

'Put some washing machines and dryers in here. There's nothing more depressing on God's earth than sitting in a launderette, pintless on a Sunday lunchtime, watching your clothes revolve around in an oversized goldfish bowl.'

Too true, Jerry, I thought as I pushed my way through the door and into the Broadway Wash 'N' Spin.

I found an empty washing machine, tipped in the contents of my laundry bag and shuffled the clothes around with my right hand in case any of the items were stuck together. The smelly pair of socks seemed to have gotten worse and I hastily shut the machine's door.

I added soap powder and five fifty-pence pieces and pressed the now-glowing red button. Nothing happened at first, but after a few seconds, I heard a whirring noise and the glass's interior blotted with white soap powder. I stole a glance at a very serious-looking man wearing glasses who was staring straight ahead at a dryer which sounded like it wanted to take off, folded up my laundry bag and walked out into the cold wind of the Broadway.

Seven

KATE

Kate was sitting at a table by the main entrance to the Spoons reading a magazine. I crept up behind her and kissed her on top of her head. She flung herself round, stood up and gave me a huge hug.

She pulled away. 'Oh, Dad; you look terrible!' she said, and began to laugh. She hugged me again and said, 'Sorry,' but she was still giggling.

'Thanks for that, sweet pea,' I said, and gently pushed her away. She was a big lady, my daughter, and her hugs could sometimes hurt.

I went to the bar and bought us both a drink: a pint of Fosters top for me and a Diet Coke with ice for Kate. I noticed the Aunty's Cornish Banger appeared to be off the menu; perhaps somebody had keeled over and died in the pub last night after drinking it.

Kate had chosen a good place to sit. It was much lighter by the window looking out over the Broadway and a tall, healthy-looking rubber plant stood in a white pot beside our table, lending the whole space a pleasant feel.

'It's a right dump, this place,' Kate said as I sat down opposite her with the drinks.

'I know,' I agreed.

She picked up the menu, a single sheet embossed with the Spoons logo in red on a white background.

'Do you want something to eat?' I asked.

'Just looking,' Kate said.

She was fourteen and my only child, the product of a six-month relationship with Julie, whom I'd met when she'd been a whacky art student at North Bitton University. Unfortunately, after Kate was born, Julie became even wackier and ran off with some other arty nutter who called himself Moon Unit 2 (apparently after Frank Zappa's cat). There was no further contact; she simply disappeared.

I'd had no idea what to do. I'd been living in Julie's student digs with Kate in a carry cot on the floor of our bedroom. The official powers of North Bitton's cathedral of learning and enlightenment seemed more interested in revenue than mine or Kate's welfare, and I was given a week's notice to move out.

Fortunately, a cousin of mine, Brian, was an expert on the ins and outs of Britain's welfare state. It wasn't that Brian was lazy – he'd just never done a day's work he'd ever reported to the Inland Revenue. He advised me to move back in with my mother. After two days, I was to report my situation to social services and they'd send somebody round my mum's to check its suitability for a new-born baby.

My mum, God rest her soul, was a good woman but smoked like Battersea Power Station used to. Her flat was small and, after four in the afternoon, almost impossible to sit in without some form of breathing apparatus. Social services deemed the property unfit for Kate to live in and I prepared to be her dad in our very own council place. Not without reservations, I had to admit, but somewhere along the way, a moral code had been installed inside me and I realised my parental duties.

Sadly, it was 1996 and tenure of at least the fourth Tory government on the trot. There was no council home for the pair of us and Kate was fostered.

'I know I'm on a diet but the all-day breakfast sounds quite nice,' Kate said.

'A lot of cholesterol, I'd have thought.'

'I know, but you can have veggie sausages instead of the normal ones.'

'I'll order you one then.'

'Thanks, Dad.' Kate beamed. 'Are you going to have something?'

The half-eaten plate of food from yesterday appeared in my mind. 'No, I'll get something later,' I told her, and went to the bar to order.

Kate chatted as she ate. Yes, her Thursday evening job at Tesco's was going OK but she didn't like her DM.

'The left or right?' I asked.

'You're not funny, Dad.'

I pretended to be hurt and she blew me a kiss.

'She's about four foot nothing,' Kate continued. 'Hair all straight across like one of them Nazis. I hate her. Reckon she's a les.'

I slipped into politically correct parent mode. 'Why are you associating a homosexual with somebody horrible?'

'Alright, I'm sorry, Dad, but she's not girly if you know what I mean.'

'That doesn't make a woman unattractive.'

'Doesn't it?'

'No,' I said, and thought of Siouxsie from Siouxsie and the Banshees who I used to have a thing for.

'She's always bossing me around and picking on me.'

'Maybe you're not doing your job properly.'

'I am!' Kate stabbed half of her veggie sausage with her fork and pointed it at me. 'She just doesn't like me.'

Time for a spot of growing-up philosophy, I decided. 'This is life, Kate. Some people like you and some people don't. You've just got to get on with it.'

'She wears this horrible black lipstick.'

'Does she?' I asked.

Kate put her fork down and said, 'You're a perv, Dad.'

I asked her about school and she said it was OK. English, History, Drama and Art were her favourite subjects, which I found a bit unusual; most kids these days seemed to be into IT and Business Studies.

Maurice and I once got talking to a teacher on a freight boat to Sweden and she told us the government were considering allowing 'text speak' to be used in English Language GCSE exams. Last year, Ross had a hernia operation and a twenty-year-old temp filled in for the six weeks she was off. Nice enough girl, but she'd never even heard of World War Two, so I was pleased Kate liked English and History. We didn't want morons running the world.

I asked her about Drama.

'It's fun,' she said, and mopped up any remaining beans, egg yolk and tomato ketchup with her last square of toast. 'I love acting.'

'I know, and you're very good,' I said. Sarah came with me to watch her in a school play at the end of the summer term and she was a natural – larger than life and very funny.

'What about Art?' This subject worried me; I didn't want her to become a deranged loon like her mother.

'It's easy,' she said. 'The teacher, Mr Hammond, lets you do whatever you want. Me and Sandi Roberts threw a load of paint over one of the walls and he said it was a great example of existential blues or something. He's a bit of a weirdo, mind. He wears dresses and high heels.'

'Each to their own,' I said.

'Yeah,' Kate agreed.

She pushed her plate to one side and burped. 'Excuse me!' She giggled.

'Do you want another drink?' I asked her.

'No, I'm alright,' she said. 'Can we go and see your flat? I still haven't seen it yet.'

I'd really have preferred her not to see it, but she was currently living eight miles away in Wallingdale and her foster parent, Marjorie, wasn't picking her up till five so I didn't have much choice.

I offered her a compromise. We'd put the washing in the dryer and then go shopping at Sainsbury's for my weekly food shop. By that time, the clothes would be dry and we'd go back to my flat and sort it all out.

'Is it a right shit-hole, Dad?'

'Kate!'

'Sorry.'

The serious man in the glasses had gone when we got to the launderette and a handsome male student-type sat in his place reading *The Outsider* by Albert Camus. Kate preened herself as soon as she saw him and fluttered her false eyelashes.

My washing revolved ever more slowly until it gradually came to a rest at the bottom of the bowl. A black and yellow shape, which I think was my Kenny Rogers T-shirt, fluttered down from above and landed on top of the pile. A loud click signified the end of the cycle and I grabbed a plastic basket from off the top of another machine and opened the door.

Kate, meanwhile, had sat herself down on the metal green bench a foot or so away from the student. He didn't appear to notice her, his novel obviously far more appealing than my daughter. He had a wonderful crop of blond ringlets, the lucky bastard, and was definitely a good-looking feller, but, alas, I thought, far too intellectual for my Kate. However, I knew she'd give it a try.

'Excuse me,' she said.

The student looked up.

'Is that your drying in there?'

I shovelled my washing into the basket and transferred it to a dryer near where the lad was sitting.

'Yes, it is,' the student answered her, and went back to his book.

'Did you use one of the washing machines first?' Kate asked.

The student looked at her again. 'No, I didn't. I use the machine in the uni digs and then come down here to use the dryer. Much cheaper.'

'But you're not allowed to do that,' Kate told him. She stood up and pointed at a sign by the door.

'*dryers can only be used by customers who wash their belongings first in our washing machines. The management, Wash 'N' Spin,*' she read.

I placed a twenty-pence piece in the slot at the top of my dryer and turned the knob beside it. The coin dropped and my clothes slowly began to rotate.

The student was flustered. 'Well, I'm sorry,' he stammered. 'I didn't realise.' He put the book down and began to get up.

'Don't worry about it, mate,' I intervened.

He gave me an apologetic look and sat down again.

I fed another six twenty-pence pieces into the dryer and picked up my empty laundry bag.

'My mum used to be an artist,' Kate announced to the student.

'Oh, really,' he replied in a 'please don't talk to me anymore' voice.

I took Kate's arm and began to guide her out of the launderette, but she stopped in the doorway and said to the student, 'Did you know that Albert Camus played in goal for Algeria?'

'Why don't you go to Iceland?' Kate asked me as we walked down the Broadway.

'Because I like Sainsbury's,' I said.

'Marjorie says Iceland is a lot cheaper.'

I ignored her. I knew Iceland was a lot cheaper but Kate hadn't been in my flat yet and didn't realise my fridge was about three feet high and the ice box at the top could only fit two trays of ice cubes or one very small, flat, frozen pizza. There was a Tesco's superstore in Pulham Park which was also probably a lot cheaper, but it meant catching a bus there and back. Besides, I'd worked out where everything I wanted was in Sainsbury's so I didn't have to flap about while I was in there. I detested shopping in all its horrible forms except for vinyl and CD buying.

I grabbed a trolley in the foyer and strode down the first aisle to the bread. I chucked in two loaves of white, thin-sliced, and noticed Kate lagging behind at the cereals holding up a box of Shreddies.

'Can I have these, please, Dad?'

'Yes, alright,' I said, and she walked over and placed them in the trolley.

My cooking skills were limited to chilli, spaghetti bolognaise and chicken curry, so I grabbed two packets of very lumpy-looking mince from the fridge food section and a ready-cooked chicken from the deli counter. I chucked in rice, spaghetti and a jar of Patak's Madras curry sauce and stopped by the fruit and veg. Kate got bored and walked off to study the magazine racks near the tills.

I once saw a really scary documentary about scurvy and knew fresh fruit and veg were essential to a healthy diet, so I picked four onions, a box of mushrooms, carrots, three apples and a cucumber. After lobbing in a block of cheese, two packets of economy sliced ham, and a jar of mayonnaise, I worked out that I now had the wherewithal to make sandwiches for my lunch every day for the coming week and cook myself evening meals every night till Wednesday.

Wednesday and Thursday evenings were still bare, so I put my head down and steamed past other shoppers to aisle 5, where I found two Fray Bentos pies and a medium-sized packet of Smash. I didn't bother with any gravy granules, as I was pretty sure I still had half a tub of Bisto somewhere back at the flat.

I paid for all the goods, which included two teen magazines for Kate as well as the box of Shreddies, using my debit card and asked for £50 cashback. This was a tricky part of the month for me as we didn't get paid till Friday. I was pretty sure I'd still just be under my overdraft limit but the moments between me placing my card in the machine and waiting for the bank's cyber approval were nerve-racking. A rejection at this point in time would be a major disaster, but the machine told me to remove my card and a receipt began to slowly unfold.

The cashier clicked open the till and took out two crisp twenties and a ten-spot. She closed the till, snapped off the receipt, paired it with the cash and held the small wad out to me.

I took it and she smiled and said, 'Have a nice day.'

The curly-haired blond student had gone when we got back to the launderette and the place was empty. The dryer had long completed its cycle, but my clothes were still hot to the touch. The sock stench had also vanished and everything smelt of Ariel. I folded up all the shirts, trousers and underpants to the best of my ability while Kate paired the socks.

As usual, one sock was missing.

My flat was situated on the ground floor of a four-storey Victorian house at the corner of Langley Avenue and Chestnut Close – a quarter of a mile south of the Broadway.

I unlocked the front door and Kate waited behind me in the communal hallway with one of the shopping bags while I fiddled with the key in the lock of my flat door. It was a bastard and you had to push on the door neither too hard nor too soft until the key accessed the barrel exactly and turned. I had nightmares of the key snapping in the lock and mentioned it to the landlord one morning when he was washing his car in the driveway, but he hadn't seemed that interested.

I finally opened the door and we walked in.

Immediately to the left was the door to the bathroom which contained a shower, toilet and sink. Opposite the bathroom was a wardrobe with some hanging space and a small, built-in chest of drawers.

Two steps further and we were in the main living area.

The single bed lay under a large sash window overlooking the communal garden. At the end of the bed sat my twenty-one-inch telly and DVD player on top of a bedside cabinet. A pine chair stood by the bed with my CD player and alarm clock stacked on top. Next to that came the Pack3-cum-laundry basket and then, parallel to the bed on the other side of the room, the 'kitchen'.

The top was divided between a sink and draining board and a small worktop upon which my Belling cooker stood. Underneath sat the fridge and the store cupboard for cleaning stuff, dried and tinned food, pint glasses, a couple of plates, one bowl and miscellaneous.

An unpleasant smell emanated from the fridge which I realised was the two frozen meals which had obviously defrosted since I'd left them there on Friday night. I took them outside to one of the bins at the side of the house and chucked them away.

When I came back in, Kate stood in front of the bed with a bemused look on her face.

'It's tiny,' she said, 'but kind of cute.'

Kate hung up all the clothes which needed hanging in the wardrobe and distributed the rest between the chest of drawers and the bedside cabinet. I put all the food shopping away except for the chicken, which I left on a plate on top of the cooker.

'Why have you put that there?' Kate asked me.

'Because I've got nowhere else to put it so I'll have to curry it this evening.'

'All of it?'

'Yes,' I said, 'but I should have enough left for tomorrow night.'

'It's a bit like this book we're reading in English.'

'What's it called?'

'*A Day in the Life of* some Russian feller who lives in a gulag in Siberia.'

I still had an hour to kill before I had to walk Kate up to the bowling alley, so I turned on the TV. Kate propped herself up on the pillows on the bed while I cleared the stuff off the pine chair and sat down next to her. *Mary Poppins* was on BBC2 which was strange; I thought it was only aired at Christmas and bank holidays.

Sarah and I watched it one New Year's Day afternoon when I was incredibly hungover. She sat on the floor while I lay comatose on the sofa and we watched the whole film. I have to say I didn't think it was that bad, probably because it didn't contain any machine-gun fire or bombs going off, and I found the bit where Julie Andrews produced a huge plant from her bag quite funny.

I think it was a bit too dated for Kate and, after the scene where they kept laughing and floating up to the ceiling, she asked me if I could turn it over. I wasn't that bothered to be honest – watching *Mary Poppins* on a Sunday afternoon was a bit like watching *2001: A Space Odyssey* or *Blade Runner: The Director's Cut* without being completely off your tits.

There wasn't a lot else on so we settled for indoor athletics from Crystal Palace on BBC2.

Kate played with her phone most of the time but stopped to watch when the men's shotput competition started. She seemed to find the contestants hilarious, especially an enormous Chinese man whose only hair on his head was a two-foot-long orange ponytail. He was called Wang and when it was his turn, he'd slump over to the space between the protective nets and place the shotput under his chin. He'd stand stock-still for a few moments and then begin to stamp his right leg before whirling around several times and releasing the shotput with an almighty roar. This reduced Kate to tears but, sadly, Wang was beaten into second place by an even more substantial Polish shotputter named Kowlaski.

At half four, I gave Kate one of the shopping bags to put in her two magazines and the box of Shreddies, and we walked hand in hand up to the bowling alley.

Marjorie was already there waiting for us, sitting in her blue Ford Fiesta in the front car park. She and her husband, Ken, had been wonderful with Kate and I was eternally grateful to them, but Marjorie liked to talk. As soon as she wound down the window to say, 'Hello,' I struck first. I asked how Ken was and told her, as always, how much I appreciated their kindness and care to Kate. I then said I had to run because I... and my mind went blank.

'Have to go to work?' Kate offered.

'Yes!' I exclaimed. 'Forty-eight-hour office job; my night shift starts at six.'

Marjorie started to say something, and I gave Kate a hug and slipped £30 into her hand.

She hugged me hard and told me how much she loved me.

I said goodbye to Marjorie and watched Kate waving at me through the back window until the car turned left at the lights on the Wallingdale Road and disappeared from sight.

Eight

HOWLING LOVE

It was getting dark as I walked back down the Broadway and the streetlamps were already lit. Kilo stood outside the Sunshine Eat talking to a tall, silver-haired man in a cashmere coat.

Must be one of his deals, I thought, and put my head down to hurry past, but Kilo held out a hand to stop me.

'Pete, how're you doing?'

'Fine,' I told him. 'You?'

'Good, good.'

Pleasantries exchanged, I made to move on. I had no intention of cramping Kilo's style, but he spoke to me again.

'Like you to meet a friend of mine: Ray Henderson.'

I froze; Ray Henderson was a renowned big shot in the area.

'Pete's missus has just thrown him out,' Kilo said to Henderson.

I liked Kilo but was beginning to wish I didn't.

Henderson held out a heavily ringed hand and I had no option but to shake it.

'Nice to meet you,' he said, and held on to my hand just that fraction longer than was necessary.

'Likewise,' I said, and noticed Paranoid Ian lurking in the alleyway between the café and the shuttered-up bookies.

'Got to shoot,' I said, and pulled my hand away but not too quickly so as not to appear rude. I'd heard the stories.

Kilo patted me on my shoulder. I nodded a goodbye and walked on.

I looked back as I crossed the road by WH Smiths and saw Henderson watching me, but his eyes were lidded and I could detect no expression.

I was shaking when I got back to the flat. Why had Kilo bothered to introduce me to that psycho?

Over the years, Henderson's notoriety had elevated him to celebrity status around these parts. He was like the third Kray, but what interest could a man like that have in an inconsequential pauper of a removal man such as myself? I fell into the category of one of those people who tell bank managers they'll close their account and take their overdraft elsewhere.

'Shut up, will you?' I said out loud; my imagination annoyed me sometimes. Kilo was a good guy; he was just trying to be friendly. All this, 'I can get you a kilo of anything,' was more than likely just simple-minded bravado. He was about the same age as Henderson so they might have gone to school together and were probably having a quick catch-up. Even people who buried other humans alive in concrete presumably liked a bit of a natter and a laugh with their old mates.

Next time I bumped into Kilo, I'd ask him for a kilo of cauliflowers.

But what was Paranoid Ian doing there and why did Kilo bother to tell Henderson Sarah had kicked me out?

Be quiet, I told myself but not out loud this time. *Think of something else.*

Food came to mind.

I pulled out my two saucepans from under the bed, gave them a quick wipe with my tea towel and placed the bigger pan on the bed and the smaller one on top of the larger ring of the cooker.

I chopped up an onion and a couple of mushrooms and chucked them in the pan to fry. I added the chicken, which I broke up with my hands, and the Patak's curry sauce, gave the whole thing a couple of stirs and turned the temperature dial to high. Belling cookers might be small but they generated heat very quickly and it wasn't long before the sauce was bubbling along nicely.

I moved the pan over to the other smaller and still dormant ring and switched the dial down to low on the larger one. I gave it a few minutes to cool down before I slid the pan back across and administered a couple of perfunctory stirs to the contents. Satisfied the flat wouldn't blow up, I walked down to Sanjays.

I knew I still had the half bottle of wine in the fridge, but I needed some form of branded lager to wash it down with. Sarah would accuse me of impending alcoholism, but I couldn't afford to hit a pub of any description tonight and I had an inkling that sleep might prove hard to come by.

The beer fridge at Sanjays was glowing with choice but I settled on a six-pack of Stella for £4.50. This meant I could have two tins tonight and one each evening till payday and the Friday Night Club.

Am I an alcoholic? I thought as I waited at the till. I suppose it depended on how you defined an alcoholic. Medical research suggests you have a problem if you imbibe only one drink a night. When I lived with Sarah, I sailed through many dry days, but I had to admit those had become almost nonexistent since our split.

A couple of weeks ago, while driving back from a job in Dorset, I decided for some reason (sheer boredom?) to confide in Leo Wainwright my concerns about my current drinking levels. I rarely got drunk, I told him, but I was having at least two pints in the pub every night after work and another can or glass of wine back at the flat.

Leo suggested I go on my own to the gym on Monday and Wednesday evenings and accompany him to rugby training on Tuesdays and Thursdays. The club was always looking for new players and he was sure I could get a game. The lads were brilliant, Leo enthused, and I might be invited to their Christmas knees-up at the beginning of December. This was held at a hotel in Banbury in Oxfordshire, and every member of the squad had to dress up as a famous female movie star. Great fun, he assured me.

The curry smell was strong when I got back to the flat and I leant over the bed to open the sash window. I moved the curry pan onto the draining board and filled the other pan with water and placed it on the larger ring. I switched the ring up to high and poured some of the wine into a glass and cracked open a can of Stella.

The wine tasted even worse than it had on Friday night, but my ploy of diluting the wine with the lager seemed to work. *Never mix the grain and the grape*, went the old adage. *Bollocks*, I thought, and perched myself on the side of the bed and pulled out my phone.

There were another two missed calls from Sarah but I still couldn't bring myself to phone her so I texted instead: *sorry both lifts broken down having to carry all up the stairs*

I was quite pleased with this text. Having shared her life with me for ten years, Sarah had learnt several things about removals. She knew I didn't like office moves, especially at the weekends, and lifts breaking down were an anathema and could put me in a very bad mood. I was, therefore, pretty certain she wouldn't try and ring me again tonight.

I was about to put the phone down when a thought hit me. I scrolled down to 'J UNSWORTH' and pressed call. Jeff answered on the fifth ring.

'Yo,' he said.

I could hear music playing in the background. 'Can you talk?'

'Yeah, hang on.' The line filled with shuffling sounds and half-voices before Jeff's voice came back on. 'What's up?' he asked, and I knew he'd walked outside the pub for a fag.

'I wanted to ask you about Ray Henderson.'

I heard Jeff whistle. 'Have you upset him?'

'No. It's just I was introduced today.'

'Who by: Al Capone?'

'Somebody I know.'

'I never had you down as mixing in those circles.'

'I don't.'

'Who's this bloke you know who knows Henderson then?'

'I don't know his real name, but he calls himself Kilo.'

The line went quiet.

'Do you know him?'

'I do,' Jeff said.

'Come on then.'

'Kilo's alright but better to keep him at arm's length if you know what I mean.'

'What about Henderson?'

'Don't go anywhere near.'

'That bad?'

'Oh yes,' Jeff said, and I could hear him puff on his fag.

Jeff exhaled. 'Look, Pete, I know you're not one of the bad boys, so to speak, but you've lived round the Bittons long enough to have heard of Ray Henderson.'

'Stories, though, only stories.'

'Henderson owns a couple of pubs and a nightclub. He also has his fingers in a lot of pies but he's no Vito Corleone. He doesn't do you favours: you do them for him or else. He also likes using people with money problems. The deal might sound good, but believe me, it won't be worth it.'

'Who's Vito Corleone?'

Jeff ignored me. 'Like I say, leave well alone.'

I changed the subject. 'Do you know what you're doing tomorrow?'

'No idea, Pete. Besides twats putting pictures in flat Pack6s, I never think about work when I'm not there.'

'What about the Stone Lion?'

'What Stone Lion?' Jeff answered, and hung up.

The room felt cold now and I shut the window. I had to stand on the bed to close the curtains, the ceiling was so high.

One nice thing about this flat: the ceiling. There was a flowery surround of white, blue and green petals on all sides, and many a night, I'd lain on the bed (or sometimes on the floor when my back was killing me) looking up at it. Suppose that's what you do more when you're on your own: look up at the ceiling,

The ring underneath the pan began to smoke. This was due to me lighting a fag a week ago off the cooker when my lighter had run out.

It wasn't really a problem, but I knew the smoke might trigger off the smoke alarm that hung above the door to the bathroom. If that went off, I'd no idea what would happen. Worst-case scenario: fire engine, landlord appearing and myself with no ceiling at all to look at, only sky.

I doubled up the tea towel and hung it over the alarm. I turned the ring down a fraction and spent the next five minutes anxiously pacing the two steps between the cooker and the smoke alarm until the water started boiling and I could add the rice and turn the heat down to a mild simmer.

My phone bleeped twice in rapid succession. Two messages. One from Kate: *love u dad xxx*, and one from Sarah: *I hope they haven't emptied the filing cabinets*

The curry wasn't great but it was filling and I ate two bowlfuls. The solitary source of heating in the flat was a storage heater which only seemed to work when it felt like it, so the place never got seriously hot. I therefore knew I could leave the rest of the curry in the pan with a lid on it till tomorrow night without it going off.

There was a loud crash from above and the couple who lived upstairs began to make love.

I'd met them a few times in the hallway when I was going out and they were coming in or vice versa. They were a very polite Iranian couple who'd told me they were studying at North Bitton university.

God knows what they got up to in their flat but, within minutes, the girl was howling. When it first happened, I nearly called the police but her partner started shouting, '*Areh! Areh!*' which I later found out was Persian for, 'Yes! Yes!'

The howling and '*Areh*-ing' subsided, and their bed began to rhythmically squeak. I decided to one day buy them a can of WD40 and turned on the television. Not antisocially loudly – I couldn't very well air any complaint about noise levels after they'd probably listened to *Sabbath Bloody Sabbath* at plentiful volume on Friday night before I went to the Lazy Lion.

I watched a repeat of *Porridge* and finished my can of Stella. There were another couple of loud crashes above and a minute's choreographed yelling of ecstasy before the bed stopped squeaking and there was silence.

I found one last fag in the packet and walked outside into the communal garden, leaving my flat door on the latch. I couldn't be arsed with the rigmarole of the turning-the-key-in-the-lock routine when I came back in.

The garden was surrounded by privet hedges and rhododendron bushes. It was a cold, still night and I could make out the wooden table and benches where nobody ever sat and the brick BBQ nobody ever used. I smoked my cigarette in the ethereal moonlight, savouring the quiet, and thought about Emily.

She was sexy and the look in her eyes when she talked to me made me think I had a chance. Love would add some much-needed spice to my life and, if it wasn't to be forthcoming, I could at least enjoy the chase.

I was smiling when I got back to the flat and realised, for the first time in quite a while, I was actually looking forward to Monday morning.

Nine

LEO WAINWRIGHT

'The Final Countdown' by Europe woke me up.

I really didn't like this song. The screeching voice reminded me of the Scorpions, another foreign band who tried to sing in English. I wasn't xenophobic by any stretch, but the lyrics were infantile and the music sounded like a rocked-up Eurovision song contest entry. Maybe I was being too harsh and this was their worst song the record company had pushed. The band, like me, probably hated it and never played it live. At least, I hoped that was the case.

I caught the earlier bus and got to the restroom at seven-thirty, the horrible keyboard fanfare still playing in my head.

There was no Maurice, only Barry Noble, the forklift driver, leant against the counter underneath the glass shutter. I made myself a black coffee and asked Barry if Maurice was on an early start.

'Off sick, by all accounts,' Barry said.

'Maurice?'

'The one and only.'

'He hasn't phoned in sick since Patrick Viera left Arsenal for Man City.'

'I know.'

Leo Wainwright walked through the office door, sunglasses and shorts, job sheet on clipboard under his arm.

Barry feigned shock. 'You're not running another job, are you?'

Leo smiled knowingly as though everybody knew he was a superb removalist and Barry's aside was merely part of a harmless, ongoing joke between them.

'I'm being serious – surely Daz isn't that thick?'

Daz opened the glass shutter. 'Leo's taking over Maurice's job,' he said to Barry.

'The shop mannequin's not doing anything today.'

Daz ignored him and said to me, 'You're with Leo, Pete.'

Leo was a bit like Europe.

'But can I have a quick word before you go?' Daz added.

'Aye, Captain,' I replied.

Daz slid a worksheet over the counter to Barry and said, 'Not that busy today but you've got to start digging out rows 24 and 25.' He hesitated for the tiniest moment. 'Magenta Carlberg's coming out of store at the end of the week.'

Barry collapsed dramatically and lay down horizontally on the restroom floor.

Daz shut the glass shutter and beckoned me through.

I walked into the office. Daz sat down at his desk and swivelled on his chair to face me.

'Do you mind?' I asked him.

'If you must.'

The office was empty besides us so I plonked myself on Trevor Blind's swivel chair whose desk was parallel and spun round three times. Feeling a touch nauseous, I middled myself, generated a bit of speed with my legs and flew down the centre aisle of the office past Kye Stoneway's glass cubicle and Ross's desk until I careened into the fire door. I backpedalled all the way, executed two final spins and faced Daz.

'Happy now?' he asked.

'Oh yes.'

Daz produced a form from the middle drawer of his filing cabinet and handed it to me. 'JOB CHAT' was written at the top in black letters.

'What's this?' I asked.

'It's the boss's new way of dealing with customer complaints.'

'Mrs Curdley?'

Daz nodded. 'Basically, I need you to take it home and fill it in. I'll also be handing one to Jeff and Maurice.'

'I'm not going on any more of those customer service courses,' I protested.

'You won't be,' Daz assured me. 'The boss is just trying to cover himself. If Mrs Curdley wants to take this any further, he's shown he's taken what he can describe as, "necessary disciplinary action".'

'She's a stupid cow.'

'I know that and so does he. Just fill in the form and do it sensibly.'

I stood up to go.

'Hang on, sit down again. There's something else.'

I sat. 'Can I fiddle with the height control?'

'No, you can't. This job you're doing with Leo today is very straightforward. Ground-floor flat in West Camwell, pack, load and deliver all to a bungalow in Purfleet. Trevor Blind says there's hardly anything there.'

'If we moved Buckingham Palace, he'd say there's only a couple of beds and a throne.'

'Stop being so sarcastic; you're getting as bad as the rest of them.'

'Sorry,' I said. I did genuinely like Daz.

'I'm putting the new girl with you: Emily.'

'The Final Countdown' stopped playing in my head. There was a ray of light. I tried to appear cool, although I could feel my heart begin to beat faster.

'Why are you putting her with us?' I asked.

'Because you're a competent man.'

'Cut out the flattery, please.'

'OK, you're more approachable and helpful than most of the others, and…' Daz paused, 'reasonably normal.'

'What about Steve Woodgit? He's probably the best removal guy we've got besides Maurice.'

Daz sighed and picked up a pen from his desk. 'Emily's just started, Pete; I want her to settle in gradually. God knows what she might think of the way Steve operates. Besides, much as I love the man, Steve's hardly the most communicative person in the world. All he says is, "Whatever," or, "Yeah," and, remember, she told us on Friday night she was a trained first aider, meaning she might have some sort of medical background. If she sees how much weed Steve smokes, she might try and refer him to an institution.'

'Anything else?' I asked.

'No.' Daz put the pen to his chin. 'But just remember to keep an eye on Leo.'

The van was parked at the back of the warehouse by the carton section with its back open. Leo leant against the side of the van holding his mug of tea with 'THE KING' written on it, chatting to Emily, who was hopping up and down again in the early morning cold. She'd been a hairdresser and was used to shop warmth, I reasoned. Exposure to the elements was obviously something new to her, but to me, she still looked goddamned sexy.

'Jeff!' she exclaimed happily.

'Pete,' I corrected her.

She put her hand to her mouth and her eyes opened fully in shock horror. 'Oh sorry, Pete! I'm terrible with names.'

'Don't worry,' I said, and couldn't help but smile when she smiled.

'We've just put all the boxes on for the job today. Gosh, it's exciting!'

Leo interrupted. 'Not quite ready to go, though, are we, Emily?'

Emily looked puzzled.

Leo held up the clipboard with the worksheet attached.

She pointed a finger at the sheet and looked at the back of the van. She did this three times.

'Ten Pack3s,' she said slowly, 'twenty Pack2s, twenty Pack6s, two wine dividers and two packs of paper.'

'And…' Leo prompted.

'Oh, tape! Silly me,' she said, and flustered off into the carton area.

I noticed she was wearing her own pair of black trousers rather than a Stoneways pair, a far tighter fit which highlighted her very appealing bottom. I think Leo also noticed.

She returned with six rolls of tape. 'Is that enough?' she asked Leo.

'Very nice,' he replied.

'I'm sorry?'

'The tape; it's very nice.'

'Is it different from the normal tape?'

'No.'

'Why did you say it was very nice then as though it was new?'

Leo was blushing. 'I just really like that tape.'

I suppose it was because I empathised with Leo that I came to his rescue. I certainly knew how to dig holes myself. 'We used to use brown tape,' I explained to Emily. 'But it was harder to tear using your fingers and was particularly prone to the heat.'

Emily, once more, appeared confused.

'It would come unstuck very easily; this white tape's much better.'

'Crumbs, there's a lot to learn.'

There certainly is, I thought.

We were using Stoneways' five-ton lorry which, in technical terms, could hold approximately eight hundred cubic feet of furniture and effects. It was built to hold two storage containers, which gave it a shape not dissimilar to a snack vehicle one finds in laybys off main roads throughout Britain and was therefore known by every member of staff as the Burger Van.

I offered Emily the window seat, but she insisted on sitting in the middle. I also offered to map read but Leo said, 'No need, Peter,' and placed his mobile phone with certain aplomb in the docking device by the steering wheel. He raised his sunglasses to study the job sheet and tapped a few buttons on his phone.

'All sorted.' He winked at Emily and proceeded to drive out of the yard.

A female voice with an American accent spoke. '*At the roundabout, take the third exit. Turn right.*'

Leo had a satnav app for his phone.

'*Turn right here.*'

'Good, isn't it?' Leo beamed.

I wasn't that bothered. I didn't like map reading at the best of times but I knew the voice would annoy me.

'I've heard they can be a bit suspect,' Emily said.

'Who told you that?' Leo was immediately defensive.

'Just something I read the other day. Apparently, a car was driving along the cliffs somewhere on the Isle of Wight and the satnav told the driver to turn left which would have plunged the car into the English Channel.'

I started laughing and she looked at me.

'Sorry,' I apologised.

She turned her attention back to Leo. 'Obviously, the driver wasn't that stupid, but I've also heard stories of people ending up down dead-end farm tracks or arriving at the wrong address.'

Having got to know Leo reasonably well during the two years he'd worked at the firm – and, believe me, his character wasn't unduly complex – I could sense he was a touch concerned by what he'd just heard. However, Leo didn't like to ever admit defeat.

'Ah yes,' he said, 'but they were probably using an inferior app.' He tapped his phone. 'This one's state-of-the-art, top quality.' Leo paused to let his words sink in. 'I bought it at Currys.'

I didn't have much chance to chat to Emily during the journey over to West Camwell. Leo talked and we listened. Well, I didn't listen.

It was the usual gaff about rugby, buying stuff off eBay and whether he and his wife, God help her, were going to build an extension on their starter home next spring. All delivered in Leo's mesmerising monotone. I sat back, closed my eyes and feigned sleep.

'Turn left here.'

Leo was telling Emily about an ongoing disagreement with his neighbour about the north-facing fence. Leo told the neighbour if he didn't play ball, he'd bring round the entire front row of his rugby team to sort things out properly. Apparently, the neighbour threatened to rip Leo's head off there and then and I heard the satnav repeat, 'Turn left here.'

Leo swung the steering wheel far too quickly and Emily was flung against me. I instinctively put my arm around her to protect her and she pressed against my chest.

She felt soft and warm and smelt far nicer than any of the other members of staff. Sadly, she pulled away as Leo righted the van and I breathed in deeply.

'Twenty yards on your left and you have reached your destination.'

Our destination was a small block of flats which lay back from the road. First thing I noticed was there was nowhere to park. All the bays on either side of the road were taken and the road itself was nowhere near wide enough for us to double park.

I pointed at a Subaru and a Volvo and said to Leo, 'I'll find out whose they are and see if I can get them moved. You drive up the road and see if you can turn round.'

I checked the job sheet – 'Mrs Laidlaw, Flat 2' – and jumped out of the cab.

Mrs Laidlaw answered the door on the third ring. She wore thick glasses and looked as though she was in her early nineties.

I introduced myself and Mrs Laidlaw seemed very pleased to meet me. I asked her about the two cars. She leant her head forward and cupped her ear. I repeated myself, speaking my words very slowly and clearly. Leo's way of dealing with old people (and, unfortunately, foreigners) was to shout at them, which I always found unnecessary and embarrassing.

'I'm not sure about the first one you said, but I think the Volvo belongs to Number 4,' Mrs Laidlaw told me, and pointed upwards at the ceiling with her stick.

An attractive, middle-aged blonde lady answered the door of Number 4 and proved extremely helpful. Yes, it was her Volvo and she'd move it straightaway. The Subaru belonged to her boyfriend who'd just nipped down to the shops and would be back in a minute. They both worked from home, she added for some reason.

Maybe they're having an affair, I thought, and rang Leo to tell him what was occurring.

Van parked, back open and ramp out, we made our way to the flat, Mrs Laidlaw still standing in the open doorway.

Leo stuck out a hand and said, 'Leo Wainwright, foreman in charge of your removal today.'

Mrs Laidlaw peered at him and said, 'Why are you wearing sunglasses?'

I saw Leo redden, but he gave a shrug and his customary, 'Ha, ha, ha,' and introduced Emily and myself.

'Please come in,' Mrs Laidlaw said.

Emily took a step forward and Leo put an arm across to bar her way.

'One moment, Emily. Peter?'

'What?'

'The floor protector, please.'

'But it hasn't rained since Friday,' I said.

Leo gave Emily an annoyingly knowing smile and said, 'I am a professional and the entrance hall to an abdobe should always, at the very least, be properly covered.'

'What's an abdobe?' Emily asked.

'One of Leo's hidden muscles,' I told her.

For the third time that morning, she looked confused. If my humour was too subtle for her, God knows how she was going to get on with some of the others.

'Floor protector, please, Peter,' Leo repeated in his best 'I'm in charge' voice.

Mrs Laidlaw's hall carpet was not overly dirty, but it was a dark, threadbare, green and looked as though it had been laid down in the mid-1970s. There was no point, but I didn't want to create a bad atmosphere, so I dutifully walked back to the van and grabbed our two-foot roll of hessian floor protector. I tucked one end under the doormat and rolled it out in the hallway upside down so there was no curl at the other end somebody could trip over.

Leo, for some reason, pressed his left foot down on the hessian twice as though assessing its quality. 'Quite happy with that,' he said to Emily, and turned to the old lady. 'Madam, if you'd like to show us round the flat and tell us what's going.'

'What's what?'

'What's going!' Leo raised his voice.

'Going where?'

'To your new house,' I interrupted.

It was Mrs Laidlaw's turn to look confused.

I tried again. 'We need to know what we can pack.'

'Oh, yes!' Mrs Laidlaw said excitedly. 'Follow me.'

Mrs Laidlaw, God bless her, was extremely hard of hearing and became easily muddled when asked a question. The-customer-showing-us-around-the-property bit was therefore a long-winded affair to say the least. Leo was soon shouting out his petty queries and confusing her further with his unnecessary explanation of how the move would progress. As he was discussing the intricacies of loading the van, Emily said she'd just remembered something and nipped outside and returned moments later with the clipboard.

'I'm sorry to interrupt,' she said, 'but it says on our job sheet, Mrs

Laidlaw, that your daughter will be coming round to help you with your move.'

'Do you want some water?' Mrs Laidlaw asked.

'No! Your daughter!' Leo shouted again.

'Yes, I'm sure she will be.'

I decided I'd better offer a suggestion. 'Leo. We basically know what's going in the main living area so why don't all three of us start packing in there until the lady's daughter arrives?'

Leo looked at me, then at Emily and then back at me again.

He turned to the lady. 'Madam, what I think we'll do is start packing up your living area until your daughter gets here.'

'Pardon?'

Emily seemed to be getting the drift and moved as quickly as me out of the flat to the back of the van.

'Are you alright?' I asked her as I untied the stack of cartons.

She smiled. 'I'm finding it quite amusing actually, poor old dear.'

I handed her a pile of Pack6s.

'One thing.'

'What's that?' I asked.

'Why aren't you in charge?'

'Think I'll take that as a compliment.'

Leo appeared in the flat's hallway with his back to us. 'I'm just going to get some Pack2s!' he roared. He strutted past us to the cab, shaking his head, and reappeared a moment later with a donut.

'Sorry about this, Emily, but the old bats as mad as a badger,' he said.

A badger?

'I think she's quite a sweet old lady, actually,' Emily replied.

'She might be sweet but she's not making my job very easy,' Leo said, and took a substantial bite of his donut.

A huge spurt of jam erupted out of the end facing us.

'Jesus Christ!' Emily yelled, and stepped back quickly. She managed to avoid the main burst, but a few globules of jam landed on the toes of her training shoes. 'What the hell are you doing?'

'Sorry,' Leo answered sheepishly, 'but they always do that when I eat them.'

'There's a hole in one end,' Emily explained patiently as though she were talking to a five-year-old. 'You're supposed to bite on that end, so the jam goes straight into your mouth.'

'Well, I never,' Leo murmured in awe, and studied the donut.

Emily pulled out a tissue from one of her pockets, bent down and dabbed at her training shoes. She stood back up and said, 'I know I'm not very experienced at these sort of things, but there doesn't seem to be that much here. What do you think, Pete?'

I was so pleased she'd finally got my name right I couldn't remember what the question was, so I just said, 'Yeah.'

Leo popped the rest of the donut in his gob and said, 'We haven't seen the bedroom yet, God knows what could be in the wardrobes.' He wiped his hands free of any sugar residue and adopted the stance of a general directing his troops into battle.

'Pete!' he ordered

'Yes, sir!' I stood to attention.

'You can make a start in the lounge while I destruct Emily here how to pack in the dining room.'

'Blow her up?' I asked.

Leo angled his head towards me as if I was an idiot. 'I'm sorry?'

'Don't worry about it.'

'Good.' Leo straightened himself and said to Emily, 'At least there's one sensible member of the crew to guide you.'

Mrs Laidlaw's living area was open plan.

Nearest the bay window, looking out over the road, was the lounge containing a small sofa, armchair, TV, coffee table and bookcase. At the other end of the room stood a dining table with four chairs. A large dresser, crammed full of breakables, occupied one wall and a tasteful-looking antique drinks cabinet sat along the other.

I taped up a Pack3 in the lounge and positioned myself in such a way I could see what was occurring in the dining room.

Leo – quite professionally, I had to admit – laid a van blanket over the dining table to protect its surface and placed a pack of packing paper on top. Emily stood watching.

Leo opened both glass doors of the top of the dresser and began to select various glasses, china plates and ornaments and place them on the table by the paper. When satisfied he had sufficient, he taped up two Pack2s, reversed the bottom one and sat the other on top. For some inexplicable reason, he left both doors of the dresser wide open.

I knew I should have said something but I'm afraid to say I was quite enjoying myself.

Leo addressed Emily. 'When packing china, glass or any fragile items, one must always layer your box first.'

'Is that a cricketing expression?' I interrupted.

'Peter, please; I am trying to teach.' Leo took several sheets of paper, crumpled them up and laid them at the bottom of the Pack2. 'This is known as rough or scrunge.'

'Scrunge?' Emily repeated.

I had to say, it was a new one on me.

'Yes, scrunge.' Leo hesitated. 'Corn language, I believe.'

'What language?' I asked.

'From Cornwall.'

'You mean Cornish.'

'Yes. Now, if you don't mind, Peter, could you please get on with your job and I'll get on with mine.' Leo turned back to Emily, rolled his shoulders and jutted out his chin. 'Now, where was I?'

'Scrunge,' Emily said.

'Ah yes, scrunge. Once the box has been protected with a bit of scrounge or a bit of rough…' Leo froze and his face reddened a touch. 'I'm sorry, Emily, I was in no way implying that you were…'

'What?' I had to interfere again.

'You know.'

'A bit of scrunge?'

'No, the other one,' Leo said. 'I'm sorry.'

Emily obviously hadn't understood any of the conversation and said, 'It's alright; please carry on.'

Leo droned on about packing while I slid three pictures down the sides of my Pack3. I placed a large china pot in the middle and padded out the carton with some scatter cushions off the sofa. I packed another Pack3 of pictures and cushions and then taped up the bottom of a Pack6 and started on the books in the bookcase.

Leo, meanwhile, had packed all the china and glass on the table and proceeded to extract more items from the dresser top. When finished, he again left the glass doors wide open.

I felt a prick of guilt. Daz had asked me to keep an eye on Leo and I owed Daz. I knew some of the lads would be bitterly disappointed, but I had to say something.

Fortunately, Emily, who was experiencing her first-ever removal, spoke first so I was covered on both sides.

'I'm sorry to interrupt, Leo,' she said, 'but shouldn't you close the doors of that dresser?'

Leo smiled his most patronising 'you know nothing' smile and replied, 'And why might that be, Emily?'

'Because—' Emily began but, at that precise moment, gravity kicked in.

Having emptied a certain amount of china and glass from the cabinet, Leo had now made the shell lighter than the combined weight of the glass doors.

I saw it going and leapt over, managing to get hold of the top before the whole thing crashed to the floor. Leo span round and also grabbed the top, and we both managed to push it back over so that it once again sat flush on its base.

Leo closed one of the doors but the other had come loose at its hinges and I propped it shut with a hardback copy of the Oxford Dictionary from the bookcase. Two panes of glass had been cracked by the sudden movement of the cabinet's contents and several breakables had fallen onto the carpet below.

Emily and I crouched down to gather up the latter. A couple

of arms had snapped off an expensive-looking figurine and handles were missing off at least three items of a Dalton tea set.

Mrs Laidlaw walked in carrying a tray with a teapot, three cups and a plate of biscuits.

'There you go,' she said, and put the tray on top of the packing paper.

Emily and I froze on the floor while Leo stood in front of the dresser, holding his arms out wide and generally trying to make himself look as large as possible.

'When are you going to start putting the Pack7s on the base things?' Mrs Laidlaw asked him.

'When your daughter arrives,' Leo replied.

'I don't drive; I always get the bus. Where are the other two?'

'On the van, sweeping and folding.'

'Why are you holding your arms out like that?'

'Yawning. Had a late night.'

'Had a fight?'

'No, a late night.' Leo raised his voice again.

Emily began to giggle. She put her arm around my back and buried her face in my shoulder.

'My late husband was very tight,' Mrs Laidlaw said.

Tentatively, I put my arm round Emily and she giggled some more.

'We hardly ever used to go out, and if we did, he'd complain about the price of everything. Oh, he was a pain. Sheila and Jessie used to always go on about me divorcing him, start a new life and stuff, but I never did. I suppose I didn't want the change and also, the sex was top notch. Would you like me to pour the tea?'

'No, thank you, madam. I'll get one of the others to do it when they get back from the van. What you could do – which would be much more helpful to us – would be to sort out the stuff in the kitchen you'd like us to pack.'

I heard the tea being poured.

'He used to have this thing about me telling him off. He'd come home from work and tell me he'd been a naughty boy so I used to dress up in my policewoman's outfit, handcuff him to the headboard and whip him. It didn't half get him going.'

'Please, can you go to the kitchen!' Leo shouted.

'I think I'll go to the kitchen and have a sit down and read the paper. Are you alright in here?'

'Fine, fine.'

'Do you want any more biscuits?'

'No!'

'I'll get some,' Mrs Laidlaw said, and I heard her shuffle out.

I really didn't want to get up; I was quite happy crouched on the floor with Emily. I wanted to peck her on the cheek and pat her lightly on the bum, but she stood up, forcing me, reluctantly, to follow suit.

Leo was holding his head in his hands.

'You alright, mate?' I asked him.

He didn't move nor answer.

Emily put the bits she'd collected on the table. I added mine and separated the broken pieces into a separate pile.

Leo finally spoke. 'Right. What we have to do is empty the dresser and lay everything on the table. I'll unscrew the doors which you can take out, Emily, while Pete and I carry the top to the back of the van. I'll tie them all to the side and blanket everything so Mrs Laidlaw won't be able to see the damage. One of you can then pack up the broken pieces and sweep up any glass with the van's dustpan and brush.'

He clapped his hands together and said, 'Let's go!'

A middle-aged woman appeared in the doorway carrying several bags of shopping. Leo immediately stretched his arms out again and I placed a couple of sheets of paper over the broken pile.

'Good morning,' Leo said.

'Who the bloody hell are you?' the woman demanded.

'Leo Wainwright; foreman in charge of Mrs Laidlaw's move.'

'Who the bloody hell is Mrs Laidlaw?'

Leo tried a different tact. 'I'm sorry, madam, but I'm afraid I'm not happy with the tone of your voice. As a matter of fact, I'd like to know who the "bloody hell" you might be.'

Leo's new approach only seemed to succeed in making the lady extremely angry and for one moment I thought she was actually going to hit him.

'My name is Linda Jackson née White,' the lady said, visibly straining to keep herself calm, 'and I am the daughter of Mrs White, who owns this flat.'

'Is she not here then?'

Linda exploded. 'I want you out of here now before I call the police!'

'Don't you want to show us round first?' Leo asked.

It's very rare I've seen somebody who is so irate that they can't even talk, but Linda Jackson née White was currently ticking that box. Emily nudged me on the arm. I had to intervene.

'I think there's been some rather large misunderstanding,' I began.

Linda turned her full, incredulous attention towards me.

I gave it my best NVQ-in-customer-service-trained voice. 'We represent Stoneways Removals and we had reason to believe we were moving a Mrs Laidlaw from this address today.' I suddenly remembered Leo's satnav. 'Unfortunately, for some reason, which I guarantee will be fully investigated, we've arrived at the wrong address.'

'Is this some sort of joke?'

I couldn't help it. 'It is quite funny, I've got to say.'

Linda whacked me underarm with one of the shopping bags, hard in the shins. It must have had something solid in there because it hurt like hell, but Emily was present and I didn't want to even flinch.

'It is not bloody funny!' Linda pointed a finger at me and I covered my nuts with my hands.

'Mum!' she cried.

Leo still had his arms outstretched.

'Mum!'

Mrs Laidlaw-White appeared.

'Oh, hello, Linda,' she said. 'Have you met them? They're a bit odd but I like the big, thick one.'

Ten

EMILY

Emily and I sat in the cab, leaving Leo to calm down Linda.

I rolled my trousers up to my knees and inspected the damage. There was a sizeable bloody welt on my left shin.

Emily reached into her bag and pulled out a tube of salve. 'Put some of this on it.'

'Thanks,' I said, and rubbed on the cream.

'Feisty lady,' Emily said.

'Can't really blame her.'

'Suppose not.' Emily put her hands on the steering wheel. 'Am I allowed to drive one of these?'

I thought about it. The Burger Van had a tachograph, so I said, 'I'm not sure.'

'Do you drive?'

Me mad, I heard Sarah say.

'No.'

'Why not?'

There were many reasons why I'd never learnt to drive: owning a vehicle too expensive, public transport on tap, parking crazy and my only ever attendance at Glastonbury when I was eighteen years old.

I hitchhiked down to the West Country on my own and it rained constantly. By the Saturday afternoon, I'd had enough, packed my tent up and walked out of the site to Shepton Mallet to try and find a B&B for the night. Wishful thinking, so I hit a pub and got chatting to a few people at the bar, where some feller who was dressed in leather took a shine to me. I told him straight up I wasn't gay and he said neither was he. We drank more and he began to slur. He said he could put me up and I, having nowhere to go as the rain shattered down on the pub windows, accepted. The landlady of the pub insisted on taking the car keys off my new mate and asked me if I could drive.

I was young and stupid but could handle my alcohol. I said, 'Yes,' and she gave me the keys.

The car was parked out front facing the road. I got in the driver's seat, switched on the ignition and reversed straight down a small hill into a tree.

I've never driven since and have also never been to an overblown rock festival when it's pissing down with rain.

'I had a go once but didn't like it,' I said to Emily.

'Is that why you're not in charge of this job, because you don't drive?'

I shrugged. I had many faults but I was fairly modest.

Leo appeared at my window, shaking his head.

'Going to make a complaint to Currys?' I asked him.

'Right. I've placcided Mrs White's daughter.'

'I'm sorry?' said Emily.

'Calmed her down,' Leo qualified. 'She's discovered the damage to the dresser and the broken bits so I've said we'll take the dresser top back to the yard and get it fixed and she can claim for the other damage. We've also got to unpack what we've packed and get moving to the job.'

'The real job?'

'Yes, the real job.'

'Emily and I'll start unpacking,' I said. 'You need to phone the office, tell them what's happened and get them to ring the right customer and tell them we're running late.'

Leo's bottom lip began to tremble and I thought there was a good chance he might actually start crying.

Under Linda's dangerously silent supervision, Emily and I unpacked the three cartons I'd packed and the half Pack2 Leo had started in complete silence as if we were working in a morgue.

Leo informed us that Daz Oatridge and Trevor Blind were driving over to the right address to begin packing and we finally got away at eleven. Leo said nothing more and looked incredibly morose while I navigated.

Trevor Blind was wearing his suit trousers and shoes but had on a Stoneways T-shirt. He was grinning broadly as I backed the van in with Emily.

'I think that must be Leo's greatest ever cock-up and there's been a few,' he said.

'How much is here?' I asked.

Trevor slapped me on the back. 'It's alright, my son. Nice job; the daughter's packed most of it.'

I slammed my hand against the side of the van to stop it and opened up one of the doors. Emily opened the other.

Daz appeared from the flat, not looking very happy. He gave me a dirty look and marched up to the driver's window.

'You enjoying your first move, Emily?' Trevor asked.

'You stupid fucking prat,' we all heard Daz say.

'It's been interesting,' Emily said.

'OK, I can slightly understand how you came to be at the wrong address but how the hell did you manage to damage an extremely expensive antique dresser top when you weren't even fucking loading?'

'I'll show you both round,' Trevor said.

'How did it happen? Please do not tell me you left the bloody doors wide open when you were packing it? Even my five-year-old son knows better than fucking that!'

For a change, Trevor wasn't lying – there wasn't much there and Mrs Laidlaw's daughter had indeed packed a fair amount. In fact, you couldn't have asked for nicer people to move. Tea was offered almost straightaway but politely refused because of the lateness of the hour.

Daz and Trevor both stayed on and we were loaded by half twelve. Daz himself got the 'we've got everything' bit signed on the sheet and apologised for the initial tardiness of the crew. Technical difficulties, he told our customer.

'You alright now?' Daz asked me as he and Trevor got into his company car.

'Fine – thanks very much,' I replied.

'I'll see you back at the yard,' Daz said to Leo, and shook his head darkly.

'Is Leo going to get a Job Chat form as well?' I asked.

'Don't push it, Pete; I'm not in a very good mood.'

We arrived outside the bungalow in Purfleet an hour later; Leo's twat-nav app was not produced.

Jenny, daughter of the real Mrs Laidlaw, met us outside and told us the sale still hadn't gone through. Her mum's solicitor reckoned about half two. I glanced at Leo, whose head was buried in the steering wheel, and told Jenny not to worry. We'd grab a bite to eat and wait.

It was a sunny afternoon so I announced I was going to walk down to the park and eat my sandwiches. Emily asked if she could tag along.

'It's up to you,' I replied in my 'I'm not bothered' voice.

'OK, I'll just stay here then.'

I began to backtrack. 'Well, you can come if you want to.'

Emily made no effort to move. 'I'm fine sitting here.'

'Well, it would be… it would be…'

'It would be what?' she asked, and smiled.

My heart melted. 'Nice if you came down to the park with me,' I said in a very quiet, pathetic voice and prayed she wouldn't be so cruel as to say, 'Pardon?'

'I'd like that,' she said, picked up her backpack and followed me out of the cab.

Leo still sat there, head in the steering wheel, and I felt for him.

'Leo?' I offered.

He raised his head and looked at me through his sunglasses. 'No, I'm alright here.'

'Sure?'

He took a while to answer. 'Yeah.' He paused and then mumbled, 'Thanks, Pete,' and collapsed back onto the steering wheel.

We found a bench to sit on in the sun. It was unseasonably warm and the last soft colours of dying autumn glowed in the trees.

My cheese, cucumber and mayonnaise sandwiches were embarrassing but I was hungry and had to eat. They tasted a bit like cardboard and globules of mayo kept falling through the slowly disintegrating, Sainsbury's thin-sliced and onto my sweatshirt and trousers.

Emily handed me a half-full kitchen roll from her backpack. I thanked her, tore off a piece and cleaned myself up. She lifted out a tartan blanket and lay it around her waist and knees. The thermos flask she had on Saturday came next, followed by a cellophane bag containing two rolls.

'A bit like Mary Poppins,' I said.

Emily unwrapped one of her rolls. God, it looked nice: soft-looking like its owner with tufts of fresh lettuce and off-the-bone ham drooping down luxuriously from its sides.

'Do you think I look like Julie Andrews?' she asked.

'No, your bag.'

'My bag?' She opened up the thermos and poured some of the contents into the cup.

'It holds a lot.'

'Oh, I see,' she said. 'Like when she pulled out the plant?'

'Exactly.'

We didn't talk as we ate. Emily's lunch had made me even

hungrier, but I was careful not to eat too quickly nor open my mouth as I chewed. I was on my last sandwich when Emily offered me one of her rolls.

'No, I'm alright; honestly,' I said.

'Peter, I'm not that hungry and you've been very nice to me today. You haven't been patronising and have treated me with respect. I'm grateful, so please have this roll.'

'Well, OK then,' I said.

'It's got butter in it.'

'Fine.'

'And mustard.'

'Even better.'

I ate it in three bites. It was incredible.

Emily stood up and shook out the crumbs from her blanket. 'How long do we have to wait until we can unload the lorry?' she asked.

'It depends,' I said. 'Solicitors won't do anything now until at least two so I should think we're looking at three. Maybe earlier, but then again, maybe later.'

'Like a piece of string?'

'Oh yes.'

'I might go and lie down over there on that bank for a while.' Emily pointed.

'Be my guest.'

She looked me straight in the eye. 'Would you like to join me?'

We lay side by side on the blanket, very close but not touching.

She told me she'd phoned Ross this morning before she came to work and had a long chat about me.

I was curious. 'What did she say?'

'She was very nice about you. Said you'd been a loyal friend since her husband died.'

'I've tried.'

'You've never thought of getting together? She's an attractive lady.'

'She's like a sister to me.'

A thrush landed nearby. It gave us a cursory look and began to peck at the grass.

'She told me about Sarah.'

I sat up. 'Excuse me, but it sounds like you seem to know an awful lot about me, but this morning you didn't even remember my name.'

'Do you think us girls are that much different to you boys?'

'What do you mean?'

'Bravado. I pretended to forget your name so you wouldn't think I was overly interested in you. Similar to when you said you were going to sit in the park and eat your lunch and pretended you weren't bothered if I came with you or not.'

'Was I really that see-through?'

Emily smiled but with a tinge of sadness and reflection. 'I can only recognise things in others which I recognise in myself.'

The thrush captured a worm in its beak and took to the air.

I lay back down. 'So, are you interested in me?'

Emily turned on her side to face me. 'Yes, I have to say I am. I think you're good-looking in a weather-beaten type of way and you're nice. Easy to get on with and, as far as I can see, not aggressive.'

Our faces were inches apart.

'Unlike your ex-husband.'

'Unlike my ex-husband.'

I leant over to kiss her but she placed a finger on my lips.

'Not yet,' she said softly. 'Can we not rush it? I've said I like you; it doesn't mean I want to have wild sex with you straightaway. I'd like to think we're both a bit older and more mature than that.'

I turned away. 'Of course, of course.'

'You are funny, you know.'

'Good.'

She sat up. 'Oh, don't be horrible.'

'Sorry.'

'Do you mean that?'

'Yes, I do.'

She picked up one of my hands and held it. 'Thank you,' she said, and kissed me on my forehead.

My phone rang: *Leo*.

'Yes, mate?'

'They've got the keys.'

'Be there in a minute.'

We stood up and Emily shook any crumbs off the blanket and folded it back into her backpack.

'Would you like to meet up for a drink sometime?' I asked her as we walked back through the park.

'Love to,' she said.

I smiled and felt pleasingly warm inside like a teenager in love.

Emily wrote down her number on a scrap of paper and handed it to me. 'One thing, though. I'm afraid we'll have to watch out for my ex. He's very jealous of me seeing anyone else.'

I made myself taller and swaggered slightly as though a small, rolled-up carpet lay under each of my armpits. 'That's OK.'

'He has a lot of eyes and ears, so please don't mention us to anyone.'

'What about Ross?'

'OK, yes; maybe Ross. But no one else, OK?

'Is he that scary?'

'OK?' Emily repeated.

I shrugged. 'OK.'

We walked on.

'Would I know this bloke?' I asked.

'Where are you from?'

'I was born in Pulham Park but have spent most of my life in North and South Bitton.'

'Then you might have heard of him.'

I had a feeling I wasn't going to like this. 'What's his name?'

Emily opened the park gate and said, 'Ray Henderson.'

We were unloaded by four but Leo offered to unpack, which was fair enough – they were lovely people and we'd been nearly three hours late. The bona fide Mrs Laidlaw gave us all a hug and a kiss and £10 each.

It was now five o'clock and I made two phone calls after we'd got back in the cab. The first was to Daz asking him if I could jump out before we got back to the yard. He said, 'Yes,' but reminded me to fill out the Job Chat form. I told him no problem and phoned Jeff Unsworth.

'Yo.'

'Where are you?'

'Just heading down the Queens for a pint. Why?'

'I'll be there in ten minutes.'

Leo dropped me off outside the pub and I said my goodbyes. When Leo checked the driver-side mirror to see what was coming, I held an imaginary phone to my ear. Emily smiled and gave me a thumbs-up.

The pub was quiet; a group of lads were playing pool and Jeff sat at the bar chatting to Ruth and nursing a pint of Stella. I decided on a Fosters top and asked him if we could sit down somewhere out of the way.

We sat at a table in the far corner of the saloon bar and the jukebox began to play 'Riders on the Storm' by The Doors.

'Unusual for you to be out and about on a Monday night, especially so near to payday. What's up?' Jeff asked.

'Can you tell me more about Ray Henderson?'

Jeff shifted in his seat. 'Why are you so interested in him?'

'I just am.'

'You're not going to do any work for him, are you?'

'A friend of mine's upset him.'

'What's he done?'

'Slept with his ex-wife.'

'Has he moved to Australia yet?'

'Jeff, be serious. Is he really that bad?'

Jeff took a sip of his pint. 'A few years ago, my brother Dan opened up a pub in Cheston. Henderson paid a visit with one of his boys, an animal by the name of Dave Kennet. Henderson wanted a cut of the takings for protection. Now, my brother could handle himself and told him no. Henderson asked him again and Dan told him to fuck off. Kennet grabbed a fork off a nearby table and gouged one of my brother's eyes out.'

Ray Manzarek's keyboards faded and a car alarm sounded in the pub's car park.

'I'm sorry to hear that story,' I said.

'People like Henderson and Kennet are arseholes of the highest order but they're also extremely nasty and vicious arseholes. Keep well away.'

'How's your brother now?'

'Let's just change the subject,' Jeff said, and I saw the hatred in his eyes.

I got back to the flat at seven and cracked open a can of Stella. I sat on the bed and thought about Emily and how much I liked her and then I thought about Jeff's brother.

I sat for a while longer before the silence began to oppress me. I couldn't face The Sabs or anything remotely heavy, so I pulled out the Pack6 from under the bed and rummaged until a compilation CD caught my eye: *The Best of Kenny Rogers*.

I put on track 5, 'Coward of the County', and played it three times.

Eleven

MANAGEMENT SKILLS

I didn't sleep well and woke up before the alarm. After I'd showered and changed, I turned on the radio. Phil Collins, 'In the Air Tonight'.

I didn't mind this track – it suited my mood.

Still no Maurice when I arrived in the restroom, only Barry Noble sitting at one of the tables eating an apple.

I pointed at Maurice's empty chair. 'Is he alright?'

Barry shrugged. 'You'll have to ask the ops manager.'

Daz opened up the shutter. 'Filled in the form for me, Pete?'

'Oh shit, I forgot,' I replied.

'Tomorrow morning, please,' he said, and closed the shutter with a snap.

'Bit tetchy,' I said to Barry.

'Wainwright's really annoyed him. Apparently, Mrs Whatever-her-name's daughter has threatened to complain directly to BAR.'

'Shit.'

'Indeed.' Barry took a bite of his apple. 'Quite amusing, though.'

'Poor old Leo.'

Barry held his apple in a pose of contemplation. 'Yes, I agree one has to show camaraderie with one's work associates and thus sympathy. However, there is no escaping the undeniable fact that Leo is an idiot.'

'We've never had anyone complain about us to BAR before, have we?'

'Not as far as I'm aware of.'

BAR: British Association of Removers, the NATO of the removal world. For a removal company to be recognised as a mover of quality, it was imperative they were members of the organisation. A direct complaint from a customer to BAR concerning one of its members could lead to that member's expulsion resulting in a severe loss of kudos and, more importantly, revenue. What was more ironic and, undoubtedly more unfortunate for poor old Leo, was that the current president of BAR was none other than our very own boss, Kye Stoneway.

'Poor old Leo,' I repeated.

'Indeed,' Barry said. 'Perhaps we should organise a mass for him.'

Emily bounced happily into the restroom. 'Hi, all. What's occurring today, then?'

'A church service,' Barry said, and took another bite of his apple.

'I'm sorry?'

'Don't worry,' I told her.

'Boys' talk?'

'Not exactly.'

Emily looked concerned.

'I'll explain later.'

'Are you alright?'

'Fine,' I said.

I noticed Barry raise his eyebrows.

'Just a bit stunned by yesterday's events,' I added.

Emily put her finger to her lips.

'No, not that,' I said, and immediately regretted it.

Daz opened up the shutter again. 'Morning, Emily.'

'Morning, Mr Oatridge.'

'Please call me Daz. Can you come through? I just need you to fill in a few forms.' He closed the shutter. Emily winked at me and stepped into the office.

Barry finished his apple and walked over to the kitchenette. 'Our Emily seems quite sweet on you, Peter.'

'Leave it out, Barry.'

'Sorry I spoke,' he said, and dropped his apple core into the bin.

'Sorry,' I apologised. 'Tad stressed at the moment.'

'You'll be more stressed on Friday.'

'It's payday, Barry; a cause for celebration.'

'We'll see.'

I recalled Daz's conversation with him yesterday morning. 'Magenta Carlberg?' I whispered.

'Selected items out of store.'

'Bloody hell,' is all I could manage.

'Bloody hell indeed,' Barry agreed, and walked out of the restroom.

Mrs Curdley, Ray Henderson and now, Magenta Carlberg. When God sees you in the gutter, he does like to come down and kick you very hard in the gonads.

Emily walked back in from the office. She held a clipboard in one hand and a set of van keys in the other.

'Running a job?' I asked.

'Don't be silly. I've got to walk down to the yard and give these to somebody called Steve Woodgy.'

I was about to tell her his surname was actually Woodgit but decided 'Woodgy' had a certain ring to it.

'Daz says he never comes up to the restroom unless he's on his way to Kye Stoneway's office for a disciplinary.'

'True,' I said, 'but he's an OK guy really. Might take you a while to get used to his habits.' I thought of Henderson talking to Kilo. 'Then again, maybe not.'

'I'm sorry?'

'Don't worry.' I changed the subject. 'What are you doing after that?'

'I've got to nip home and get my driving licence, fill in a couple more forms and then drive over in a transit van with Jeff Unsworth to help Steve Woodgy on his job.'

'Don't mention your ex to Jeff, will you?'

'I never mention him to anyone,' she replied, and then lowered her voice. 'When are you going to ask me out for that drink?'

'Tonight?' I offered, and then remembered I was skint.

'Where?' She was very close to me now and I noticed how brown her eyes were and how clear her make-up less skin was.

No way the Queen's Head or the Spoons, I thought. Somewhere a touch classier was the order of the day. 'Have you heard of the Lazy Lion in South Bitton?'

'Of course.'

'Eight o'clock?'

'Look forward to it,' she said, and was off out of the restroom, leaving me in the slip stream of her beautiful fragrance.

Daz opened up the shutter. 'You look really stupid,' he observed.

I pulled myself together. 'What am I doing today?'

'This afternoon, you, Leo and Freddie are going to start going through Magenta Carlberg's containers.'

'How many's she got?'

'Thirty-five.'

'I don't feel very well,' I said, and coughed a couple of times.

Daz ignored me. 'This morning you're with me.'

'You?'

'Yes, me. We're going to pick up cartons from somebody you moved recently.'

'Who is it?'

'I'll give you a clue. She's owns a garden ornament called Curly.'

'Have I upset you?' I asked Daz as we drove over to Sunningford in the Burger Van.

'No more than usual,' he replied.

'Carlberg and Curdley.'

'Don't forget Curly.'

'Don't think I'll ever forget him.'

We pulled up at the Bragstone lights. 'Why couldn't you bring Jeff?' I asked.

Daz looked at me. 'Because, Pete, as I've tried to tell you before on several occasions, you're more tactful and less volatile. Jeff could make matters worse. I'm not having a go – that's just his way – but at the moment, I really don't want a second complaint to BAR.'

'Is that woman from yesterday really going to complain?'

'I'm hoping not and that's why I need you to fill in the Job Chat form ASAP.'

'Has Jeff filled in his?'

'He's sitting at my desk right this minute filling it in under Trevor Blind's supervision.'

'At gun point?'

The lights changed and we turned into the Bragstone Road.

'That reminds me,' I said. 'I thought you said yesterday morning that you weren't going to put Emily with Steve Woodgit.'

'Didn't have much choice. Maurice was going to run the job but he's off sick.'

'What's up with him?'

'Bad back.'

'In a minute,' I said, 'I think you'll find out why.'

The electric gates stayed shut as we drove up and I had to get out of the cab to ring the buzzer.

'Just second,' I heard Rosa say, and the gates began to open.

A pile of ripped cartons, sodden by the rain, lay in a heap by the metallic grey 4x4 which sat there like the silent, killer robot in the black and white classic *The Day the Earth Stood Still*.

I smiled to myself. There was one thing both Daz and the boss detested: complete disregard to the value of company materials.

Rosa came out of the house and asked us pleasantly if we wanted tea.

'I'm not touching those,' Daz told her, and pointed at the cartons.

Rosa looked alarmed.

'No, thank you, Rosa,' I said. 'We're fine.'

She eyed us nervously and walked back to the house.

'It's not her fault,' I said to Daz.

'Good morning,' we heard a voice say, and turned to see Mrs Curdley walking purposefully down the spiral staircase from above the garage. She looked stunning, I couldn't deny, and I noticed Daz caught for a moment in the glare of her cosmetic headlights.

'Mrs Curdley, I presume?' Daz said, and held out his hand.

'And who might you be?'

'Darren Oatridge, Stoneways Removals. I've talked to you several times on the phone.'

Several times?

'Oh yes.' She shook his hand with a flash of a limp wrist. She glanced disdainfully at me and, once more, I peered into the depths of her dark, shallow soul.

She held my gaze and tutted before turning back to Daz. 'Your men refused to do what I asked them.'

'And what would that be?'

'Place my lion where I wanted it to go.'

We followed her to the corner of the garage where Curly stood.

'I wanted him on top of the garage by the BBQ. Your men consistently ignored me and drove off.'

Daz looked at Curly and asked, 'Can you show me exactly where you want the lion placed?'

'On top of the garage,' she said as though Daz was the most stupid person on the planet.

But Daz was calm – I suppose composure was the essential difference between the general and his frontline troops. 'I'm sorry, Mrs Curdley, but I would like to know precisely where on top.'

Mrs Curdley turned on him. 'Why are you being so particular? I just want him on top of the bloody garage. Is that plain enough English for you?'

Daz's tone changed just that fraction, imperceptible to her but apparent to me. 'Not really, I'm afraid.' He smiled a touch patronisingly. 'You see, we'd need to know exactly what spot to position the crane.'

'The crane? Why on earth would you need a crane?'

Daz patted Curly on its back. 'This is made of stone and, at a rough estimate, would weigh…' He put his hand to his chin. 'A ton? Maybe more.'

'So?'

At that moment, I felt an anger rise up inside me that I hadn't felt for an enormously long time. If Mrs Curdley were a man, I would have been tempted to punch her straight in the mouth.

'The hire for the crane would be £400,' Daz said.

'Why can't your men carry it up?'

'You might also want to seek advice from a roofing company to ascertain whether the spot Curly eventually rests upon would need re-enforcing. Otherwise, the lion might end up sitting in the driver's seat of one of your cars in the garage.' Daz chuckled at his little joke. 'Altogether, not a cheap operation I'm afraid.'

'I'm sorry, Mr…?'

'Oatridge.'

'Mr Oatridge, but I still don't understand why the two of you just can't carry my garden ornament up there right here and now.'

'Health and safety, madam.' Daz pointed at his shoes. 'I'm not wearing my steel toe-capped boots.'

Mrs Curdley's face reddened and I watched as she tried desperately to find words to vent her anger, but Daz had stumped her. Try as she might, she couldn't speak and settled for shuffling her right foot back and forth across the gravel like a bull about to charge.

'If you and your husband decide on the crane option, please give us a call and we would only be too happy to help.' Daz held out his hand.

Mrs Curdley ignored it. Her face had turned a sickly pale hue and she looked ten years older. One day, I thought, she'd visit a beauty parlour and the beautician would say, 'I'm sorry, madam, but we can't polish a turd.'

'What about your boxes?' she asked in her best threatening tone.

Daz looked at the rotting pile and said, 'No use to us now. Ask your gardener to burn them. Good morning, Mrs Curdley, and please don't hesitate to ring.'

'Got to admit, you're quite good,' I said as we drove down the road.

'I learnt a long time ago to always keep calm,' Daz said. 'Play them at their own game and let *them* lose their temper. When they do that, you've got them.'

Daz's phone rang. He pulled it out of his pocket and handed it to me. *T Blind*, the screen read.

'Trevor, it's Pete – Daz is driving.'

'Great news,' Trevor said happily. 'Mrs Curdley has just rung up to complain about him.'

'I'll tell him,' I said, and handed the phone back to Daz.

'I heard,' he said, and put the phone back in his pocket.

'You don't seem that bothered.'

'Like you said, she's a silly cow but that doesn't mean you don't have to fill in that Job Chat form.'

'Are you sure you don't want to take a few photocopies of it first in case we run out?'

'Management don't have to fill in forms like that.'

I could have had a go but I remembered my date at the Lazy Lion.

'Daz?' I asked politely instead.

'Yes?'

'Is there any chance of lending me twenty sobs till Friday?'

Daz beeped at a cyclist who spun off the kerb five feet in front of us. He reached into the pocket of his jacket with his free hand and produced a thick-looking black wallet.

'I bet that's nearly as heavy as Curly,' I said.

Daz fingered a £20 note and held it out to me. 'Job Chat form completed and handed in to me tomorrow morning.'

'Without fail,' I told him, and took the note.

Twelve

YARD GAMES

Barry Noble lined up ten storage containers in the yard along either side of the main entrance to the warehouse.

I wrote down the number of each container on a slip of paper while Leo and Freddie took off the doors. On the front of one of these, somebody had written in tall, black marker-pen letters: 'CARLBERG, PROBABLY THE WORST MOVE IN THE WORLD'.

I took the slip of paper up to the office and Daz selected the corresponding inventory lists. Every item the customer wanted delivered to the new address, Daz had indicated with red highlighter. Our job was to remove these items from each container and load them onto STONE 42. I was entrusted with all the paperwork while Freddie and Leo would be responsible for most of the physical graft.

There was no enmity felt – both Leo and Freddie knew I was the only one of us capable of deciphering the lists and they also knew that any mistake would be down to me. Boring, boring work and worse was the thought that there were still another twenty-five containers to go through before Friday. It was still sunny but the cold easterly wind blowing across the yard only added to the general unpleasantness.

Leo was his usual, annoyingly positive self – he'd never moved Magenta before. 'Should knock these ten out in an hour,' he said to me. 'I'll get Barry to dig out another fifteen for later.'

'We'll see,' I said to him.

Magenta Carlberg was an attractive woman in her late thirties who'd recently divorced her billionaire Texan husband. Their marital home in Knightsbridge had been two six-bedroomed houses on five floors knocked together. Rumour had it the hubby, whom we'd never met, had been caught more than once with his trousers around his proverbial ankles and Magenta, understandably incensed, decided to strip the property of its entire contents. Hence, the thirty-five containers.

One could never call Magenta a horrible person – she was always unfailingly polite and blissfully ignorant of her good looks. No Mrs Curdley but she also had absolutely no concept of reality.

As a consequence of her divorce, Magenta discovered religion. When we moved her into store out of Knightsbridge, I was appointed the task of packing the main kitchen (there were at least two others). I laid out a hundred or so glasses on one of the worktops to pack and she told me her priest, Father somebody-or-other, had advised her to get rid of a lot of her belongings before she moved.

She said, 'He told me that when I died, I couldn't take them with me.' She looked at me in wonder. 'I'd never thought of that before.'

A Hanging Wardrobe carton can hang up to ten items of clothing. Magenta insisted she wanted to pack her own clothes and, despite our constant prompting, decided to begin packing them at gone three on the last afternoon of the move. She painstakingly divided her clothes into spring, summer, winter and autumn, and after listing and loading eighty-four wardrobe cartons, we finally closed up the last container in Knightsbridge at two in the morning.

To put it mildly, Magenta Carlberg was – most probably – the worst customer I'd ever moved.

The first container immediately caused a problem. According to Magenta's list, she wanted us to extract a 'Jacobean Hunting Table'. Daz had highlighted 'TABLE – UPSTAIRS LOUNGE'. There were three different types of table in the container.

I rang Daz and asked him if Arthur Negus was available. He told me to get on with it.

Needless to say, the afternoon progressed extremely slowly and Freddie quickly became bored. After we closed up the second container, he sat on one of Magenta's thirty-eight dining chairs and began playing with his phone.

Leo had a go at him and I had to intervene and tell Freddie to at least try and look interested. Freddie descended into one of his black strops and I threatened to call his mother down from the office.

At half past three, we opened up the fifth container. Daz had highlighted 'FOOTBALLS AND MISC – 3RD FLOOR PLAYROOM – PACK3'. Freddie found the carton, tore it open and extracted one of the footballs.

'Freddie,' I warned him, but he was off booting the ball around the yard.

Leo wasn't happy, but I told him to leave Freddie be. He was a youngster, I explained, and needed to let off some steam. We'd carry on without him and I'd help stack the van. Leo told me Freddie should be sacked and I mentioned the potential complaint to BAR. It shut Leo up and we managed to progress a bit faster without Freddie.

I had a problem deciphering the writing on the inventory list of the sixth container which, according to the paperwork, had been loaded at 10.15pm on that fateful last night. Leo himself became bored and started to play football with Freddie.

It was funny watching them; I couldn't work out who was the tearaway sixteen-year-old and who was the supposedly sensible, married rugby player in his late twenties.

Leo was a lot bigger but much slower. His idea of getting the ball off Freddie was to assault him, but Freddie was too quick and sped round Leo's charges with ease. Leo suggested they play a penalty shoot-out using two of Magenta's Pack3s as goalposts. Freddie insisted it should be rush goalkeepers and they both grabbed another two Pack3s to form a set of goalposts opposite.

Freddie went one-nil up, nutmegging the charging Leo and letting the ball roll into Leo's goal without further touching it.

Leo placed the ball on what I assumed he estimated was the halfway line. 'My turn,' he said, and took a run-up. He booted the ball but mishit it and the ball looped up into the air.

Freddie volleyed it and the ball smashed into Leo's forehead, knocking off his sunglasses.

Freddie was laughing as he ran on past the stricken Leo and tapped the ball between the two boxes to make it two-nil.

However, Freddie was too cocky with his goal celebrations and Leo ran after him and caught him. There was a bit of wrestling and fake fighting, but Freddie emerged first and picked up the ball.

'My turn,' he said, and ran back and placed the ball roughly on the spot which Leo had previously decided was the halfway line. Freddie was still giggling and his ball control deserted him. Leo barged him over, took charge of the leather and sidestepped it into Freddie's goal. Two-one.

Leo's turn again and he kicked the ball from the halfway line purposefully slowly towards Freddie.

I could see Freddie falter. He knew it was a fifty-fifty ball but decided to go for it.

They both met at the ball. There was some spirited defiance on Freddie's part but Leo, utilising his superior weight, threw Freddie to one side and scored. Two-all.

My phone rang and I pulled it out of my pocket. I clocked the name but decided, on the spur of the moment, to go for it.

'Sarah,' I answered.

'How are you?'

'Great.'

'Can you talk?'

The sky was tinged with the red of approaching twilight as Freddie picked up the ball from the side of STONE 42 and ran back over to Leo.

'Yes,' I said into the phone.

'Why haven't you answered my calls?'

Leo and Freddie were arguing.

'I texted you I was busy.'

'Oh yes, the twenty-four-hour office move.'

'Forty-eight, actually.' I was one of those better liars; I could usually remember them.

Freddie was insisting, as it was the deciding goal, they should have a drop ball.

'That means you should be able to help me out with the rent for this month then.'

That was the problem with lies; they could get you into trouble.

I decided to come clean. 'I lied.'

'No shit, Sherlock.'

Freddie and Leo walked over to me.

'Just a minute,' I said to Sarah.

'Can you drop the ball for us?' Leo asked.

Freddie gave me the ball and they followed me up to the halfway line. I booted the ball as hard as I could over the top of the barbed-wire fence at the back of the yard to the wasteland beyond.

'That was one of our customer's balls!' Freddie exclaimed, and started laughing again.

'Are you still there?' I said into the phone.

'Of course.'

'I can't pay you any more rent,' I said.

'I wasn't asking you.'

'Good.'

There was a pause on the line before Sarah asked, 'How's Kate?'

'She came round to see me on Sunday.'

'She OK?'

'Seemed alright.'

There was another silence.

'Pete.'

'What?'

'Do you want to come back?'

I heard Phil Collins' drums rolling around my head.

'Not at the moment,' I said.

'Just asking.'

'Got to go.'

'Talk to you soon, then.'

'Yeah.' I clicked off the phone.

Freddie walked up to me. 'Are you alright?' he asked.

'Why, what's wrong with me?'

'Nothing,' Freddie said. 'You just look a bit odd.'

Leo, now stripped down to his T-shirt and covered in sweat, grabbed a Hanging Wardrobe carton and carried it onto the back of the van.

'Have you got a girlfriend?' I asked Freddie.

'Sort of.'

'Have you?' I was surprised.

'I haven't screwed her or anything yet. Think she's a bit frigid.'

'Playing hard to get,' I said.

'There's another girl I like better.'

'Who's that?'

'A girl called Liz. She's meant to be a right old bike and let's anybody shag her.'

'Are you still a virgin, Freddie?'

'No!' he replied indignantly.

'Freddie, it's me you're talking to.'

He was quiet for a moment. 'Alright, yeah: I'm still a virgin.'

We got through eight containers and decided to call it a day at 4.30. Leo parked up the lorry and Barry began to put the containers away while Freddie and I walked up the passageway to the restroom. Freddie carried on through to the office to talk to his mum and I handed Daz the completed inventories through the shutter.

He counted them. 'You've only been through eight,' he said.

'Fuck me, you should be on *Countdown.*'

Daz held up his right hand and rubbed his thumb against the other four fingers. 'Twenty sobs?'

'How long are you going to hold that against me for?'

'As long as it takes for you to treat me with the respect and deference I deserve.'

'You've been reading the dictionary again.'

Daz separated the eight completed lists and fastened them together with a bulldog clip. The two remaining he placed with the other twenty-five lying on the desk return by his phone.

'Has Woodgit finished yet?' I asked indifferently.

'Should be back soon – Steve and Jeff don't tend to hang about. Why?'

'Just wondering.'

'Then again, they might both have spent too long trying to chat up Emily.'

'Why would that be?'

Daz looked at me. 'Are you alright?'

'Everybody keeps asking me that.'

'Well, are you?'

'What time tomorrow?'

'Eight.'

'Magenta's storage?'

Daz nodded.

Ross appeared at the shutter with her coat on.

'I'm going shopping on the Broadway,' she said to me. 'Do you want a lift?'

'Freddie not coming?' I asked as I got in Ross's car.

'Football training. His mate's dad's picking him up from work.'

'Did a bit of training this afternoon.'

'I know, I watched some of it on the cameras. Why didn't you stop them?'

'I wasn't that bothered. The job was shite and they were enjoying themselves.'

We drove out of the estate and turned left down London Road.

'How are you anyway?' I asked.

'OK, can't complain. You?'

I suddenly felt the urge to talk to someone and who better than Ross? 'Good.' I paused. 'And bad.'

'Come on, tell me.'

'Which first?'

Ross pretended to think. 'The bad.'

'Can that wait?'

'OK, the good then.'

'I'm going for a drink with Emily tonight.'

Ross smiled broadly. 'Oh, that is good news. She's a nice person.'

'This is strictly hush-hush.'

'You can trust me.'

'I know, but don't even tell Freddie.'

'Where are you meeting her?'

'The Lazy Lion.'

'Bit trendy for you, isn't it?'

'What are you trying to say?'

She tapped her hand on my knee. 'I just don't want you to try and be someone you're not. You're fine as you are.'

'Thank you,' I said, and meant it.

We joined the A3 at the Purfleet roundabout. Night had fallen and the dual carriageway was dotted with the car lights of rush hour.

'And the bad?' Ross asked.

'Her ex-husband's a psychopath.'

She began to laugh.

'It's not funny.'

'Sorry, it was just the way you said it.'

'He's the jealous type according to Emily.'

Ross indicated to overtake. 'You'll be alright,' she said, 'as long as he's not a deranged ex-SAS war veteran or some nutter like Ray Henderson.'

'What?' I blurted out, and put both hands on the dashboard.

Ross pulled back from overtaking and an angry car horn beeped behind us.

She looked worried. 'Are you alright?'

'What name did you just say?'

Ross began to repeat his name, but a flash of realisation spread across her face when she got to the first syllable of the surname.

'Oh, shit,' she said. 'You're kidding.'

I said nothing.

'I can't believe Emily could have ever got herself involved with an arsehole like that.'

'Do you know him?'

'Don't be silly, but I know of him.' She indicated to overtake again. 'Oh, Peter; what have you got yourself into?'

I rang Jeff when I got to back to the flat.

'Yo.'

'Where are you?'

'Where do you think?'

I heard a muttering of background chat and glasses clinking.

'Do you know the Lazy Lion?'

'South Bitton?'

'Yes.'

'Wankers pub. C-drinks and overpriced continental lagers.'

'But has you-know-who got anything to do with it?'

'Idi Amin?'

'Ray Henderson.'

'What is your problem with this bloke?'

'Just answer me, please.'

'Extremely doubtful. No bullet holes in the walls.'

'Are you sure?'

'About the bullet holes?'

'Henderson.'

'Are you alright?'

'Sort of.'

'OK,' Jeff said. 'Henderson's got no class. Thinks he has but I don't think he'd be seen dead in a place like that. Besides, it's owned by ex-Old Bill and not the "he fell down the stairs" type. The governor would know who Henderson was and wouldn't let him in.'

'Certain?'

'What's up, for fuck's sake?'

'Nothing.'

Jeff was quiet for a moment. 'This bloke you know who's seeing Henderson's ex – it's not you, is it?'

'Don't be stupid.'

There was another pause. 'OK. Anything else or can I get on with the crossword?'

I cracked open a can of Stella and cooked myself a chili con carne without the kidney beans. I ate a bowlful and decided I'd better spruce myself up. I had a shower, put on *Back in Black* by AC/DC and got dressed into my black jeans, plain black T-shirt and black V-necked jumper. I checked myself in the mirror and thought I looked pretty cool.

At a quarter to eight, I donned my leather jacket, a woolly hat and a pair of sunglasses. If one of Henderson's snitches saw me, they'd tell the man his ex-wife was seeing the lead guitarist of The Sisters of Mercy.

Thirteen

THE LAZY LION

The Lazy Lion was quiet – empty tables, piped jazz music playing and no bouncers on the door.

Before I got to the bar, an attractive female in her early twenties with 'LL' splayed across her blouse in glittery golden capitals, approached with a menu.

'Would you like to eat, sir?' she asked, and shined a lipstick smile.

'No, thank you,' I replied. 'I'm here to have a drink with a friend.'

'This way then, please,' she said, and led me to a table.

She lit the solitary candle and handed me a drinks menu. 'When your friend arrives and you've decided what you'd like, give myself or one of my colleagues a wave.' The lipstick stretched again and she walked back to the bar, her bottom wiggling pleasantly in her tight black skirt.

I looked around. There was only one other couple in the whole place, sitting at a table at the far end of the bar underneath what looked like an enormous picture of Des Lynham, so I decided to dispense with the hat and sunglasses. I picked up the drinks menu, flicked through the wine and champagne section, and had a quiet chuckle at the list of bottled C-drinks before arriving at the draught lagers (real ale drinkers were obviously not catered for). I'd never heard of any of them and was also gob-smacked at some of the prices. The most expensive, a Bavarian brew beginning with an 'L', was £9.75 a pint. 8.1%, mind, but I not only wanted to stay sober; I also wanted some cash left to buy Emily chips afterwards if need be.

You really know how to treat a lady, I heard Sarah say.

Tough, I thought. *If she likes me, she'll have to get used to it.*

Somebody prodded me on the arm: Emily.

'Hi!' she said, and I stood up.

She offered me her cheek and I clumsily pecked her ear which made her giggle.

We sat down opposite each other and she took off her jacket, revealing a tight-fitting red top.

'This is nice.'

'Yes,' I agreed. 'Have you been here before?'

'Oh, years ago when it was the Grey Swan or the Lingering Death, as it was better known.'

'Bullet holes in the walls?' I quipped.

She looked at me. 'No,' she said, and the smile froze on my face.

'Sorry,' I said.

'It's alright.'

'Would you like a drink?'

'Yes,' she enthused, and her natural friendliness returned. 'A glass of Merlot would be great.'

I turned to the bar and nearly snapped my fingers, but the waitress was already making her way over.

'Are you ready to order?' she asked.

'Yes, please. Could I have a glass of Merlot?' I said.

'Large or small?'

I looked at Emily.

'Small, please; I'm driving.'

Thank fuck for that, I thought.

'And, could I have a pint of one of these, please?' I pointed at the second-cheapest lager on the menu.

'Certainly, sir. A small Merlot and a Weihenstephaner Kristall Weissbier.'

'Exactly. Couldn't have put it better myself.'

'Anything else? A sharing platter, perhaps?'

I glanced at Emily again.

'No, I'm fine. I ate before I came out.'

'Are you sure?' I asked, and prayed she'd say yes.

'Yes, honestly. Maybe we could grab a portion of chips later or something.'

I was falling in love.

The waitress disappeared back to the bar and I asked Emily how her day had been.

'Interesting,' she said, and laughed.

'Steve?'

'Oh, he's nice enough; I just can't believe how much dope he smokes.'

'You don't mind?'

She scrunched up her eyes. 'I wouldn't say I don't mind. It doesn't offend me – each to their own and all that – I just think…'

'What do you think?'

'Well, it's not very professional. I mean, our customer must have noticed. The van absolutely stunk of it and it's not the most pleasant of smells.'

'He has been told to smoke it away from the vehicles.'

She was incredulous. 'You mean the management know?'

I thought I'd better change the subject. Trying to explain the culture of Stoneways was not possible in words. You could only begin to understand it through experience and Emily had only worked there for three days.

The waitress reappeared with the drinks and a small bowl of roasted peanuts.

'A Weihenstephaner for you, sir, and a glass of Merlot for the lady.'

'Thank you. Shall I pay now?'

'No rush, sir; when you're finished. Enjoy.'

I'm not bloody tipping you, I thought, and considered telling Emily not to eat any of the peanuts.

'Cheers,' she said, and held up her glass.

I clinked it with mine. She smiled and I admired her perfectly white teeth. Did she have any faults? *Baggage*, I thought. Big, bad, horrible baggage and I wasn't thinking about her son.

'Excuse me a sec,' she said. She took off her bobble hat and shook her hair down over her shoulders.

God, she was stunning.

'Anyway, how was Jeff?' I asked.

'Oh, he's nice. Very helpful and quite funny. He showed me how to do some export wrapping.'

Export wrapping was one of the hardest aspects of the job to master. It involved covering furniture with specially designed paper blankets to ensure its protection during transit overseas. Every space on a shipping container had to be filled which meant a sofa would be wrapped to look like a sofa you could actually sit on. Truly skilled. I once worked with a guy from a firm in Fulham who was so good he used to sign some of the pieces he'd wrapped.

'How did you get on with that?' I asked.

'It's difficult. I had to wrap this chest of drawers and it's really hard to keep the paper blanket thing tight.' Emily stood up. 'So, I held one end with my hand and had to hold my leg up like this to keep it all together before I taped it.' She jutted one leg out at a ninety-degree angle like a ballet dancer.

'I'm sure Jeff enjoyed that,' I said.

'Oh, don't be silly.' She sat down again. 'He's old enough to be my dad.'

'You can't be that young.'

'How old is he?'

'Fifty-one.'

'You're joking.'

'Hard life.'

She sipped her wine. 'How old are you?'

'Go on, have a guess.'

'Ninety-five.'

'Thanks.'

'Only kidding.'

'Thirty-eight,' I said quickly in case she really did insult me. 'And you?'

'Slightly younger.'

'How long were you married for?'

'Too long.'

I knew I shouldn't have pushed it, but I'd never been renowned for my subtlety. 'What was he like?'

'What was Sarah like?'

'Touché,' I said, and took a drink of my lager. It was too cold and I felt a sharp pain in one of my upper molars.

'Can we change the subject, please?' she asked, and leant over the table towards me.

Her cleavage looked great. 'Of course,' I said.

She talked about her son, Charlie. He wasn't Henderson's. 'A product of a one-night stand with a very handsome rock star,' she said.

'Rock star?' I was impressed. 'Who?'

'OK, that's a bit of an exaggeration but he once played guitar on an Oasis track.'

'Oh right.' I didn't really like Oasis; a sort of cross between Slade and The Sweet spruced up with a bit of modern technology.

She seemed to sense my drift. 'Not your scene?'

'Not really. They're OK. Bit boring, I find.'

'I don't like them: shouty, cocky and bland.'

Good taste and *beauty*, I thought. 'Who do you like then?' I asked.

She thought for a minute. 'Sabbath, AC/DC, Motorhead, but my favourites are Hawkwind.'

This was too good to be true, but I checked my enthusiasm. In my experience, opposites in relationships could work better.

'Well,' I began slowly, trying to mask my excitement, 'which is your favourite Hawkwind track?'

'"Dingo Wilderness", she replied.

'Christ, I don't think I've ever heard that. What album's it on?'

Emily looked upwards and rolled her lips around in thought. '*Merlot Surprise*,' she said, and then burst out laughing.

'I'm sorry,' she said when her mirth finally began to subside. 'I just couldn't keep it up.'

Jeff Unsworth, I thought. *Bastard*.

'You're settling in quite well at Stoneways, aren't you?' I asked her in a stony voice.

'Oh, don't be angry.' She stretched out her hand and placed it on one of mine. 'I thought you working-type men were a bit more thick-skinned than that.'

I forced a smile. 'Yeah, course we are.' I should have left it but felt I had to carry on and try and explain myself. 'You see, I know it might sound strange, but I really do like Hawkwind.'

She withdrew her hand and sipped her wine, her face adopting a serious manner.

I ploughed on. 'A lot of people think I'm mad. "What, Hawkwind?" they say. Instrumentals that go on for ever: pseudo-space-imagery, repetitive guitar riffs and nonsensical lyrics. But they don't get it. Hawkwind were, and still are, a brilliant band.'

'Quite,' Emily agreed.

'*Space Ritual* and *Hall of the Mountain Grill* are two of the best albums ever made, while *Shot Down in the Night* is a great live album. I'll lend them to you if you want.'

Emily looked into my eyes. 'I'd love that,' she said, and then burst out laughing again.

'Sorry, sorry,' she kept repeating.

I wasn't happy and began to sulk. Sulkiness was another of my traits Sarah disliked, but I couldn't help it nor disguise it.

I stood up. 'I'll go and pay for the drinks and make tracks.' I yawned falsely and checked my imaginary watch. 'School night and all that, but thanks for your time and I'll see you in the morning.'

'Oh, Peter; sit down, please!'

I stood stupidly.

'You're very nice and I like you.'

'Oh, do you?' I replied with intended sarcasm.

'Yes. You wear your heart on your sleeve, which is a very rare and touching quality. So, please sit back down.'

I sat and took another drink of my lager and noticed there was no reaction from any of my molars. I still had the choice. I could finish my drink, pay and go, or I could stay.

I stayed. 'You promise not to be nasty about the Hawks again?'

'Cross my heart,' Emily said, and smiled.

She'd never really got into music like I had, she told me. She'd liked dance music when she was growing up, but the popularity of guitar bands like The Smiths and The Stone Roses miffed her and she found the grunge scene depressing and unlistenable. Charlie arrived when she was eighteen and she gradually found pop music as engrossing to her as the wallpaper in her mum's lounge.

'I've heard of Hawkwind,' she finished, 'but I can't say I've listened to any of their music.'

'You're a virgin, then?'

'A Hawkwind virgin?'

I smiled. 'I'll begin your education with *Space Ritual*.'

'I can't wait.'

I finished my lager and cautiously asked her if she'd like another drink.

'No, I'm alright,' she replied. 'I'm driving and I'm not really a big drinker. You have another one, though.'

'I'm OK,' I said trying not to show my relief. 'Like you, I don't really drink a lot.'

A knowing smile crossed her features and a shot of a possible future flashed before my inner eye. It came and went too quickly like a fading déjà-vu but I realised that smile might attain some significance if a relationship ever truly blossomed.

'Portion of chips, then?' she said.

'Yeah,' I replied, 'I'll just settle up.'

I walked up to the bar to pay. I'd already mentally totted up the cost of the two drinks in my head and knew the twenty would cover it.

A dapper-looking barman approached me, the waitress nowhere to be seen.

'Yes, sir, how can I help you?'

'I'd like to pay, thank you.'

He whisked the top chit off a spike by the till. 'A small Merlot and a Weihenstephaner?'

'That's right.'

He placed a key attached to a ribbon around his neck into a slot in the bottom of the till and tapped the screen a few times with one of his fingers. 'That's £21, please,' he said, and held out the palm of his hand.

'Just a second,' I said in a lower tone so that Emily hopefully wouldn't be able to hear. 'The Merlot is £9.50 and the lager is £8 a pint. By my calculations, that means the total should come to £17.50.'

The barman smiled. 'Waitress service,' he said.

I gave him the twenty and my last fiver, pocketed the change and hoped Tony hadn't raised his prices at the chip shop since I'd last been in. I got back to the table, put my sunglasses on and pulled my bobble hat down low over my forehead.

'Just playing the percentages,' I told Emily.

'He's in Manchester,' she said. 'He phoned me tonight.'

I took off the sunglasses and we walked out of the pub.

It was a cold, clear night. Stars flickered in the sky above the fluorescent glow of the street lights and our footsteps crunched on the pavement beneath in expectation of a morning frost.

Emily slipped her arm through mine.

'Does he often phone you?' I asked.

'All the time.'

'And you always answer?'

She stopped outside the advertising light of an estate agent's window. 'He gives me money for Charlie.'

'I didn't know you snorted that stuff.'

'You're not funny, I promise you.'

'Sorry.'

'He's generous and he doesn't have to be. I feel I should at least answer the phone to him when he calls, OK?'

'OK.'

We kissed.

It was nice to kiss. It meant a new journey, a journey which might only last a day or two or maybe longer.

We walked into the chip shop. Tony was cooking, but he saw me and waved from behind the fryers. I ordered two portions of chips and grabbed a couple of wooden forks. A man was playing the fruit machine in the corner with his back to us and a group of lads sat on the plastic chairs by the yucca plant. I remembered my daydream from Sunday morning and grinned.

'What's tickled you?' Emily asked me.

'Don't worry about it,' I replied, and leant down and kissed her again.

The man playing the fruit machine turned round and said, nervously, 'Hello, Pete.'

I froze: Paranoid Ian.

'Ian,' I acknowledged, and turned to Emily. 'I've got to nip outside,' I told her, and hurried out of the door before she could answer.

I paced up and down in the cold. Paranoid Ian obviously knew Henderson: why else would he hang around with him and Kilo? If he was on the payroll, he'd undoubtedly grass me up, but would he know who Emily was?

I had to find out.

I walked back into the chip shop; Emily still stood at the counter. Paranoid Ian had just been handed his carry-out in a paper bag with 'The Great British Tradition' written on it in green and a skeletal fish drawn underneath in blue.

'Sorry, I just need to have a quick word with this gentleman,' I said to Emily, and followed Ian out of the door.

'What's up, Pete?' he asked with some agitation.

I decided to be direct. 'Do you work for Henderson?'

'Who, who's Henderson?' he stuttered.

I grabbed the collar of his coat. 'Do you work for him?'

'You're scaring me, Pete.'

I released my hand. 'Sorry,' I apologised, and Ian was off, sprinting up the Broadway and shooting left down an alleyway.

'Shit,' I said out loud.

Emily was by my side with the chips. 'What was that all about?' she asked.

'Did you recognise that man?'

'Never seen him before. Why?'

'It doesn't matter.'

'Sure?'

'Yes. I'll tell you later.'

'OK.' She shrugged and lifted up the bag. 'Where shall we eat these then?'

I really didn't want to, but I had to offer. 'My flat?'

'Is it far?'

'Half a mile.'

'I'll bring the car.'

Her car, a gleaming red Mini, was parked in a bay on the other side of the road. We drove down the Broadway, past Sanjays and down Langley Avenue in silence. We pulled up outside the house and I said, 'It's a bit small.'

'Depends how you use it,' Emily commented in a deadpan voice, and it took me a moment to realise what she'd just said.

I opened up the main door. There was silence; the Iranians weren't at it yet.

I put the key in the lock of my flat door. 'I hope it's not too messy,' I said, and turned the key. It didn't open. I twisted the key again and pushed but, perhaps because of my nerves, I pushed too hard and the key snapped off in the lock.

'Shit,' I said.

Emily laughed. 'Back to mine then.'

I was hungry and ate my portion of chips on the way. Emily picked at some of hers as she drove and said she'd heat the rest up later.

She lived in a two-bedroomed maisonette on a private estate halfway between Fleet Town and Purfleet. The lounge was sparsely furnished but tasteful. Charlie sat on the sofa, engaged in youthful multitasking – playing with his phone and watching TV. He got up when he saw his mum and kissed her on her cheek.

Emily ruffled his hair. 'You remember Pete from Sunday?'

'Yeah.' He held out a hand and I shook it. 'I'll go to my room.'

'No, please; you stay here,' I said.

'It's alright, I've got some homework to do. I'll say goodnight later.'

'He's a nice lad,' I said when he'd gone.

'Sometimes,' Emily answered cryptically.

She walked into the kitchen while I stood awkwardly between the sofa and the armchair. I glanced around the room and spied several framed photos dotted around on the coffee table and on top of the sideboard next to a fish tank. Emily and Charlie, Charlie on his own, Emily on her own, an elderly couple (parents?), but no pictures of Henderson.

Emily came back in with a bottle of wine and two glasses.

'Sit,' she ordered me. I went for the armchair and she said, 'Don't be stupid.'

We sat next to each other on the sofa and she poured out the wine and asked me about Paranoid Ian.

I told her the truth. 'I thought he worked for your ex.'

She was thoughtful. 'Possible, I suppose.'

'But you've never seen him before?'

'Pete, besides phone calls, I've had no physical contact with Ray for over a year. He transfers money directly into Charlie's account. I would have no idea who would be working for him.'

'Dave Kennet?'

I could feel her stiffen beside me. She leant forward on the sofa, turned her back to me and took a sip of her wine. 'Don't mention that name, please.'

As usual, I'd fucked up: any hint of romance had fled the room.

I placed my wine glass on the coffee table. 'Where would you like me to sleep?' I asked her in the same manner I'd ask a Travelodge receptionist where my room was.

'In the bus shelter at the top of the road,' she replied without looking at me.

I sighed and stood up.

'Sit down,' she ordered again.

I sat.

'And hug me,' she said.

We cuddled and she kissed me on the lips. She smiled, stretched herself out on the sofa and lay her head down on my lap.

She traced the lines of my face with one of her hands and said, 'I feel comfortable with you.'

'Likewise,' I said.

She rested her hands on her stomach and closed her eyes. I watched her breathing become more regular and finished my wine.

'Mum?' I heard Charlie call from outside the door.

Emily sat up. 'Yes, luv?'

'Can I come through to the kitchen?'

'Course you can.'

Charlie nodded at me and I smiled sheepishly back. He walked into the kitchen and Emily stretched out her arms and yawned hard.

'I'll nip out and see if he's OK,' she said.

I waited till she'd gone and eased myself slowly up off the sofa. Although I still wasn't yet forty, the ravages of removals had begun to take their toll, and I felt and even heard several things crack in my back and legs as I gingerly got to my feet.

Charlie appeared with a drink of orange and some sort of sticky bun. 'Goodnight,' he said to me.

'Goodnight, Charlie,' I replied.

He stopped at the door of the lounge. 'Don't make too much noise if you bang my mum,' he said, and ran up the stairs before I could go red.

'He's a cheeky little sod,' I told Emily when she came back in.

'Just ignore him; he thinks he's funny.'

'It's OK. I've heard a lot worse.'

'What are you doing? You're not going, are you?'

'I'm sorry, but I have to stand up for a bit. My back and stuff, but I can go if you want me to.'

'Don't be silly; I want you to stay, but are you alright on the sofa?'

'Fine.'

She kissed me on the lips again. 'I really do like you,' she whispered, 'but can we learn to walk before we can run?'

'Absolutely,' I said, although I hadn't got a clue what she was on about.

She bent down and produced a duvet and two pillows from underneath the sofa while I admired her lovely bum. She led me through the kitchen into the bathroom and pulled out a brand-new toothbrush still in its packaging from the cupboard under the sink.

'If you need to brush your teeth,' she said, and I kissed her again.

She was more responsive and her tongue flicked into my mouth. I held her tighter and our tongues travelled deeper, but she stood back and gently pushed me away.

'Sorry,' I said.

'No, I'm sorry, but please give me more time.'

I noticed her face was flushed and her breathing more laboured. 'Of course,' I said.

'Thank you,' she said, and kissed me quickly on the cheek.

I lay awake on the sofa in the dark listening to the gentle murmur of the fish tank's motor. I'd wanted to make love to Emily but her rebuttal was fair and, somehow, made me feel closer to her.

I'd take a kicking for her or maybe even dish one out, I thought, and buried my head in the pillows.

I was standing outside the Lazy Lion, Kennet and Henderson opposite me. I decked Kennet with a powerhouse right.

Henderson pulled out a gun and aimed it at me. Emily cried out, 'No!'

He was momentarily distracted and I karate kicked the gun out of his hand. I swung my other leg round and caught him in the side of the neck. He collapsed on the pavement next to the unconscious Kennet.

I walked over, picked up the gun and stood over Henderson. I broke it down, pulled out the six bullets and put five in my pocket. I showed the last one to Henderson, placed it back in the barrel and spun it.

'Want to play a game?' I asked, and pointed the gun at his head.

'You're fucking crazy!' Henderson almost screamed, and I noticed the dark spread of urine darkening the crutch of his charcoal-grey trousers.

Somebody switched on the lounge light. Charlie.

'Sorry, Pete,' he said, 'but Mum said I could heat up the rest of her chips.'

'Be my guest,' I replied.

Charlie walked into the kitchen and I heard the low whir of a microwave oven and then a bling. He re-emerged with a plate of chips. 'Want one?'

'Wouldn't say no,' I said, and took a chip off the plate.

'Have another.'

'Cheers.' I took another couple.

Charlie ate one himself and said, 'Mum not giving out then?'

Fourteen

NO LIFT AND NO STAIRS

'Hands off cocks, on socks,' a voice spoke in my ear. I opened my eyes: Charlie.

'You're beginning to annoy me,' I told him.

'I've just read Kes.'

'Good for you.' I made to push the duvet back but stopped myself.

'Aren't you going to get up?'

'In a minute, now bugger off.'

Charlie walked over to the kitchen door. 'Mum, Pete's got a hard-on.'

'Go and get ready for college and stop embarrassing our guest!' I heard Emily say.

'OK,' Charlie answered. He stood by the sofa for a moment and raised his arm.

I sat bolt upright. 'Don't you fecking dare, you little shit.'

'Peter! Stop being so rude to my son!'

Charlie laughed and zoomed out of the room.

Emily walked in from the kitchen wearing a dressing gown and carrying a mug of coffee.

'Nescafe?' I asked.

'Tesco's economy.' She sat on the sofa and stroked my hair. 'Sorry about Charlie.'

'It's OK.'

'You've got to remember, he's only sixteen.'

'Do you think he'll live much longer?'

She leant over and kissed me on the lips.

I pulled her closer.

She flicked my nose with her finger. 'Come on, it's nearly seven.'

'Can I have a shower?'

She kissed me again and stood up. 'I'll grab you a towel.' She disappeared through the kitchen and I lifted up the duvet to check if my morning glory had subsided.

'The red towel's clean,' Emily told me as she came back in, 'and I've put a bottle of Charlie's shower gel on the side.'

'Thanks.'

'Put your pants and socks in the laundry basket and I'll dig out some of Charlie's for you.'

When Sarah first kicked me out, I hadn't quite worked out the launderette system and experienced several periods of wearing the same pairs of socks and underpants for two or three days at a time. It hadn't been pleasant.

'It's not necessary but appreciated,' I said.

After I'd showered, I wrapped the towel round my waist and walked back into the lounge. The bedding had been put away and my clothes lay neatly folded on the coffee table. On top of the pile were a pair of socks and a pair of blue Y-fronts with 'RH' emblazoned in red letters either side of the pouch similar to a boxer's shorts.

I got dressed and Emily appeared moments later in her Stoneways uniform, car keys in hand.

'Ready?' she asked.

'The Y-fronts?'

'Afraid they were Ray's.'

Emily switched on the car radio. Jackie Wilson, 'Higher and Higher'.

'Great tune,' I said.

'Not Hawkwind?'

'No, but I like it.'

We turned into the London Road and the song was cut off scandalously early by an inane DJ. I blamed Chris Evans; I'm sure he was the first DJ who thought his humour was more entertaining than the actual music.

'Sorry about Charlie,' Emily said.

'I've said it's alright.'

'You've got to remember his real dad never took any interest in him and the only father figure he's had in the last five years was Ray, and God knows what he might have taught him when I wasn't around.'

'He's good at football.'

'Do you have problems with Kate?'

I pictured Kate's chubby, cheeky face. 'Not really, I must admit. She's a sweetheart most of the time. I've been lucky with the foster parents.'

'That's good.' Emily was silent, staring straight ahead at the road and I sensed things at home with young Charlie were sometimes far from rosy.

We turned into the industrial estate.

'Look,' I said, 'do you mind dropping me off outside the B&Q warehouse? I'd be more than happy to drive into Stoneways with you in a confetti-strewn Roller but I think it might be easier for both of us if we kept last night quiet from some of our workmates.'

'I agree,' Emily said, and pulled the car over. 'If I don't see you later today, can you give me a ring tonight?'

'Of course,' I said, and we kissed. No tongues but it was nice.

I did like her a lot, but I felt a strange relief when she drove off. Maybe I was getting too used to being single or perhaps the horrible baggage now included Charlie.

There'd been an overnight frost and it was cold but the sky was a clear blue – no clouds, only Heathrow vapour trails. I thought about Sarah as I walked. I was still a bit stunned by her asking me if I wanted to come back. Must have had a row with the builder boyfriend. Bastard.

Daz opened up the shutter as I walked into the restroom, Emily nowhere to be seen.

He eyed me curiously.

'Went out for a quick pint last night,' I explained. 'Got back to the flat and the key snapped in the lock. Had to stay the night with a friend and came straight here, uniform-less.'

'You look like the keyboard player from Depeche Mode,' Daz said and produced a thick wad of inventories on a clipboard. 'No Job Chat form then?'

I stayed silent.

He tutted. 'Grab a spare work shirt from the store cupboard. Barry's put out the two containers you didn't do yesterday. I want you to get them sorted and twelve others before you go home tonight.'

'*Jawohl.*' I saluted.

The morning was murderously dull. Any amity which might have developed during yesterday afternoon's footy had disappeared, and Leo and Freddie were soon bickering.

Another example of Magenta's unrealistic idiocy manifested itself during the sorting of the second container. She'd requested a Gideon Bible and a paperback copy of *The Lord of the Rings*. Daz had highlighted all five Pack6s of books. I gave the job to Freddie while Leo and I selected and loaded the other items.

Freddie's method was entertainingly stupid and managed to provide a rare moment of humour during the morning's monotony. He grabbed a book carton, opened it, took out all the books, lay them on the concrete and then checked them. After emptying a third box, he finally found the two books Magenta had asked for.

Barry Noble, obviously interested in Freddie's modus operandi, parked up his forklift and walked over with a made-up Pack3.

Now, a Pack6 is the smallest carton we use mainly for packing heavy items such as tools, magazines and books. A Pack3, the largest carton, is meanwhile primarily used to pack light items such as tall pictures, duvets, cushions and pillows.

'It would be easier if you use this to repack the books,' Barry told Freddie, and placed the Pack3 in front of him. 'Saves space,' he added, and patted him on the back.

Freddie was sixteen and, like most lads of that age, only really interested in actually moving things in order to increase his strength and develop muscles to impress the fairer sex. Packing was, in his mind, not only boring but unfathomable. He thanked Barry for his advice and began bunging all the other books besides the Bible and Tolkien's tome into the Pack3.

Leo started to say something but I caught his attention and pressed a finger to my lips. Leo didn't seem to quite grasp the significance of the gesture but said nothing and continued loading the van.

After Freddie had filled the Pack3 and taped it up, Barry reappeared.

'Well done,' he said. 'Now put it back in the container.'

Freddie bent down to lift up the box. I could see him redden with effort but the box didn't move an inch. He looked at me.

'It weighs a ton,' he said.

Barry tutted and slowly shook his head. 'Things have changed since our day, haven't they, Pete?'

'You could lift things like this?' Freddie was stunned.

Barry toed the Pack3. 'We didn't have these types of boxes then, just tea chests. Not only did you get splinters from the wood but the metal round the edges used to flake off and cut your fingers to pieces. I remember moving this bloke who filled them all with concrete. Remember him, Pete?'

'Will never forget him, Barry,' I replied.

'Concrete?' Freddie was beginning to become suspicious.

'Arty concrete; sculptures and such.'

'Oh, right,' Freddie said. 'Christ, they must have been heavy.'

Leo stopped loading and walked over to stand behind Freddie.

'Tell them about the load-up, Pete.'

'No, you tell them, Barry.'

Barry stared straight ahead in the direction of the black shipping container by the east fence which currently housed excess metal racking and some spoilt little brat's lifesize toy tank, seemingly lost in the horror of the memory.

'Nineteenth-floor flat,' he began, 'no lift and no stairs. Just a piece of rope dangling down.'

'Jesus,' said Freddie.

'Under constant fire from the Germans,' Barry continued.

'Bastards,' said Leo, and shook his head in disgust.

We managed to get through seven containers by twelve. I was hungry and told Leo and Freddie to have a bite to eat. They both had sandwiches, they said, and walked up to the restroom.

Four pounds in my pocket, I headed out of the yard and up to the road to Jill's snack bar, phoning my landlord on the way. There was no reply so I left a message on his answerphone, explaining what had happened to the key and could he get it fixed ASAP.

Trevor Blind stood at the snack bar chatting to Jill as she cooked.

'Alright, love,' Jill greeted me. 'What you having?'

I checked the prices on the side of the trailer – I hadn't been there for a while. 'Bacon burger with onion rings,' I told her.

'How's Magenta's storage going?' Trevor asked.

'As well as ever.'

I liked Trevor. He'd worked on the vans for ten years before graduating to the office and, despite his sometimes abysmal estimating, he knew the score and often batted our corner against Kye Stoneway when the latter became irrationally incensed by customer complaints. He had a naturally stocky build but, in recent years, the muscle had begun to turn to fat and he now resembled more Les Dawson than a white Mike Tyson.

A couple of suits approached and we moved over to the table where the sauces stood.

'Bit of a change of plan this afternoon,' Trevor said to me.

I felt a glimmer of hope. 'What's that?'

'The boss is doing the rest of the calls and you and me are going out on a job together.'

'What about Magenta's storage?'

'Daz is taking your place.'

'Excellent,' I said. 'What's this job then?'

Jill called over to us. 'Bacon burger with fried onions and a half-pounder with cheese and chips?'

'And chips?' I repeated.

Trevor ignored me but then did a strange thing. I pulled out my £4 to pay and he said he'd get it. This was unusual; Trevor was renowned for his short arms and deep pockets. I was immediately on guard and would have said no but payday was still two days away and I was pretty certain the landlord would try and charge me for fixing the lock.

'What's the catch?' I asked.

'No catch, you're a mate.'

I didn't believe a word of it. Trevor had made a cock-up and needed me to help him in some way. The free lunch was my reward.

I hadn't eaten anything since last night's chips and ate half my burger as we walked back to the yard. When we got to the office, Trevor told me to sling a few boxes on the Sprinter and be ready to leave at one. I carried on through to the restroom where Leo was telling Freddie about the latest bidding on his six-door, glass-fronted wardrobe he was trying to sell on eBay. I made a quick coffee and headed down to the yard and sat in the cab of STONE 42 to finish my burger.

The driver's door opened as I was wiping the mustard off my sweatshirt. Nobody appeared at first and then Ross's head and shoulders gradually came into view.

'Just a second,' she said, and launched herself up onto the seat. 'Do you have to be a certain height to get into one of these things?' she asked me, and grabbed the steering wheel to help her sit upright.

'The doors are a bit high, I must say.' I didn't bother asking her why she'd got in. Ross was a woman; the answer was obvious.

'Come on then, tell me how it went?' she asked immediately.

'It was alright,' I replied as casually as I could.

Ross was studying me with wide, inquisitive eyes. She prodded me in the arm. 'Come on, tell us.'

I told her about Emily coming back to mine, the key snapping in the door and then going to hers.

'Did you spend the night?' Ross sounded excited.

'Yes.'

'Did you, you know?'

'You know what, Ross?'

'You know. Oh, come on, Pete, tell me!'

'Tell you what?'

She punched me lightly on the arm. 'Did you...' She paused and then adopted a Demis Roussos-type voice. 'Make luuurve?'

'You're worse than a bloke,' I said, and then thought, if she had actually been a bloke I might have lied but, because she was a woman and my friend, I told her the truth.

'No, we didn't.'

She looked puzzled. 'Seriously?'

'Seriously.'

'Oh, I think that's romantic.'

'Do you?'

'Yes. It shows you have respect for each other.'

'It left me with a dirty great hard-on in the morning.'

'Peter!'

'Sorry.'

'Where did you sleep then?'

'On the sofa.'

'Did you see her boy?'

'Unfortunately.'

'Oh?'

'Cheeky little sod.'

'What, and Freddie isn't?'

I didn't answer.

'You've only just met the poor lad. If Henderson was married to his mum, he must have a pretty warped view of any of her subsequent boyfriends.'

'I suppose so,' I half agreed.

'When are you seeing her again?'

'I'm ringing her tonight.'

'Oh, good.' Ross rested her chin on the steering wheel and looked out over the wasteland beyond the chain-link fence. An early fox appeared and trotted stealthily across our view before darting into a bush wrapped in stinging nettles.

'Sarah rang me yesterday,' I said.

Ross looked at me. 'Oh,' was all she said.

For some reason, they'd never properly got on. They'd never slagged each other off to me but there'd never been any noticeable warmth between them either. If anything, they merely pretended to like each other.

'She asked me to move back in.'

'Really?' Ross was suddenly curious.

I nodded.

'What did you say?'

'Not at the moment.'

Ross accidently beeped the horn of the truck.

She put her hand to her mouth. 'Ooops!'

I looked at my watch: 12.50. 'I'd better get moving,' I said.

'Me too,' she sighed, 'but it's hard to tear myself away from a stud like you.'

'Sod off,' I said, and kissed her quickly on the cheek.

Fifteen

RUPERT

'Right,' Trevor said as he settled his ever-expanding backside into the driver's seat of the Ford Sprinter. 'Our customer's name is Charlotte Grellier and she hates me.'

'Why are you going then?' I asked.

'Because Maurice is still off and she's never met me; we've only conversed over the phone.'

'Is that a mathematical term?'

'The boss saw this job, not me, and he booked it into the diary for the 4th of December.'

'Next week?'

'Exactly.'

We drove out of the yard and a beeping noise began to sound. Trevor tutted and put on his seatbelt.

He began again. 'Mrs bloody Grellier has been on the phone all morning asking where her removal crew is. Because Ross is sorting out Leo's cock-up on Monday, I've had to deal with her. I've told her the jobs not booked in till next week but she's having none of it.' He mimicked a high-pitched, snooty voice. '"Mr

Stoneway specifically informed me your men would carry out the quoted work on Wednesday, the 28th of November", i.e: today. Silly cow.'

'Is that what you called her?'

'Not quite but she doesn't like me.'

'What's the job like?'

'According to the paperwork, it's a piece of piss. Pack and load a hundred foot and deliver it to her son's house in South Bitton.'

Before I could say anything, Trevor added, 'Yes, Daz says you can jump out when we've finished.'

'Very nice of him.'

'When we get there, whatever you do, do not call me by my real name.'

'What, twat?'

'Call me John or Simon or something else but not Trevor.'

'What about Rupert?'

'I'd prefer twat.'

We pulled up outside Charlotte Grellier's residence, a large, detached house on a gated estate in West Purfleet. Trevor's phone rang.

He checked the screen and said to me, 'It's Kye. Knock on the door and introduce yourself while I answer it.'

Mrs Grellier was a smartly dressed lady in her sixties. I introduced myself and she shook my hand warmly.

'Pleased to meet you, Peter, I'm so glad you've come,' she said.

'If you wouldn't mind waiting,' I told her, 'my colleague will be with me in a second. He's on the phone to his wife.'

'Not a problem.'

I lowered my voice. 'She's filed for a divorce.'

'Oh dear.'

Trevor got out of the cab.

'Don't mention anything, will you?' I said to the lady.

'Of course not.'

Trevor walked purposefully over, smiled cheerfully and shook the lady's hand.

'This is Rupert,' I said before he could speak.

The job was indeed a piece of piss.

Mrs Grellier led us to a room on the ground floor. There was a chest of drawers, an armchair and several, small separated piles of books, china and glass.

'Anything else?' Trevor asked.

'Oh yes, I nearly forgot. There's an ornament in the garden.'

I cleared my throat. 'A stone ornament?'

'I think it's made of stone,' Mrs Grellier replied. 'Would you like to see it?'

'If we may,' Trevor said, and we traipsed out through the house and into the back garden.

'There it is,' Mrs Grellier said, and pointed at a full-size steamroller lying underneath an oak tree.

'Jesus Christ,' I said.

'No, not the steamroller!' Mrs Grellier laughed. 'The little gnome beside it.'

Mrs Grellier made us tea and chatted as we packed. She told us she hoped to move herself next summer. Her husband died two years ago and she found the house was just too big and the garden far too much trouble. Today was the first tentative step, she said – clearing out her son's stuff. Her daughter was coming down from Edinburgh next Sunday to go through her bits and pieces, and then the three of them would get together and decide which of her items she, herself, should take with her and which she should get rid of.

'You'll be moving somewhere smaller, I take it?' I asked.

'Oh, yes,' she said, 'so I'll have to get rid of a lot of things.'

Trevor straightened himself in salesman mode. 'We're always available to give you a quote, madam.'

For the first time, Mrs Grellier became slightly hesitant. She rubbed her hands together and said, 'We'll see how this afternoon goes, Rupert.'

We were loaded within an hour and I was able to pick up the gnome with one hand.

Before we left, Mrs Grellier handed me a detailed road map she'd drawn to show us the way to her son's house in Lytton Gardens, South Bitton. I told her not to worry as I only lived round the corner. She seemed pleased with this and added that her son wouldn't be there, so if we got there first, could we wait for her as she would be letting us in.

The afternoon traffic was fairly light and we got to Lytton Gardens at three. There was no sign of Mrs Grellier's car so I asked Trevor if I could nip home and see if the landlord had sorted out the new lock.

Trevor said, 'Yes,' as long I didn't call him Rupert again.

A light-blue van with a huge, black key painted on the side was parked out the front of the house. I opened up the main door and saw a grey-haired man, dressed in overalls, crouched down on a dustsheet outside my flat.

'Alright, mate,' I greeted him. 'I live here. How's it going?'

'Fine,' the man replied. 'The old lock was buggered; should have been replaced years ago. Take me another half an hour to fit the new one. Do you want to hang on till I finish and I'll give you the key?'

'Sorry, but I've got to go back to work.'

'Where do you want me to leave the new key then?'

I thought quickly. 'Under here?' I lifted up the china umbrella stand by the front door which never had any umbrellas in it.

'No probs.'

'I take it you're billing the landlord?'

'I am indeed,' the locksmith replied. 'By the way, are the couple upstairs making a porn film or are they trying to kill each other?'

Mrs Grellier's car was parked in the driveway when I got back; Trevor sat on the back of the van with a mug of tea.

'Sorted?' he asked.

'Yeah, thanks.' I noticed another mug by where he was sitting. 'Is that mine?'

Trevor nodded and said, 'Right, all the china and glass boxes are going in that room there.' He pointed at a downstairs window facing us. 'And the books are going to a bedroom at the back on the first floor.'

'Chest of drawers?'

'Another room upstairs I haven't seen yet and the armchair's going in the lounge.'

The gnome was standing by the front door. 'See you've managed to move the garden ornament,' I said, and sipped my tea.

The chest of drawers was the last thing off. We carried it up to the landing and asked Mrs Grellier which room she wanted it put. For the second time that afternoon, she appeared anxious.

'Can you put the chest down for a minute please, boys; I need to show you something.' She opened up a door to her left and we followed her in. 'I'm sorry,' she said, 'but I didn't tell Mr Stoneway this when he came round, but where that sofa bed is there,' she pointed, 'is where my son wants the chest of drawers to go.'

'So, you'd like us to move the sofa somewhere else?' I asked.

She was rubbing her hands nervously again. 'The conservatory, if you wouldn't mind, but it's awfully heavy.'

'No problem at all,' Trevor said.

Mrs Grellier clapped her hands. 'Oh, you're both so lovely.'

We had another mug of tea before we left and Mrs Grellier happily signed our sheet. She also wrote underneath her signature: *Peter and Rupert were terrific!*

She handed us £20 each and we both told her she didn't need to (myself less vocally than Trevor I had to admit), but she insisted.

'You've both been wonderful. I was so nervous about this move. Your man in the office was simply horrible.'

'Really?' I said, feigning surprise.

'He was rude and brusque and very short-tempered with me.'

'I wonder who that could be?' I pondered and turned to Trevor. 'Oh, I know!' I slapped him on the shoulder. 'It's that new bloke, Trevor.'

'That's it!' Mrs Grellier exclaimed. 'Trevor Deaf or something.'

'Blind,' I said. 'Nobody likes him, madam. Do they, Rupert?'

'Bacon burger at lunch,' Trevor muttered through tight lips.

'He's slimy, nasty and he smells,' I continued to Mrs Grellier.

'Does he?'

'Doesn't wash properly.'

'How awful.'

'Letting you go home after this,' Trevor muttered again.

'Finishing jobs at ten at night cos you couldn't be arsed to look round the whole house,' I muttered back.

'Anyway, Rupert; we'd better be off,' I announced.

Mrs Grellier shook both our hands. She held on to Trevor's a touch longer. 'There are times when things may look dark,' she said to him, 'but look for the cloud's silver lining and, always remember, there are plenty more pebbles on the beach.'

The new lock sat proudly on my flat door when I got home and the key, as promised, had been placed underneath the umbrella stand. The Iranian couple walked down the stairs as I turned the key smoothly into the lock.

'Fits like a glove,' I said to them.

They looked confused.

'Had a new lock fitted,' I explained.

'Oh, brillo!' the woman said. 'My lock is very greasy.'

'It is not so smooth,' her partner added.

'Oh dear,' I said, and opened the door.

'We have to lubricate.'

'Which end?'

'Both,' the man said. 'One night, we came home and it was very difficult to get it in. I had to shove and shove.'

'Very hard,' the lady added.

'I'm sure it was,' I said.

'We going for a drink,' the lady said. 'You like to come?'

'That would be nice,' I replied, 'but I've got a few things to do at home first.'

'We going to the Weatherforks,' the man announced.

'Yes.' The lady smiled and she suddenly looked quite sexy. She lifted an imaginary glass to her mouth and said, 'Get a bit pisso.'

I lay on the bed in my flat and looked at the ceiling. *Twenty-four pounds in my pocket, why not?* I thought, and put on my leather jacker and walked out the door.

Sixteen

RAY HENDERSON

Wednesday was curry and a pint night at the Spoons. The curry was usually rank and the cheap pint was nothing stronger than Fosters, but at £4.50 for the two, it attracted a reasonable trade.

Once again, I studied the real ale pumps and settled on a pint of Harry's Tonsils, a six per cent beer brewed in Cowdenbeath. I spotted my Iranian neighbours and walked over.

The man stood when he saw me and pumped my hand enthusiastically. 'Ah, my friend, please join us.'

I sat on a chair opposite them and gave them my best smile which Sarah always said made me look like a prat, but the Iranians didn't seem bothered and smiled avidly back.

'I'm Peter,' I said after a prolonged bout of inane grinning.

'Like Peter Townsend,' the man said.

'Yes!' I replied, impressed. 'And you?'

'I name, Shayan.'

'And I, Faezeh,' the girl said, and her eyes twinkled as she smiled.

'I don't know any rock stars called that,' I commented, and they both exploded into laughter.

'Sorry,' Faezeh explained. 'We drink very little most times so already a bit bollox.' They both laughed again.

'That's OK, but watch out for the hangover in the morning,' I said, and tapped the side of my head.

'Oh yes, can be very bad,' Faezeh replied.

I noticed how naturally brown and friendly her eyes were. I also saw a flashing sexiness which, combined with the gymnastics I often heard taking place in their flat, was making me feel a touch randy.

They were from a city called Hamadan about two kilometres west of Tehran, they told me, and were on a year's exchange course to study Environmental Science at North Bitton University.

'It is our government's version of détente,' Shayan said.

'Make love not war,' Faezeh added, and I smiled.

'Do you like England?' I asked.

'Some things,' Faezeh said, 'but it is very different. People are not so friendly, I think.'

'You like the shopping,' her boyfriend countered.

'Oh yes, of course.' She looked at me. 'Maybe, I miss my family.'

'I understand,' I said.

She smiled at me radiantly with a hint of otherness that forced me to press my thighs together underneath the table.

I dragged my eyes away. 'What about you, Shayan?'

'I like it.' He sipped his drink. 'I always wanted to come; culture, music, mainly. I love Sex Pistols, Who, Stones, oh, lots of things. Iran is very behind in such matter.'

'Do you like Hawkwind?' I had to ask.

'Hawk?' Shayan uttered, unsurely.

'Wind.'

'No, sorry.' Shayan shook his head. 'Good?'

'I'll lend you a CD.'

He put both his thumbs up. 'That would be very nice.'

Faezeh stood up. 'You like drink, Peter?'

I covered the top of my glass with my hand. 'No, thank you; I'm alright.'

'I insex.'

'Pardon?' I said.

'I insex.'

'Insist, Faezeh,' Shayan corrected her.

'Oh sorry, insist.'

'Well, that's very kind of you. Half a Harry's Tonsils, please.'

'Half Harry what?' she queried, and we all laughed.

Shayan and I watched her walk to the bar. She wore tight-fitting leggings and, yes, her bum was a tad on the large side, but its considerable wiggle did nothing to dampen my ardour. I remembered I'd said I'd phone Emily later and thought, after another beer, my conversation could get quite suggestive.

Shayan asked me about my job and I was deliberately evasive.

In general, when I tell the majority of academic and 'professional' people I worked in removals, they usually say, 'Oh right,' and disappear from sight. This normally didn't bother me but, despite having a slight crush on Faezeh which I knew was only harmless fantasy, I genuinely liked this couple. I went with one of Maurice's and told Shayan I was, 'A purveyor of fine arts.'

It was by no means an out-and-out lie and Shayan seemed suitably impressed. He did, however, then stand up and say he had to, 'Go pee,' but I think he seriously needed the loo rather than saying it as an excuse to get away from me.

I sipped my pint and a shadow partially covered the glare on the table from the overhead lights. I looked up, expecting it to be Faezeh with the drinks.

Kilo.

'Hey, Pete,' he said, and caressed my shoulder. 'Come over and have a quick chat with me and my friends.'

'Sorry, Kilo, but I'm with people myself.'

'It'll only be for a minute.'

I let myself get annoyed. 'Kilo, I'm with my friends, alright?'

Kilo's hand squeezed a pressure point on my shoulder and the pain was quick but intense.

'When my friends say they want to talk to you, I think you should come. If not,' Kilo leaned his head to my ear, 'they'll come over here to see you themselves and they won't be happy.'

'Who are they?' I asked.

'Friends who want to offer you a little deal.'

I knew I didn't have a choice. I didn't want Shayan and Faezeh involved and, if it was Henderson, we'd still be in the pub and there'd be no chance of any violence.

Or so I hoped.

'Can I just explain to my friends why I have to leave them?'

Kilo patted me on the back. 'Good man. We're sitting over there,' he said, and pointed at a table half-covered by a pillar. I could make out two bodies, but their faces were hidden to me.

Faezeh came back with the drinks more or less at the same time as Shayan returned from the loo. They both sat down and Shayan said, 'Peter is an artist.'

Faezeh's eyes lit up. 'Pisso artist?' she asked, and I laughed with her.

'Sorry, sorry,' she said, and reached out and put her hand on mine.

'It's OK, it's good,' I said. 'You're learning to make jokes in English.'

'I talk to building man at university,' she said. 'I tell him rude words in Iranian and he tells me English ones.'

They both raised their glasses and said, 'Bottoms!'

'Bottoms,' I replied, and we clinked glasses and drank.

I noticed Kilo standing by the pillar watching me.

'Look, I'm sorry about this,' I began, 'but I have to go and see someone for a minute.'

'Now?' Faezeh asked.

'Yes.'

They both looked hurt.

'Only for a minute; I'll be back soon and buy you both a drink.'

Shayan's voice was sad. 'Please go; we understand.'

'No, please; I won't be long.' I stood up. 'Business,' I added.

'Goodbye,' Shayan said, 'and take your drink with you.' His voice had lost its warmth.

I picked up the quarter-full pint glass and left the fresh half on the table. 'I'll take this and come back in a minute. Promise.'

'Whatever,' Faezeh said, but she didn't smile.

Kilo had his arms crossed and was adopting an impatient air. I had to go.

'Sorry,' I said, and walked quickly over to him without looking back.

There were two men sitting at the table.

'Peter, sit down, please.' Ray Henderson addressed me.

My legs were trembling and I was glad to sit. Kilo stood behind me.

'This is David.' Henderson indicated the other man.

'Hello,' I said.

The man said nothing. He had a large shaven head and a bulbous nose that looked unbreakable. He wore an ill-fitting suit and his enormous shoulders jutted out at impossible right angles from his massive neck.

Dave Kennet, I thought.

Henderson himself looked dapper in comparison. Smartly dressed and handsome in a lean, saturnine way, his hair was a closely cropped blond rather than silver. He was undoubtedly older than myself or Emily, but he radiated health and fitness and was somehow more dangerous-looking than the monster who sat to his left.

'We met the other evening,' Henderson said.

I feigned ignorance.

'On the Broadway with Paul.'

Paul? I turned and looked at Kilo, who remained impassive.

'Oh, yes,' I said to Henderson. 'I remember.'

Henderson put one hand to his chin and studied me. 'Do you not know who I am?'

'Well, I do now,' I said with a little snort, but Henderson didn't smile and I noticed Kennet shift in his seat.

'I'm known as a man with a certain...' Henderson paused, as though searching for the right words, '*influence* in these parts.'

Fuck me, I thought. *He thinks he's the head of Spectre.*

'Anyway, that is all by the by. Paul tells me you work for Stoneways.'

I was taken aback. Why the hell was he interested in who I worked for?

'Well, do you?'

'Yes,' I said, and felt I might have been too abrupt. I reminded myself that this man had more than likely murdered a few people. 'I do,' I added quickly.

'I have a connection there,' he said, and smiled.

I'd never met anybody who smiled quite like he did. There was no warmth. It was a gateway to his soul and he might just as well have said, *I'd really love to break both your legs.* Mrs Curdley's soul had been shallow and vain, but Henderson's was truly black.

More pressing to me, however, was who the hell his connection was? Emily immediately sprang to mind but my instincts and heart shouted, *No!*

'I believe you're moving a Mrs Carlberg soon.'

What the fuck had Magenta got to do with anything?

He leant forward and, as if on a string, so did Kennet.

'I want you to give this to her for me.'

Kennet produced a manila envelope and placed it on the table. There was something written on the front, but the lighting was too dim for me to be able to read it.

'What is it?' I asked.

Henderson smiled again. 'That I'd prefer not to tell you, but it's not drugs or anything illegal; you have my word.'

'You want me to give this to Magenta Carlberg?'

'Perhaps not *give*; perhaps hide somewhere where she will certainly find it. The advantage with you, removal people is you have almost unlimited access to all your customer's possessions.' He paused. 'You will be paid £1,000 in cash for your troubles.'

'It's not going to kill her, is it?' I blurted out.

'Don't be silly, Peter. It definitely won't kill her but it will make her extremely angry with somebody who has...' again he searched for the right word, 'how shall I say, *upset* me somewhat.'

'Something like this could jeopardise my job,' I protested.

Henderson laughed a surprisingly shrill laugh. Kennet raised his eyebrows and grinned for a tiny second as if I were a complete buffoon.

I got the message. 'OK,' I said, and slipped the envelope into the inside pocket of my leather jacket.

'Good man.' Henderson leant over and patted me gently on the cheek, and I could feel the cold sharpness of one of his rings on my skin.

Kennet pushed another envelope towards me, plain white this time.

'There's £500 in there,' Henderson told me. 'You'll have the rest when I'm made aware the job has been completed.'

Stay well clear, I heard Jeff say, and I hesitated for a moment before putting the new envelope into the same pocket as the other.

Shayan and Faezeh had gone when I got back to their table. All that remained were two empty wine glasses and my untouched half of Harry's Tonsils.

I felt lousy and downed the half in one and was about to go when I thought of something. I looked round. Nobody close by seemed to be taking any notice of me so I grabbed the two wine glasses, shoved them underneath my leather jacket and zipped it up.

I was shaking when I got back to the flat and sat down on the bed to try and calm myself. *Who's this 'mole' at Stoneways?* I thought. What had the manila envelope got to do with Magenta Carlberg and why the fuck had I got involved with Ray Henderson?

I pulled the two envelopes out of my jacket pocket and threw them on the pillow. I felt sick and put my head in my hands.

The sick feeling eventually passed, and I got up and rinsed out the two wine glasses and placed them upside down on the draining board. I opened the plain envelope and counted out £500 in used ten and £20 notes. I peeled off three twenties and stuffed them in my back pocket, put the rest back in the envelope and hid it at the back of the cupboard underneath the kitchen sink.

I put on some gloves and picked up the manila envelope. On the front was written, 'TO MAGENTA WITH LOVE X' in printed block capitals. *Fuck it*, I thought, and flicked on the kettle.

A minute later, I held the envelope over the steaming spout. The flap quickly un-gummed and I gingerly pulled out an unmarked DVD. I slipped it into the player and turned the TV on to the appropriate channel.

The production was grimy and amateur. A naked man sat on an armchair playing with his half-erect penis. A naked blonde woman entered, wearing a Catwoman mask. She straddled the man and I turned it off. Nearly all my male acquaintances found it near impossible to believe, but pornography had never interested me.

Although I'd seen neither of the participants before, I made an educated guess that the man was either Magenta's ex-husband or a current suitor. Who the woman was, I had no idea.

Still wearing my gloves, I put the DVD back in the envelope and, very carefully, applied some glue to the flap and fastened it. To ensure it sealed securely, I placed it flat down on the carpet underneath three blocks of CDs. Satisfied with my work, I put on my jacket and walked down to Sanjays.

Kilo was standing by the wall outside the house smoking a cigarette.

I glared at him and continued walking.

'Peter!' he called out. 'Please can I have a word?'

'Sod off,' I said.

'I don't like Henderson either!' he called out again.

I stopped at the corner of the road and looked at him.

He held his hands out to his sides. 'Honestly,' he said, and his face in the moonlight appeared almost angelic. 'You can find me at the Squat.'

I paused for a fraction of a second but then turned and hurried off.

I bought a bottle of Merlot and a bottle of Sauvignon blanc, which Sanjay assured me was a decent white wine, and walked back to the flat.

Kilo had gone.

I opened the top drawer of the bedside cabinet which was used exclusively to house my entire Hawkwind collection. Choosing your favourite album of your favourite band for a novice to hear is a nigh-impossible task, but I settled for two compilations which also featured some superb live recordings.

I walked up the stairs to Shayan and Faezeh's flat and was about to knock when I heard a noise not akin to somebody jumping off a wardrobe. I therefore decided to leave the bottle of wine outside their door with the two CDs balanced on top.

By the time I got back to my flat, the screaming had started and a vision of Faezeh's bum crossed my mind. I felt a twinge down below and picked up my phone.

Emily answered practically straightaway which was a good sign.

'I was beginning to think you wouldn't call,' she said. 'Daz told me you'd jumped out at four.'

Shayan was '*Areh*-ing' very loudly and I could hear Faezeh shouting out 'Bottoms!' for some reason.

I had to raise my voice. 'Had a quick drink with the neighbours.'

'There's no need to shout.' Emily sounded offended.

'Sorry, it's just the fire alarm's going off in the flats over the road.'

'I *can* hear something,' she said.

The volume of the vocals subsided into a steady, rhythmic grunting, but the bed was squeaking so badly I thought they and it might soon land on my head.

'Anyway, are you alright?' I asked, enunciating every word in a similar manner to how I spoke to the bogus Mrs Laidlaw on Monday morning.

'OK,' she said.

'Pardon?'

'OK!' she shouted.

There was a final vocal crescendo of ecstasy, the squeaking ceased and there was silence.

'All quiet on the Western Front,' I said in my normal voice.

'Oh, good.'

'You sound a bit blue.'

'A touch.'

'What's the matter?'

'Charlie's gone out and I was wondering if I could come over and see you.'

I panicked. God knows what she'd make of my hovel but a vision of *her* lovely bum and cleavage now crossed my mind. 'If you'd like,' I said.

'You don't seem too keen.'

'No, it would be great.'

'I'm just sick of being on my own in this tiny house.'

'Wait till you see my flat,' I said, and swore I could see her smile. 'Can you remember where I live?' I asked.

'Sort of, but tell me the postcode just in case.'

I hesitated.

'I've got a satnav and I didn't buy it at Currys.'

I got off the phone and hurriedly tidied up the flat. I stripped the bed, remade it and sniffed the bedding. There was a vague odour of stale feet and I sprayed everything with deodorant. I had a quick wash, brushed my teeth and dried the wine glasses.

I put the CDs on the floor back in the Pack6 and hid the manila envelope with Henderson's cash. She liked dance music, I remembered her saying, so I selected a few CDs from the carton before shoving it back under the bed: *The Best of Motown*, *Madonna's Greatest Hits* and a Dr Dre album in case she liked a bit of rap.

I cracked open a Stella and alternated sitting on the bed and pacing between the room and the bathroom while I waited.

The buzzer sounded at 7.15 and I let Emily in through the front door.

'I won't say it again,' I told her, and pushed open the flat door. She walked in first and I stood nervously outside in the hallway.

'Where are you?' I heard her say after a minute.

I crossed myself and walked in, her sweet fragrance now dominating the space.

'It is quite small, I must admit,' she said, 'but I like it.'

'Similar to what my daughter's mother said. Here, let me take your coat.'

'Where shall I sit?'

'On the bed, if you don't mind.' I hung up her coat on the back of the bathroom door; there was no room in the wardrobe.

The storage heater had kicked in for a change and the room was warm. She took off her fleece, revealing another low-cut top.

'Merlot?' I asked, and picked up the bottle.

'Please,' she said.

I was caught once more in her gaze and smiled my prat smile.

She laughed.

I poured her a glass of wine and decided to stick with my can of Stella.

'Where are you going to sit?' she asked.

'I'll clear the chair.'

'Don't be silly,' she said, and patted the bed beside her.

I sat and we both sipped our drinks.

'How was your day?' I asked.

'Alright, I suppose. We've finished the job.'

'Did you get a tip?'

She was interested. 'I didn't know we got tips.'

'Not always, but it's one of the job's few perks.'

'Not that I'm aware of. The couple we moved weren't over-friendly.' She paused. 'Steve wouldn't have pocketed it, would he?'

'No, he's a good man. If any gratuity had been forthcoming, he would have dished you out.'

She smiled. 'Removals seems to have its own language.'

'Indeed, it does.'

She arched her head towards mine.

'Just a second,' I said. 'I'll put on some music.'

I put on the Motown album, relieved the CD player was within reaching distance – I didn't think walking would have proven to be very comfortable at that particular moment.

Jackie Wilson, 'Higher and Higher'.

'The day's ending as it started,' Emily said, and we kissed.

She was as charged as I was and everything became a blurred passion of tongues and discarded clothes until I was on top of her and we were making love. It was frenzied, noisy, sweaty and simply wonderful. My whole body juddered when I came and I'm pretty sure I saw a few stars. I collapsed beside her and we clung to each other – mainly because the bed was so small – breathing heavily.

'Are you alright?' I asked softly.

Her head was buried in my chest and she mumbled something.

'I can't hear you,' I said.

She looked up. 'You're a proper romantic, aren't you?'

'Well, it's just you were mumbling.'

She kissed me. 'I said, oh yes.'

'Oh, good,' I said, and looked at the ceiling and spotted two cobwebs.

She slept for a while, but my back began to hurt and I had to shift her ever so gently to one side in order to gingerly stand up and crack some aching bones.

I looked down at her. Her skin was so smooth and unblemished, her hair so wild and free. *She's beautiful,* I thought, *but what the fuck is she doing with me?*

I realised something else: I hadn't eaten since Jill's burger at lunchtime and was hungry. I found a takeaway menu for the nearby Golden Spice and sat down carefully on the bed. I might not like porn, but I was a normal man in the sense that I adored curry.

I carefully tapped Emily awake. She yawned and kissed me.

'I'm going to order a takeaway curry,' I said.

'Down in the Tube Station at Midnight'; that was the reason I bought The Jam album, I thought.

'That would be nice.'

'Do you want some?'

'More.' She giggled.

'No, curry.'

'You are funny,' she said, and kissed me again.

'I'm serious: I'm hungry.'

'I'll eat some of yours.'

I rang up the number on the menu and a male voice answered, 'Golden Spice.'

I ordered a lamb madras, pilau rice, onion bhajis, Bombay aloo, three poppadoms and two keema naans. Smokey Robinson started singing 'The Tears of a Clown' on the CD player.

Emily sat up behind me and wrapped her legs round my waist. She balanced her chin on my shoulder and said, 'It's been a very unusual evening.'

'It certainly has,' I replied. 'I can't remember the last time I ordered a takeaway curry two days before payday.'

Seventeen

STEVE WOODGIT

My phone woke me up: *Daz.*

'Hello.'

'Where are you?'

'What time is it?'

'Ten past eight.'

'Fuck, I've overslept. Be with you soon as.'

'Get changed and stay where you are. I'll get Steve to pick you up.'

'Thanks.'

'What are you going to bring in with you?'

'A set of golf clubs?'

'Completed Job Chat form.' He hung up.

I sat up on the bed, head in hands, a dull ache in my temples. The flat was a mess. An empty bottle of wine lay on its side on the floor besides a not quite empty glass, a stain of red visible on the grey carpet. Two dirty bowls and three curry containers sat on the worktop, a spoon and another container on the floor, my clothes and several CD cases strewn everywhere.

Last night began to piece itself together. We had sex again after the curry arrived and at one in the morning before she left. I smiled to myself. Despite the headache I felt great and my mood only got better when I found there was still enough lamb madras, pilau rice and Bombay aloo left for breakfast.

I knew Steve wouldn't hurry so I showered and had a quick tidy of the flat. I loved curry but it always got everywhere and was a bastard to clean up. The wine stain was as indestructible if not more so and I made a mental note to ask Ross how to get rid of it when I next spoke to her.

Steve arrived at nine in the Burger Van, joint on the go.

'Sleep well?' he said when I got in.

'Too well,' I told him.

'Daz told me to tell you something but I can't remember what it was.' Steve stared out of the window and shook his head. 'Nope, won't come.'

'Think and drive,' I said in my best Brooklyn accent. 'I want to get to New York today.'

'Don't think we've got enough diesel.'

'It's a line off *The Godfather*.'

'Oh, right.'

'Have you seen it?'

'No,' Steve said. He started the engine and pointed at a job sheet lying on the dashboard. 'Small job to do this morning.'

I picked up the sheet. 'Mrs Walsh: Pack and load selected items into store. Address: 3, The Flower Gardens, Cox Lane, North Bitton.' We'd both moved loads of flats in the Flower Gardens which meant I didn't have to map read.

Steve offered me the joint.

'You know I don't anymore.'

'Oh yeah, forgot.'

There wasn't much conversation on the way and I spent most of the journey sat bolt upright in my seat. I wasn't so bothered about

Steve's lack of memory, but it did worry me when he forgot to check his mirrors when he overtook. We cut up two cars on the A3 and nearly knocked over an irate cyclist on North Bitton Hill.

My phone rang as we pulled up outside the gated entrance to the Flower Gardens.

'Ross, how are you?' I answered.

'Fine but got to be quick.'

'Fire away, then.'

'I've just had a complaint from a member of the public about Steve's driving.'

'Christ, I thought you were going to tell me something unusual.'

'Look, the boss is in a very bad mood this morning mainly due to complaints from Mrs Curdley and Mrs White's daughter. He does not need any further aggravation, I warn you. So please tell Steve to *regardez la rue*.' She paused. 'That's French, by the way.'

'Is the daughter really going to complain to BAR?'

'The boss doesn't know yet, but if she does, say goodbye to the Friday Night Club and any Christmas bonus.'

'OK, I'll tell him.' I looked over at Steve. His eyes were as red as my floor.

'Ross?'

'What?'

'How do you get rid of red wine stains?'

'With great difficulty.'

'Shit.'

'I'll talk to you later,' she said, and hung up.

'Somebody's complained about your driving,' I said to Steve.

'Whatever,' he replied.

I got out of the cab and rang the buzzer for Flat 3.

'Hello?' a well-spoken, female voice asked.

'Stoneways.'

The intercom crackled and the gates began to open.

Mrs Walsh met us at her flat door, an attractive lady I'd have put in her mid-forties. We introduced ourselves and shook hands.

'Before you come in,' she said, 'I must ask you both if you have any problems with dogs – fears or allergies?'

'No, we're fine,' I assured her. I'd learnt over the years, when working with Steve, it was far easier if I did most of the talking.

'Oh, good,' she said. 'He's quite lively but very friendly.'

'No problems.'

The hound in question was a springer spaniel who barked and wagged his tail excitedly when he saw us.

'Bradley!' Mrs Walsh admonished him. 'Go to your basket.'

Bradley's tail drooped slightly and he dutifully trotted off down the hallway.

'Sorry about that,' Mrs Walsh apologised.

The flat, like many on the estate, was on two floors. Mrs Walsh led us upstairs first and showed us the contents of two sparsely furnished bedrooms. Although fitted wardrobes covered one wall of each room, there wasn't a lot in them. An ottoman and a chaise longue were also going in the lounge, and she showed us four or five cupboards of packing in the kitchen.

'And that's everything?' I asked.

'Is it more than you thought?'

'No, it's absolutely fine.'

Although Steve's driving could be terrifying and his conversation sometimes monosyllabic, he was probably the easiest and most competent person to work with at Stoneways.

The van had two empty storage containers on board. We took the door off one and Steve covered the wooden floor with van blankets. Without saying anything to each other, we went upstairs and dismantled and loaded the two divan beds, mattresses, bases and bed ends, filling three quarters of the container.

Steve liked to pack and load at the same time which suited me. He asked me to pack the kitchen and went upstairs. After half an hour, the lady made us each a cup of super strong ground coffee which killed off any remaining vestiges of my late night. Steve wandered off to the landscaped gardens which gave the flats their name to smoke another reefer while I sat on the back of the van throwing a ball for the dog.

We started work again and Bradley seemed to take to Steve. I could hear him pounding down the stairs after Steve every time he carried a box out to the van.

Mrs Walsh sat in the kitchen with me while I packed. She was an affable person and conversation was easy. The topics shifted from the recession to her dislike of social media to people's manners in general and back to the recession again. Her politics were a bit too right-wing for me, but her views were down-to-earth and we shared a couple of politically incorrect chuckles.

I watched Steve through the kitchen window as he stacked a Pack2 at the front of the container and jotted something down on the inventory, Bradley following his every move, tail revolving like a helicopter blade.

Steve appeared in the kitchen, the springer spaniel beside him. 'Excuse me,' he said to the lady. 'There's a safe in the corner of the wardrobe in...' he pointed at the ceiling above the breakfast table, 'that bedroom. Is it going?'

'Oh no, Steve,' Mrs Walsh replied. 'It stays, but thanks for asking.'

Steve walked out, Bradley hot on his heels.

'He's a lovely dog,' I said.

'Thank you, my husband and I are very fond of him.'

'He's certainly taken a shine to Steve.'

'Yes, he has, which is a touch unusual. Don't get me wrong, he likes people, but he's not normally as fascinated with them as he is with your Steve.'

'Probably the smell of his feet,' I joked.

'Could be,' Mrs Walsh said. 'You see, we rescued him last year.'

'Was he badly treated?'

'No, nothing like that – thank the Lord. He was a sniffer dog at Heathrow Airport.'

On the way back to the yard, we parked up round the corner from Cheston High Street and grabbed a KFC. I had a Spicy Zinger

Burger Meal and Steve bought a £9.99 Bargain Bucket for Four. *Severe case of cannabis-induced hunger*, I thought – I hated the term 'munchies'.

I wondered about Henderson's 'connection' as we ate. The obvious candidate was Emily, but I would not let myself believe that. She'd been so passionate last night; she couldn't have been faking it, surely? Maybe she did genuinely fancy me and the deal with Henderson was just a side issue – a debt she owed to him for his generosity to her son. No, it didn't add up.

Another thing bothered me. She *was* a very attractive woman. I mean Sarah was alright, but Emily was in a different class.

I pulled out my phone and rang Ross.

'Is this about wine stains?' she answered.

'I'd forgotten about them.'

'What do you want then?'

'You don't sound very happy.'

'Sorry. Kye's in a foul mood and annoying everybody. He's upset Daz, Barry and even Maurice.'

'Maurice?'

'He came in this morning.'

'Oh right.'

'What do you want anyway?'

'Do you think I'm good-looking?'

'Why are you asking me that?'

'I was just wondering.'

'Have you and Emily… you know.'

'Why are you asking me that?' I imitated her.

'Because, Peter Booth, I've known you a long time and you're very see-through. You've obviously bonked Emily and your inferiority complex has kicked in and you're wondering if she's got some ulterior motive for participating in the deed rather than the fact that she really does like you.'

'So, do you think I'm good-looking?'

'No.'

'Seriously?'

'Cross my heart.'

'Oh,' was all I could muster – I was actually hurt.

'Just a minute, Daz is saying something.'

I heard muffled voices.

'He's asking me about your Job Chat form.'

I lowered my voice. 'Shit, I've forgotten to fill it in.'

'He's done it,' I heard her say.

'Ross?'

Her voice came back on the line. 'Funnily enough, I found a spare copy in my drawer this morning. Do you want me to fill it in for you?'

'But you won't know what to put.'

'Jeff's in the yard; I'll have a chat with him. When you get back, ring me and I'll come down and give it to you. All you'll have to do is sign it and hand it to Daz.'

'You're an angel.'

'You owe me,' she said, and hung up.

I put my phone back in my pocket and considered other possible company moles. Jeff, definitely not; Maurice, likewise. Trevor Blind? Daz? Barry? Freddie? Leo? All no.

Steve had finished the whole Bargain Bucket and was rolling another joint.

'Steve.'

'Yeah?'

'Do you know anybody called Ray Henderson?' I asked, and watched him closely.

'Yeah.'

'You do!'

'Yeah.'

'How do you know him?'

He popped in a filter. 'I get him some gear from time to time.'

'Ray Henderson?'

'Yeah.'

'When did you last see him?'

'Yesterday morning when he dropped off the electric bill.'

'You pay him for your electric?'

'No.'

'So how do you know him?'

'He's my postman,' Steve said, and lit up the reefer.

Eighteen

KYE STONEWAY

The boss's Range Rover sat outside the front of the building in his favoured parking space nearest the main door. When he was away on holiday or business, no other member of the office staff would dare park there in case he decided to come back early. The boss had his idiosyncrasies and his tempers.

We drove round the back to the yard and I rang Ross.

'I can see you on the cameras,' she said. 'I'll be down in a mo.'

It was overcast but still dry and six of Magenta's containers stood either side of the entrance to the warehouse; van blankets, boxes and sticks of furniture were scattered in front and around their sides. Barry Noble sat on the bench outside the carton area eating his lunch but there was nobody else in sight.

We parked up next to STONE 42. Steve went and sat in his car, purposefully positioned between the diesel tank and the shipping container and invisible to the CCTV.

Ross appeared through the open warehouse door and walked over. I opened the driver's door and she hopped in.

'Here we are,' she said, and handed me the Job Chat form.

I studied her printed capitals. 'Daz will know it's your writing.'

'I shouldn't think he'll be bothered as long as you sign it.'

'Can I read it first?'

'If you must.'

'NAME, ADDRESS, POSITION IN THE COMPANY' all filled out accurately. Underneath 'PROBLEM ARISEN', Ross had written:

> *The customer, Mrs Turdley, requested us to place an extremely heavy lion ornament on top of her garage. The only access was a spiral metal staircase. Maurice, Jeff and I told her, due to health and safety concerns, we would not be able to fulfil her request. Mrs Turdley became vociferous in her demands and we had no option but to depart the premises as politely as possible.*

'I like it,' I said, 'but her name's Curdley.'

Ross grabbed the form off me and laughed. 'Oh dear; typo, I'm afraid.' She took out a pen. 'I'll change it.'

'No, leave it,' I said, and quoted one of Jeff's favourite sayings: 'Little victories.'

'I suppose if she complains further,' Ross said, 'Kye will send her a copy and it would be nice to picture her face as she read it. She sounds horrible on the phone.'

'She's horrible in person.'

'Daz said she was a very attractive woman: blonde, big boobs – every male's fantasy.'

'Saggy bum,' I said, and something struck me – a thought, an image – but I couldn't hold it.

'Are you alright?'

'Yes.' I shook my head quickly. 'Fine.'

'Kye wants to see you in his office at two,' Ross said. 'You'd better sign your form and give it to Daz before you go in.' She opened up the cab door.

'Red wine stains,' I prompted.

She sat back in the seat. 'Difficult, but try covering the stain in salt. Leave it overnight and then give it a good scrub in the morning.'

Stoneways originally began life as an iron-mongers in North Bitton High Street in the mid-1920s. Legend has it that a friend of the family approached the then owner and founder Victor Stoneway and asked if he could borrow the shop van for a small fee to move his furniture and personal effects to his new home. As the van was only used once a fortnight to pick up supplies from North London, Victor readily agreed and, naturally, the wheels began to turn in his business-honed brain.

Within ten years, Victor had sold the shop, purchased three more vans and an old farmyard without the fields near Mossford and Stoneways had become one of the earliest fully fledged removal companies in the South East of England.

Kye Stoneway was the first member of his family to attend university and initially turned his back on the family business, instead trying his luck in insurance. For reasons still largely unknown, his forays into the world of the City were unsuccessful and Kye returned to Mossford and began to work under his father, Arthur Stoneway.

As with most generation gaps, Kye's views on running the business were far more progressive and forward-thinking than his father's. He certainly brought the company and Arthur kicking and screaming into the dawn of the twenty-first century when, in 1997, he sold the old yard in Mossford and borrowed the balance to build the modern warehouse and offices we now inhabited on the Fleet Town industrial estate.

Arthur was mortified by the move. Borrowing money was surrendering to the Zionists, in his view, and his arguments with Kye during the transition period became increasingly turbulent and nasty.

But Kye was a shrewd businessman. He saw the future laid in storage and the new warehouse could hold eleven hundred purpose-built airtight containers. The old yard, commonly known as the Farm, could not even store half that capacity. More embarrassing was the manner in which customers' belongings were actually being stored.

The main storage area comprised of two corrugated cow sheds which were knocked together one summer by Arthur, two of his cousins and some hired help. Huge pyramids of furniture, tea chests and boxes, some over ten feet high, were dotted around the tarpaulin floors with the customer's name written on pieces of A4 paper and taped to all four sides of the stack. Often, two neighbouring stacks would slowly dislodge themselves, rather like cliff faces eroding, and their contents would collide.

Due to the fact that most of the time nobody could remember which item belonged to which stack, customers often received items that weren't theirs. One famous example was the delivery of a three-legged BBQ which only possessed one wheel to the King of Denmark's official UK residence in the highly sought-after Wentworth Estate. Its counterpart, a £5,000 Australian 'Outback' contraption which could cook for two hundred people, meanwhile ended up in the back garden of a council house in Bermondsey.

Other items simply could not be found, and a double mattress Maurice had thrown in the yard's skip when his wife, Janet, had decided to buy them a new bed, was wrapped in plastic and stacked in a shipping container bound for the Middle East. The fact that Janet was forced to invest in the new bed due to a late-night 'accident' after her husband had overindulged one evening at the Friday Night Club added a certain lurid humour to the attempted cover-up.

Several damp, weed-strewn-out buildings were also used for storage and, on occasions when business was brisk, we weren't able to gain access to the restroom as the space had been filled wall to wall and floor to ceiling with customers' furniture. A preposterous and increasingly financially damaging situation which, given our supposed reputation as a quality removal company, Kye quite rightly decided had to be changed.

So, we moved and Arthur accepted it (most probably when he saw the size of his cut) but, although officially retired, he couldn't let the business go. He was a regular visitor to the new warehouse in its early days, dropping in mornings and afternoons for a chat with all of us on the vans. He was a thick-set and nice enough man but always talked removals.

One morning, Daz discovered that all the van keys had gone missing. Another evening, we walked into the restroom and every table and chair had been stacked into a column which nearly touched the smoke alarm on the ceiling.

A few days later, Arthur received a court order prohibiting him to come within two miles of Stoneways' new warehouse. Arthur broke the order within a week and was arrested, leaving Kye no option but to have his father committed.

Although a generation gap often produces very different outlooks on life, genes are inherited and Kye displayed many of his father's personal traits such as Arthur's manic intensity, old-fashioned frugality and slightly unhinged psychological state.

For example, when Kye was divorced from his first wife on grounds of serial adultery, Maurice and myself picked up a double bed and a few other knick-knacks from the marital home and brought them back to the yard. Kye made himself a bedroom out of an empty storage container and lived in the warehouse for three months. First thing in the morning after Kye had risen, Barry would close up the container and forklift it up to the top of a stack and, every evening before he went home, he would forklift it back down. The rest of the staff weren't meant to know but, naturally, Barry told us all straightaway. In Barry's defence, it was quite a hard fact for Kye to successfully cover up. Often, on early starts or when we worked Saturday mornings, we'd find the boss, bleary-eyed in his boxer shorts, socks and an old T-shirt, wandering round the building munching on a bowl of cornflakes.

I walked into the restroom and found Maurice arguing with Leo about the superiority of football over rugby.

'Why the fuck's it egg-shaped?' Maurice was saying. 'Some berk boots it and all you thick wankers chase it up the field trying to catch the stupid fucking thing as it bounces in all different bloody directions.'

'It's aero-dynamite,' Leo countered.

'Dynamic,' I had to correct him.

I didn't think Leo was a terrible bloke, merely thick and annoying. I knew he had no chance against Maurice in a verbal battle and I sometimes felt sorry for him and felt obliged – to not exactly bat his corner – but at least deflect a few bouncers.

'It's much more exciting than football,' Leo said.

'Oh, right,' Maurice answered, and began to gather steam. 'Let's start with the kick-off. One of the tarty boys with the tight shorts boots the egg-bladder up the field straight at a troglodyte. If, by some miracle, the troglodyte catches it, he's immediately battered by a load of other Neanderthals and they all collapse on the turf. Referee blows whistle. Penalty for no reason at all except the ref thinks it makes him look important. Another pretty boy boots the egg-bladder into touch and a load of the heavies trundle up and stand in a line opposite each other. A really thick-looking short arse with a broken nose and cauliflower ears throws the thing in; somebody half catches it and falls over. Ref blows his whistle: scrum. What's so fucking exciting about that then?'

'Nice to see you back, Maurice,' I interrupted.

'Thank you, Pete.'

'How's the haystack?'

'Iffy.'

The office door opened and Daz appeared.

'Have you seen the boss yet?' I asked Maurice.

'Concerning Curdley's Curly?' Maurice replied, and chuckled at his alliteration. 'I have and I'm sure you'll enjoy your turn.'

I left Maurice deriding the scrum as some form of pagan ritual for deranged homosexuals. Why else would anybody want to stick their head in some ugly, smelly Welshman's crotch? I heard him reason.

I followed Daz through the office door and handed him the Job Chat form.

He flicked through it and smiled. 'It looks suspiciously like Ross's writing, but I like the "Mrs Turdley" bit.' He indicated Kye's office. 'He's waiting for you.'

Kye Stoneway's personal domain was window-facing and separated from the rest of the office by three glass walls. He sat at a right angle studying his computer, stacks of paperwork lined up in neat piles covering his desk.

The door was open, but I still knocked.

He turned. 'Ah, Peter. Please take a seat and close the door.' He glided majestically to take up a position opposite me.

His swivel chair was red and sleeker-looking than all the other office chairs in the building. I'd always promised myself that, one day, I would have one magical spin on it before I left Stoneways either of my own accord, impending retirement or death.

Kye pressed a button underneath his desk and the white blinds on the glass walls rolled slowly down. I didn't think this reflected on the severity of the matter at hand; it was more to do with the fact that Kye enjoyed playing with his toys.

'Mrs Curdley,' he began, then took off his glasses, wiped them and put them on again. 'A customer of ours,' he added, and steepled his fingers.

I hadn't been asked anything so stayed quiet.

'The fact is,' Kye said, and stood up. 'Mrs Curdley has demanded the resignation of you, Jeff and Maurice or else she will complain to BAR.'

I got angry. 'But she's a silly cow; that thing weighed a ton. There was no way we were going to be able to carry it up a spiral staircase to the garage roof.'

Kye held out a hand and sat down again. 'Calm yourself, Peter. I would not sack any of you. I've known you all for many years and trust your integrity.'

'Seriously?' I was surprised.

'Seriously. Maurice has worked for this company for thirty years and, like Barry Noble, was employed by my father.'

'How is Arthur?' I politely enquired.

'Not too well,' Kye sighed. 'According to the nurses, he wanders around the hospital with a notebook estimating the cubic capacity of every ward and continually dismantles his bed and wardrobe and puts them back together again. A psychiatrist was called in and suggested to the staff to tell him he's on a perpetual tea break, which calms him down for a day or two, but then he's back at it.'

'I'm sorry to hear that.'

He pressed another button under his desk. There was a crackling sound and a sharp stab of feedback. I heard Daz say, 'Yes?'

'Sorry, Darren,' Kye said. 'Pressed the wrong button.'

He stood up again and I could see he wanted to wander, to get his thoughts out, but there wasn't enough room, so he sat down again.

'You see, Peter, I am the current president of BAR, and if we get a complaint, it doesn't look good on me. In fact, it looks terrible.' He used his hands to push himself away from his desk and sped over to me on his swivel chair, looked me straight in the eye and then shot back.

'Can you make it go up and down?' I had to ask.

'Watch this,' Kye said, and lifted one of the arms. He zoomed downwards so only his head was visible over the desk.

'And up?'

Kye lifted the other arm but stayed where he was. He tried again but there was still no movement.

'Bugger,' he said, 'I'll have to try and fix it.'

'Do you want me to go?'

'In a minute,' Kye replied. 'I've manged to calm Mrs White's daughter down and she's withdrawn her complaint, but we live in a vain world where everybody thinks they're more important than they actually are and the current legal system encourages them to complain *and* claim.' He paused. 'Excuse me, Peter, what's so funny?'

'It's not what you're saying,' I said, 'but can't you stand up? You look ridiculous sitting there like that.'

Kye stood. 'What I'm trying to say, Peter, is we need to be especially vigilant in respect to our relationships with our customers.'

'I'm with you.'

'Good. I will pay Mrs Curdley a visit and try and placate her. So far, I've only spoken to her on the phone.' He lowered his voice. 'I've been told she's quite attractive.'

'If you like that sort of thing,' I said, and again, an image flashed through my brain, but it wouldn't stick and floated out of my mental grasp like a dandelion seed in a spring breeze.

'Are you alright?' Kye asked.

'Yes, sorry. I keep thinking of something but can't quite grasp it. Do you ever have that?'

Kye looked at me for a moment and then asked in a stern voice, 'Any other questions?'

I knew I'd crossed the line between business and personal but decided I had to push it. 'Well, there is one thing,' I said, and stood up.

'Yes?'

'Do you know anybody called Ray Henderson?'

There was just that tiny moment, a millisecond before Kye answered, 'Never heard of him,' and I knew he was lying.

I realised I couldn't go any further so I thanked him for his time and walked out the door.

How does he know Henderson? I thought, and, *Does that mean Kye's the 'mole'?*

Nineteen

MR DELWAR

Maurice was joking with Mary, the company cleaner, who was polishing the tables in the restroom.

Mary must have been in her early fifties and could easily be described as 'simple', but she carried a sadness with her which hinted at a past emotional complexity. She was also painfully shy and only ever seemed to smile when Maurice or Barry were present. When she saw me, her smile vanished and she hastily walked over to the kitchenette and turned on the taps.

Maurice stood up. 'Come on, Booth, we've got a job to do: you, me and that bellend Freddie Keating.' He handed me a handwritten sheet of A4 paper.

Daz's handwriting: a name, 'Mr Delwar', and two addresses in Purfleet. 'Move upright piano, ground floor to ground floor.'

'I thought you had a bad back?'

'I'm there to supervise,' Maurice replied, and his eyebrows arched mischievously up and down.

We walked out of the restroom and along the pebbled passageway to the yard.

'By the way,' Maurice asked me, 'how did you find our noble leader?'

'More like his father every day.'

Maurice stopped walking and said, "Tis a shame. Arthur was a good man – mad as a gnat's jazzer but a good man.'

'Amen,' I said.

I put a set of piano wheels on the back of the Sprinter and grabbed Freddie, who was sitting on a pile of van blankets with his head in his hands, sulking. Leo was jogging up and down on the spot and performing the occasional star jump while Jeff stood by two taped-together, upside-down wardrobe cartons trying to make sense of Magenta's remaining inventories and generally looking very pissed off.

Emily was standing by the forklift chatting to Barry. I caught her eye and she smiled.

Although she must have been standing twenty yards away, the distance dissolved and all I could see were her eyes. It was like *West Side Story* when Tony first saw Maria but set in a removal yard rather than a 1950s New York youth club for delinquents. I smiled back and gave her a little wave.

As soon as he sat in the van, Freddie grumpily pulled out his phone and said nothing. Maurice gave it a few minutes before he began to sing a ditty to the tune of 'The House of the Rising Sun'.

There was a boy called Freddie Keating,
Who had the tiniest dick,
He pulled it often and far too hard,
Until, one day, it shot him.

'Bit obvious,' I said.

'Oh, sorry, Peter Dylan. I'll try harder next time.'

Mr Delwar was a friendly man of Asian descent who shook mine and Maurice's hands warmly. Freddie was still in a strop and lingered at the back of the van, mobile phone in hand.

Mr Delwar showed us into the lounge where a woman and two little girls sat. 'This is Moorish and Peter,' he introduced us.

'Maurice,' Maurice said.

'More Ease?'

'That will be fine.'

The lady smiled politely and the two little ones hid their faces in her sari.

'And this is the piano!' Mr Delwar exclaimed.

It was slightly bigger than a normal upright but nothing untoward: two pedals and no German insignia. (Three pedals and a Steinways logo always meant *bloody heavy*.)

I told Freddie to grab the piano wheels and roll out the hessian floor protector. Maurice removed the music rest and I leant down and opened up the bottom panel to check for a glass or bowl of water.

Freddie and I edged the piano out from the wall and Maurice picked up the piano wheels. I saw him grimace and told him to give the wheels to Freddie – I knew what a bad back was like.

'What do you want me to do, then?' Maurice asked me in a strangely unsure voice and, once more, I saw the shadow of the older, more vulnerable man cross his face.

'Just put your foot on the bottom on your side and stop it from moving while I tip it over,' I told him in a respectful tone.

'You're too much of a pansy,' Maurice replied. 'The girls here would be more help than you.'

They both raised their heads and smiled shyly at Maurice.

'Just steady the bloody thing and shut up,' I whispered to him.

'Such manners,' he said to the two girls, and they both began to giggle.

I leant down and grabbed the bottom of the piano and then remembered my own back. The piano hadn't felt unreasonably heavy when Freddie and I had pulled it away from the wall, but I liked to play the percentages. 'Freddie, give us a hand to tip it over.'

'See!' Maurice said to the two girls. 'When I was their age, I'd have strapped the Joanna to my back and carried it out on my own.'

I could tell the girls hadn't got a clue what he was on about, but they laughed anyway. Freddie helped me ease the piano over till we achieved point of balance. He broke away and put the wheels underneath, angling them so they rested smoothly underneath the piano as I lowered it.

'My God, you have learnt something, young Keating,' Maurice said, and I noticed a faint tickle of animated pride on Freddie's face.

Freddie and I trundled the Jo out of the house and pushed it up the ramp onto the back of the Sprinter. Maurice tied it to the side and I told Mr Delwar we'd meet him at the other address in ten minutes. Mr Delwar beamed and told us how wonderful we were.

Maurice composed a new ditty on the way to the unload. I froze as soon as I heard the first line.

> Emily, Emma, Emily,
> > Peter's gonna show you the smallest willy this world has ever
> seen.
> > Emily.

Maurice guffawed and nudged Freddie who was grinning despite himself. I decided Maurice had no idea there was anything between Emily and me and was just generally taking the piss because she was an attractive woman and I was a single man, so I said nothing.

We arrived at the unload address, Mr Delwar already there with the two young children in tow.

'I hope you don't mind, More Ease,' he said to Maurice, 'but the girls have taken a shine to you all and wanted to come along.'

'Not a problem,' Maurice replied.

Freddie and I wheeled the piano into the hall and asked Mr Delwar where he'd like us to put it.

He looked slightly worried. 'I'm afraid I neglected to inform Mr Deaf—'

'Blind,' Maurice corrected him.

'Mr Blind that I'd really like the piano upstairs in the girls' bedroom.' He winced when he finished the sentence.

I glanced at Maurice.

'I understand how difficult that would be,' Mr Delwar continued, sensing our hesitation, 'but I am willing to give you three, personally, £100 each for your efforts.'

Maurice and I immediately looked up at the staircase. It looked tight.

'Can you let Pete check something first?' Maurice asked.

'By all means,' Mr Delwar replied.

The staircase was separated into two flights of approximately ten stairs apiece by a small stairwell where the piano would have to rest vertically on one end. I checked the ceiling and gauged there would just be sufficient height.

'Could we have a quick conflab between ourselves?' I asked Mr Delwar.

'Of course,' Mr Delwar answered. 'Look, please; if it can't be done, it can't be done.'

'We'll have a chat,' I said, and Maurice and I walked out to the back of the van, leaving Freddie with the piano.

'It'll go,' I said to Maurice, 'but what about your back?'

'I haven't actually got a bad back,' Maurice replied in a small voice.

This was difficult to fathom. One could accuse Maurice of a lot of things, but skiving off work was not one of them. 'What was wrong with you, then?' I asked.

'I'll tell you later, but I could certainly do with the hundred sobs.'

For some reason I thought of Henderson's blood money. 'Likewise,' I agreed.

I grabbed three webs and two van blankets off the van, and we walked back into the house.

'We'll give it a go,' Maurice told Mr Delwar.

'I am so grateful,' he gushed, 'but please, please: do not hurt yourselves.'

'Hopefully not,' Maurice said, 'but can you tell the girls to go in the lounge?'

'Girls! Girls! Come on, into the lounge.'

'Can we watch from the door?' one of them asked.

'Course you can,' Maurice told her, and they both skipped through into the lounge and closed the door to. A moment later, their pretty little heads appeared in the gap, one on top of the other.

I laid a blanket on the stairwell and another by the piano. Maurice tied a web around the circumference of the piano just below the keyboard and I helped him tip it off the wheels so it rested upright on the blanket. I tied the other two webs to Maurice's web at top and bottom, and we swivelled the piano round so its underneath pointed directly at the staircase.

I took the top, walked backwards up to the fourth stair and tilted the Jo over towards me. Maurice and Freddie crouched down at the bottom and, after three, we humped the piano up one step at a time until we reached the last step before the stairwell. I grabbed the lower web and heaved the piano almost vertically upwards while the other two pushed until it slid onto its end on the stairwell van blanket.

Freddie steadied the top while Maurice and I grabbed either side of the van blanket and slid the piano round to the second staircase. We repeated the same process as on the first staircase and, twenty minutes after webbing it up, the piano stood on the landing. Freddie and I walked it into the appointed bedroom and the excited girls showed us where they wanted it placed.

When we got back to the van, 'Old Macdonald Had a Farm' tinkling away upstairs, Freddie suggested we partake in a group hug. Maurice ignored him and grabbed the sheet of A4 out of the cab.

Mr Delwar signed and said, 'It was the girls who wanted the piano in their bedroom, not I. I'm afraid I am an overindulgent father who would try to do anything to make their dreams come true. I am extremely grateful.' He flipped open his wallet, pulled out a huge wad of folding and gave us each £120.

He was such a nice man, we all immediately protested that £100 was what had been agreed, but he closed up his wallet and waved his finger at us in fake admonishment. 'That includes your tip,' he said.

The girls came out to wave goodbye and I felt a warm glow in my heart. For all the Mrs Curdleys in the world, there was at least one Mr Delwar. *If people like he possessed most of the world's money,* I thought, *the planet would be a much better place to live in.*

Maurice parked the van by the canal in Purfleet to kill a bit of time. It wasn't yet four and if we got back to the yard too early, we'd only be roped into sorting out the rest of Magenta's containers.

Freddie asked if he could walk home. Maurice began to protest for no other reason than to annoy Freddie, but I intervened and told him he could go. Daz wouldn't give a shit and, besides, I wanted to talk to Maurice on my own.

'Why were you off then if you didn't have a bad back?' I asked him after Freddie had slipped off.

'You won't tell anybody?'

I felt insulted. 'Come on, Maurice. It's me you're talking to.'

'Bit of trouble with my good lady.'

'Go on.'

'Why should I tell you?'

'Because I confided in you about Sarah.'

'More fool you.'

'Well, I know that now,' I said. 'Come on, tell me.'

'Had a bit of a session down the rub a dub, Sunday lunchtime. Well, more of an all-dayer. Didn't get home till half nine that night.'

I waited.

'Woke up on the lounge floor at three in the morning, went upstairs and mistook the laundry basket for the khazi.'

'Janet not too pleased?'

'You could say that. She chucked me out and I had to kip round my brother's.'

'But why didn't you come in to work?'

'He lives in Skegness.'

'Oh, right.'

'I came home yesterday afternoon.' Maurice flicked down the sun visor and checked his reflection in the mirror. 'I don't really understand what all the fuss was about,' he said, and combed down what was left of his hair with his fingers. 'I mean, the bloody thing's the same sort of shape as a toilet. I was pissed; how was I to know?' He snapped the visor back up. 'Luckily for her I didn't sit on it.'

All the other lorries were parked up when we got back at five and the yard was empty of people and containers. We parked in front of the diesel tank and walked along the pebbled passageway to the restroom.

'Can I ask you something else?' I asked.

'If you must,' Maurice replied.

'Do you know anybody called Ray Henderson?'

Maurice looked at me as if I was an idiot. 'Was Dennis Bergkamp the greatest player to ever grace a football pitch? Of course, I know bloody Ray Henderson.'

'Personally?'

'I went to school with him.'

We'd reached the door to the restroom. It opened and Jeff Unsworth appeared.

'Ah, it's Thunderbolt and Lightfoot,' he said. 'Fancy a quick pint?'

'I'm up for one,' I said. 'Maurice?'

'I'll drive you there,' Maurice answered in a noncommittal voice, 'but I probably won't stay.'

'Are you alright?' Jeff asked.

Maurice looked at me. 'You tell him. I'll nip in and see Daz and find out what's happening tomorrow. Might be an early start. I've heard on the grapevine that mad Carlberg woman's on the move again.'

He disappeared through the fire door and I told Jeff about the laundry basket incident and the brother in Skegness.

'I can sympathise,' Jeff said. 'When you're half-asleep and pissed they can look like khazis. It's similar with wardrobes resembling toilet cubicles.' He paused. 'That's why my Suzie kicked me out.'

Maurice drove us down to the Queens and I persuaded him to come in for a drink; I was desperate to learn more about his knowledge of Ray Henderson.

I bought the round: a Fosters for me, Stella for Jeff and an orange juice and lemonade with ice for Maurice.

'Don't laugh,' Maurice said as I put his drink down on the table.

'Why would we?' Jeff said. 'It looks very refreshing,' He took a swig of his Stella and said to me, 'Anyway, how come you're so flush on payday eve?'

I told him about Mr Delwar and the £360 tip.

Jeff whistled. 'Very nice.'

Maurice picked up his drink, sniffed it and then put it back down on the table, untouched. 'Pete, here's been asking me about Ray Henderson,' he said to Jeff.

'He keeps asking me as well.' Jeff looked at me. 'Come on then, tell us what's going on.'

'I will,' I said, 'but can Maurice first tell me what he knows about Henderson?'

Maurice sighed and put his hand around his glass. 'Henderson's a prat. Yes, he was always quick with his hands and his head, but he's never really been that hard. Made his rep knifing some ex-con in the Wheatsheaf in North Bitton one night.'

Maurice put his glass to his lips and then placed it back on the table, still untouched.

He continued. 'Reputations are like rumours; they quickly grow out of proportion, but Henderson was clever and encouraged the exaggeration and the lies. He went into protection and made money which, like shit, attracts vermin. In Henderson's case, big, nasty vermin.'

'Like Dave Kennet?' I asked.

'Like Dave fucking Kennet,' Maurice answered.

'Not a popular character, I take it?' I said, and immediately wished I hadn't.

Jeff and Maurice both stared at me and, for one second, I actually felt threatened.

Jeff broke the silence. 'So, Pete, tell us why you're so interested in these toss-pots?'

'Between us three?'

'Yes,' Maurice answered impatiently. 'Just get on with it.'

I told them about Kilo, the meeting in the pub, the manila envelope, the porn film and the money.

'Kilo put you up to this?' Maurice asked, surprised.

'You know Kilo?'

'Known him for years but he hates Henderson.'

'He was the one who introduced me,' I said.

'How do you know Kilo?' Jeff asked Maurice.

'Past life,' Maurice told him. The conversation was nearing its end.

'One last thing,' I said. 'Has Kye Stoneway had any dealings with Henderson?'

Maurice sighed once more as though he were dealing with an inquisitive toddler. 'When we were on the Farm before either of you worked here, Henderson tried to muscle in on the business. Legend has it Kye started to give in to him, but old Arthur got wind of it, gave Henderson a slap and chased him off the property with a pitchfork. Whether Kye had any more dealings with Henderson, I don't know, but one thing I do know was the supposed God-bloody-father of North Bitton and surrounding areas was always shit-scared of old Arthur Stoneway.' Maurice picked up his glass again. 'Any other questions?'

'Yeah,' Jeff said. 'Why did Alan Curdley call you Mike?'

Maurice ignored him and took a long swig of his orange juice and lemonade. Immediately, his face turned a crimson red and he put his free hand up to his throat. Alarmed, Jeff slapped him on his back.

I stood up. 'He's choking!' I shouted.

Maurice broke into a coughing fit and Jeff continued whacking him. Eventually, the coughing subsided and Maurice pointed at his glass.

'That's disgusting!' he said.

I caught the bus back to the Broadway, my head spinning and not from the solitary pint of Fosters.

Henderson had dealings with Kye Stoneway back in the day. Arthur interfered, who was then sidelined from the business by his own son. Was Kye in cahoots with Henderson? Did Henderson lend him the money to pay for the balance on the new warehouse or use his influence to secure the loan? Was Kye, therefore, the 'mole'? Also, If Kilo hated Henderson, why was he acting as his gopher?

I walked into Sanjays and bumped into a man on his way out: Paranoid Ian. He recoiled in fright and bolted down the Broadway before I could collar him. What the fuck had Ian got to do with it all, or was he just a mad red herring in this increasingly convoluted plot?

My phone rang: *Daz.*

'Leo's picking you up on the A3 slip road at ten past seven in the morning.'

'Magenta Carlberg?' I asked.

'Afraid so,' he said, and hung up.

An early start so I bought another four-pack of Stella to try and dull my pinballing thoughts and help me sleep. I remembered the wine stain and added a packet of salt. A bottle of Merlot in case Emily stopped by? *No,* I thought. I'd call her but give tonight a miss – Magenta Carlberg always spelt 'long day'.

The flat smelt of spilt wine and curry and, after spending a minute inhaling the tantalisingly beautiful, spicy aroma of the latter, I opened the sash window. I tossed my jacket on the bed, opened the packet of salt and began sprinkling a quantity on to the wine stain, eventually covering it in a granular sea of white. Satisfied, I cracked open a can of Stella and pulled out my phone to call Emily.

There was a knock on the flat door and I froze. I eased myself off the bed, opened the drawer under the sink and grabbed my onion-cutting knife. 'Who is it?' I called out in my deepest baritone.

'It's us,' a voice answered. Shayan.

I put the knife back and opened the door. Shayan and Faezeh stood there, a polite foot away from the opening.

'Would you like to come in?' I asked tentatively.

'No, we are just going for walk,' Shayan replied politely. 'But we want to say thank you for wine and brilliant Hawkshower.'

'Wind,' I corrected him.

'Sorry, wind.' Shayan smiled in apology.

'You like it?' I asked with nervous anticipation.

'I love "Spirit of Age",' Faezeh said.

'Me, "Motorway City",' Shayan added. 'Brilliant guitar.'

I was stunned. 'Two of their greatest tracks,' I stuttered. 'I'm so pleased.'

They both beamed. Faezeh handed me a Tupperware box. 'I make these for you, today,' she said. 'Ghorabiye: Persian biscuit. Very nice.'

I was touched. 'Well, thank you very much. It's very kind of you.'

She smiled her coy smile and I smiled my imbecilic one back.

'We go now,' Shayan said.

'We go for drink together soon?' I asked.

'Define,' they both chimed happily.

I watched them walk out of the front door of the house and admired Faezeh's posterior once more. Saggy and wobbly, perhaps, but undoubtedly sexy.

The image which had momentarily gripped and eluded me in the cab of the Sprinter when I was with Ross and in Kye's office later at last crystallised in my mind. I closed the flat door, opened the cupboard under the sink and pulled out the manila envelope. I didn't bother putting gloves on nor steaming it open and slit the flap with my onion-cutting knife.

I played the DVD again but fast-forwarded it through till the end when the woman ripped off her mask and smiled seductively at the camera.

I pressed pause and stared into the face of Mrs Curdley.

Twenty

MAGENTA CARLBERG

Mick Jagger sang the opening lines of 'Honky Tonk Women' and the blue light of the alarm clock flashed 5.50am.

Very early to be getting up, but the Stones were always a welcome start to the day.

I'd been fortunate during my time with Stoneways to have moved people the length and breadth of the British Isles and to and from the majority of the other main countries of Western Europe. Amongst the beauty, I'd seen the arse of Paris, Berlin, London and Glasgow, but in my view, I'd never stood in a more depressing place than on the London-bound A3 slip road off the Broadway roundabout – the easternmost tip of the suburban sprawl of South Bitton.

The roundabout itself was thirty metres in diameter, crisscrossed underneath its barren concrete by two graffiti-strewn subways where not even Ray Henderson himself would dare venture in the midnight hours. To the south stood South Bitton Tower, a twenty-storey architectural monstrosity of glass and concrete, once owned by the MOD. Its top five floors were now let by commercial businesses while the rest of the building was given over to a Travelodge, a definite candidate for the worst-situated hotel in England.

To the east was the Broadway Bowl: a thirty-lane bowling alley which, in 1996, tendered an application to host the World Ten-Pin Bowling Championships. The application was unsuccessful, but if the Bowl's main bar had entered a reality TV competition for the UK's most violent place to have a drink on a Friday night, it might have made it through to semi-finals week.

Directly opposite where I stood in the freezing wind lay acres of barren wasteland, untouched since the prefabs of the MOD and the MAFF had been bulldozed in the early 1990s. It was a testament to the merits of government cuts and the holy free market. The government balanced its books and slashed the civil service, sold the land cheaply to a certain private enterprise (which, in essence, was no different to a private monopoly) and the latter sat on its new asset, thus artificially inflating the rents of its other commercial properties.

You can't argue with the suits – they'll blind you with economics and the principles of the free market – but all I've realised, during the transactions of billions of pounds between the government and the conglomerates in the name of privatisation, was that I, the low-income tax-payer, received not one solitary penny.

The A3 was a human-made wind tunnel and it was bitterly cold. I checked the time on my phone – 6.58 and, for the first time in two years, I wished Leo would arrive early.

It took me a long time to get to sleep last night, even after three cans of Stella.

I phoned Emily and could tell she wanted to chat, but too many things were ricocheting around my head. Although we'd taken the first steps, I still didn't feel I knew her well enough to confide my innermost thoughts, especially when her ex-husband loomed so large in the background. I told her I was shattered after our night of passion and needed to catch up on some sleep, but I'd love us to get together on Friday night. She said she looked forward to it and promised to give me a little treat.

This reminded me of the porn film and Mrs Curdley, and I agonised over what I should do. I needed to talk to someone, to share my load, and I considered phoning Sarah. She'd always had a practical head and knew me as well as anyone. She could sift through all the needless, speculative delusions, fantasies and conspiracy theories I always bought to the table when I was distressed and help me concentrate on the essentials.

I dismissed this idea after five minutes because I knew she'd have a go at me for watching filth and we'd end up arguing.

STONE 42 appeared over the horizon and I could make out Leo's sunglasses and the lived-in face of Jeff Unsworth in the passenger seat. The truck pulled over and Jeff opened the cab door.

'Bunk or seat?' he asked me.

'Bunk,' I said, and he shifted his legs so I could slip past him and climb into the back.

Magenta's new abode lay somewhere between Sloane Square and Brompton Road, and I hated map reading in that part of London. Also, if I sat in the passenger seat, I'd be in direct fire of one of Leo's monologues, so I viewed the bunk to be the best option.

Jeff must have wanted to watch the crumpet in the King's Road, I reasoned.

I made a pillow of my backpack and bomber jacket and tried to make myself as comfortable as possible. Leo was rabbiting on about something or other but, from where I was lying, there wasn't much difference between his monotone and the drone of the lorry's engine.

I ended up phoning Ross and telling her everything: the meeting with Henderson and Kennet, the money, the manila envelope, Kilo outside my flat, trying to tell me he didn't like Henderson, the porn film and Mrs Curdley's starring role.

She told me I was an idiot for getting involved with Henderson and I protested I didn't have much choice.

'Did he know you'd recently split up from Sarah?' she'd asked.

I told her, for some reason Kilo mentioned it to him during our very brief first meeting on the Broadway last Sunday evening.

'That's what people like Henderson do,' Ross said. 'People your age who have recently split up with wives or long-term partners are generally short of cash and therefore more susceptible to his shady deals.'

'How do you know all this?'

'Because when Bill died, Freddie was only eight and I was financially vulnerable.'

'You got involved with Henderson?'

'Not Henderson but somebody like him.'

'Why didn't you ask me?'

'Pride, Peter, pride.'

The truck slowed to a standstill and I arched my top half up to look out of the windscreen: traffic lights at Roehampton Hill. Leo's voice became clearer as the engine ticked over. I noticed Jeff was feigning boredom, but Leo was relentless.

'So, I said to my missus, why don't we paint the spare bedroom tortoise, but she wouldn't have it and wanted it done in violent pink in case she had a baby and we could turn it into a nursing home. I must say, I'd love to have kids, I really would, but there are drawbridges. For instance, can we afford one? Archie Deacon, who's the first team's openside wanker, had a sprog in June and now he never comes for a protein shake in the café after rugby training.'

'Wanker?' Jeff interrupted.

'You what?'

'Archie Beacon.'

'Archie Deacon?'

'Whatever, but he's a wanker, right?'

'No, he's a flanker,' said Leo.

'OK, carry on then.'

Mercifully, the lights changed and we began to move, the noise of the engine once more drowning out Leo.

I lay back on the bunk and thought about Emily. All of yesterday, I could physically smell her on my clothes, my hands, my fingers. Often, her face was so clear in the air in front of me like an apparition, but there was always a creeping darkness around the edges, barely visible and just out of reach. Henderson and little Charlie, yes, but something else also that I couldn't quite put my finger on.

The engine's drone was steady, Leo's voice distant and I closed my eyes.

We were in the Lazy Lion, Faezeh sitting on my lap, Shayan opposite with his arm round Mrs Curdley. Henderson was standing at the bar and we were all smiling at one of Dave Kennet's jokes, but Kennet had become Mr Delwar and Charlie was lying on top of a piano. Maurice tipped the piano on its end and Charlie fell off onto a sofa next to Ross, who was snogging Kye Stoneway. Barry Noble burst through the doors of the pub, stacked four chairs onto our table and then began to prod me in the arm, harder and harder until it began to hurt.

I woke with a start.

Jeff's face loomed over me. 'Hands off the tiddler,' he said, 'we're here.'

Magenta's new house was equally as tall as the last one but definitely not as wide; divorce had taken its spatial toll. Her usual maid, Fatima, greeted us at the door and informed us that madam wasn't awake yet, but would we like a coffee while we waited? Jeff and I said that would be brilliant, but Leo, who was a Magenta Carlberg removal virgin, was chomping at the bit.

'This is ridiculous,' he told Fatima. 'It's half past eight already and I've told our operations manager we'd be back at HQ by one to wash a few vans and sweep the yard ready for Monday morning.'

Fatima smiled, asked him if he'd like sugar and disappeared back into the house.

'Calm, Leo, calm.' Jeff held up his hand.

'Have you heard of The Velvet Underground?' I asked Leo.

'Is it a ride at Alton Towers?'

'No. The Velvet Underground were a seminal 1960s rock band, and one of their famous tracks was called "I'm Waiting for My Man".'

Leo looked confused.

'Basically, the singer is waiting to score some drugs off his dealer with $26 in his hand,' I explained. 'He's desperate and the dealer doesn't appear on time, but he wants the drugs.'

'What's that got to do with the price of an orange and carrot smoothie?'

'You what?' Jeff butted in.

'It's one of my jokes,' Leo told him proudly.

'Christ, I'd hate to hear a bad one.'

'Hang on, hang on,' I said. 'What I was trying to say, Leo, is that the first thing you learn about moving Magenta Carlberg is you just have to wait.'

'Well, it's very inconvenient,' Leo grumbled.

Fatima bought out the coffees and we thanked her. She told us it was Turkish, very strong.

Leo looked at the small cup with distaste. 'Not much of it,' he muttered with disdain, took a sip and immediately spat it out over the pavement. 'That's revolting,' he told Fatima.

Fatima looked alarmed, but Jeff said, 'Don't worry, sweetheart, this man has absolutely no class.'

Fatima smiled unsurely and walked back into the house.

'How much is on the truck?' I asked Jeff.

'About three quarters full.'

'Like I say, we should be done by lunchtime,' Leo told me, and rested one of his elbows on the side of the van.

'Leo,' Jeff said, 'do those funny pointed things on either side of your head actually work?'

Leo took off his sunglasses and studied them.

'Your ears, I think Jeff means,' I said. Once again, I was starting to feel sorry for Leo.

'Well, yeah, why?' Leo asked, and put his sunglasses back on.

'Because,' Jeff told him, 'we could have two boxes on the truck and we'd still be here this afternoon. Magenta Carlberg is not from this planet.'

'Where's she from then?'

'Leo, just forget it,' I said, and turned to Jeff. 'Must say, I could do with not being stupidly late.'

'You won't be.' Jeff pointed to our left. 'Check out the parking suspension.'

In the most well-heeled parts of the capital, it was customary for the office to book a parking suspension in order for us to park the lorry within at least striking distance of our customer's door. The suspension would be posted on the relevant lampposts two weeks before the move took place and any vehicles parked in the suspended bay on the day of the move would be towed away. On occasion, the offending vehicle would be owned by a VIP, a member of the Royal Family or some other obscenely wealthy person and the clampers would simply move the vehicle further down the road.

Our suspension read: 'THE SPACE BETWEEN NO'S 19–27 INCLUSIVE WILL BE SUSPENDED ON 29/11/2010 FOR REMOVALS BETWEEN 7AM AND 4PM ONLY'.

This meant, no matter how full or empty the lorry was, at 4pm we had to pack up and leave.

'That's amazing,' I said to Jeff. 'Who?'

'Good old Trevor Blind by all accounts.'

'I want to have his babies,' I said.

Magenta finally appeared at just after ten and could best be described as Stupidly High Maintenance. She was auburn and beautifully preserved with perfectly formed facial features and light-blue eyes, but I never thought of her as sexy. She was of an older era: Jane Austen 'handsome', an English rose.

As always, she was very pleasant and asked us how we all were and how were our families.

Jeff told her his oldest son had been banged up for armed robbery and his daughter had just started a new career as a high-class prostitute in South Croydon.

Magenta said that was nice.

Leo told her he and his family were as well as could be expected, although his mother was awaiting an operation for an ingrowing toenail. Magenta sympathised and said how painful that must be. Leo then told her he was in charge and could she show us around the property. Magenta thought this was a good idea and we dutifully followed her up and down the six floors.

Bedrooms 4 and 5 were on the top floor, bedrooms 2 and 3 on the third, and her bedroom and adjoining boudoir took up the whole of the second. Lounge and dining room were on the first floor, kitchen and playroom on the ground, and gymnasium and wine storage in the cellar.

We returned to the van and Leo said, 'A few stairs, I've got to admit, but basically, the job's a piece of crust. As I said, we'll be unloaded in a couple of hours if we get a woggle on.'

Jeff and I said nothing.

First item off the van was a Pack2, presented to Magenta by Leo which read 'CLOTHES AND LINEN – BEDROOM 7'. Magenta thought about this for several minutes while Jeff and I stood behind her carrying a lawnmower. She asked Leo to put the Pack2 on the floor and open it, which Leo duly did. Magenta unfolded a pair of boys' grey school trousers and stared into space. Finally, she said, 'These trousers can go back to store.'

Jeff and I put the lawnmower down on the pavement outside and nipped down to a nearby Tesco Express to grab a bite to eat. We came back and sat on the back of the van where Jeff ate his Scotch egg and I had one of my coronation chicken sandwiches.

Jeff lit up a fag and told me he was taking Suzie out for a drink on Saturday night, which surprised me.

'I thought you'd become the archetypal bachelor,' I said.

'I've been experiencing the male menopause,' Jeff replied with unusual candidness, 'but I think I'm through that now. By all accounts, Suzie's still a right old sort so I should be OK.'

I nearly told him about Emily but decided against it.

Jeff finished his fag and we picked up the lawnmower and walked back into the house. Leo and Magenta were crouched over the same Pack2 in the hallway.

Magenta held up two pairs of socks.

'Bedroom 4?' Leo asked.

'Perhaps bedroom 3,' she said. 'What do you think?'

By 12.30, we'd managed to unload two Pack2s and a wine rack, which, for some reason, ended up on the top floor in bedroom 5. We sat on the back of the van and Leo ate two huge cheese rolls. I ate my remaining coronation chicken sandwich and Jeff smoked another three fags.

Leo admitted things weren't going too well and it was time for us to adopt another approach.

'Go down the pub?' Jeff suggested.

'Don't be so unprofitable,' Leo reprimanded him. 'What we'll do is leave all the boxes to one side and dig out the furniture.' He stood up and began to unstack the load while Jeff and I stayed where we were.

Leo uncovered a tier of three beds. 'Right!' he announced with some excitement. 'She must know where these are going.'

Jeff and I reluctantly got up, grabbed a double mattress and walked it into the house.

Magenta was drinking a herbal tea in the kitchen and we called her through into the hallway.

She studied the mattress for a moment. 'What's that?' she asked.

'It's a sideboard,' Jeff told her.

Magenta looked puzzled for a moment but then smiled and patted Jeff on his arm. 'You are funny,' she said.

'Where would you like it, then?' I asked.

'What?'

'This mattress,' Jeff said.

'Oh, silly me, yes.' She sipped her tea.

We waited.

'Did you want something?' she asked.

'We'd like to know where you'd like this mattress,' I said.

'Is it mine?'

'I believe so,' Jeff told her.

'Bedroom 6,' Magenta decided.

'I'm sorry, Magenta, but you haven't got a bedroom 6,' I said.

'Oh, sorry, yes, of course.' She sipped her tea again.

'Bedroom 2?' I prompted.

'Do you think so?' she asked.

'Why not?' I replied, and Jeff and I carried the mattress up to the third floor and leant it against the wall of bedroom 2.

We walked back down the stairs to find Leo holding a headboard.

Magenta nursed her tea and walked around Leo and the headboard twice. She stopped and said, 'Bedroom 2.'

'There seems to be some progress,' Jeff said, and took the other end of the headboard and helped Leo guide it up the stairs.

I walked out to the van and grabbed one end of another double mattress. Jeff appeared first and we carried it into the hallway.

'Another sideboard,' Jeff announced.

'Bedroom 2,' Magenta said straightaway.

The remaining sections of all three double beds went into bedroom 2, plus a wheelbarrow, three nests of tables, a two-seater sofa, a dishwasher, three armchairs, one half of a dining table and six dining chairs. Magenta was very pleased with herself, and Jeff and I agreed with her how well she was doing. Leo, meanwhile, had collapsed onto the back of the van with his head in his hands.

At 2.30 Magenta said she needed to have a bit of a siesta as she'd been working so hard. I told her that was a good idea, and Jeff and I nipped upstairs and moved one of the mattresses across the landing into bedroom 3 for her to lie down on. Fatima made Jeff and I another cup of Turkish coffee and gave Leo a glass of water.

Leo looked as though he were about to suffer a minor coronary. 'What are we going to do?' he asked us.

'Wait till four and bugger off?' Jeff said.

'But where will she sleep and eat her dinner?'

'Probably at some incredibly expensive hotel in Mayfair.'

'Really?'

'Leo, will you stop worrying?' I intervened. 'Magenta Carlberg, in case you hadn't noticed, is as mad as a box of frogs. She is also stinking rich. Thanks to Trevor Blind, we'll drive back to the yard in an hour and a half. If we can't fit Magenta in in the next two weeks, somebody – maybe us – will unload the lorry back into store and Magenta will completely forget about her storage for another year until her or her ex-husband's accountant says she has to get rid of it due to the ludicrous cost of it gathering dust in our warehouse combined with the expense of putting her up in the Dorchester.'

'The Savoy, I think you'd find,' interrupted Jeff.

'Whatever,' I said, and my phone rang. *Daz*.

'I'm parked up at a meter in Sloane Street,' he said.

'I'll be right there,' I replied, and hung up.

I made up an excuse to Jeff and Leo, grabbed my backpack out of the cab, and headed up the road.

Daz was feeding coins into the meter. 'Twenty pence for three minutes,' he told me in disgust. 'Kye'll go mad.'

I handed him the manila envelope.

Daz shook it. 'This better be worth his while. You know what a tight git he can be.'

He had a valid point. Kye possessed a bewildering ambivalence towards money. You could break a £5,000 vase and he wouldn't bat an eyelid, but spending £3 on parking in London could transport him into an apoplectic frenzy.

'We'll have a drink in the Queens tonight, don't you worry,' I assured him.

'I bloody well hope so, for your sake.' Daz dropped the envelope on the passenger seat of his Volvo. 'How's the job going?'

'As smoothly as ever.'

'How much are you going to bring back?'

'Most of it.'

'That'll please the boss as well. He's told me her storage alone nearly pays for the yearly mortgage on his flat.'

Magenta rose an hour later and ventured down to the back of the van in a Stella Mcartney number clutching a Gucci handbag. She peered at the stack and said, 'Gosh, is this really all mine?'

'Afraid so,' Jeff told her.

Magenta sighed. 'I've just been chatting to a couple of my friends on the phone and they've asked if I could meet them at the restaurant in Peter Jones for a bite to eat.'

'What a great idea!' I exclaimed before Leo could say anything.

She looked at her watch. 'I should be back about half five and then we'll carry on.'

'Brilliant,' Jeff said.

She smiled coyly. 'I think we're doing very well.'

'We certainly are.'

'See you later.' She smiled and we watched her pretty figure amble up to the corner of Cadogan Place. She turned, gave us a wave and disappeared.

Jeff and I gave it a couple of minutes and then we both leapt up onto the back of the truck and began to secure the stack, dropping cartons and furniture down onto the floor and filling in any gaps with empty, made-up cartons and piles of van blankets. I tied two webs across the top and middle of the stack, and Jeff shifted a confused Leo off the back of the van and onto the pavement. I jumped down and Jeff closed the tail lift with a thud.

We faced Leo and said at the same time, 'Let's get the fuck out of here.'

Twenty-One

THE SQUAT

I managed to grab the bunk on the way, back albeit for the price of two pints of Stella, but I needed time to think.

Last night, Ross helped me with my plan. The ploy with the DVD had so far worked well. Kye now had the evidence he needed to hush up Mrs Curdley and there would be no repercussions for us in terms of bonuses and free booze on a Friday night. I would be in his good books and, although I knew Magenta was a pain in the neck, she wasn't a bad person and didn't deserve to be humiliated by that detestable woman. Thus, my karma felt relatively untouched.

Now came the hard part. The plain envelope containing Henderson's blood money was in my backpack, topped up to its original £500 by some of my share of Mr Delwar's tip. Leo would drop me off at South Bitton and I'd take the money to Kilo in the Squat, explaining I'd forgotten to bring the DVD and was terribly sorry so could he please return Mr Henderson his money and the film would follow the next day.

Ross and I agreed this part of the plan had more holes than Blackburn, Lancashire, but could work in the sense that it would portray me as a bumbling, harmless idiot whom Henderson would never consider employing again.

'If you have to see him at any point after this, pretend to be thicker than you normally are,' Ross had added.

After I'd dropped the envelope off at the Squat, I'd nip home, get changed and phone Ross. She'd zoom over and drive me to the Queens to have a pint with the lads and, hopefully, meet up with Emily.

It was payday, I still had £50 in my pocket without visiting the hole in the wall and I'd been promised a treat by a very sexy lady. Things were looking good.

I asked Ross why she put herself out for me like this. She said it was because I'd been a very good friend to her and Freddie since Bill died and she felt she owed me. I told her not to be so silly and blew her a kiss down the phone.

I was smiling to myself and, experiencing a sudden urge to be sociable, I sat up on the edge of the bunk between Jeff and Leo.

We'd actually managed to leave Magenta's at a quarter to four and, although it was POETS Day, the traffic was light and we'd already reached Parson's Green. At this rate, I'd be at the Squat in half an hour and sitting in the Queens by six. Perfect.

Jeff asked Leo how many times he banged his missus every week.

Leo tried to change the subject and pointed at a Chinese takeaway by a tattooist. 'That used to be an Indian,' he said.

'No, come on, Leo,' Jeff insisted. 'How many times do you bat your missus?'

'They used to do a Special Meal for Three for £20 – very reasonable, I always thought.'

'Six times? Seven? More?'

'A lot of the rugger lads used to like a hot curry, but I always preferred egg and chips.'

'I bet a feller like you indulges in shit-loads of foreplay before you get on board.'

Leo looked at Jeff with a puzzled expression on his face.

'You know, like a warm-up,' Jeff said.

'Press-ups and running on the spot and stuff?'

'Whatever floats your boat.'

'Does it turn them on?' Leo asked.

'What, doing press-ups and running on the spot?' I had to say.

'Yeah.'

'Could do, I suppose.'

'So, come on then, Leo,' Jeff said, 'answer the question: how many times a week do you and your missus have a bit of How's Your Fathers?'

Leo was quiet and pulled up at the first of the many pedestrian crossings on Putney high street.

'This last year,' he said slowly, staring straight ahead, 'we did it twice.'

'Twice more than me, then,' Jeff said.

'I had sex three times on Wednesday night,' I announced, and they both turned and stared at me.

After a moment, Jeff said to Leo, 'Don't worry, mate – Pete's including handwork.'

'Handwork?'

'Yeah,' Jeff said. 'Like choking the chicken.'

'Choking the chicken?'

'Yeah.'

Leo remained blank.

'You know, strangling the old parrot.'

'We haven't got a parrot.'

'Let's get back to Archie Beacon,' Jeff said as we pulled up at another pedestrian crossing.

The Squat was situated behind the back of South Bitton Tower on the edge of the Moon Shine Estate.

The building, an eight-bedroomed Georgian mansion, was still, to this day, the official private residence of an entrepreneur by the name of Jonah Richards who made his fortune buying and installing condom machines on Spain's Costa Del Sol during the initial onslaught of the AIDS epidemic in the mid to late 1980s.

Sometime in the early '90s, while holidaying on a cruise ship in the South Atlantic, Jonah's pre-dinner, gin and tonic was spiked with peyote. The entrepreneur discovered God and converted the mansion in South Bitton into a quasi-religious temple for the shelter and spiritual nurturing of other fellow souls who'd dabbled in hallucinogenic drugs.

The mansion was renamed the Rainbow and, for the first few years, Jonah's social experiment was remarkably successful and he was awarded an MBE in 1997. With this award came publicity, and the original residents and devotees to the cause – the college drop-outs and fucked-up kids of the middle and upper classes – were gradually ousted by the speed freaks and pill-poppers of the council estates.

Jonah became increasingly Christ-like and welcomed his new children with open arms. At the turn of the twenty-first century, his new line in glow-in-the-dark, ribbed rubbers with a little cross on top, proved incredibly popular and Jonah's personal wealth increased to astonishing levels. So much so, it's said, that one bright morning he walked out of the front door of the Rainbow, leaving the keys with an ex-Hells Angel of the Windsor Chapter known as Filthy Fred the Hedgehog Eater, never to set foot in the house again.

The Rainbow moniker was rarely used thereafter and Jonah's South Bitton residence quickly became known as the Squat. Jonah was knighted in 2005 by Tony Blair for his outstanding contribution to industry and the building became virtually untouchable to the forces of law and order. In short, a perfect set-up for a person who promised he could get you a certain metric quantity of anything you wanted.

This was the first time I'd ever been to the Squat but Kilo's whereabouts wasn't hard to find. The West Wing had been converted into a separate house with an overgrown front garden and a sign on the gate read 'KILO'S PAD'.

I walked up the path past a rusting Triumph Bonneville with one wheel and rang the doorbell.

A recorded voice said, *'If you require speed or pills, ring the doorbell twice. Solid or green, three times and any A class, please email: kilo@ squat.com Any other enquiries, please use the knocker.'*

I lifted up the large cast-iron badger's head and whacked it against the heavy oak door.

Nothing happened.

I whacked it again.

The voice said, *'Are you the Filth?'*

I was about to say, 'No,' when the door opened and the short, stocky frame of Kilo stood there, aiming a double-barrelled, sawn-off shotgun directly at my chest.

I felt a loosening in my bowels and put my hands straight up above my head as far as they could go.

'Is this a friendly visit?' Kilo asked, and I nodded vigorously.

Both barrels of the gun moved up level with my eyes. 'What's it about?'

'Henderson.'

'What about him?'

'I want you to give him back the money he gave me in the pub the other night. I'm not going to do his dirty work.'

'You're not blaming me for anything?'

'No, I promise.'

Kilo lowered the gun. 'Come in then.'

'How do I know you're not going to shoot me?'

Kilo rested both barrels of the gun on my shoulder, took aim at the fence behind and pulled the trigger. There was no detonation, just the recorded voice of Arnold Schwarzenegger saying, *'You're terminated, fucker.'*

Kilo led me into a lounge and patted an armchair for me to sit on. He put the gun on a coffee table and sat on the sofa opposite.

'Very lifelike,' I said, indicating the gun.

'Bought it in a specialist toy shop in Texas after the second *Terminator* film,' Kilo said. 'Carried it with me everywhere – bars, restaurants, banks, shops, and even sat with it on my lap on the plane from Houston back to Heathrow. Nobody batted an eyelid until I disembarked at Terminal One.

'Within minutes, I was face down on the concrete, arms forced up to the top of my back at impossible angles and surrounded by crew cuts in suits and sunglasses armed with sub-machine guns. At first all I could hear were radios and excited chit-chat from the other passengers but then Arnie's voice sounded, loud and clear.

'One of the crew cuts had tried breaking the toy down. Everything went quiet for a moment and then people began to laugh. Arnie kept repeating, "*You're terminated, fucker,*" and I was picked up by two of the suits and dusted down.'

'They didn't arrest you?'

'I was given a warning but they seemed to generally find the whole incident a bit of a chuckle. Two of the security guys even made me write down the name of the store in Texas I bought the gun from. Half an hour later, I collected my luggage and walked through the green light at customs, out of the terminal, into a cab and home: £300,000 richer.'

'I don't understand.'

'That was the street value of the cocaine hidden in the lining of one of my suitcases.' Kilo leant forward on the sofa. 'Do you want something to drink?'

I shook my head and pulled the envelope out of my backpack.

'You sure about this?' Kilo asked.

'Positive.'

'What about the other one he gave you?'

'Before I answer any more questions,' I said, 'what's your relationship with Henderson?'

'Let's just say we have dealings with each other.' He stood up and walked over to the French windows. There were no curtains and it was pitch black outside. Drops of rain pattered on the glass.

'There's an old saying, Peter: "Keep your friends close but your enemies closer."'

'Don Corleone.'

'It's in the book, not the movie.'

'I've read the book more times than I've seen the film.'

'Then you know where I'm coming from,' Kilo said. He turned and rested his arms against the back of the sofa. 'I owe that bastard and he'll get it before this cancer gets me.'

I put the plain envelope on the coffee table.

'Where's the other one?'

'I've left it at home.'

Kilo laughed. 'Who's your script writer, the guy who wrote *The Pink Panther*?'

'OK, Kilo; for some unknown reason I trust you,' I said. 'The other envelope contained a porn film which featured some dude and a bitch of a customer we've recently had dealings with.'

'Aaron Carlberg and Carmen Curdley.'

I was stunned. 'You know them?'

Kilo said, 'Henderson wanted you to plant it so Carlberg's ex-wife would find it. Is that right?'

I nodded.

'What have you done with it?'

'Tell me how you know the Carlbergs and this Curdley woman?'

Kilo sighed. 'You're a tough little fucker, Peter Booth.'

He sat on the arm of the sofa and I noticed a spiderweb of pain appear around the corners of his mouth.

'Aaron Carlberg owes Henderson big time – details of which I can't disclose, but Henderson hates being stiffed. If Magenta finds this film, she'll fuck her hubby over to the tune of a couple of mil at least. Henderson will then contact Aaron Carlberg and tell him he's got another film.'

'And Carlberg pays him off?'

'Well done, Peter. But this all begs the question: why didn't you just plant the film, take the grand and be done with it?'

'Magenta Carlberg is as crazy as hell and a nightmare to move,' I said. 'But she's not a horrible woman and she's fragile upstairs. Something like this could push her over the edge and I don't want to be a part of that.'

'Morals,' Kilo said. 'Very dangerous things.' The rain on the windows became louder. 'You're a tough little fucker, Peter Booth,' he repeated, 'but, also, bloody stupid.'

'I can't stand that Curdley woman either.'

'What's your beef?'

'She's made a serious complaint about me and two of my workmates and says she'll take it to a higher level which could have serious repercussions for our firm and, therefore, our financial welfare. It's not only that; she's just a horrible old bag.'

'So, where's this film then?'

I hesitated but the mouth was beginning to dislodge itself inexorably from the brain. 'I've given it to my boss, Kye Stoneway.'

'Jesus fucking Christ,' Kilo said, and began to laugh.

Twenty-Two

STATUS QUO

I got back to the flat, phoned Ross and got changed. There was no time for dithering; I was on a tight schedule, so I chucked on my favourite pair of Levis I'd bought in a charity shop in North Bitton ten years ago and my Bee Gees 'Jive Talkin'' T-shirt. I looked in the bathroom mirror and thought, *Fuck 'em; Peter Booth's here.*

My phone rang.

'I'm outside,' Ross said.

'Be there in a sec,' I told her, hung up and checked myself in the mirror again.

I'm not going anywhere if you're going to wear that, I heard Sarah say.

I changed my T-shirt twice more before I ran out of the front door of the building, through the pouring rain and into Ross's passenger seat.

'I love you,' I said.

Ross gave me a fleeting look and eased off the handbrake. She checked her mirrors and drove the car at a right angle towards the opposite pavement. We stopped and she spun the wheel and reversed.

'Do you want me to see you back?' I asked.

'Just shut up and tell me what's occurred,' she said, and completed the three-point turn.

She was pleased I'd done what I'd said I'd do with the money and the DVD but made a face when I told her Kilo didn't think the 'I've left it at home cos I'm a bumbling idiot' approach would work.

'Well, we always knew that was the weakest part of the plan,' she said, 'but as long as you make sure Kye burns himself a copy and you get the original back to Henderson, I can't see what could go wrong. I suppose he might get a bit pissed off and give you a slap.'

'A slap?' I repeated, alarmed.

'You know, a punch in the nose or something.'

'I know what a "slap" means, Ross.'

'Why are you asking me then?'

'Well, I don't like the idea of being hit.'

'Oh, stop being such a wimp. It's better than having a pair of electrodes strapped to your meat and veg.'

'Ross!'

'Sorry, only teasing.'

The rain was teeming down now and, although this part of the A3 was a well-lit, busy dual carriageway, vision was impaired and Ross cut her speed down to thirty.

'Do you think he's ever done that to someone?' I asked.

'How do I know? It's just one of those common torture methods you read about in crime novels.'

'It makes me wince thinking about it.'

'You'll do more than wince if he finds out about you and Emily.'

'Maurice reckons he's not that hard – more mouth than trousers.'

'Maurice Bagley is a nutcase; I've never known him to be scared of anybody except Janet. Anyway, tell me about this Kilo feller again; he sounds quite interesting.'

'Ross, can I ask you something?'

'Of course.'

'I get the impression you're quite taken with these hard men, criminal types.'

Ross was quiet for a moment. 'Yes, I suppose I am.'

'I don't ever remember Bill being like that.'

She smiled. 'Bill was a lovely, lovely man and I still think of him most days. So kind and generous and good to me, but if pushed, he could certainly handle himself, as you blokes say.'

We drove along in silence and Ross pulled out a tissue from her pocket and blew her nose. I put my arm around her and she leant her head against my shoulder for a moment.

She lifted her head back up and indicated to come off at the Purfleet turn-off. 'So, tell me about Kilo,' she said.

Last Friday of the month and the bar in the Queens was two-deep – the monthly PAYEs had joined the weekly cash-in-handers.

Ross pointed out the Stoneways crew sitting in the corner of the saloon bar by the gents' toilets and I could see the boss, pint in hand, standing over the curly top of Daz Oatridge and the near-white billiard ball of Barry Noble's bald head. The boss was laughing and generally looking exceptionally pleased with himself. *His plastic was definitely over the jump*, I thought.

'What you having?' I asked Ross.

'Pint of Stella.'

'What?'

'Want to attract a hard case,' she said.

Ruth, the landlady, spotted me as I queued and held up one finger.

'Two,' I mouthed, and saw her reach down and pull out two Stella glasses.

I grabbed the two pints and made my way through the throng. A wandering arm spilt some of the lager from one of the glasses and a big man in paint-splashed overalls turned and apologised. I gave him my most pissed-off stare and detected a hint of worry in his eyes.

'Look, I said I'm sorry, mate,' he said defensively. 'I'll get you another one.'

I held his gaze for a moment longer and said, 'Forget it.'

He stood aside and I walked through the gap feeling pleased with myself – it must have been the T-shirt.

The usual suspects were all there but no sign of Emily. I gave Ross her pint and leant against the radiator by Jeff and Maurice.

Maurice studied my T-shirt. 'Status Quo?' he read, and began to laugh.

I was hurt. 'What's wrong with them?'

'They're shit, that's what's wrong with them. It's the sort of thing that rugby prat over there would wear.' He pointed at Leo.

Leo looked over.

'Do you like Status Quo, Leo?' Maurice asked him.

'I've seen them four times,' Leo said proudly, and I zipped up my leather jacket.

The usual chit-chat progressed, but there was a more cheerful, raucous atmosphere than last Friday. It was payday, the boss was in the chair and an extended free drinking period was on the cards with the possibility of a curry later for the die-hards in the Mansoori Heights in West Purfleet.

Leo was targeted by Maurice and Barry Noble.

Barry told Leo that the police were looking for a large, thick-looking bloke in shorts and sunglasses who gained entrance to the homes of old ladies with ongoing dementia by pretending to be a removal man and then proceeding to damage various items of their furniture for no reason at all.

Maurice added that the culprit was eventually apprehended whilst fleeing across a field from the scene of one of his crimes. An astute policeman booted a rugby ball over the escaping villain's head, which the latter began to chase. By the time the idiot managed to catch the erratically bouncing pig bladder, the chasing posse of law and order caught up with him, bundled him to the ground and read him his rights. The handcuffed reprobate then demanded to see his lawyer as his pursuers were in an offside position when they'd apprehended him.

I stayed quiet and drank my Stella, shooting glances towards the pub doorway for any sign of Emily.

'Are you alright?' Jeff called over.

'Yeah, fine.'

'Oh, come on, Peter,' Maurice said. 'Sit down and have a chat with the lads. I was only joking about the Quo.' He took a long draught of his Fosters. 'I saw them at Butlins in Minehead with my dad when they first started out.'

'Really?' I was interested.

'Yeah.'

'What year was that?'

''68, '69?'

'Must have been when they'd just released "Pictures of Matchstick Men".' I was quite excited.

'No, they didn't play that.'

'Great song, though.'

'In fact, they didn't play anything.'

'What do you mean?'

'They won first and second place in the Biggest Wanker's Haircut Competition.'

Daz and Trevor Blind came over and asked what we wanted to drink. I looked at my half-full glass and said, 'Stella.' *Might as well*, I thought. It didn't look like Emily was going to turn up.

'What did you say?' Daz shouted across the table.

'I didn't say anything,' I said.

'Well, your lips moved.'

'Sorry, pint of Stella.'

Kye Stoneway approached me. 'Evening, Peter,' he said.

'Kye.'

'Appreciate it.'

'Appreciate what?'

'The film.'

I could feel myself beginning to sweat and wanted to take my jacket off but I was still reluctant about showing off the Quo, God bless them. I leant over so I was closer to Kye's right ear.

'Have you watched it?' I asked.

'Twice,' Kye told me. 'It's definitely her.'

'Good,' I said, and plucked up courage. 'Can you give me back the original then?'

'Not tonight, unfortunately. Can you pick it up tomorrow morning?'

'Where?' I asked.

Kye thought for a moment. 'My office at ten?'

Trevor Blind edged around the table with a pint of Stella for me and I remembered the parking suspension outside Magenta's.

'Thanks for the suspension,' I said to Trevor.

'The four o'clock finish? Thought you'd like that.'

'Magenta Carlberg?' Kye pricked up his ears.

'The very one,' Trevor said.

'How much did you unload?' Kye asked me.

'Not enough to affect your mortgage repayments,' I replied with a grin.

Kye continued to stare at me and I felt the smile freeze on my face. 'Tomorrow morning at ten, then,' he said curtly.

He was always touchy about his or the company's finances. I'd forgotten as usual and felt I had no choice but to agree, although the place and time was inconvenient.

'See you there,' I reluctantly said.

Half an hour later, the crowd began to thin. Barry was first to leave, followed shortly afterwards by a very cheesed-off Maurice. Kye had just announced he was going to book a couple of tables at the Mansoori Heights for 8.30 and wanted to know how many of us were interested.

Maurice had hastily gone outside to phone his wife to ask permission but returned fairly quickly with a sick expression on his face. 'No go,' he grumbled, put on his jacket and walked out of the pub.

I sat down in his seat opposite Jeff.

'What about you?' Jeff asked.

'I hope so,' I said.

'What do you mean, you hope so?'

Somebody kissed me on the back of my neck and I turned round.

Emily. She'd obviously gone home straight after work and got changed. She was dressed casually: leggings and a black V-necked jumper. Her hair ran free in an avalanche of dark curls and she wore just that hint of make-up which accentuated all the sharp, beautiful features of her face.

'You look stunning,' I said.

She sat down next to me on Barry's vacant chair and put her hand on my knee.

I felt myself blushing and noticed Jeff and Leo staring at us.

Emily grabbed one of my hands and pressed it gently against the surface of the tabletop in full view of both of them. 'Yes,' she announced, 'Peter and I *are* an item.'

She looked at me. 'Aren't we?' she asked.

'I think so,' I said quietly, and Jeff began to laugh.

I suppose we had our first ever slight tiff in the pub that night. Emily wanted to have one drink and then we'd go back to hers. She'd rustle us up something to eat and perhaps we'd have an early night. This last bit was suggested with a twinkle in her brown eyes and a sultry smile on her lips.

This was all very appealing but the lamb madras in the Mansoori Heights was second to none, and their samosas and onion bhajis were top quality. I proposed we go for a curry first and then back to her place. She was quiet and I decided to push my idea further by telling her that having a curry with the lads was an essential piece of monthly team-bonding and our attendance would greatly please Kye Stoneway.

Emily stood up and started to put her coat on. 'That's fine,' she said. 'Hope you have a nice time and give me a ring over the weekend if you feel up to it.'

Strangely enough, it was Leo who saved the day. He said, 'Why don't you tell the boss you've got to go home but could you order a takeaway from the curry house by phone?'

This had the potential of being an incredibly good idea and I couldn't believe Leo had the intelligence to suggest it.

'Have you got their takeaway menu at home?' I asked Emily.

'No,' she said, and sat down next to me again. 'But I can pick one up from there on the way back.'

'That OK with you?' I asked.

She kissed me on the lips. 'Of course it is,' she said, and Jeff and Leo started clapping.

We stayed for another half hour, long enough for Emily to drink a small glass of Merlot and me to finish my second pint. She laughed and chatted with everybody, held my hand, hugged me sporadically and generally showed everybody I was her beaux. I could tell by their demeanour, Daz and Trevor were taken with her and pleased for my new-found happiness.

Steve Woodgit and Freddie disappeared, most probably out to Steve's car for a doobie, but Ross was still there with a fresh pint of Stella in front of her. At one point, Emily popped to the loo and I walked over to Ross and whispered in her ear that I hoped she was getting a cab home. She planted a big wet kiss on my forehead and told me to bugger off.

Eventually, we said our goodbyes and Kye told us to order what we wanted from the Mansoori Heights and tell them to put it on his bill. Ross's chair was empty and I looked around the bar to see if I could spot her before we went.

She was standing by one of the fruit machines, lager-flushed face beaming at the big man in the paint-splashed overalls who leant over her with lecherous intent.

I felt a pang in my chest which I at first considered to be caused by a sense of brotherly protection but realised, with a sense of confused surprise, there was a tinge of jealousy mixed in there too. Perhaps it was because I believed I was perched on an untouchable plateau because of Emily and thus all the other women I knew should only be interested in me, but I realised there was something else there that made me feel wistful and uncomfortably sad.

I waved, but she didn't see me and I walked out of the pub with Emily into the pouring rain.

Twenty-Three

FINDING THE FACILITIES

Charlie was sitting on the sofa, eating crisps and watching TV.

Emily warned me he was at home in the car on the way back and made me promise to ignore his sarcasm and try and be pleasant.

'Alright, kiddo,' I said cheerfully as we walked into the lounge.

Charlie gave me a look and then turned his attention back to the telly.

'We're going to order a takeaway curry,' Emily said to him. 'Would you like something?'

Charlie shrugged.

She sat down by him. 'What's the matter?' she asked.

'Nothing.'

This was said in a manner which reminded me of Sarah. Many a time, I'd be chatting away to her quite happily – usually about my favourite bands, I must admit – and would then notice an ominous silence. I'd ask her if she was alright and she'd answer, 'Fine,' which meant there was something very wrong and an unpleasant scene was brewing.

'Suppose you want to sit here with him and snog and stuff?' he said.

'Charlie!'

'It's alright; I'll go to my room.' He got up and strode out of the lounge, the door banging shut behind him. One of the framed photos of he and his mother fell face down on the sideboard.

'Do you want me to go?' I asked.

'Don't be silly,' Emily said. 'He's upset because I'm no longer giving him my undivided attention. I'll let him stew for an hour or so. He'll be alright.'

I remained standing.

'Look, for Christ's sake, sit down and order the curry!'

I'm afraid to say that, as per usual, my natural selfishness clicked in. *I'd have to get a cab back to the flat,* I thought, *sit there on my single bed and get mindlessly and depressingly drunk.* Also, Emily was looking decidedly hot and I really wanted a curry.

'OK, then.' I sighed, sat down on the sofa and opened up the takeaway menu.

She chose a chicken balti, keema rice and a naan, while I opted for my favourites, plus boiled rice. Rice, in my view, was always best served plain.

'What about Charlie?'

'I forgot he's not that keen on curry. I'll stick a pizza in the oven for him later.'

I ordered and Emily switched off the telly and put on a CD. The haunting opening guitar sequence of 'Gimme Shelter' began.

'*Let It Bleed*,' I said. 'Great album.'

'Thought you might like it.'

She leant over and kissed me. I kissed her back and she put her tongue in my mouth. I was instantly erect and began to kiss her neck.

I made my way down to her cleavage, but she pulled away.

'Come with me,' she said, and took my hand and led me through the kitchen into the bathroom. She bolted the door and took off her top.

'Just a quick one before the curry,' she whispered.

'What a wonderful thing to say,' I whispered back.

The curry arrived ten minutes later than they'd said, which to be quite honest didn't make any difference – it could have arrived twenty minutes earlier.

I had my strides and T-shirt on, and Emily wore her dressing gown as we ate.

As usual, it was of a high standard and the madras had a particularly zesty zing to it. I purposefully left an onion bhaji for the morning and noticed Emily had only eaten half her balti and hadn't even touched her naan.

She cleared the plates and the containers off the coffee table and walked through the open kitchen door. She pressed her foot on the lever of the pedal bin and the top sprang open.

'No!' I shouted.

She turned, startled.

'Don't throw it away,' I told her. 'I'll eat it in the morning.'

'What?' she asked.

'The curry. Spoon the rest of into a bowl and leave it on the side. I'll have it for breakfast.'

'Cold?'

'The only way.'

She looked at me as though I were mad but did as I said. She pulled a pizza out from the fridge, unwrapped it and stuck it in the oven.

She came back into the lounge. 'Look, I'm going to ask Charlie if he wants to eat his pizza and watch a DVD with us. Is that OK?'

'Fine,' I said, and then thought it might have been said in very much the same tone as Sarah would have said it. 'I mean it,' I added quickly.

Emily kissed me on top of my head and said, 'You are funny, you know.'

Charlie came in and sat between us on the sofa. *Maybe he's one of those mad, fucked-up, homicidal kids I often read about who embark on mass-murder sprees in the deep south of the USA*, I thought.

The film was *Casino Royale*: the 2006 version starring Daniel Craig.

I'd never seen any of his Bonds before but I thought he was good. Not quite Sean Connery but better than Roger Moore. The fight scenes and car chases were great, but my favourite bit was when his drink was spiked during the big poker game. He realises he's minutes away from a fatal coronary and rushes out to his super-duper Aston Martin in the car park and plugs into a direct line to MI6 in London where Q, with the aid of the love interest, save his life. Fully recovered, he walks back into the casino and, much to the barely disguised shock of the dastardly baddy, sits back down at the table and says, 'Sorry about the delay but that last hand nearly killed me.'

Not as good as *Goldfinger*, when Sean Connery was nearly lasered in half and wakes up, sat in a plane sipping a martini. Honor Blackman appears and introduces herself as Pussy Galore and he asks, 'Have I died and gone to heaven?' But not bad.

The only thing which annoyed me was the long, drawn-out romance between him and the main bird. James Bond was like Judge Dredd: fictional characters far too cool to fall in love.

I expressed this thought out loud when the film finished.

Charlie, surprisingly, agreed with me. Emily stood up and switched the lights back on and I noticed she'd been silently crying.

She blew her nose and said, 'You two have got no sense of romance.'

'He's there to blow people away, Mum,' Charlie said. 'Not go all gooey and lovey-dovey over some dolled-up tart with stupidly long legs.'

'She was quite tall,' I agreed.

'She was very beautiful,' Emily commented, and blew her nose again.

'She's not dead, Mum, it's just a film.'

'I know,' she said, 'but it seemed real at the time.'

'I used to always cry at films and sad TV programmes,' I said.

'Did you?' Emily asked.

'Yes, I did. *Little House on the Prairie* used to destroy me.'

'And me.' Emily smiled. 'But *The Waltons* was worse.'

'Do you remember the one where Grandad nearly died?'

'Oh, shut up, you two,' Charlie interrupted. 'You're making me puke.'

'Charlie.'

'Sorry, Mum.'

'That's better.' Emily looked at her watch. 'Crumbs, it's half eleven. I'm going to have a bath. Will you two to be alright?' There was a tiny hint of worry in her voice.

'Suppose so,' Charlie mumbled.

'OK, be back soon,' she said, and walked out through the kitchen door.

We sat in awkward silence. I heard the bath taps begin to run and Charlie said, 'Ray'll kill you if he finds out about you and Mum.'

'He can try,' I told him.

Charlie looked at me for the first time. 'Are you a hard bastard like him?'

I returned his stare and left it a moment. 'No,' I finally said.

Charlie laughed. 'Didn't think so. Freddie Keating says you're a right prick.'

'Did he really say that?' I was offended.

Charlie smiled. 'No, he says you're cool.' He pulled his phone out of his pocket, looked at it and then put it away again. 'I'm sorry if I was rude earlier,' he said.

'It's alright.'

'Just, I don't want Mum to be hurt again.'

The only one that'll get hurt is me, I thought but said instead, 'Hopefully she won't be.'

'I didn't like Ray. Fancied himself, if you know what I mean. I hate people like that.' He pulled his phone out again. The bath taps fell silent.

'How long have you been playing for Leysham?' I asked.

'Just a couple of weeks.'

'You're a good player.'

'Thanks.'

'Better than Freddie.'

'That's not hard,' Charlie said, and then immediately put his hand out towards me. 'Don't tell him I said that, for fuck's sake.'

'I won't, and don't tell him I said you were better than him.'

'Cool,' Charlie said, and returned to his phone.

I leant back on the sofa with my hands behind my head and studied the ceiling.

Charlie began texting and said, without looking at me, 'By the way, Mum thinks Status Quo are shit.'

I woke up in the middle of the night dying for a pee, Emily curled up asleep beside me.

I gently eased her arms and legs away and sat on the edge of the bed. I didn't want to risk turning on a light in case I woke her, so I spent a minute trying to adjust my eyes to the dark before I made any sort of move. If I were in my flat or Sarah's, this wouldn't have been a problem, but I'd only ever seen Emily's bedroom with the lights on once and that was a couple of hours ago and only for about twenty minutes.

I gradually made out a very thin, lighter shade of dark surrounding a tallish, oblong structure which I guessed must have been the door. I was naked but decided trying to find my strides would be near impossible, so I crept off the bed towards the shape, holding my hands out in front of me until they touched wood. I found the handle, opened the door and tip-toed out.

My hands felt along the wall until I found a light switch and flicked it on.

There was a corridor, one closed door either side and one at the end. I switched off the light – it was too bright – and decided the khazi must be through the door at the end.

I got there in the dark, opened the door and could immediately walk no further; some form of shelving was blocking me. I reached in and felt a fluffy but coarse fabric: towels. I was in the airing cupboard.

I had to think quickly; my bladder was about to explode. Where would Charlie sleep? In the room next to her or opposite? He was a headstrong lad, I knew, but was also very fond of his mother. I took the plunge, decided he slept opposite and opened up the door adjacent to Emily's bedroom.

My left hand searched the wall but could find no switch. I walked into a space, both arms once more stretched out before me until I again touched wood. I was actually now in pain and assumed there was a bath or shower to my left and this was another door I was now feeling which led to a separate toilet. I opened the door and aimed Percy down towards the middle where the porcelain must surely be.

I was just about to mercifully let go when lights flooded the room. I was looking at a row of shirts hanging up in a wardrobe. I whirled round both hands, covering my aching willy. A terrified Charlie was sitting up in his bed.

'What the fuck are you doing?' he screamed.

I was lying with my head under the duvet when the landing light went out and the bedroom door opened. Emily came in and purposefully allowed her knee to press painfully into my groin as she clambered over me to her side of the bed.

An elbow dug in my ribs as she made herself comfortable. She lay still for a moment and then said, 'He didn't want me to turn off his light and says he's going to call Ray in the morning to come over and duff you up.'

'Sorry,' I mumbled.

'Why the bloody hell didn't you go downstairs and use the bathroom off the kitchen? You could have turned on as many lights as you liked and even eaten your bloody curry.'

'Sorry,' I mumbled again.

She let out a long sigh and I felt her turn in the bed away from me.

My eyes were wide open and I watched the air above me crystallise into minute, dark particles. The silence was somehow audible and reminded me of the low drone of the beer fridges in the Spoons.

Emily shifted onto her back and said, 'And you were just starting to break the ice with him.'

I tried humour. 'What's happened to this treat you promised me?'

'Here it is,' she said, and snatched the pillow from underneath my head and whacked me with it.

'Ow,' I said.

Emily turned away again and I lay there thinking it might be an idea to get up, get changed and go. It was roughly a five-mile walk home and it would be a bastard to get a cab, but I could no longer hear any rain. Back to the flat, bachelor once more, sad but aware of my place in the scheme of things. Potential alcoholic, maybe, but at least I'd never experience moments like this again.

Emily began to giggle. She swivelled round and kissed me on the cheek. 'You are an idiot,' she said, 'but you are funny.'

Morning arrived and I had a shower in the bathroom off the kitchen. I smiled when I saw the blue toothbrush I'd used on Wednesday night lying on the side of the basin by the taps.

I'd finally worked out the layout, so I draped the towel round me and walked through the kitchen and lounge and up the stairs into Emily's bedroom. My Quo T-shirt and Levis lay neatly folded on the bed, a pair of fresh, 'RH'-emblazoned Y-fronts and socks on top.

Fully changed, I walked out onto the landing and Charlie's door opened. Emily.

'Now that you're decent,' she said, 'can you come through and have a quick word with my son?'

I nodded, took a breath and followed her in.

Charlie was sitting up in the bed wearing a Spurs shirt in almost exactly the same position he was in when I disturbed him in the night.

Emily led me to the foot of the bed and said, 'Peter wants to apologise.'

'I'm sorry,' I began, 'I thought your wardrobe was the toilet.'

Charlie stared at me in silence.

'I have made this mistake before,' I admitted.

'Have you?' Emily interrupted.

'Unfortunately, yes.'

'When you were a small child?'

'No.'

'Well, when then?'

'Not that long ago.'

Charlie was suddenly curious. 'Did you actually have a wee?'

Emily had her arms folded and was staring at me.

'Yes,' I said.

'Euuugh, gross.' Charlie made a fake retching noise.

I thought of Maurice and Jeff. 'It can happen to many men of my age or older.'

'Whose wardrobe was it?' Emily asked in horror.

'My ex's: Sarah's.'

'He's not going to stay again, is he, Mum?'

'Doesn't look like it,' I said.

'How often does this… this middle-aged weeing problem happen?' Emily asked.

'Very rarely,' I assured her, already seriously regretting I'd ever mentioned it.

'Good, I'm bloody glad.'

'Wait till I tell Freddie and his mum,' piped up Charlie.

I didn't think Ross would give a shit. I remembered Bill telling me once, after a particularly heavy session, she'd found him peeing in the fridge-freezer.

'Look, I'm sorry I even mentioned it; I was trying to be funny,' I said.

'Funny?' repeated Emily.

'Is this something to do with alcohol?' Charlie asked.

'Yes, I'm afraid it is,' I told him.

Emily clapped her hands. 'Right! This seems to have cleared things up nicely.' She turned to me. 'Thank you, Peter, for your apology to my son for trying to pee in his wardrobe. If you don't mind, I'll just go and check if mine's alright.' She stormed out of the room.

Charlie laughed. 'Last night, when I saw you there trying to cover up your archbishop, I was really scared. I thought you were a perv or something but now I know you're just a complete idiot.' He shook his head. 'Poor Mum,' he added, and began to laugh again.

Things were being slammed on the kitchen worktops as I ate my breakfast standing in the lounge. Curry always tasted nearly as good as it did the night before and I wiped the bowl clean with the last of the naan.

I checked my phone for the time: ten past nine. I had to make tracks. I stood by the kitchen door and watched Emily accidently drop a plate on the floor. It broke and she wrenched open the door underneath the sink and pulled out a dustpan and brush.

'Suppose you want a lift home,' she said without looking up.

'It's alright, I'll get the bus.'

Charlie appeared by my side. 'Mum, I'll clear that up. You give this plonker a lift and don't worry. I think he's alright really. Much more entertaining than Ray and all the others.'

Twenty-Four

UNDERPANTS AND CURTAINS

The rain had stopped and the sun was trying to shine its way through the clouds. *All the others?* I kept thinking as we drove along in silence.

We turned onto the dual carriageway by the BP garage outside her estate. 'There weren't any others of importance,' she said.

'I wasn't asking.'

'Well, I'm telling you,' Emily said without looking at me. 'After Ray, there were "others". Mostly blokes who asked me out for a date – a drink, a meal, the cinema – and, yes, I went. Because I was flattered, mainly, and because of how Ray used to treat me.

'He liked to control my life and he did his darndest to make me feel unwanted, ugly. So, after I finally got rid of him, I responded to these new advances – it made me feel attractive again, sexy even, but I never really fancied any of them. Mostly, after one date, I'd put them off and they accepted it, but there was one feller who was more persistent than the others. We got drunk one night and slept together.'

She stopped talking, put both hands on the wheel and stared out the windscreen.

'Did he pee in the wardrobe?'

'I knew you were going to say that. No, he didn't, but I didn't enjoy it. It was seedy and drunken and messy and horrible. It was as if I was another notch on the bedpost. I told him to go at five in the morning. He never had a shower nor a clean pair of underwear.'

'Have you seen him since?'

'Once,' she said, and paused. 'A few days later in North Bitton outside the Black Horse. He had a black eye and was walking on crutches. Ray had somehow found out.'

The noise of the engine seemed to become louder and, for the first time, I noticed the yellow air freshener tucked in beside the central mirror.

The turn off for the industrial estate was approaching. 'Do you mind if we come off here?' I asked.

'Work?' she queried.

'Yeah, I have to see Kye concerning the Mrs Curdley incident,' I half-lied.

We drove down London Road and into the estate. She pulled over by the B&Q warehouse. It was a Saturday morning and the car park was empty.

'Before we get to the yard, I need to say a couple of other things,' she said.

'It's over?' I offered.

'No – not on my side anyway. I just want to say, although you undoubtedly have a few odd habits, I feel very comfortable with you. You make me laugh when I'm with you and smile when I think of you.'

She fell quiet and I realised I was meant to say something, but for once I wanted my grey matter to be properly engaged before I opened my mouth.

'So, what do you think?' she prompted.

'About?' I managed to say.

'Us, you bloody idiot,' she said, and whacked me playfully on the arm.

'Ow.'

'Sorry,' she said. 'You're worried about Ray. I understand.'

I thought as quickly and as lucidly as possible. 'OK, I really do like you and want to make something of it. I know I'll annoy you; I've annoyed every woman I've ever been with.'

'And how many of those have there been?'

I thought of 'arty' Julie. 'Besides Sarah, one other whom you'd call a "serious" one, the mother of my daughter whom I haven't seen for nigh on fourteen years.'

'I'm not really that bothered as long as there's nobody else right now.'

For some reason, I thought of Ross. 'There isn't,' I assured her.

'What about Ray?'

'I'll confront him.'

'Seriously?'

'Yes.'

'Why don't I tell him?'

'What about: together?'

She thought for a moment. 'That might be an idea, but are you sure?'

'Yes,' I said, and we kissed.

She dropped me off at the yard and asked me if I wanted her to wait.

'No, it's OK,' I told her.

When there was a lot going on in my head, I liked to walk and the sun looked like it was there to stay. After I'd seen Kye, I could make my way back home along the canal and enjoy the freedom only moving solitude could bestow.

'Will you come round later and stay?' Emily asked. 'I think Charlie's getting used to you.'

'Love to,' I said, and kissed her.

I waved goodbye as she drove off and, once again, felt a strange relief. I decided, since splitting up with Sarah, I'd discovered my personal freedom was something to value, but I also believed I was better off *in* a relationship rather than not and I did really like Emily.

There were two cars parked outside the front of Stoneways, Kye's Range Rover and a highly polished black Mercedes E-Class I'd never seen before. I pressed in the code on the keypad on the wall and the entrance door buzzed open.

When the warehouse was built, Kye installed a state-of-the-art security system. All entrances to both the actual building and the yard, front and back, were alarmed and needed either a code or a personal fob to access. CCTV covered every nook and cranny (except Steve Woodgit's car) and when the main alarm was set, hidden sensors could pick up any internal movement. Once triggered, the noise was not only deafening but the system would transmit a direct signal to North Bitton Nick and the Old Bill could be there within ten minutes.

The only intruders we'd had so far were a couple of pigeons and a field mouse who'd made its home in a container stacked purposefully at the very back of the warehouse due to the expense of the contents. The container had not yet been delivered and Kye was still working out what to say to the hedge-fund manager owner when he discovered his Andy Warhol had a two-centimetre hole in its canvas.

Directly opposite the main entrance was the warehouse proper where the one thousand-plus containers sat, evenly distributed either side of a seven-metre gangway, ten rows deep and neatly stacked in columns of four.

To my left was the grandly named 'Packing and Restoration Area', a carpeted space where items of damaged furniture lay awaiting repair – Leo's latest faux pas, the top of Mrs White's dresser, included. Beyond that were the two fire doors leading to the restroom.

I turned right through the shop, where brand-new packing materials were stacked on two rows of racking which a visiting customer could purchase at extortionate prices. For example, a

Hanging Wardrobe carton was priced at £12.50 and the essential bar, upon which the customer's clothes would be hung, cost an extra pound.

The shop's bald mannequin stood on guard dressed in the Stoneways uniform of red T-shirt, fleece and black trousers. The mannequin used to wear a pair of shiny, size nine, health and safety-approved steel toe-capped boots, but they'd mysteriously disappeared a couple of years back. Rumour had it a skint Jeff Unsworth purloined them one quiet Monday morning after his only pair of boots had completely disintegrated.

There were another two floors above my head containing endless racks of archive storage boxes. Each box cost a business 12p a week to store and, by law, could not be destroyed for seven years. The facility stored twenty thousand boxes and was a further example of Kye's uncannily good business sense.

I walked through the fire door at the end of the shop and immediately right through another fire door and into the office. The shutters were down on Kye's cubicle and the door was closed shut.

I knocked politely.

'Come,' I heard Kye's regal voice announce, and I walked in.

Kye sat in his red swivel chair, eyes downward, empty coffee cup on top of his desk. The door slammed shut behind me and I turned round to see the monstrous form of Dave Kennet blocking the exit.

Ray Henderson stood by the fire-proof filing cabinet to my left. He wore a black open-necked shirt revealing a silver cobra-head medallion.

'Ah, foolish Peter,' he said, 'please take a seat.' He pointed to a blue swivel chair halfway between Kennet and Kye.

'Please,' Henderson added politely, 'or David here might have to make you.'

I sat.

'Your boss and I go back a long way, don't we, Kye?' Henderson said.

Kye said nothing.

Henderson walked over and crouched down in front of me. He smelt of expensive aftershave and the eyes of the snake head sparkled green as a ray of sunlight shot through the shuttered window.

'Needless to say,' he said, 'I'm not very happy about you failing to complete your half of the deal.'

'You've got your money back and the film,' I countered.

'Yes, but that's not the point. I expect people to do what I tell them.' He stood and walked back to the filing cabinet, leaving myself a clear view of the eye-gouging Kennet.

'Why don't you just post the film to Magenta?' I said.

'Because I wanted to try you out. A firm like mine could always do with new recruits.'

'I've decided I don't want to be one.'

'Obviously not.' Henderson turned to Kennet. 'David, please go ahead.'

Kennet took a step towards me.

'Wait!' Kye Stoneway cried out.

Kennet stopped.

'What's the matter, Kye?' asked Henderson, his voice remaining quietly uninterested.

'You said you wouldn't hurt him. That was part of our deal.'

Henderson took his time to answer while I kept my eyes on the giant who was now only a foot away from me.

There was no visible definition of muscle anywhere. Both his arms were massive trunks of flesh finished off by hands nearly as large as my head, and I hated to think what damage a roundhouse blow from either one of them could do to my countenance.

'I suppose so,' I heard Henderson say, 'but Peter here does need a little lesson.'

Kye began to protest but Henderson held up a hand to him.

'Just a bit of fun.' He smiled. 'Only his pride will be hurt, I promise.' He turned back to Kennet. 'Trousers, please, David.'

Kennet took another step towards me and snapped open the blade of a flick-knife. 'Stand up,' he said.

I stood.

'Take off your strides,' Kennet said, 'or I'll cut them off.'

Henderson laughed his shrill laugh. 'Peter, don't look so scared. Kye's already told me that you don't drive and you always get to work by bus so I thought your punishment would be to return all the way home in your underpants.' He laughed again, almost pleasantly, and Kennet joined in with an impossibly slow, low: 'Ha, ha, ha.'

Christ, these two have a mature sense of humour, I thought but did as I was told and dropped my strides. I shoved them to the side, underneath Kye's desk, and an ice-block suddenly struck my heart.

Henderson stared at a pair of his own Y-fronts and I watched his face slowly drain of colour. One of his pale blue eyes began to twitch and his hands began to clench and unclench into fists.

'Well, well, Peter,' he said, but his voice was no longer sanely controlled. It shook with an approaching storm. 'This puts a different – how shall we say? – aspect on things.'

I heard a knock and the door was pushed slowly open.

Kennet took a step sideways towards Henderson and Mary, the company cleaner, appeared in the doorway.

'Oh, I'm very sorry, Mr Stoneway,' she said, her hands wringing together with uncurbed nervous energy. She looked at Kennet and Henderson and then at me. 'I didn't realise you had a meeting. I only came in to ask if you wanted some more coffee. I'm so sorry.'

I saw my chance, dropped back into the swivel chair, placed both feet on the ground in front of me and propelled myself towards Mary. She jumped out of the way and, with another huge shove, I bolted out of Kye's office.

I raced past Ross's desk, through the first fire door and careened into the wall. I shifted my balance left out of the other door and into the shop. I built up speed again, knocking over the mannequin, which crashed to the floor, dislodging its head, and sped right into the warehouse.

I zoomed past the rows of silent containers to the closed shutter at the end and jettisoned the swivel chair. It clattered into a stationary forklift truck and I hit the green 'OPEN' button above Barry Noble's wooden desk.

The shutter began to slowly crank upwards.

I turned to see a red-faced Kennet charging around the corner from the shop and pressed the 'OPEN' button again. The shutter stopped a foot above the ground and I dived underneath, thinking a fat bastard like that would never be able to squeeze through.

I ran to the diesel tank, balanced myself on top of a large ceramic pot which sat amongst the other oversized, outdoor storage items and heaved myself up onto the flat roof of the tank. I jumped over the top of the barbed-wire fence and landed painfully on top of a gorse bush in the wasteland beyond. Fuck me, it hurt, but Henderson's Y-fronts seemed to be made of stern stuff and I didn't think there was any serious damage to the boys.

I bolted up the slope and through the undergrowth until I found the hole in the fence I'd discovered one summer afternoon with Jeff when work had been quiet and we'd been bored shitless washing vans all day. I slipped through into the Redbridge estate and started to run in the vague direction of Fleet Town train station.

I spotted an old curtain hanging on top of a half-full skip, grabbed it and tied it as best as I could round my waist. It stopped me from properly running anymore, but there was nobody following and at least, I thought, to a passing stranger, I'd look more like a run-of-the-mill weirdo rather than a trouser-less perv.

The estate was also known as Poet's Corner and I walked up Chaucer Avenue and into Wordsworth Street, gradually steadying my breathing and pondering my situation. I'd worry about Kye's connection to Henderson later, but for the time being, I realised I was in deep shit.

My mobile phone, keys and wallet were in the pockets of my Levis.

If I managed to avoid any ticket inspectors and jump the barriers at both Fleet Town *and* North Bitton (which was more easily achievable on a Saturday morning, I had to admit), what would be the point? I couldn't go back to the flat; that would be one of the first places they'd check. Walking to Ross's was a possibility, but I'd have to traverse at least a couple of miles along three main roads which Henderson would surely be keeping an eye on. Also, did I really want to get Ross too involved? Kennet had been about to break at least one of my bones before I'd escaped, so what might he do to Ross?

I could try and sweet talk a passing stranger into borrowing their phone, though that would probably prove to be pretty difficult to do while wearing a pair of curtains, but where would that get me? Ten years ago, I used to be pretty good at memorising landline numbers, but nobody ever seemed to answer them anymore and, for the life of me, I could never remember mobile numbers.

Except one, I realised.

Twenty-Five

SARAH

On the corner of Tennyson Close stood Redbridge Stores, a squat, one-storey building which sold newspapers, sweets, tobacco, foodstuffs, alcohol, pornography and other essentials to the local citizens of the estate: a similar establishment to Sanjays but with more barbed wire.

I waited across the road until a man in his thirties came out carrying a loaf of bread and studying his mobile phone.

'Excuse me!' I called, and the man stopped. 'I was wondering if you could help me,' I smiled my most innocent 'I'm OK' smile and started to cross the road, but he walked off rapidly towards Redbridge Towers, two ten-storey blocks of flats known locally as the Gorbals of Fleet Town.

I sat on a wall and waited another half an hour before a pretty girl about Kate's age approached along Wordsworth Street. I caught her eye and smiled sheepishly. She smiled back and walked into the shop.

She's definitely a possibility, I thought. She'd smiled so she must be cool with weirdos and all people her age had mobile phones. I rehearsed my lines and mannerisms until she walked out of the shop carrying a litre of milk and a box of tea bags.

'Excuse me,' I said.

She looked over the road at me, her face suddenly more suspicious than friendly. 'I'm not interested,' she said, and carried on walking.

'Please!' I said, and couldn't hide the desperation in my voice.

She stopped. 'What do you want?'

'I've been mugged,' I told her.

'Go to the Old Bill, then,' she said.

Obvious answer, I thought. I'd have to revert to something more like the truth.

'OK, I haven't been mugged but a couple of badasses are looking for me. They made me take off my trousers but I managed to escape and found these curtains in a skip in John Betjeman Street.'

She folded her arms and I noticed a hard, lived-in edge to her features.

'Look, I work at Stoneways, the removal firm, and live in South—'

'Do you know Trevor Blind?' she interrupted.

'Yeah, course I do.' Things were looking up.

'He's my dad's brother, my uncle.'

'Phone him up and tell him I'm Peter Booth. He'll vouch for me.'

'Last time my dad saw him he was in bed with my mum.'

'Oh,' was all I could come out with.

'Anyway, why don't you phone him?' she asked. 'You can tell him Dad says he'll break both his legs if he ever sees him again.'

'That's the whole point, I can't! My phone was in my trousers and the badasses have got them.'

'You want me to phone the Rozzers then?'

I hesitated. This was an idea but the cop-shop which would be most likely to take the call would be North Bitton and they'd probably just deliver me straight to Henderson.

'They wouldn't help.'

'You mean you don't trust them?'

'No,' I said.

'I understand. Nobody in the Towers trusts them either.' She paused. 'So, what do you want me to do then?'

I realised I couldn't ask her if I could borrow her phone. She'd think I was going to nick it, start yelling and I'd most probably receive a good kicking from the Redbridge Massif. I tried another tact.

'If I tell you a number of a friend of mine, can you ring it for me?'

'Alright, but you stay right where you are.' She pulled out her phone. 'What's the number?'

I told her and she dialled.

'It's ringing. What's your friend's name?'

'Sarah,' I said quietly.

'Who?'

'Sarah!' I shouted.

'Alright! Don't get your curtains in a twist.' She tittered at her own joke.

I waited as she pressed the phone to her ear.

'Answerphone,' the girl told me. 'If I was you, mate, I'd piss off. They don't take kindly to strangers wearing a pair of curtains round here.' She put her phone back in her pocket and began to walk towards the Towers.

I sat back on the wall and put my head in my hands. I decided I'd have to take my chances and walk to Ross's; there were a few alleyways along the route I could easily escape down if need be. I was about to get up when I heard the beginning of Lady Gaga's 'Born This Way'.

The girl stopped walking, pulled out her phone and the frighteningly polished music ceased.

'Hello?' she said into the phone. 'Are you Sarah?' She turned to look at me. 'I've got some bloke here who wants to talk to you.' She listened. 'Just a sec.' She covered up the phone. 'What's your name again?' she called out to me.

'Peter Booth.'

'Peter Booth,' the girl repeated into the phone. 'OK.' She held out her mobile. 'She wants to talk to you.'

I began to walk slowly over the road towards her.

'You ain't gonna nick it, are you?'

'I swear on my kid's life.'

The girl handed me the phone.

'Sarah,' I said.

'What's going on?'

'It's really hard to explain but I'm in serious trouble. Can you come and pick me up?'

'Now?'

'Yes.'

'It's a bit inconvenient.'

'Please.'

The line went quiet.

'Sarah?'

'Where are you?'

I told her, hung up and handed the girl back her mobile.

'I really appreciate this,' I began. 'You don't know wha—'

'Is she coming to pick you up then?'

I said nothing.

'Sarah,' she said.

I was suddenly miles away contemplating ten years of life released in short, stabbing jolts of raw emotion; occasionally love but mostly pain.

'Are you alright?' the girl asked.

'Yes, yes,' I answered.

'So, is she coming to pick you up?'

I nodded.

'My name's Christine,' the girl said.

'Hello, Christine.'

'Is Sarah your girlfriend, then?'

'Was.'

'But you still get on?'

'Sort of.'

A tall Asian man appeared in the shop doorway. He gave me a dirty look and said to the girl, 'Are you alright, Chris?'

'Yeah,' she said, and pointed at me. 'Baz, this is Pete.'

Baz nodded.

'Some heavies took Pete's trousers, but he escaped and they're looking for him.'

'What's he done?' Baz asked.

'I don't know. What have you done, Pete?'

'The top baddy thinks I'm seeing his ex-wife.'

'Who's the baddy then?' Baz asked me directly.

I didn't want to tell them. They might know Henderson and admire him in the same way the East Enders allegedly looked up to the Kray twins back in the '60s.

'Come on, Pete; you can tell us,' Christine prompted. 'The big man round here's Ted Croker. Isn't he, Baz?'

'Suppose so,' Baz replied. 'Bit past it now, mind.'

'Still hard, though.'

'Yeah,' Baz agreed, but the tone of his voice indicated he had doubts.

'You wouldn't mess with him,' Christine said.

'Maybe, maybe not,' Baz told her, and then quickly glanced round the corner behind him in case Ted Croker was listening in.

'So, come on, Pete, tell us who's after you for porking their missus?'

'Language,' I couldn't help saying.

'I agree, mate,' said Baz. 'My kids don't swear like that.'

Christine blushed slightly. 'Alright, sorry. But come on, tell us? We might be able to sort him out. Mightn't we, Baz?'

Baz shrugged.

I decided to go for it. 'OK. The bloke who's after me is called Ray Henderson.'

'I've got some pricing to do,' Baz said, and disappeared into the shop.

Christine was looking at me wide-eyed.

'Take it you've heard of him then?' I asked her.

'Course I have,' she replied. 'He's a real headcase – different league to old Croker.' She pulled out her mobile phone, checked it and put it back in her pocket. 'I've got to go,' she said, 'but you watch yourself, Pete. If Ray Henderson gets hold of you, you can kiss your Lionel Ritchie goodbye.' She gave me a wave and strode off towards the Towers.

Sarah arrived ten minutes later in her silver blue VW Golf and I got in.

She eyed the curtains. 'Put your seatbelt on and pull yourself together.'

'Did you just make that one up?' I said. 'It's so funny, I think my sides are going to split.'

She looked at me with granite eyes. 'Don't push it.'

'Sorry,' I acknowledged, and settled back in the seat. 'I do appreciate this, you know.'

'I should bloody well hope so.' Sarah pulled out a tissue from where an ashtray used to be and wiped at a spot on the windscreen.

'First of all, where do you want to go?' she asked.

'Can we go back to yours? I'm sure some of my clothes are still there.'

'This isn't some sort of involved scheme to worm your way back into my life again?'

'Hang on a minute,' I said. 'The other day, you asked me if I wanted to come back.'

'I was having a weak moment.'

We drove down Wordsworth Street and turned into Dryden Road. 'Why can't you go back to your place, then?' Sarah asked.

'I'm in trouble; people are after me.'

'Who?'

'Have you ever heard of Ray Henderson?'

'The snooker player?'

'No,' I said. 'He's a nasty bastard who wants to chop off my Lionel Ritchie.'

'Your what?'

'My archbishop.'

'What are you on about?'

'OK: my willy.'

'Crikey. How have you upset him, then?'

'He thinks I'm bonking his ex-wife.'

These last words hung in the air and Sarah was quiet until we reached the A3.

'Are you?' she eventually asked.

'How's your builder boyfriend?'

She said nothing and indicated to move over to the outside lane.

'OK, I shouldn't have asked that,' she said.

'Likewise,' I replied.

'But why did you ring me instead of "her" or one of your other mates?'

'Because my phone's in my trousers which are currently under Kye Stoneway's desk and yours was the only number I could remember off by heart.'

'The plot thickens, but I'm quite flattered my number was the only one you could remember.' She looked at me and I detected the glimmer of a smile.

It was strange going back to the flat. I hadn't been there for six weeks and it seemed smaller than I remembered it. The furniture in the lounge was exactly the same and Sarah hadn't decorated, although there was a space on the wall where my Van Gogh print had hung.

She told me any clothes I'd left would be in the wardrobe in the spare bedroom and for me to go in and help myself while she made coffee.

I purposefully closed the door to the lounge behind me and had a quick peek in the main bedroom. It looked the same but a touch more feminine which pleased me. *No sign of a cohabitating male*, I thought and then realised my eye was still green. Maybe not jealousy, I reasoned: more likely, vanity.

I found an old pair of jeans in the spare bedroom which no longer had a bed in it because it was in my flat, put them on and walked back into the lounge.

We drank our coffee, me sat on the armchair and Sarah on the sofa, I noticed we were both perched forward rather than sat back as though our presence together again in this flat was uncomfortable. Conversation was also strained; we knew each other too well to pretend. Too many bad words had passed between us which would never be forgotten.

Eventually, she asked me what I was going to do and I told her I really didn't know.

'Was your wallet in your trousers?' she asked.

I nodded.

'Well, first of all, you need to get your trousers back.'

'Yes, but how? Kye won't be there and I'd need a key to get in and the code to disarm the alarm – neither of which I possess. Also, how do I know my strides will still be there? They might have chucked them, got rid of the evidence, as it were.'

'Tell me exactly what happened in Kye's office,' Sarah said.

I told her and she made me go over it again.

When I'd finished, she sipped her coffee said, 'I would think, after you'd got out of there, they would have panicked. You said you threw the trousers under Kye's desk. I'm betting they're still there.'

Sarah left school with six GSCEs and got a minor desk job for the local council. Over the years, she'd watched many better qualified but less able minds rise above her, but she stayed patient and slowly and painstakingly climbed the ladder. She was now chief procurement officer for Surrey County Council, commanding a salary of £45,000 plus a year. She was a very astute lady and, despite our many differences, I'd always respected her intelligence.

'Is there anybody else who you trust who's got a key and knows the code for the alarm?' she asked.

Yes: Daz, Barry and Trevor Blind, I thought, but their mobile numbers were on my phone. I had a vague idea where they lived, but did I really trust them fully not to phone Kye and tell him what I was up to? Not because I thought they were in cohorts with whatever conspiracy was unfolding, but by informing Kye, they'd be earning kudos. Kye was renowned for rewarding grasses and I'd worked at Stoneways long enough to realise these three were susceptible to gaining brownie points. All innocently and even playfully done but, at this point in time, extremely dangerous to my physical well-being. *Too big a risk to take*, I thought.

'Nobody I fully trust,' I said.

Sarah looked at me over the top of her coffee mug. 'What about Ross?'

I detected the familiar edge and hesitated before I spoke again. 'Yes, she would have the key and the code, but her numbers on my phone.'

'I've got her number.'

I decided to be frank. 'But you don't like her.'

Sarah sighed and put her mug down on the coffee table. 'It's not that I don't like her; I think she's a good woman. It's just...'

'It's just what?'

'I suppose I was jealous of her. You always seemed to get on far better with her than you ever did with me.'

'She's like a sister to me.'

'I know,' Sarah said. She pulled out her phone, pressed a couple of buttons and put it to her ear. 'It's ringing,' she said, and handed me the phone.

Ross answered. 'Sarah?' Her voice was unsure.

'No, it's me,' I said. 'I'm round Sarah's and she's leant me her phone.'

'Oh.' Ross paused. 'Are you back together?'

I glanced at Sarah, but she looked away.

'No,' I said. 'Look, Ross; I need you to do me a huge favour.'

'Here we go.'

'Please. This is really important.'

Ross was quiet. 'OK, fire away,' she said at last.

Sarah made us both a sandwich and we sat in the kitchen together. She asked me how Kate was and I said I saw her last Sunday. Sadly,

Kate had been another obstacle in our relationship. Sarah was a career lady, not a children person. Kate wanted love and Sarah had never properly given her any. She was never nasty but there was always an atmosphere when Kate stayed over.

I watched Sarah wash the dishes. She was tall, blonde and graceful, and I still felt something for her. What, I didn't quite know. Not necessarily love, but perhaps an affection or nostalgia for somebody I had loved and whom I'd known intimately for a very long time.

I got up and moved towards her. She turned and I put my arms round her. She stiffened at first but then hugged me back and rested her chin on my shoulder. We stayed like that for a couple of minutes before she gently pushed me away.

'Thank you for helping me,' I told her softly.

She smiled a sad smile and wiped a tear from her eye.

Her phone rang and she handed it to me.

'Ross,' I said.

'Bingo! Got your trousers.'

'Under the desk?'

'Tangled up in the wires of Kye's computer.'

'Are my wallet and phone in the pockets?'

'Affirmative.'

'Are you still there?'

'Just leaving.'

'No Kye?'

'Nobody, but there's a funny smell of disinfectant in the air.'

'Mary the cleaning lady's been in,' I said.

'No, not a normal cleaning smell. More overpowering than that. Like a hospital.' Ross paused, gathering her words. 'Almost as if somebody's very recently died in here.'

Twenty-Six

THE FIRE

A car horn beeped outside.

Sarah looked through the curtains in the lounge and said to me, 'It's Ross. Please tell her to come in.'

Her car was parked by the path leading to the flats. Ross lowered her window and held up my trousers.

'Thanks,' I said, 'but Sarah asked if you could come in.'

Ross made a face.

'Please,' I said.

I led her into the flat and Ross stood in the doorway. Sarah walked up and hugged her. Ross hugged her back.

'I'm sorry,' I heard Sarah say.

'And me.'

They sat down on the sofa next to each other and Ross handed me my trousers: phone, keys and wallet intact.

'You're not going to check your wallet, are you?' they both asked, and smiled at each other.

Sarah made me sit on the armchair and tell Ross what happened in Kye's office and then Ross made me tell Sarah about the 'deal' with Henderson and the porn film.

My throat felt dry when I'd finished and I walked into the kitchen to get a glass of water.

I heard a low murmur of voices in the lounge, but they stopped mid-sentence when I came back in. Both girls looked at me.

'What?' I asked.

Sarah got up and perched herself on the arm of the armchair. At first, I didn't understand this movement but then realised it was intended to make me feel surrounded.

'Where are you going to stay?' Ross asked.

'I'll have to go back to my flat.'

'Don't be silly. That's the first place they'll look. Emily's, the same.'

'Is that her name?' Sarah asked Ross.

'He hasn't told you?'

'He's insinuated he's seeing this gangster's ex-moll but hasn't disclosed any other details. What's she look like?'

'Alright, I suppose,' Ross answered tactfully.

'Big boobs?'

'They come in two minutes before she does,' Ross said, and they both laughed.

I shrugged. 'I've no choice.'

'You can stay here,' Sarah said.

'Or at mine.'

'But you'll have to sleep on the sofa,' they both said at the same time, and laughed again.

They've gotten on better in the last five minutes than they have in the last ten years, I thought.

'Look, I really appreciate this, but these people are dangerous. I don't want either of you to get involved.'

'They don't know where either of us live, Pete,' Sarah said.

'People like that can find out.'

'I don't care, the offer's still there.'

'Likewise.'

I was genuinely touched. 'OK, thank you, both of you, but I've still got to go back to my flat to pick up some clothes and stuff.'

'No Hawkwind CDs,' Sarah said.

'No CDs, full-stop,' Ross added.

'Oh, come on, that's not fair.'

'Oh, shit, I've just thought of something,' said Sarah.

'What?'

'Can you put him up tonight?'

I caught Ross mouthing something and Sarah nodding back.

'No problem,' Ross said.

Builder boyfriend, I thought.

Ross said she'd take me back to my flat and then we'd go back to hers. I asked her if she minded waiting in the car for a moment and she nodded. That was the beauty with Ross – she understood certain things and asked no questions.

I walked back in and hugged Sarah and thanked her again.

She told me she and Ross were planning to get together for a drink after all this had been ironed out and I said I was glad. She also told me to only stay two nights with Ross at a time. Not because she was jealous but because she thought I'd drive her up the wall.

I told her I'd see her on Monday night and kissed her goodbye.

In the car, I asked Ross about the smell in Kye's office.

'For the last two years of my mum's life, she lived with my sister,' she said. 'Mum's MS gradually got so bad, Becky converted the lounge into her bedroom. When she finally died, my sis had the whole room professionally fumigated. Kye's office smelt like that – as though somebody had just died in there.'

An idea struck me. 'Do the CCTV cameras cover his office?'

'They cover the whole building.'

'Do you know how to rewind them?'

Ross looked at me. 'You're not much of a detective, are you?'

'What do you mean?'

'Do you really think Henderson and co would have left the

camera on in Kye's office while they gave you a good kicking? I don't think they'd be that thick.'

'You mean you can turn them off?'

'Yes, or tamper with them.'

'Maybe they didn't think the building had any CCTV?'

'Can you please stop being so stupid?'

'Sorry, just an idea.'

We pulled up outside the house in Langley Avenue. It was a typically quiet Saturday afternoon and the street was deserted save for a couple of lonely kids roller-skating back and forth along the pavement.

'Any unusual cars you can see?' Ross asked.

I searched for the black Mercedes E-Class but there was no sign. Everything appeared as usual. 'No, it looks OK,' I said, and got out of the car.

'Be careful,' Ross called out softly.

'I can hear the music,' I told her, and walked up to the main door.

I peered through the letterbox and made out the door of my flat. It was shut and I couldn't detect any shadows of a very large man nor a very lean one.

I unlocked the door, flung it wide open and crouched back in the small porch. The door hit the side wall and flew back, slamming shut. *There goes my element of surprise*, I thought, and unlocked it again.

The hallway was empty and nobody I knew was small enough to hide in the fake grandfather clock by the stairs nor skinny enough to hide behind it.

I scanned my flat door. There was no sign of forced entry, but what about the locksmith who was here in the week? Even Baz and Christine knew who Henderson was so there was no reason not to believe that the locksmith could also know him and be part of his network.

They could be in there now waiting: Henderson sitting on the bed, Kennet on the toilet seat.

I heard a door open above me and turned to see Shayan standing at the top of the stairs.

'Peter,' he said. 'I need talk to you.'

'What's wrong?' I asked.

'Come up to our home.'

I hesitated. Were the dastardly duo in their flat waiting for me or did Shayan and Faezeh want me to join them for a threesome?

'Please,' Shayan said, and I saw tears in his eyes.

Their flat was a similar layout to mine but at least three times bigger. The bathroom door to my left was open and I saw an actual bath with a curtain rail as well as a toilet and basin. The main living area contained a double bed, sofa and armchair. Colourful prints of the Middle East, leafy houseplants and the view of St Mark's Church through the sash window, misty in the low afternoon sun, combined to give the whole room a touch of ambience.

On the bed lay Faezeh, her head propped up by two pillows. Her cheeks were puffy and swollen, one eye horribly blackened and her pretty nose red and splattered to one side. Her one good eye looked at me, but there was no sparkle, just a glint of recognition, and perhaps, I imagined, accusation.

I stood stupidly at the end of the bed. Shayan's voice behind me was low and unsteady.

'An hour ago, there was knocking on the main door. Loud, not stopping. I went downstairs to open it and there were two men; one was very big. They said they wanted to see you. I didn't like them and I said you were out. The big man pushed past me. I argued, said I would call the police. Faezeh heard and came downstairs also. The big man grabbed me by the throat and Faezeh started hitting him on his arm.'

Shayan stopped talking and I stared into Faezeh's one eye.

'The man punched her,' Shayan said, 'and now she like this.'

Something snapped inside me. I felt it as clearly as if a pair of shears had cut off my soul.

'She has to go to the hospital,' I said.

'We have no money for such things.'

'Shayan, this is England. Medical things are free here.'

'Not for us, Peter; we are foreign.'

'Oh, bollocks!' I said. 'I'll pay for it!'

'Peter, please; not loud, please. We need peace.'

'I'm sorry,' I stammered.

'I will stay with her and nurse her. She's strong. Then, when she is better, I go and find this man and kill him.'

I walked out to the car, blood pounding around my head, and got in.

'Where are your things?' Ross asked.

'I can't stay with you,' I said. 'Nor Sarah.'

'What's happened?'

'I can't talk about it, but I need to sort this thing out *now*.'

'You're shaking.'

'Go home, Ross. I'll ring you later.' I got back out of the car.

'Peter!'

'Please! Things have gone to another level. If I stay with you, you'll be a target and I can't let that happen.'

I began to walk up the road but stopped and turned to look at her. 'I love you, by the way.'

'Oh, sod off,' she said, but she smiled.

The Squat and Kilo was my destination, but I decided to take the back streets rather than walk down the Broadway. A battered-up Ford Cortina pulled up beside me on Lily Street. The driver wore shades and a woolly hat: Paranoid Ian. *At last,* I thought, *somebody smaller than me I can beat the fuck out of.*

I checked no one was sitting in the back and sprinted round to the driver's door. Before I could reach the door handle, Ian drove down the road another hundred yards and stopped. I realised it was no use me trying to chase him and, also, that I'd reacted from anger rather than reason. I had to think logically, lucidly, like Sarah would.

Ian got out of the car. 'Kilo's sent me to pick you up,' he called over to me, nervously.

'Not Henderson?' I called back.

'No, I swear.'

Ian could have weighed no more than ten stone, at least two and a half stone lighter than me, and had never been renowned for his fighting ability. I decided to chance it and walked up to the Cortina.

I was five yards away when Ian held up a hand to stop me. I stopped.

'I thought I'd better let you know,' he said, 'I had my six-monthly assessment last week. The doc takes my blood pressure and checks my heartbeat and a psychiatrist asks me a few questions. They've upped the head-med and told me I'm not only a schizophrenic but also a manic depressive with suicidal tendencies.'

'So?' I shrugged.

'If you start any funny stuff while I'm driving you to Kilo's, I'll accelerate straight into a wall or an oncoming truck.'

'I'll sit still and put my seatbelt on.'

The last time I saw Ian smile must have been when he was six. He definitely wasn't smiling now and backed away from the car to the pavement on the other side of the road as I got into the passenger seat.

I leant over and called through the driver's open window, 'Ian, I can't drive, so if you stay there, we won't be going anywhere.'

Ian looked up and down the deserted street twice before cautiously approaching the car. He stopped at the driver's door and said, 'Definitely, no funny stuff because I don't mind killing myself.'

'I promise.'

He got in and we both put on our seatbelts.

We drove down the Broadway at just under twenty miles an hour. If I'd tried to assault Ian and he'd driven into a wall, I think it would have hurt less than being kicked in the shins by a passing sparrow.

We stopped at the pedestrian crossing outside Sainsbury's, although there were no pedestrian crossing and I tried to make small talk.

'How's your brother?'

'Why?'

'Just asking.'

A car beeped us from behind and Ian drove on, a touch slower than before.

'How often do you have to take your pills?' I asked.

'I don't.'

'Why do you go bother going to the docs then?'

'I don't want to talk about it.'

We finally arrived at the Squat and Ian pulled up outside the West Wing.

We got out of the car and walked through the gate to the front door, me in front, Ian lagging a few steps behind.

I made to press the doorbell and Ian hollered, 'No! I don't like the voices!'

'How's Kilo going to know we're here, then?'

Ian thought for a moment. 'I'll phone him,' he said, and quickly walked back to the car. He opened the boot and pulled out an old Motorola which he carefully strapped around his shoulders. The phone was an antique, one of the original mobiles that must have dated back to the early 1990s. Ian punched in a number and every button he pressed emitted a piercing, beeping noise. He waited nervously and although the temperature could have only been a few degrees above freezing, I noticed several beads of sweat appear on his forehead.

The dialling tone was as loud as a foghorn, but Ian still had to tell me it was ringing. There was a touch of awesome feedback which reminded me of the intro to 'I Want to Be Your Dog' by The Stooges and Ian dropped the receiver.

The front door opened and Kilo appeared. He wore a pair of black jeans and a black T-shirt which read, 'THOU SHALL NOT KILL.' His feet were bare.

'Come in,' he said.

We sat in the lounge again: this time, myself on the sofa, Kilo on the armchair and Ian standing, looking out through the French windows.

I told Kilo about what happened in Kye's office.

Kilo laughed. 'He has his own Y-fronts initialled?'

I nodded and decided to be direct. 'What's the connection with Kye Stoneway?' I asked.

Kilo sighed and addressed me. 'It was to do with the old man, Arthur Stoneway. Henderson had been sniffing around your old yard for years and made a couple of offers to buy the land, but Arthur didn't like him. Not because Henderson was a man of shady repute – that didn't bother Arthur. He'd been no angel himself and, over the years, he'd done more to a few people's toes than merely trodden on them, but he didn't like Henderson's *style*. Arthur had certain morals, Henderson didn't, but he underestimated old Stoneway and threatened him. Story has it, Arthur twatted him and chased him off the land with a shovel.'

'Pitchfork, I was told.'

'Whatever, but Henderson's pride had been pricked and his rep damaged. He wanted revenge, but he was wary of Arthur, scared of him. When Kye took over the business, Henderson sidled up to him and secured the extra money Kye needed to buy the warehouse in Fleet Town. The interest was low but there was one condition: make sure Arthur comes to a sticky end.'

'He was committed.'

'Sticky enough, I'd have said.'

'But he'd gone mad.'

'How do you know that?'

I told Kilo about the missing van keys and the furniture stacked up in the restroom.

'Did anybody see him do these things?'

'Well, no, but it was obvious.'

'Was it?'

I couldn't answer that. I thought back to my dealings with Arthur. There hadn't been many and they'd all been years ago. Yes, he'd been a boring old sod and a bit mad, but not many people I'd ever met could be classified as completely sane.

'But Kye told me only the other day that he was causing havoc in the nut house he's in.'

'Who told you?' Kilo asked softly.

I didn't reply.

'Henderson's got a hold over your boss,' Kilo said. 'When you told Kye about the porn film, he told Henderson. From what you've told me, mind, you have to give your boss his due – he didn't want you to get hurt. It wasn't his fault that you're dumb enough to bang Henderson's ex-wife.' Kilo took a handful of nuts from a bowl on the coffee table and popped them in his mouth. He wiped his hands together and asked, 'How is Emily, by the way?'

I was immediately defensive. 'You leave her out of this.'

Kilo held his hands up. 'I was only asking. She's a nice girl – just fell in love with an arsehole.'

Fell in love?

'OK, but can we not talk about her?' I said.

'Fine.'

I remembered the smell in the office. 'Would there be any reason for Henderson to murder Kye?'

'Murder him?'

'Yeah.'

'Why do you ask that?'

I told him what Ross had said.

'Sounds like ammonia, which *is* used to cover up the smell of death.' Kilo thought for a moment and then shook his head. 'No, I can't see any reason why he'd want to kill Kye. This is South Bitton, Pete, not the Bronx. I'm not saying Henderson or Kennet's not capable of it, but murder attracts unnecessary attention – something Henderson wouldn't want so, no, I don't think he'd kill Kye Stoneway.'

'I know that name,' Ian suddenly piped up from the French windows. 'Stoneways: a removal company. I've got to do a job for them.'

'What sort of job?' I asked.

'Why are you asking?'

'For fuck's sake, Ian, just answer the bloody question.'

Kilo interrupted. 'Ian works for a machine-hire company in North Bitton. He drives a hi-ab. Stoneways obviously want him to move something heavy. Is that right, Ian?'

'Might be.'

'A body?' I asked out loud.

'Earth calling Peter, can we come back to reality, please?' Kilo said.

'Sorry.'

'Do you want a pill?'

'I thought you only dealt in kilos?'

'Think of it like when you go in one of the posher supermarkets like Waitrose or Marks and Spencer and a couple of smart-dressed smilers offer you a nibble of some cheese you've never heard of.'

'A taster?'

'Exactly.'

'Thanks, but no thanks.'

'Joint?'

I shook my head.

'Beer?'

'I wouldn't say no.'

'Ian, get Pete a beer from the fridge.'

Ian walked out the room.

We watched him go and Kilo said, 'Before you ask, Ian's a decent guy: odd, maybe, but OK. Better than a lot of people I know.' He leant forward. 'Now, tell me why you're so angry.'

I told him about the Iranian neighbours and Kennet hitting Faezeh.

Kilo sat back. 'Nice bloke, Dave Kennet.'

Ian came back in and handed me an ice-cold can of Kronenberg. I cracked it open and took a long swig. 'Cheers,' I said. 'You two not having one?'

'Ian's got some driving to do and the juice isn't my bag.'

'Fair enough.' I took another drink. 'Now, it's your turn. What's your gripe with Henderson?'

Kilo stood up and walked towards the door we'd come through. He stopped, pulled off his T-shirt and turned round to face me. A birthmark stretched from just below his neck to the waistband of his jeans, covering most of the left side of his torso. Except it wasn't a birth mark; the wound was too raw, the colouring too lurid.

'It ends here,' Kilo said, and leant down and fingered a bright red splash just visible at the top of his bare left foot.

'Five years ago, I was living in a squat in Pulham Park. There were some Angels living there, mad fuckers but coded. Played hard and tipped the scales occasionally but could distinguish the Bad from the Real Bad. They liked their speed, their blow, their women and their wine.

'They came back late one night, a couple of them bruised and bloody but in high spirits. They told me they'd had hassle in a pub in North Bitton – landlord and a couple of heavies got arsey with them and they trashed the place. In their eyes, it was a battle won and they spent the next forty-eight hours partying, they and their women. Didn't bother me, I made a killing supplying with them bombers and whizz and, besides, they were good boys.

'On the third night, we all slept and somebody torched the place. Only me, the Hedgehog Eater and Crazy Jane got out; the rest of them died in the flames. The docs told me the burns caused my cancer. Terminal, they say.'

I stared at the mark on his chest, saw the curling of the flesh and the minute yellows, whites and blues amongst the red.

Kilo walked over to a bookcase, picked up a framed photograph and held it up. A pretty, wild-haired girl with a ring through her nose and gap between her front teeth smiled out at me. 'Crazy Jane,' he said. 'She died two years ago. Never was the same after the fire.'

He put the picture back and said, 'I've got my troops lined up.'

'Troops?'

'You'll find out,' Kilo said, and I saw a gleam in his eyes that unnerved me.

'Where do I come into all this?' I asked.

'Have you ever been fishing, Peter?'

'A few times. Why?'

Paranoid Ian turned to look at me.

'Oh, shit,' I said.

Twenty-Seven

KILO

I sat in the back, Kilo in the passenger seat, Paranoid Ian driving.

We reached the Chinese takeaway by South Bitton Tower just before the A3 roundabout and stopped. Ian turned to Kilo and said, 'It's too scary, man. I just can't do it.'

Kilo undid his seatbelt and got out the car. Ian did the same and they crossed over: Kilo driving, Ian now in the passenger seat.

Kilo gunned the engine and we flew round the corner of the Tower and straight into the middle lane of the roundabout. He overtook a Lamborghini and then cut across to the outside lane and hit the left indicator.

'Cheston?' I called out from the back.

Kilo nearly lost control and I heard the screech of the tyres and the smell of burnt rubber like thunder after lightning. We managed to stay on four wheels and Kilo steered the car through the bowling alley's car park and left down a one-way street.

Halfway along, Kilo pulled over, and he and Ian changed places again.

We trundled on down the road at twenty miles per hour and Kilo turned round to me and said, 'Maybe.'

Cheston was dead as usual. We drove through the high street and headed south, the houses beginning to space out until there was open countryside on one side and the woods I'd got lost in last Sunday morning on the other.

Ian took a right down a dirt track. After two hundred yards, we pulled up by the Mercedes E-Class which sat like the Angel of Death in front of a large, cobble-stone house. All its windows were boarded up, and judging by the length of the grass and weeds surrounding the driveway, the house had been derelict for some time.

'I can't believe I'm trusting you,' I said.

'You'll be fine,' Kilo told me. 'Just act as though you're my prisoner.' He pulled out a sawn-off shotgun from underneath the passenger seat and said, 'Let's go.'

We both got out of the car and Kilo said to Ian, 'You stay here and, if we come out running, get in the passenger seat and I'll drive.'

The front door of the house opened and Henderson stood there in a Crombie overcoat. 'Come in, boys,' he greeted us. 'How very nice to see you both.'

We followed him along a dimly lit corridor and down a staircase, the smell of neglect and decay far worse than even S&S's storage facilities.

'Touch musty, I must say,' said Henderson, 'but very convenient for our meeting.' He opened another door and we walked into a cellar illuminated by a solitary lightbulb hanging from a dark ceiling.

A wooden chair sat in the middle of the room, Dave Kennet standing in the shadows nearby.

'Please sit down, Peter,' Henderson said, and Kilo prodded me in the back with the gun.

I sat and Henderson slapped me across the face, open-handed. I felt blood drip down the side of my face where one of his rings had cut my cheek.

Kilo stood silently to my right, an inscrutable look on his face.

'Ah, that does make me feel better,' Henderson said. 'I was going to let you off lightly, but you've not only contravened the unwritten wording of our agreement, you've also been fornicating with my ex-wife.'

My fear was waning. I recalled Faezeh's face and the anger was returning. 'She's her own person,' I said.

Henderson slapped me again, this time with his other hand. I rocked back and then leapt at him. Henderson ducked and a huge hand grabbed me round the throat.

Kennet lifted me off the ground and began to squeeze. My arms and legs felt like jelly and a galaxy of white dots flashed in front of my eyes. I was helpless; I couldn't breathe and a blind panic possessed me as I realised I was being strangled to death.

'Leave him!' Kilo shouted, and levelled the shotgun at Kennet.

The monster dropped me and I fell to the floor clasping my throat, trying to breathe like a snared fish squirming on a dry riverbank.

Kennet smiled. 'Come on, Kilo; you brag too much. Everybody knows the story of you and the pop gun at Heathrow. But if you want a row, that's fine by me.'

He took a step forward and Kilo pulled the trigger.

The noise was deafening. Kennet was spun three hundred and sixty degrees, his left arm almost severed from his shattered shoulder. He stared at Kilo in comical surprise and collapsed. He started to slither to the other side of the cellar, making strange, high-pitched, mewling noises; an enormous snail trailing a secretion of blood.

Kilo broke down the shotgun and two empty shells chinked on the stone floor. He pulled two fresh cartridges from his jacket pocket, reloaded and snapped both barrels shut.

'Sorry. mate,' Kilo said cheerfully. 'I was in a bit of a rush when I left home so I must have picked up the wrong gun.' He stood over Kennet and lowered the sawn-off so it was inches from his face. 'But, in case you're missing my little toy, I'd just like to say, "You're terminated, fucker."'

I turned away as the detonation echoed around the cellar. I saw Henderson open the cellar door and run up the stairs.

'He's gone,' I tried to say, but no words would come out of my ragged throat. In my mind's eye, I saw what was left of Kennet's arm and vomited.

Kilo sat patiently on the chair while I retched, the shotgun lying across his lap.

'Finished?' he asked, and handed me a tissue.

I nodded and wiped sickly spittle from my mouth and chin.

'What about Henderson?' I asked in a hoarse whisper.

'We'll catch up with him later, don't worry.'

I looked over at the soles of Kennet's boots. 'Him?'

Kilo stood up and offered me his arm. I took it and he pulled me to my feet.

'Henderson owns this place,' he said. 'He'll get rid of the body, and if he doesn't, who cares? The cops won't give a shit if Kennet goes missing and won't rush to find him. They wouldn't search here anyway. No, some nosy kids, a tramp or some desperate lovers will find him one day, or what's left of him after nature takes hold. There'll be no evidence to incriminate me, and even if there is, I'll be long dead myself by then.' Kilo shrugged. 'Mind you, the forensics might check your chunder for DNA.'

He slapped me playfully on the back. 'Only kidding.'

'Where do you want to go, then?' Kilo asked me as Ian drove us slowly back through Cheston towards the Broadway.

'My flat,' I replied with some discomfort – my throat was still swollen and raw. 'I need to get cleaned up and change my clothes.'

'Sounds good to me. Henderson won't go back there.'

'How can you be so sure?'

Kilo tapped his nose and said, 'Trust me.'

'Do you know where he'll be?'

'I've got a pretty good idea.'

I still didn't fully trust Kilo, but if there was one thing I'd learnt today, I was now more scared of him than I was of Henderson.

Twenty-Eight

THE TROOPS

The flat was the same as I'd left it yesterday morning. Shayan and Faezeh had, at least, managed to prevent the gruesome twosome from entering. I'd have to check up on them later and insist on Shayan taking some money from me for treatment for Faezeh. If I ran short during the month, I could get a small loan from Kye to see me through, but where was Kye, and after what happened this morning, would he ever dare appear at Stoneway's again?

Unless the evidence was removed, the thought hit me, and I realised my life was still in danger.

I showered and changed and put my jeans and Status Quo T-shirt in a Sainsbury's bag. I wanted to burn Henderson's boxers but decided to chuck them in as well.

Where to go now? I thought, and picked up my phone.

Emily answered straightaway.

'Pete, I've been so worried about you,' she said and, I could tell by her voice she'd recently been crying.

'Are you alright?' I asked.

'Ray came round earlier with that monster thug of his.'

'What time?'

'About twelve. He said he was looking for you.' Her voice began to break.

'Emily?'

'Sorry,' she said. 'He was horrible and threatened me. Thank God Charlie had already gone to football. I managed to run into the garden and start screaming. A couple of windows opened and I shouted for someone to phone the police.'

'What happened?'

'Ray told me he'd post me your ears and then he and the other brute left.'

'Any sign of them since?'

'No, Ray won't come back here.'

'How can you be so sure?'

'He won't. Believe me, I know him too well. Besides, I've informed the police.' The line went quiet. 'What's happened, Pete?'

'I'll tell you later.'

'Can you come round?'

I said nothing.

'Where are you? I'll pick you up.'

'OK, I'll come over, but don't pick me up. I'll make my own way.'

'I love you, Pete.'

'Love you too,' I said, and hung up.

It was fully dark and there was a fresh breeze in the air. I wore my long, waterproof coat I bought at a fishing shop when Sarah and I went on holiday to the west coast of Scotland, sunglasses and a woolly hat.

Once again, I took the back streets and chucked the Sainsbury's bag in a dustbin in Bond Road. I ran up and down two alleyways to try and confuse any would-be pursuers until I reached the bus stop at the end of the Broadway outside Blockbuster.

It started to rain but I didn't sit on the bench underneath the plastic shelter – it was too well lit. Instead, I buttoned up the top of my coat and stood in the shadows between Blockbuster and Kissy's, the unisex hairdressers.

Several shoppers hurried by, their faces hidden underneath umbrellas, and I saw a couple of smokers outside the Spoons opposite, standing several feet apart and staring into space. It was early Saturday evening and the Broadway was beginning to close down for the night.

A slender figure appeared at the bus stop wearing a bulky duffel coat which reached down to her knees, where laddered black tights led to tatty slippers. A Number 82 double-decker bus towards Purfleet slowed down in front, the sheeting rain glimmering in the electric lights of the street.

I ran over and stood on the steps of the bus behind the figure as she paid the driver with change from her purse. She wore no hat and her greying hair was matted to her skull by the rain. She finished paying, took her ticket and walked down the aisle to the middle of the bus. I flashed my Oyster card and saw her half-profile as she turned at the stairs.

'Mary!' I called out.

She glanced towards me at the sound of her name. I smiled a friendly smile, but she looked quickly away and hurried up the stairs.

I sat at the back on the lower deck, face almost pressed against the glass of the window, staring out at the passing lights and the wash of the teeming rain.

I got out at the BP garage, sheltered underneath a large oak tree and phoned Emily.

'Where are you?' she asked.

'Five-minute walk away,' I told her. 'You on your own?'

'Yes,' she said.

'OK, I'll see you in a bit.'

I darted along Purfleet Road and left into her estate, ducking my head if any car passed by.

Emily made me take my coat off as soon as I came in. She shook it outside on the front step and hung it up in the hallway.

'You're drenched,' she said. 'Take your shirt and trousers off and come and sit in the lounge.'

I sat on the sofa by the electric fire in my underwear and a long cotton shirt of Emily's.

She brought me in a mug of hot chocolate and sat next to me. 'You've changed your pants,' she observed.

'The last pair I was wearing caused me rather a lot of trouble.'

'Explain.'

I told her about what happened in Kye's office.

She laughed. 'Sorry,' she said, 'but I'd loved to have seen Ray's face.'

'It was quite a picture, believe me.'

'Come on, drink your chocolate; it'll warm you up.'

I put the mug to my lips and smelt something. She said he'd been here at midday; the smell should have gone by now.

I put the mug down and stood up.

'What's the matter?' Emily asked, her voice sounding strained and unnatural.

I followed my nose to the lounge door.

'Please, Peter; sit down. You're scaring me.'

I flung the door open.

Ray Henderson stood there holding up something in one of his hands. I heard a sound similar to a spraying aerosol and suddenly my eyes and face felt like they were on fire. I staggered backwards and somebody grabbed me round the head and forced one of my arms up painfully between my shoulder blades. My eyes were still burning and I couldn't see, but I knew it was Henderson's ringed fist that uppercutted me in the groin.

I hit the deck, tears stinging my blinded eyes, dark nausea crawling up into my guts. A heavy form sat on my back and my hands were forced behind me. Cold steel wrapped around my wrists and tightened with a click. Handcuffs.

I managed to lift my chin up from the carpet.

'Was that my treat!' I shouted as loudly as I could.

I heard Henderson's monotone from a distance. 'It would have been far easier if you'd have drunk your hot chocolate, Peter. Emily drugged it, you know.' His voice came closer. 'You would have woken up two hours from now exactly where I wanted you to be.'

The voice moved away. 'The man currently sitting on top of you is called Dominic. Please say hello to Peter, Dominic.'

A hand whacked me across the top of my head.

I wanted to say 'fuck off' but was scared the bile might come up and I'd need to vomit.

The weight shifted off my back and I lifted my head to breathe freely again. My eyes were clearing and I could make out the colours in the carpet.

Henderson was talking. 'The late Mr Kennet was a wonderful help to me in my business, but he's gone now. He will be missed, but he is only one. Dominic, here, is one of many others.' Henderson's voice came closer until I felt his breath on my ear. 'Paul took me by surprise this afternoon. It won't happen again. Besides, the next time we meet, he'll only have the schizo to help him.' He paused. 'You, of course, will be long gone. Pick him up, Dominic, and we'll escort him to the car.'

Strong arms lifted me to my knees. My vision had fully returned, and Emily and Charlie's faces smiled at me from their frames on top of the sideboard.

I stood up, tensed my neck muscles and snapped my head sharply backwards. It hit flesh and bone, and I heard a yelp behind me. I spun round and confronted Dominic for the first time. He was holding his nose between two gnarled hands, blood seeping through his fingers. He was bigger than me but not as big as the late Kennet, and I kicked him as hard as I could in the bollocks. It hurt my shoe-less toes, but it appeared to hurt Dominic more and he roared in pain like a bull-elephant with a hard-on whose potential mate had just given him the slip.

I ran to the front door, balanced my foot on the door handle and shoved. The door sprung open and I ran out into the night.

A dark figure caught hold of me and shoved me into the passenger seat of an idling car. I didn't struggle; I could smell the petunia oil on Kilo's leather jacket.

Two sets of powerful headlights lit up Emily's front door, catching the pursuing Henderson and Dominic in their glare like two guilty schoolchildren. Dominic ran off right and wasn't followed. Henderson tried the same but was immediately pounced upon by dark figures.

He struggled but to no avail, and I watched as he was carried past me by two men in dark overcoats, hats pulled low, Henderson's saturnine face bleeding. The boot of the car opened behind me and a sudden weight caused the back of the vehicle to sink down.

The boot slammed shut and the two men hurriedly climbed into the front of a Mitsubishi Shogun parked to our left.

A small figure appeared in the house's doorway: Emily. She was crying and her hair looked wilder than I'd ever seen it before. Both sets of headlights cut out.

It was the last time I ever saw her.

Kilo jumped in the back behind me and the car reversed back into the road and we began to drive out of the estate, the Shogun following.

The spaciousness of the car, the sweet smell of the leather upholstery and the myriad softly glowing lights of the dashboard signified comfort and wealth.

'Are you alright, Peter?' Kilo asked from the back seat.

'I think so,' I replied. 'A bit cold maybe.'

'I'll turn the heating up,' the driver said in a soft, refined accent with a hint of the deep American south. 'Don't think we've met,' he added, and held out his left hand.

I was still too wary to accept it, and the man smiled at me and withdrew his hand. He was middle-aged, greying, good-looking and smelt expensive.

'I understand, but you're safe with me,' he said. 'In fact, I'm very obliged to you for not planting that unfortunate film amongst my ex-wife's possessions. Aaron Carlberg's the name and I'm extremely pleased to meet you.'

I shook my handcuffed hands at him.

'We'll sort those out before we drop you off,' he said. 'The other two gentleman in the Mitsubishi are "hired help" but completely trustworthy.' He looked in the mirror at the top of the windscreen. 'Now, Kilo, are you going to introduce our other passenger?'

I turned round to look in the back seat. A thin pale man with an eye patch sat next to Kilo. He nodded and I realised I was staring into the wan face of Jeff Unsworth's brother.

'The troops?' I said to Kilo.

'In one,' he replied.

Twenty-Nine

THREE WEEKS LATER

Besides the hoover, the last thing left in the flat was the Pack3. A lonesome sock dislodged itself from underneath one of the flaps and fell to the bottom as I picked up the box.

Kate was dragging a duster back and forth over the windowsill. 'Hasn't your new girlfriend got a laundry basket of her own?'

'I'm sure she has, but as I keep telling you, I've got to completely empty the flat or else I won't get back my deposit.'

'I've cleaned the bathroom.'

'Thank you. This room needs a quick hoover and we'll be off.'

'What about that?' Kate pointed her duster at the still-visible wine stain on the carpet. The salt theory hadn't quite worked and the stain brought back memories of my one and only night spent here with Emily.

'What is it?' Kate asked.

'Never you mind.'

'Is it blood?'

'No.'

Steve Woodgit appeared in the doorway and took the Pack3 off me. 'Is that it?'

'Just the hoover,' I told him. 'Can you give me five minutes to have a final clean round?'

'Yeah. Can I have a walk in the garden?'

'Of course,' I said.

It was the Saturday morning before Christmas and Daz had lent me the Sprinter free of charge. I'd asked Steve to help and told him I'd bung him £50 when we'd finished. I'd also told him Kate wanted to be involved, so I knew his visit to the communal garden hadn't sprung from any sudden horticultural interest.

I plugged in the Henry and began sucking up the cobwebs which hung from the walls where the furniture used to be.

Kate stood looking out the window. 'Wow, that's a big cigarette Steve's smoking. Is it a reefer?'

'What's a reefer?' I asked over the noise of the Henry.

'Those things you used to smoke when I was younger.'

'They were cigars.'

'I'm not stupid, Dad.'

'Alright, but I don't want you touching anything like that.'

'Lots of people at school do.'

'Well, they shouldn't.' I fitted the extension onto the nozzle and began to hoover the carpet.

Kate turned away from the window. 'Don't worry, Dad; I don't like the smell and, one day, Karen Myres gave me a puff on a normal fag and it tasted horrible and nearly made me throw up. Besides, the kids who smoke that weed stuff are really stupid. They giggle and say, "Cool," and, "Man," and generally act like right prats. They listen to really shit music as well; full of bleeps and weird noises that go on forever with some dork saying, "Groove and live," or some other rubbish every ten seconds.' She opened the door of the wardrobe for me. 'Bit like the crap you like.'

There was a knock on the flat door and I switched off the hoover.

'Come in,' Kate announced in her deepest thespian voice.

It was Shayan and Faezeh. They were holding hands and smiling.

Faezeh had almost fully recovered from her wounds, although the bad eye still didn't fully open and was streaked by the violent red of a blood clot.

On the Sunday, after the final showdown with Henderson, I'd knocked on their door and insisted Shayan take the £200 I offered him to get her proper treatment. He refused and I threw it on the bed and ran out. That evening, an envelope with the £200 in it was slid underneath my door.

I slid the envelope back underneath their door on the Monday night only for it to reappear, untouched, underneath my door an hour later. This time it contained a handwritten message: *Take back money or Hawkwind CDs get it!*

'We miss you gone,' Faezeh said. 'You ring us please and we go bollox?' She handed me a slip of paper with a number written on it.

I smiled. 'Of course. You've been really nice neighbours and I'm so sorry about what happened.'

'You find these men?' Shayan asked, his voice cold.

'Yes,' I said. 'Me and the troops.'

Shayan put the edge of his hand against his throat and slid it across.

I patted him on the shoulder. 'You won't ever see them again.'

'I hope they are in Duzakh.'

'Is that a place in Iran?'

Faezeh smiled. 'Yes,' she said, 'bad place in Persia.'

'Like Southend-on-Sea?'

I don't think either of them had ever heard of Southend-on-Sea but they laughed anyway. We had a group hug in the hallway and they made me promise I'd ring.

Kate sat in the middle of the cab between us. 'Have you met Dad's girlfriend yet?' she asked Steve.

'Yeah.'

'What's she like?'

Steve seemed to take an inordinately long time to answer, so I had to say something.

'Come on, Steve; tell my daughter what you think of my new bird.'

'"Bird". I don't like that word,' Kate interrupted. 'We're women.'

'Alright, my new "woman".'

'Have I met her?' Steve asked.

'Yes!'

'Oh yeah, her.'

'What's she like, then?' Kate almost shouted.

'Reasonable.'

'Reasonable?' I repeated.

'Have you got a girlfriend, Steve?' Kate asked.

'Yeah.'

'What's she like?'

Steve's girlfriend was an actress who'd been on stage and had had bit parts in *EastEnders* and *Holby City*. She was quietly spoken and absolutely stunning to look at. Maurice always said her relationship with Steve was the Eighth Wonder of the Modern World.

Steve took another age to reply. 'She's OK,' he finally said.

Aaron Carlberg and crew had dropped me off outside my flat with their captive still in the boot.

The Mercedes E-Class was found parked on a side road a hundred yards from Emily's maisonette. Henderson's drowned corpse was found a few days later, eighty miles away at St Margaret's Bay near Dover.

The police statement read: *'There were no suspicious circumstances. Mr Henderson suffered from coronary problems and had been undergoing treatment for clinical depression.'*

The body was released two weeks later and the funeral held at North Bitton Crematorium. Kilo, Jeff and Jeff's brother, Dan, attended. Jeff told me the crematorium was nearly full, a dozen or so people who were related or worked for Henderson and fifty others like themselves, who just wanted to make sure his coffin burnt.

Emily and Charlie weren't present.

It was December the 21ˢᵗ, the winter solstice, and a thickly clouded sky hung over the half-hearted Christmas decorations of the Broadway.

'I never really got on with Sarah, did I, Dad?'

'Sadly not,' I answered.

'Did you ever meet her?' Kate asked Steve.

'Yeah.'

'Did you like her?'

'Yeah.'

'Do you always answer "yeah" to everything?'

'No,' Steve said.

Kate laughed. 'I mean, she was alright,' she continued. 'Not bad-looking and all that, but she was a bit…'

'A bit what?' I asked.

'I don't know, priggy.'

'Priggy? What does that mean?'

'Like a library person: priggy.'

'She always asks after you when I talk to her.'

'Does she?'

'Yes, so try and be nice to her when you see her.'

Kate put her hand to her mouth. 'Oh my God. Are you going back out with her?'

'You'll have to wait and find out,' I said.

Kate gave me a hug. 'I wouldn't mind if you did go back with her, Dad.'

'You honestly wouldn't mind?'

'No.'

'But would you be nice to her?'

'Yeah, promise.' She turned to Steve. 'Sarah's loaded; she always used to give me £50 on my birthday and at Christmas.'

'Nice,' Steve commented.

'Hang on a minute,' Kate said. 'You're not allowed to drive if you've been smoking that funny stuff. The police could arrest you.'

'How would they know I've been smoking it?' Steve asked her.

'They'd test you.'

'How would they do that, then?'

'I don't know. Make you pee in a bottle.'

'But I might have just had a pee and wouldn't be able to go.'

'They'll give you a couple of cans of lager to drink. That'll get you going. Dad pees loads when he's been drinking lager, don't you, Dad?'

'Can we change the subject, please?'

'But Steve could be arrested.'

'But he won't be able to pee in the test bottle for at least an hour after he's drunk the lagers,' I argued. 'And, by then, any traces of the wacky-baccy in his blood might have gone.'

Kate was quiet for a moment and I could see her thinking up a counterargument. 'I know,' she said. 'They'll pull Steve over and tell him a stupid joke, like "Why was six scared of seven?", and he'll wet himself laughing because he's high as a kite and they'll bang him up.'

'Why *was* six scared of seven?' Steve asked.

Kate sighed. 'Because seven ate nine.'

Steve indicated to turn left onto the A3. He and I both shook our heads and said at the same time, 'No, I don't get that.'

Work had been busy; December always was. Lots of people wanting to make that final move before Christmas.

Maurice, me and Jeff spent four days moving a religious American family. On the second morning, I was packing and shifting the playroom while the two kids sat cross-legged on the floor asking each other questions from a board game called Holy Knowledge. I carried out a box to the truck, and when I came back in, one of the boys said to his brother, 'That's easy: John the Baptist, stupid.'

It was already dark when we finished unloading everything into the new house on the last afternoon. Americans weren't renowned for tipping despite the fact that their entire culture seemed to be based on the practice. We'd also been offered neither tea nor coffee during the whole move, so the odds of us receiving a gratuity were pretty slim. However, it was nearly Christmas and they were God-fearing people, so there was still a chance.

The customer, a young, good-looking blond feller who insisted on us calling him DJ, stood by the front door. Maurice handed him the sheet while I stood behind, hands in coat pockets, Jeff beside me, smoking a cigarette.

DJ signed and addressed us. 'I'd like to thank y'all for your help over the last few days.' He called into the hallway. 'Mabel!'

Mabel, his wife, appeared: a slim, serious-looking lady who'd still overseen her home Bible-reading classes every morning during the upheaval of the move and looked as though she'd never laughed once in her entire life.

'We'd like to give y'all something for Christmas as a sign of our appreciation,' DJ said.

Jeff and I pricked up our ears and Maurice's right knee began to tremble.

Mabel handed DJ a bottle of red wine and a box of chocolates which he, in turn, proudly presented to Maurice.

Maurice mumbled, 'Thank you,' and gave the customer's hand a perfunctory shake.

Jeff muttered, 'Tight bastard,' under his breath, and he and I trudged back to the lorry. Jeff opened the cab door and we were about to get in when we heard DJ say, 'I'd also like to give you three hundred of your English pounds to share between you.'

Jeff and I were immediately back at the front door pumping both the gent's and Mabel's hands and thanking them profusely. Maurice couldn't help himself and gave Mabel a kiss on her cheek, and she not only blushed but actually smiled.

Kye Stoneway had disappeared.

It was not uncommon for the boss to go 'walkies' – neither darken the yard nor answer his phone – but these occasions would normally last no longer than three or four days at most. Eventually, he'd reappear and we'd see him sitting in his office, unshaven and bleary-eyed quizzing Daz and Trevor about what had occurred during his absence. After a week, when there was still neither hide nor hair of him and bills were due to be paid, Daz became worried.

The police were called in and, after another seven days' no-show, Kye Stoneway became an official *Missing Person*.

On my request, Ross checked the CCTV footage of the Saturday morning I last saw him with Henderson and Kennet. She called me over to her desk one evening when the office was empty and we watched Kye pull up outside the main door at 9.32am in his Range Rover and walk into the building.

Ross altered the perspective to Camera 2 and we saw Kye enter his office and sit at his desk. The door opened and Mary came in with a cup of coffee. She left and, at 9.45am, the film went blank.

Kilo must have been wrong, I thought. *Henderson murdered him, but where's the body?*

I decided to go to the police. They took a statement off me and, naturally, I became a suspect. Kye's office was cordoned off and forensics found prints of myself, Henderson and Kennet.

Baz and Christine were also questioned and confirmed they'd met a distraught man wearing a pair of curtains who called himself Peter at approximately 11am on the morning in question. The police still considered me a suspect, but the story was so mad it had to be true and I was placed way down the list. I think they agreed with me; if Kye had been murdered, it must have had something to do with Henderson.

Stoneways was now faced with a huge problem. If neither wages nor bills could be paid without Kye's signature, the company would cease to exist by the New Year. Daz hired a lawyer who discovered the company still traded under the name of Stoneways and Sons. A new titular managing-director could be installed on a temporary basis while the current one remained missing; an MD whose signature carried as much legal weight as Kye's.

Heeding the lawyer's advice, Daz arranged for the day release of Arthur Stoneway on Tuesdays and Thursdays *only* to visit the warehouse, authorise bills and pay rolls and generally wander round the yard boring all and sundry with removal tales of the past.

We were happy to see him. He'd saved our jobs, but Mary, the cleaner, seemed happier than anyone else. She doted on him when he visited and festooned him with biscuits and cakes. The affection was mutual and Arthur's smile was always broader when she was near.

One lunchtime, while we were sitting in the cab during DJ and Mabel's move, I asked Maurice about it.

'I've always told you, Arthur's a fine man,' Maurice began. 'Yes, he might be slightly unhinged and a boring old fart, but he has a good heart. There were rumours that Mary was his illegitimate daughter – never proven – but Arthur has always been very fond of her. Believe it or not, she was an attractive woman in her day, intelligent, confident and happy. In fact, our current forklift driver had quite a thing for her.'

'Barry Noble?'

'The very one. Of course, this was well before he met Angela, but nonetheless, I think he still holds a candle for Mary even to this day.' Maurice paused and gave me a stern look. 'That's strictly between you and I, Booth.'

'Understood,' I said.

'It had better be,' Maurice warned.

'On my daughter's,' I assured him.

He kept his eyes on me for a moment longer before continuing, 'Alas, she spurned Barry's advances – and possibly those of other potential suitors – and got involved with a violent man whom Arthur detested. He tried to warn her off him, but she ignored Arthur and fell pregnant. One night, the father-to-be revealed his true colours and beat Mary black and blue. She lost the baby and, several weeks later, attempted suicide. She was committed but she hated the place and continually tried to escape. Arthur stepped in and moved her to a private residential home paid for by him where she still lives now. He also got her the job as Stoneways' cleaner on a permanent contract and I'm pretty certain her hourly rate is a lot higher than yours or mine.'

'Kye must have liked her as well to have kept her on,' I said.

Maurice paused. 'Not certain about that. I believe there was some legal stipulation on Arthur's part that Mary's contract was permanent. She never liked Kye.'

'Why?'

'She always blamed him for having Arthur committed. Remember, she, herself, hated being in an institution and she would never have wanted the same for her Arthur.'

The two kids came charging out of the front door, dressed in fourteenth-century Crusader costumes, one chasing the other with a plastic sword.

'Has she always been a cleaner?' I asked.

Maurice shook his head. 'Oh no, before she lost the baby, she was a sister at North Bitton Hospital.'

'Like a matron at Billy Bunter's boarding school?'

'You are an idiot, Booth. A sister in a hospital is a very important position these days.'

'Making the beds and darning the socks?'

Maurice tutted at my stupidity and said, 'They're in charge of dispensing all the drugs to the patients.'

Steve announced he had to put some juice in the van and we pulled up at the BP garage outside Emily's estate. First the wine stain, now here.

Kate was engrossed in her phone, so I cadged a fag off Steve and crossed the garage forecourt to stand on the grass verge by the bins, smoke and watch the Saturday morning traffic zip by on the dual carriageway.

During the following twenty-four hours after Henderson's abduction, I received a barrage of calls from Emily. I didn't answer and deleted all the answerphone and text messages without listening to or reading any of them.

She didn't turn up for work on the Monday or Tuesday. Daz called me into the office on Wednesday morning and asked me if I knew what was going on. I told him we'd split up.

On the Thursday, he received an email from her tendering her resignation for personal reasons.

News at Stoneways always spread like an Australian bushfire, and by Friday, everybody knew our fling was over. I don't know what was said behind my back and I didn't care, but to my face, the lads were respectful. For at least a week, even Maurice walked around me in hushed silence as though somebody dear to me had died.

I held her image away from me as far as I could, but she crept through, not only in the sleepless midnight hours but in broad daylight when I was walking in the park or even taping up a Pack3 in a four-bedroom semi. Had I loved her? No, it was probably more lust, but we'd shared something and she'd hurt me badly.

Last Saturday morning, Jeff and I helped Leo pick up two of the double beds we'd delivered to Magenta to be returned to store. Daz assured us Magenta wouldn't be there and the maid would let us in so we should easily be done by midday. Daz was true to his word and we'd loaded the beds in Knightsbridge by ten. Fatima signed the sheet and handed Leo an envelope addressed to 'PETER BOOTH + CREW'. There was £600 in fifties inside and a handwritten note wishing us all a very merry Christmas signed by Aaron Carlberg.

We unloaded the beds into a container back at the yard and Jeff and I headed straight to the Queens at opening time. I drank too much and phoned a cab to take me home. On the way, I made the driver pull up outside Emily's.

I knocked and a woman opened the door, an inquisitive tot hiding behind her knee. The lady who'd lived there before with her son moved last Tuesday, she told me. I convinced her she was my sister and the woman handed me a forwarding address on Woodford Hill near Windsor where the cheapest property was a million and a half.

My Emily had certainly done very well for herself after her ex-husband had died.

Steve and Kate were waiting for me when I got back in the van.

Steve pointed at the estate opposite. 'Is this where that other woman lives?' he asked me.

Kate was all ears. 'What other woman?'

'Never you mind,' I said.

She whacked Steve on the arm. 'Come on, Steve, tell me.'

Steve indicated to pull back out onto the bypass. 'What was her name?' he asked me.

'Emily,' I mumbled.

'Who?'

'Emily.'

'That's a nice name,' Kate said.

'Yes, but not a very nice woman,' I told her.

'Nice bum,' Steve commented.

'Stop being so sexist!' Kate said, and whacked Steve on his arm again. She turned back to me. 'Come on, Dad, tell me about her.'

'I don't want to.'

'Oh, please.'

'No!' I raised my voice and saw fear and tears appear in my daughter's eyes. I immediately hugged her. 'Sorry, sorry,' I said.

'You scared me,' she whispered into my shoulder.

'I'm sorry; I really am. I'd never hurt you, I promise.'

She pulled away. 'It's alright, Dad. I've got to learn to stop being so nosy.' She kissed me on the cheek.

Steve saw a gap in the traffic and we pulled out of the garage forecourt and away from the estate.

'So, what was this Emily like then?' Kate asked Steve.

The taxi dropped me off back at the flat and, after an alcohol-induced kip, I walked down to Sanjays to get some more beers. I bumped into Paranoid Ian outside the bookies and he told me Kilo had been admitted to the Davenport Cancer Ward at North Bitton Hospital.

I got up early on the Sunday morning and had a fry-up at the Sunshine Eat. I avoided any eye contact with Tula when I paid Frank at the till – I didn't want to upset any more psychos – but Frank insisted the breakfast was on the house. Tula was engaged to be married to a fine Turkish man with good connections and the overheads running the café had nose-dived in the past two weeks thanks to me. No one was collecting protection money anymore. Some chancer called Ted Croker from Fleet Town had tried his luck last Thursday, but even Manny, Frank's wife, had managed to shoo him off.

I caught a 75 to North Bitton Hospital and walked through the main entrance to the reception desk and asked the solitary receptionist if I could visit a friend of mine in the Davenport Ward.

The receptionist studied his computer. 'Name, please?' he asked.

'Peter Booth.'

The receptionist studied his computer again and said, 'I'm afraid there is no patient in the Davenport by that name.'

'No, that's my name,' I told him.

'Sorry, sir, but I was asking for the patient's name,' he said, and eyed me with a hint of suspicion.

'Oh, yes. Kilo.'

The receptionist's head dropped back to his screen.

He looked up again. 'Is that with a "K" or a "C"?'

'K,' I said.

'Surname?'

'I don't know his surname,' I admitted.

The receptionist stood up and called out, 'Security!' to a passing security guard. The guard stopped and walked over to the reception desk.

'This gentleman wants to see a patient,' the receptionist said to him.

'That's what most people who come in here wish to do during visiting hours,' the security guard replied.

'Yes, but he doesn't know the patient's surname.'

The security guard looked me up and down and turned back to the receptionist.

'First name?'

The receptionist sat down and looked at his computer again. 'Kilo,' he said. 'With a "K".'

'Davenport Ward?' the guard asked.

'That's the one,' I said.

'I'll handle this,' the guard told the receptionist. He signalled to me. 'This way, please, sir, if you would.' He pointed at the double doors leading to the wards.

I followed him down a long corridor passing trolleyed patients and children's crayoned pictures hanging on the walls until the guard stopped at a door to our right. He unlocked it and said to me, 'This way, please, sir.'

I walked into a cleaner's cupboard. 'This isn't a ward,' I said, and felt the first pinpricks of alarm. 'Who the hell are you?'

The guard shut the door behind him. 'Please don't be alarmed. It's just Paul Mackenzie – Kilo – isn't serving at present.'

'Serving?'

'Providing.'

I clicked. 'Sorry, you're talking to the wrong bloke. I'm an acquaintance of his. I have nothing to do with his...' I hesitated, 'his business.'

'Ah.' The guard's face reddened and he opened the door.

We carried on walking and the guard started telling me he thought I'd like to see how well-equipped the cleaner's cupboard was.

'Very impressive,' I told him.

He opened another set of double doors and beckoned me through. 'Second bed on the left,' he said.

Kilo's head was propped up on two bulky, comfortable-looking pillows. He'd lost some of his natural ruddiness and his face seemed gaunter, but the rocker's quiff was still intact.

'Peter!' he greeted me. 'Where's my chocolates and grapes?'

I pulled up a plastic chair and sat to one side of the bed. 'Personally, I'd like to remove one of those pillows from behind your head and suffocate you with it.'

'Oh, Peter, whatever's the matter?'

'How well did you know Emily?'

He feigned innocence. 'Why?'

'Because since her ex-husband has departed this mortal coil, she appears to have done extremely well for herself.'

'What are you trying to say?'

I glanced round. The bed to Kilo's right was empty and a frail old man was asleep to his left, a tube attached to one of his nostrils.

I leant forward. 'To further your fishing analogy, I was double-hooked. Emily and you were in cahoots from the start. I was the bait to sort out Kennet first and then Henderson later.'

'Not entirely true,' Kilo said.

'But not implausible.'

'I've known Emily for a little while and we've always shared a mutual sentiment.'

'Your dislike of Henderson?'

'Crikey, Peter; you are better than Clouseau. She let on to me that Henderson had left her a substantial amount of dough in his will.'

'Were you screwing her?'

'No!' he replied, offended. 'She's not my type.'

'I don't believe you.'

Kilo shrugged. 'Do you want me to phone Ian so he can spell things out to you?'

'Paranoid Ian?'

'Please don't call him that; we don't like it.'

The light dawned. 'You mean you and Ian are…'

'You can say it out loud, you know. It's no longer an offence.' Kilo paused. 'In this country, at least.'

'It's just I'm surprised, that's all.' I thought for a moment. 'What about Crazy Jane?'

'She was my sister.'

'OK, OK; so, you weren't screwing Emily.'

'Wasn't even in the queue.'

I stood up. 'The queue?'

'Sit down, Peter; you're attracting attention.'

I sat down and lowered my voice. 'What do you mean by "the queue"?'

'Oh, Peter, you are a bit wet behind the ears sometimes.'

'She told me she'd only slept with one bloke since she split up with Henderson and she said it was a disaster.'

'Arfa.'

'Arthur who?'

'Arfa Surrey.'

'What a bitch,' I said in a low tone.

'OK. I can see you're upset, but that's what women can be like.' Kilo thought for a moment. 'And blokes,' he added. 'If it makes you feel any better, she did genuinely like you and had second thoughts about setting you up. Anyway, I heard on the old vine, you'd found someone else.'

'I have, but I don't want you going anywhere near her.'

Kilo put up his hands. 'I thought we were mates?'

I ignored him. 'Right, let me get this straight. You used me as bait in Cheston to lure Henderson but you only stiffed Kennet. Why not Henderson as well?'

'How many people have you killed, Peter?'

I didn't answer.

'None. No shame in that, but killing people isn't that easy. Henderson was on his way out of there as soon as he heard the first blast. There was no way I could have got him as well. In fact, I was lucky he didn't have a shooter himself; I took a chance.'

'So, all along, you'd planned to get him at Emily's later.'

'With the troops, yes.'

'And once again, I was the bait.'

'You're alive, aren't you? If it hadn't been for me, Henderson would have got hold of you eventually and I don't think he intended to give you a bloody kiss.'

I hadn't thought of this. 'OK. I suppose you're right in a way.'

'Mates?' Kilo asked.

'Still not sure,' I said. 'What was your share of Henderson's dough?'

'Peter, Doc says I'm definitely on the way out – maybe a year if I'm lucky. The money's for Ian. He can't hold a job down and he needs looking after.'

'I thought he was driving a hi-ab for a machine-hire company?'

'At the moment, but he gets confused about securing the loads on the crane. He'll have an accident soon and they'll get rid of him.'

I caught Kilo staring out to an invisible distance, perhaps thinking of Ian or Crazy Jane. At that moment, he didn't look like a big-time drug dealer capable of murder. He resembled more a cuddly teddy bear or a kind-hearted pussy cat with its claws withdrawn.

'I'm sorry,' I said.

Kilo turned to me. 'Mates?'

'Yeah,' I said, and we tapped fists.

A nurse appeared at the end of the bed with a trolley. She handed a plastic cup to me. 'Would you mind giving this to Mr Mackenzie? It's his medication.'

'Of course,' I told her, and handed the cup to Kilo.

'Thank you, Sister,' he said, and the nurse smiled and moved on to the next bed.

I waited till she exited the ward. If there was somebody who was an authority on drugs it was the man lying in the bed before me.

'That's the sister, right?' I said to Kilo.

'Right.'

'And she's in charge of administering all the medicine to the patients in the ward.'

'Right.'

'Does she prepare them as well?'

'She does.'

'Could she make a lethal cocktail?'

'I've no idea what you're trying to get at, Peter, but I'm already keeping some of the pills to one side in case the pain ever gets too bad. So, if I could make one, I'm sure she can.'

'Easily?'

'With my eyes closed,' Kilo answered, and a jag of pain crossed his face.

We pulled up outside the flat and Sarah opened the door.

'This isn't where you used to live with her, Dad,' Kate said.

I ignored her and got out of the cab and gave Sarah a hug.

'How much is there?' Sarah asked.

I opened up the back of the van and she looked inside.

'Is that it?'

'I'm afraid so,' I said. 'All my worldly possessions.'

'Do you want me to show you where it's going?'

'That might help.'

'Don't be cheeky,' Sarah warned.

Steve and I unloaded in twenty minutes while Kate sat in the van pretending to play with her phone. There was only one slight blip when Steve asked Sarah where my box of CDs was going.

'I'd hide it somewhere if I was you,' Sarah suggested.

When we'd finished, Sarah made us a coffee and asked me about Kate.

I shrugged. 'I'll leave her; she'll come in when she's ready.'

'What have you told her?' Sarah queried.

'Not a lot, I must admit.'

'Does she think I've moved here and you're moving in with me?'

'I haven't indicated otherwise.'

'You are cruel,' Sarah said. 'I'll go and have a word.'

Steve followed her out the door with his coffee and wandered off down the road to smoke a joint while I sat on the sofa wondering if I'd done the right thing. I'd been in this flat so many times and slept on this sofa on countless occasions, but it all seemed new and different to me now I was actually moving in.

The thing which most frightened me was how quickly it had all happened. I'd never loved Emily – perhaps not even Sarah – I'd always loved someone else, and it was that bloody painter and decorator in the Queens who'd finally made me realise it.

Kate bounded into the room and jumped on the sofa next to me. Sarah stood in the doorway.

'Oh, I'm so happy, Dad. No offence, but I always preferred her to Sarah.'

'Kate!'

'Sorry, sorry!'

Sarah was smiling. 'It's alright,' she said.

'Anyway,' Kate gushed, 'Sarah says her new boyfriend's really nice. Well, good-looking and got loads of money. Much more romantic than you ever were and tickles all her right bits. Isn't that right, Sarah?'

Sarah was blushing. 'I didn't actually say that. I said he made me laugh.'

'Same sort of thing.'

'Didn't I ever make you laugh?' I asked.

'Yes, you did.'

'See!' I said to Kate.

'But not intentionally.'

Thirty

THE AWAY GAME

Ross was standing on the touchline with a dozen or so other Leysham Village parents and friends. Normally, both sets of supporters would mix freely with each other, but this was an away game against Redbridge Rovers on a council pitch off Byron Street. The Towers stood silently above the unruly privet hedges behind the home crowd opposite which outnumbered us by two to one.

A year ago, at this very venue, Leysham won 5-0 and the Redbridge crowd charged us. I'd grabbed Ross's hand and run like buggery to the nearby scout hut where we barricaded ourselves in until the police arrived. *I won't run today*, I thought. *Not after what I'd been through.*

Freddie told me the form on the Friday afternoon at work. Redbridge were a strong outfit this season and topped the league by five points. Leysham, meanwhile, were languishing in the bottom half and had a couple of key players missing. To get a point would be a miracle, Freddie reckoned.

The first half hour of the game reflected Freddie's low-down. Leysham were stuck in their own half under constant pressure from the home side. Their main problem, in my opinion, seemed to be a lack of a creative player. Their captain was injured and they missed Charlie's mazy runs through midfield to alleviate the pressure. When in possession, the Leysham players took to hoofing the ball hopefully up the pitch where it was easily retrieved by the Redbridge defence and ping-ponged skilfully back into the away team's penalty area. Eventually, the resistance was broken by Redbridge's Asian centre-forward, who adroitly volleyed in from a corner.

The home crowd sang, 'Can we play you every week,' which I was OK about, but Kate and especially Ross became more vocal. Redbridge added a second just before the ref blew for half-time and I was satisfied Leysham were going to end up getting tonked and there'd be no trouble after the game.

Sarah said she had to go and we all kissed her goodbye. Even though the home team were winning, it was still too dodgy to try and purchase a drink in the clubhouse, so Ross handed Kate a can of Diet Coke and Steve and I a cold Stella each from her bag. Steve took his and wandered over to the roped-up cricket square to smoke a joint while I cracked open my tin.

In the opening minutes of the second half, Freddie threw himself into a fifty-fifty challenge with their second goal scorer and the latter came off worse. The Redbridge manager and one of the linesmen rushed on and gave him a spot of physio but to no avail and the goal scorer hobbled off. The home crowd bayed for Freddie's blood and an incensed Ross ran over to their side of the pitch and told them to lay off her son or else they'd, 'Get some.' The ref managed to calm her down and led her back over to our side, but I could sense the atmosphere was turning ugly.

The injury proved to be a pivotal point in the game and Leysham suddenly came into their own. Their striker hit the bar and the Redbridge keeper made a couple of sharp saves but could do nothing to stop a thunderbolt from the boot of the Leysham centre-back which nearly burst the net.

Twenty minutes to go: two-one and all to play for.

It became a very entertaining game with chances at both ends but my enjoyment was muted due to the increasing hostility emanating from the other side of the pitch, where a worryingly aggressive and out-of-tune chorus of, 'You're gonna get your fucking heads kicked in,' began to become a constant refrain.

A goal-mouth scramble in the Redbridge penalty area with five minutes to go was punctuated by a long shrill blast from the ref's whistle. He pointed to the penalty spot and at least six lager-fuelled Redbridge supporters of both sexes surrounded the ref. Ross charged over with Dave Whitlock, the Leysham manager, and Pod, the grumpy barman, and a few minor scuffles broke out. I told Kate to stay with Steve and marched towards the melee, though not quite as quickly as the advance party had.

Once again, Dave Whitlock received a vicious-looking knee in the nadgers, but Ross whacked his attacker around the head with her bag, which she later told me contained two bags of flour and five kilos of rice. The recipient, a large, tattoo-covered, peroxide-blonde lady, fell over and Ross had her arms grabbed from behind her by a tall Asian man. I started to run towards them and the Asian man let go of Ross and stepped back.

'Leave it!' he shouted to the other Redbridge supporters, and the aggro immediately ceased.

'Alright, mate,' the man greeted me nervously.

'Fine,' I said. 'How's Christine?'

'Yeah, she's good,' he replied.

'Baz! What the fuck's going on!' a stocky, shaven-haired man demanded. 'Let's sort these bastards out now!'

'Leave it, Will,' Baz cut him off sharply. He whispered something in Will's ear and I heard Henderson's name mentioned.

'Shit,' said Will. 'Well, we'd better get on with the game then.' He pulled the peroxide-blonde to her feet. 'Come on, Sal, fights over.'

'What you on about?' She pointed at Ross. 'I'm gonna kill that bitch.' Will pulled her close to him and whispered in her ear.

'Fuck,' she said, and looked at me in awe. 'Right,' she said to Ross, 'hope the best team wins.'

Baz led his entourage back to the touchline and there was talk between them and the rest of the home crowd.

Freddie took the penalty.

He stepped back and then ran up and whacked it as hard as he could. The ball hit the goalkeeper full in his face. The keeper collapsed and Freddie toe-poked the rebound into the left corner to equalise.

There was polite applause from both sets of fans.

The last three minutes of the game were played in Redbridge's half. The home team stroked the ball around without venturing over the halfway line while the Leysham team made shadow runs in their own half also without crossing the halfway line.

It reminded me of one of those final group games in the World Cup when it was best for either team not to score. I wanted to boo but I thought that might be pushing it.

I thanked Steve and sorted him out the cash and got in the car with Ross and Kate. We drove out of the car park and Kate said, 'That was one of the best games I've ever seen. It was mad. I nearly wet myself when Freddie's penalty hit that dork on his nose.'

'Kate!' Ross said.

'Sorry.'

'Behave,' I said.

'Who are you talking to?' they both asked.

'My daughter,' I confirmed.

'Are you a bit of a hard man, Dad?'

'Why do you ask that?'

'It looked as if it was going to really kick off when the penalty was given and then you walked over and they all backed off.'

'Your father has a bit of a reputation,' Ross said. 'Don't you, darling?'

Darling – I liked that. 'I suppose so,' I said.

'Come on, Dad: tell me!'

'I can't.'

'Why not?'

'Because if I tell you, I'll have to kill you.'

'Oh, shut up, Dad. I'm not a baby anymore.'

Ross said, 'They think he killed a baddy called Ray Henderson.'

'Wow,' Kate said. 'Did he used to play for West Ham?'

When we got back to Ross's, Kate pleaded with us to let her stay the night.

I looked at Ross.

She shrugged, 'It's your choice as well, you know.'

'You'd better phone Marjorie then and tell her,' I told Kate.

'Yes!' Kate punched the air and took her phone out of her pocket.

I suddenly thought of something. 'Hang on a sec,' I said to Ross. 'There's only your bedroom and Freddie's, so if Kate sleeps on the sofa bed, where am I going to kip?'

Ross looked at me in askance.

'Oh yes,' I said, realisation slowly dawning. 'With you.'

On Sunday morning, Kate helped Ross put up the Christmas decorations while I went for a walk on Oxam Common. It was a beautifully crisp, clear day and I stood on top of Telegraph Hill and looked out over the woods to the distant A3 and the rooftops of Cheston. The world of Henderson, Kennet and Kilo seemed miles away, and I realised that any feelings I might have still harboured towards Emily had vanished.

I was happy and, on the way back to my new home, I thought of asking Ross about getting a dog.

Kate greeted me dramatically at the front door of the flat, hugging me tightly and telling me how much she loved me, so I knew something untoward had occurred.

Freddie was sitting grumpily on the sofa playing with his phone. He sat in the middle in a spread-out manner as if to warn off any intruders.

I asked Ross in the kitchen what had happened.

They'd argued about what should sit on top of the Christmas tree, she told me. Kate wanted a black angel as a sign of racial harmony. Freddie had no problem with the message but wanted the angel to be a plastic model of Didier Drogba from his Chelsea collection. Kate was OK about having a footballer but argued that Drogba was a diving dork and a Manchester United player such as Rio Ferdinand would be a far better choice. Like most Chelsea fans, Freddie couldn't stand Manchester United and a huge row commenced. Insults were thrown and Freddie told her she wasn't allowed to stay at the flat again.

Ross made us all sit at the kitchen table and eat lunch together. Kate picked at her food and generally acted like a spoilt five-year-old. Freddie took on the air of Man of the House and started talking removals.

I said to him I'd made a new rule.

'What's that?' he asked.

'We never talk work over lunch.'

'What about supper?'

'You won't get any unless you start behaving,' Ross told him.

'Yeah, Freddie!' Kate said.

Freddie looked at me.

'And you,' I told Kate.

Kate put her fork down. 'But Marjorie's picking me up in an hour so I won't be here.'

I did love my daughter. That big heart was always on her sleeve and she said the last with a tear not too far away.

Freddie spoke up. 'Well, maybe next time you can stay a bit longer.'

'Good boy!' Ross exclaimed, stood up and then sat down again.

'Oh, shut up, Mum.'

'We might have a dog by then,' I said, and they all looked at me.

The first time I ever slept with Ross, she had one of those beeping alarm clocks which also ticked during the night. I had to ask her to get rid of it; I told her I wouldn't move in otherwise. This was our first disagreement since we'd become official but I won and my radio alarm took its place.

Unsurprisingly, 'Manic Monday' by The Bangles woke us up on Monday morning, but it was a decent song and I reflected on how much better the charts were in the 1980s. The songs were well-crafted and less glitzy. OK, you still had prats like Duran Duran and Spandau Ballet, but most of the stuff they play on the radio from that era was less in your face, the anger more subtle, the normality of daily life more prominent. Everything nowadays seemed to scream, *Look at me! I'm so important; me, me, me!*

I told Ross this over a piece of toast and coffee, and she said it was because I was getting old.

Ross didn't start work till nine while I always had to be in at eight at the latest. She offered to give me a lift and then hang around for an hour or so, but I decided this was a perfect opportunity for me to try and get a bit fitter. OK, I wasn't badly overweight and I rarely smoked, but I drank too much and could generally do with a bit of trimming up around the edges.

Freddie leant me his old bicycle and I decided, in future, I would always cycle to work and back. Besides, we were only working Monday and Tuesday morning and then wouldn't be back in till after New Year, so this would just be a short trial period to see how I got on.

Helmeted Lycra-clad cyclists whizzed past me and at one point I had to make way for a middle-aged woman with a shopping basket attached to the middle of her handlebars. I considered stopping and vomiting halfway up the small hill approaching Fleet Town Train Station, but I nobly persevered, although I spent the last ten minutes of the journey working out if I could fit the bike in the back of Ross's car on the way home later.

I cycled round to the back of the yard and padlocked the bike to the fence by the diesel tank. I knew nobody at Stoneways would nick it but, a couple of months ago, Jeff Unsworth – shortly after paying an extremely rare visit to the doctors – started cycling in to work and used to lean his rusting Raleigh, unlocked, against the side of the warehouse. One morning, not long after Jeff's new fitness regime had begun, Maurice and Barry Noble purposefully included the bike in a small consignment out of store which was stacked onto a visiting Britannia van to be eventually delivered to an address in Dumbarton, ten miles west of Glasgow.

A truck was standing in the yard opposite the warehouse entrance, but it was owned by the Filbert brothers from East Camwell who specialised in house clearances and general waste disposal. Every so often, the yard and warehouse would become overloaded with unwanted furniture and junk and the Filberts would be called in to dispose of it. There were usually a few items they could sell and thus they offered Stoneways a much cheaper price than what the company would have had to pay if we were to load the stuff on one of our own trucks and take it to the dump in Fordingbridge.

One of the Filbert brothers – I could never remember their first names (Burke and Hare, Maurice called them) – leant against the side of the cab with his foot up on the wheel-arch, rolling a cigarette. He was a tall man dressed, as always, in yellow hi-vis overalls, steel toe-capped boots and a black bobble hat slung low to the tops of his constantly alert eyes. Like his brother, his complexion was dark from continual exposure to the elements and the natural dirt and grime of his vocation.

He nodded at me as I walked past and lit his cigarette. I nodded back and noticed the front half of their curtain-sider was already loaded with the cardboard and other junk which had surrounded the skip.

Barry Noble drove out of the warehouse on his forklift carrying a storage container and began to fork it onto the truck.

This was unusual. 'Dumping a container?' I asked Barry.

'Afraid so,' he answered, shifted some gears and placed the container onto the lorry, its front edge overhanging by a few inches.

'Does Daz know?'

'He does,' Barry said, and slid the forks out from underneath the container. 'As far as I'm aware, it's empty, but I can't get the door off. Whether due to rust or some kind of sealant I'm not sure, but it can't be used and is just cluttering up the warehouse.' He placed the forks on the wooden base of the container and pushed the whole box fully into the truck. 'There's also a funny smell coming from it.' He shrugged. 'Probably an entire family of mice this time so best to get rid of it.'

I clocked the number on the door: ROW 7/14. 'Isn't that the container Kye used to sleep in all those years ago?'

'Indeed, it is. Don't think he'll be needing it now, mind.'

'Suppose not,' I said, and headed for the pebbled passageway.

The restroom was empty bar Maurice, who sat at his usual place by the toilets, glasses on, sipping a can of Tizer and reading the *Daily Mirror*.

It was only 7.45 so I had plenty of time to make a coffee without being assaulted.

'Ah, Mr Booth.' Maurice addressed me as I flicked the switch on the kettle. 'There's a story in today's paper which might interest you.'

'What's that then?'

'Shall I read it to you?'

'Fire away,' I said, and selected a mug from the draining board.

'*Carmen Curdley,*' Maurice read, '*a resident of affluent Sunningford, was rushed to hospital on Saturday morning after a heavy stone lion fell onto the roof of her car as the garden ornament was being hoisted on top of her garage by a crane.*

'*Carmen's spouse, Alan Curdley, told ambulance staff that the crane operator, Mr Ian Coulson of South Bitton, had looked extremely nervous when securing the load. A spokesman for LIFT-EASY, the firm who hired out the crane, said Mr Coulson had been temporarily suspended pending a full enquiry.*'

Maurice finished reading, took off his glasses and said to me, 'It would appear that Carmen Curdley is in critical condition after being crushed by Coulson's catastrophic craning of Curly.'

'How long did it take you to work that one out?' I said.

The shutter above the counter opened and Daz stuck his head through.

'Good morning, Mr Oatridge,' Maurice greeted him. 'And what delights have you got in store for us today?'

ACKNOWLEDGEMENTS

I'd like to thank the following people.

My readers – Peter and Janine Buchner, Jenny Parker, Alan Harris, Marje Simms, Jon HD and Peter Dyer (if you ever visit the Hampshire coast and like a decent bit of rock and roll, check out Peter's band, Dogruff), who all read my novel – in some form – to the end. It was much appreciated and your kind comments kept me going.

Chris Fielden, who runs the wonderful comic short story competition To Hull and Back and drums for the excellent Little Villains. Thanks for your much-valued advice during the writing, but you need to take Hawkwind more seriously.

And that goes for most people I know.

Hugh Whitlock and Mike Barnard, for their advice and time. Hugh and Mike are guitarists and backing vocalists for the Rambling Men, Milford on Sea's premier rock/pop trio.

Obviously, my Anna, who listened to my increasingly mad ideas about how the tale would unfold with a straight face and put up with all my other bullshit in between.

To all the good people at the Book Guild, who have helped make one of my dreams come true.

And, lastly, to the unfortunate people I worked with who tried to teach me that unfathomable trade and anybody else who believes the sight of an empty removal truck – late on a Friday night after an incredibly hot, sweaty summer's day – is far, far, far more pleasing on the eye than any of the Seven Wonders of the Modern World.